Hammer of Titan

A Fantasy Adventure

Paul Mouchet

Paul Mouchet Publishing

CONTENTS

To my wife, who believes in me, even when I struggle to believe in myself. Without her support and infinite patience, I would have never realized my dream of becoming an author.

And, to my big sister Louise, thank you for helping me bring my stories to life.

Chapter One

Sweet Sixteen

The morning sun came pouring into Kit's room and gently woke her from what had been a deep and dreamless sleep. She opened her eyes to find that she was on the floor, her body curled up against her dire wolf's deep black fur, with her oversized golden retriever pressed close to her chest. Even though the sun was right in his eyes, Runt, the dire wolf, was still snoring peacefully. Kit closed her eyes and wrapped her arms around Lump, the golden retriever, and savored every sweet moment with her canine family. She smiled to herself, remembering how her two pals had tried to share her bed with her, and eventually had knocked her off her thin, straw-filled mattress and onto the floor. Where many people may find their antics to be a nuisance, Kit reveled in their behaviors. She adored the way they expressed their love for her – and her bed.

A loud bang at her door roused the boys, causing Lump to start barking wildly. Without her furry comforters, Kit instantly shivered, her naked little body instantly becoming covered in goosebumps. Kit scowled at the door and slipped on one of her priestly robes. She took a quick look in her mirror and cringed at the way her mass of black hair was knotted and tangled into a horrific mess on her head. Only hours ago, Lin had used her enchanted comb to make it look perfect. Apparently, she was meant to go through life looking permanently disheveled. She still wasn't used to the thick stripe of red that had found its way into her otherwise obsidian hair. She also wasn't used to the gold ring that now surrounded her once deep brown eyes. She wasn't used to it, but she liked the look of it.

"C'mon Kit, no time to waste!" shouted a voice that sounded a lot like Silverleaf's. There was a flurry of hushed voices, one of them sounding like Amara berating the young half elf.

"Happy Birthday, Kit," Amara called through the door. The giantess' voice was a deep baritone with an innocent, gentle sweetness to it. Like all Gigas, Amara was an amazing fighter – and a pacifist. It was an unlikely combination, but her people loved combat, but only as a sport. Her culture strictly forbade killing except for food or to protect the clan. Even then, it needed to be an option of last resort.

After a brief attempt to flatten her unruly hair, Kit opened the door to her friends. "I was sleeping," she whined. "Couldn't this have waited for a few more hours?"

On cue, Silverleaf, Amara, Slate and Indie all shook their heads in perfect unison. Each of them had a stupid grin on their face. Kit wasn't sure if they were laughing at how she looked or if they were simply happy to prevent her from getting any sleep.

"Where's Danny?" Kit asked, rubbing the sleep from her eyes. She waited a moment for her friend to leap out from the hallway, but it never happened. Her friends' faces all went blank at the question, except for Indie's. His face went dark. He averted his eyes so as not to look directly at Kit.

"Indie. Where is he?" Kit pressed. Danny and Indie didn't get along too well, and Kit had a sinking suspicion that Indie, her boyfriend, had something to do with her long-time friend's absence. She glared at the young man while she scratched her butt-cheek.

"He left last night," Indie said as he handed Kit a small scroll. "He asked me to give you this."

Kit stared blankly at the gift as she tried to blink away her tears.

"He didn't want to say goodbye?" She stared up at Indie, her tear-filled eyes now the size of saucers. "I don't understand."

Before she had a chance to say another word, Indie took Kit into a deep hug. She buried her face in his tunic. Her tears immediately stained the white fabric.

"He didn't say, not exactly anyway. But I think he was afraid to tell you in person. I think he feared that saying goodbye would be too hard, and he'd never leave."

"Why did he have to go?" Kit's voice was muffled as she spoke into Indie's chest.

"It might have been my fault," Slate said, rubbing the back of his neck. The young dwarf sounded terrified, fearing Kit might unleash holy vengeance upon him for sending her friend away. Slate, along with the others, were Kit's first and best friends at the Temple. At fifteen cycles, the dwarf was no older than Kit, but he sported an impressively thick orange beard. Even though Slate was among her best friends, she knew almost nothing of his past. It wasn't something he spoke of.

"What?" Kit asked as she pulled away from Indie. His tunic was wet and rumpled where she had pressed her face against him. She tried to quickly iron out the wrinkles in the linen with her hand, but with no effect.

She wiped an errant tear from her cheek as she turned her focus on Slate. "What do you mean?"

The dwarf continued to scrub the back of his neck. He looked at his friends for support, but they all had the same questioning look on their faces. "I received a letter from one of my kin; he's a member of the Fair Traders Union."

"A member of what?"

"The Fair Traders Union. They're a group dedicated to supplying goods to the ports along the Gaelinora Sea and beyond. They are the last bastion against the frookin' slave traders, the Auctioneers. But that's not important right now. My kin's crew were delivering a shipment of tea and wine to the Berrathian capital of Ravenlord, when..."

"Slate! What have I told you about swearing?" Amara interrupted.

"Ravenlord?" Kit said, ignoring Amara's protests about Slate's choice of words. "It's not the capital, Taseko is."

"Not anymore," Slate replied. "The ruler of Ravenlord declared it the capital city after Taseko fell to a new, even more cruel group of Berrat slavers." He waited a moment for this information to sink in. Berrat had turned on their own and were selling people from their own villages. "From what I've heard, this new group is utterly ruthless. They are killing and capturing Berrat from all the surrounding villages."

Kit's eyes went wide with shock. "Danny's from Taseko; his whole family is. Why didn't he say something? I'd have gone with him."

"Because you're not a phoenix," Silverleaf interjected. "It would take you well over a moon to travel there, even by horse. Based on how fast he is, Danny could fly there in less than a day."

"You knew?" Kit's question was filled with pure venom. Her eyes scanned the entire group; all of them shared the same look of shame. "You all knew, and none of you would tell me?"

"Danny asked us not to," Amara replied, taking a knee so that her head was almost level with Kit's. "The people who took control of the city are ruthless, brutal murderers. He didn't want you anywhere near them."

Kit wiped away some more tears that had managed to find their way down her cheek. "And what? He didn't think I was capable of defending myself?" Her fury with Danny's decisions, and with her friends for not telling her, was causing Kit's temper to boil over.

Amara laughed lightly and shook her head. "Not at all, but if he had told you himself, you would have stopped him from leaving on his own – and that would have been a delay that he couldn't allow."

"I wouldn't have stopped him," Kit said with a pout. Lump and Runt moved in beside her, offering the full weight of their support, nearly knocking the girl off her feet in the process.

"Maybe you should just read the note he left for you?" Indie finally suggested, trying to break Kit out of her mood.

"Later," Silverleaf said, as he took Kit by the hand and dragged her away. "You need cheering up right now. Nobody's allowed to be sad on their birthday."

"I don't want to be cheered up," Kit replied as she feebly tried to pull her hand away. She was staring down at the scroll, wondering what Danny might have shared with her.

"And that's exactly why you need to be cheered up!" Amara added, helping to shoo her out the door. "We've got some birthday presents for you." Both Runt and Lump barked, like they, too, wanted Kit to receive her presents.

"Let me get cleaned up first," Kit objected as they corralled her out the door.

"You look beautiful just the way you are," Indie said with an easy smile, eliciting some whistles from both Slate and Silverleaf.

The group hustled Kit out the back door of the dormitory to the courtyard. From there, they took the path leading to the Temple's outbuildings. Standing in front of the stables was the small roan Kit had ridden to Templeton. The horse had a huge red ribbon wrapped around her neck, with a giant bow dangling precariously off the side of her head.

"Happy Birthday, Kit!" Amara and Silverleaf shouted with glee. "We bought her for you!"

"You what? It's too much!" Even though Kit was protesting, she had a huge smile on her face.

"How can you afford this? Acolytes don't get much in the way of a stipend."

Silverleaf smiled sheepishly. "We didn't have to pay for the horse, not with money anyway. When we asked Father Hoarfrost, he said we could pay for it by doing extra duties."

"What sort of extra duties?" Kit asked, her eyes glued to the festively decorated little horse. Kit would have never considered herself a horse-lover, but she had developed a close connection to this animal during her adventures at Templeton. Through thick and thin, she was a stalwart little mare.

"He wouldn't say," Silverleaf responded, "but he had an evil smile on his face when he agreed."

"An evil smile? Hoarfrost?" Indie didn't seem to understand. The words evil and Father Hoarfrost didn't fit together in his head. Kit laughed as though she might have an idea of what the *duties* might be.

"Indie and I got together to get you something to go with the horse," Slate said. He was practically vibrating, like he couldn't wait for Kit to question him about it.

"Slate was able to get two griffin feathers," Indie added, "and I got the Watch's head smith, Morty, to place the speed enchantments on her. She's even faster than Char now."

"Not just regular speed enchantments either," Slate added, his bright-orange facial hair now dancing on his cheeks. "Morty also added two barding enchantments. They will protect your horse like she's clothed in full plate armor."

"I'm pretty sure those were Harding's doing," Indie said. He's the one who introduced us to Morty. Without him, we'd never have gotten in to see him. "Oh, and Morty added a first level carrying enchantment to the horse before he put the others on. I think he wanted to be included in the gift giving."

"My horse has five levels of enchantments on her?" Kit blinked in disbelief. Second and third level enchantments were expensive, but with five levels of enchantments on the little roan, well, she would be one of the most valuable things Kit had ever seen, let alone owned. Her stomach was churning. She had never experienced such generosity. As her face reddened, she turned away, undeserving of such wondrous gifts.

"You know," Indie said, giving Kit a bit of a nudge with his elbow, "you're going to have to give her a name. You can't keep calling her *horse*."

"My name is Angel," a voice said in Kit's mind. Whatever anxiety she was feeling about her friends having given her such an extravagant gift vanished instantly.

"You can talk?" Kit asked, her eyes wide. "How's that even possible?"

"It was a gift from your not-so-secret admirer, and you should probably just talk to me in your mind and not out loud. Your cohorts think you've gone bonkers."

Kit tried to surreptitiously steal a glance over at her friends, and sure enough, they were gawking at her like she was *not right in the head*.

"What?" she asked, trying to cover her embarrassment. "She's got very expressive eyes! It's like she's talking to me."

"What do you mean, my secret admirer?"

"That wonderful young man, Tyr. He's very dreamy. You two would make wonderful foals together."

"He is not a wonderful man! He's a Fate! He's a raving lunatic and a complete menace!" Kit had meant that comment to be in her head, but the notion of being *romantic* with Tyr, well, it pushed her over the edge.

"You're doing it again. Your friends are staring."

Amara took a step closer and held her palm out to Kit. "Is everything okay? Who's a menace?"

Kit grimaced. She didn't want to have this conversation. Tyr confused her, muddled her brain. He seemed to be a friend, but she wasn't sure about him. "It's nothing. I was just..."

"So, what are you going to call her?" Indie asked, rescuing Kit from the awkward conversation.

"Her name is Angel," Kit replied. "That's what I see when I look into her eyes. She's an angel." The small roan nickered at Kit in response. "See, she likes the name."

"Nice job on the cover-up," Angel laughed. *"I see why you're an honest person. You couldn't lie to save your life."*

"I'm a bad liar because I don't like to lie," Kit replied, smiling inwardly. *"It's not something I ever want to be good at."*

"Wow," Indie said, interrupting Kit's mental conversation. "You two already have an amazing rapport. I can see it just by the way *Angel* looks at you."

Kit gave Indie a caring smile as she gently stroked her horse's soft nose. "How about we take her out? Try out her new speed enchantments."

"I could use a good run," Angel whinnied, nudging Kit. *"I'd like to try out these enchantments, too."*

"I'm going to need some tack," Kit replied to Indie as she ran her hand down Angel's graceful neck. "I don't think I can ride her bareback."

"I won't let you fall," Angel snorted. *"I am yours and you are mine. I will never let harm come to you."*

"Look on the hitching post," Slate said. "It's from Captain Harding." Kit's eyes managed to get even wider, and her mouth dropped open. She gaped at the brand-new saddle and brightly patterned horse blanket. "The bridal she's wearing is also from the captain."

"It's a bit utilitarian for my liking, but if you need me to wear a saddle, I think it will be okay."

"Harding gave me an actual present?" Kit clasped a shaky hand over her mouth. "Why would he do that?"

"You did save the city," Amara said with a broad smile. She sighed heavily. "I wish that man paid me that sort of attention."

"You know he's married, right Amara?" Indie said, taking a few steps away from the Gigas, fearing perhaps that the giant might swat him like a horsefly. Even though she was a pacifist, she was not against knocking someone onto their backside – in a friendly sort of way.

"A girl can dream, can't she?" Amara's face was flushing, so she headed over to the hitching post to pick up Kit's saddle.

"Let me," Kit said with a shrug as she stepped in front of her friend. "I'd like to do it."

Amara gave Kit a mock-bow with a broad grin. She appreciated that Kit didn't give her a hard time. She was still blushing heavily and there was no way her tiny friend didn't see it.

Kit went to pick up the saddle when she noticed a pair of chainmail gloves laying on top of it.

Holy Helja, he remembered.

When Kit had talked with the captain in his office, she had joked that she would like a pair of chainmail gauntlets for her birthday. Never in a million cycles would she have thought that he'd actually buy her a gift. The girl's cheeks suddenly reddened. She grabbed the gloves off the saddle and tucked them into one of the many pockets in her robes.

In just a few minutes, Kit had the blanket and saddle on Angel's back. Even though it did look like a military saddle, it was a beautiful piece of tack.

"You look very nice with this saddle on you," Kit said through their bond. *"But I'll try to learn how to ride bareback, so you won't have to wear it any more than necessary."*

"The saddle is quite comfortable," Angel nickered. *"We can go bareback for fun, but the saddle will be important when we're adventuring together."* Her

priestly robes were not particularly well suited for horseback riding, but Kit didn't care. She hopped up onto her horse's back and wiggled her butt in the saddle.

"Comfy!"

"This saddle is wonderful," Kit exclaimed. "So, let's ride."

Indie whistled at the stables and Char came trotting out a moment later. With amazing grace, the young man swung himself up and onto the big stallion's back. Kit found herself staring. Her heart was beating a little faster than it should.

"Kit, that bridal you're using, it has no bit. You're not going to be able to properly control her." Indie had neither a saddle nor bridle on his horse. His long legs dangled down the side of the animal, his hands sitting comfortably on his thighs. Kit wondered if he shared the same bond with Char as she shared with Angel.

"They can't talk to each other like we can – but they have a very deep connection. They can feel each other on a – spiritual level."

"No need," Kit retorted, patting her roan on the neck. "Isn't that right, Angel?"

Angel knickered. Char knickered back.

Kit's friends were all staring at her, each with a dopey looking smile on their face.

"Aren't you coming?" she asked. Angel was prancing about, eager to get out into Aarall's open grasslands.

Silverleaf gave Kit a knowing wink. "Nah, you two go. We'd just slow you down." He looked to Amara and Slate; both of them nodded in agreement. "Go have a ride; we can get together for breakfast."

Not wanting to wait for an objection, Indie wheeled Char around and trotted off.

"Thanks for everything," Kit said, giving her friends a shy wave. Without Kit taking any action or saying a word, Angel spun around and followed after Indie and Char. Runt and Lump immediately gave chase, barking at their heels.

CHAPTER TWO

THE RACE

As Runt got closer to Angel, she shied away from him slightly. *"That dog smells like wolf. He's made me nervous since the first time I saw him."*

Kit gave her horse a reassuring pat. *"That's because he is a wolf. A wolf in a dog disguise."* Kit sensed a sudden uneasiness in Angel as soon as she told her that Runt was a wolf. With the spell broken, the horse then saw Runt in his natural form. She bolted away from the dire wolf and threw out her hoof to keep him at a distance.

"Don't be afraid. He's our friend and our protector."

"But he's not just a wolf. He's a dire wolf!" Angel fought hard to maintain her composure, the whites of her eyes showing as she raised her head, on the verge of bucking. *"How can that be?"*

"That's a long story, Angel. One that I'll share with you when we have time. But for now, we need to hurry up a bit. Indie is getting too far ahead of us." Angel relaxed slightly with Kit's reassurances, but the horse's fear still rippled through their connection. Angel calmed a bit further as the small horse's thoughts drifted to Indie's magnificent mount.

"Char is a beautiful stallion," Angel commented as she picked up her pace. There was a longing in her voice. Kit's heart swelled.

Even though Angel was only trotting, Kit was amazed at how quick she was and how smooth her ride was. In just a few minutes, they caught up to Indie and Char. The pair rode in connected silence until they reached the front gates to the city.

"Where do you want to go?" Indie asked as they cleared the bustling market-place. Char had already moved into a light canter, clearly wanting to run. Angel kept pace, nodding her head, coaxing Char to run faster.

"Race around Lake Titan?" Kit suggested.

The locals had quickly named the new lake formed by the melting sculpture in honor of the statue that had created it.

"Let's try out your new enchantments, Angel."

It didn't take much encouragement from Kit for Angel to take off. She headed off at an easy gallop, quickly leaving the others in her dust.

"She's definitely faster," Indie said with raised eyebrows as he pulled up alongside of Kit. "Char's having to put some effort into keeping up."

Lump and Runt, affectionately referred to as *the boys*, both barked in agreement as they loped alongside the horses. Indie gave Kit a boyish grin as Char suddenly surged forward, quickly putting distance between himself and Kit and the boys. Not wanting to be left behind, the two canines surged forward as well, closing the distance on Char.

"Your friends are very fast," Angel nickered. *"Let me know when you want me to actually start running."*

A wide grin spread across Kit's face at the joyful exuberance in Angel's voice. "I'm ready when you are," Kit laughed out as she took a stronger grip on her reins.

"I'll try not to embarrass them," Angel said as she continued increasing her speed. *"Hold on!"*

Angel broke into a full gallop, her strides getting longer and longer by the second. The rush of the growing breeze on Kit's face was exhilarating. Her heart pounded harder and harder with each hoofbeat. She shook out her hair, letting the wind catch hold of it. Kit's long black mane flowed behind her, snapping in the wind. Kit's heart soared as the crisp morning air bit at her cheeks. Her eyes watered slightly, heightening the joy of the experience.

"This must be what it feels like to fly," Kit said. She closed her eyes and let her senses take over. *"The feeling is – incredible!"*

Angel's withers shuddered at Kit's words. Like her rider, she drank in the freedom of racing across the rolling countryside. She reveled as she sliced through the air like an arrow loosed from a bowstring.

Before Angel had started *trying*, Indie and the boys had a sizable lead on them, but by the time they reached the far end of the lake, Kit had closed the gap and was ready to pass.

"Your canine friends are exhausted," Angel said. *"They'll both run until their hearts burst. For their sake, we need to stop."*

Kit pulled up alongside Indie and called out to him, having to scream to be heard over the rushing wind.

"The pups need a break!"

Indie nodded, and Char slowed to an easy trot. Both Lump and Runt were panting heavily, their tongues dangling out from the sides of their mouths. Their faces were a picture of joy and enthusiasm.

Sensing that the race was over, and needing a drink, the two boys changed direction and headed towards the lake's grassy shoreline. The cold, pristine waters cooled them and satisfied their thirst. Water poured down from their muzzles when they finally pulled their faces from the water. Seeing the horses approaching, the boys gave way to Char and Angel as they followed suit.

Char drank deeply, his front legs knee deep in the water. His chest was heaving; a thick lather covered his charcoal coat. Indie slid down from the horse's side into the lake. Cupping it in his hands, he drank his fill before using the water to cleanse the sweat from his face and neck. He ran his hands over the horse's shoulder and gave him some hardy pats.

Kit's heart raced again as her eyes lingered over the young man's water-soaked tunic.

"I think Char was trying to impress you," Kit said through her bond. *"He ran harder than he should have."*

"No more than your man was trying to impress you."

Lump shimmered just before he transformed into his shaggy, golden-haired human form. Holy Helja, he was as beautiful as a man as he was as a dog.

Angel whinnied at the sight and took a few awkward steps backward. *"He's a shifter? You keep very strange company, Kit."*

"No, he's a dog, but Tyr gave him a gift that lets him shift between dog and human forms." Kit patted Angel on the neck, reassuring her that everything was okay. It was only then that she noticed her hair was bone dry. She had barely broken a sweat from the exertion of the race.

"That was so much fun!" Lump exclaimed as he shook out his shaggy hair. He scratched absentmindedly behind his ear. He stared down at his hand like it was wondrous. "Why'd we stop? I thought the race was around the whole lake."

"Tell them we stopped because he and Runt were tired," Angel replied in Kit's mind. There was a strange, almost pleading tone in her voice. The sudden tension in Angel told Kit everything she needed to know. Angel wanted to stop because Char was overexerting, not because the boys were in distress.

"It was a much longer run than I had anticipated," Kit replied. "You and Runt needed a break."

Lump just shrugged. "I was tired, but I could have run longer. I don't think I could have kept up that pace, though. It took everything for us to keep up with Char." Lump's eyes were absolutely sparkling as he spoke. Even in human form, his big brown eyes were exactly the same as his doggie-eyes.

"We should keep going," he continued, rubbing his stomach. "I'm hungry."

Indie and Char came trotting out of the lake. Water was still dripping down from Char's muzzle. Indie's wet tunic clung to his muscular frame.

"I agree," Indie said with his quiet calmness. "Let's keep going. Char and I are starving, too."

"I'm ready when you are," Kit replied. "Maybe we can take it easier on the way back. No need to run the animals into the ground." As she said the words, Angel sniggered in her mind.

Smooth as silk, Indie sidled up next to Kit. "Angel's enchantments are amazing. She's much faster than Char now."

"Wow," Angel laughed, her ears perking straight up, swiveling them to face Indie. *"It's not very often that a man is willing to admit that sort of thing."*

"Did you see how her hooves sparked on the ground when she was running?" Lump asked. "If she ran any faster, she'd probably have set the ground on fire."

"I am amazing," Angel laughed again, causing Kit to laugh along with her.

"I could eat," Kit said as she coaxed Angel into a slow, graceful canter. Her stomach rumbled. Kit had never really understood why she was always so ravenous lately. Was it the spirit of Amaruq, the father of Runt, that supposedly inhabited her, that brought on the constant need for food? The thought flew from her mind as the wind once again whipped about her face and hair. Kit closed her eyes and pictured herself soaring through the skies, hundreds of feet above the ground.

⸎

The ride to the Temple was effortless. Kit was surprised at how quick the trip was, even without trying hard. When they arrived at the stables, two young acolytes came out to greet them. "We'll look after your horses, Sister Kit." A young Nomad girl of no more than twelve cycles took Angel's reins after Kit dismounted.

"They care for us well," Angel said in Kit's mind. *"They're all very kind, and this one brushes me very nicely."* The small roan turned her head towards Char and huffed. *"And I like watching when they brush Char down. I love the way his hair glistens. When his skin twitches..."*

"You're incorrigible," Kit laughed. *"As long as it's okay with you."* The horse was already clopping alongside the acolyte, happy to be taken inside and have her needs taken care of.

As the acolytes took the two horses into the stables, Indie took Kit's hand in his. "Ready for some breakfast?" Kit's heart raced a bit faster at the warmth of Indie's skin. She stole a look down at their coupled hands. She was just about to respond when three soldiers approached. They were dressed in City Watch uniforms and their demeanor was stiff and formal.

"Hail, Indigo. Hail, Sister Kit," one of them said as they got closer. "We're sorry to interrupt, but the captain requires Indigo's presence."

"I'm just on my way to breakfast," Indie protested, squeezing Kit's hand as he did.

"It's not a request," another of the guards replied, his freshly shaven jaw set firm. "You can eat at the barracks before we head out."

Kit pulled her hand back from Indie. "Head out?" She asked as she planted her hands on her hips and stepped slightly in front of her friend.

"Field training, Sister. We'll be gone for at least four days, maybe more." The guard's voice sped up, and several beads of sweat appeared along his hairline.

Indie dipped his head for a moment as he considered the situation. He stood silently. His feet shuffled slightly.

"Go with them," Kit said with a sigh. She gave Indie a soft smile as she took his hands in hers. She stared up at him, breathing in his manly fragrance. "Finish your training. There will be time for *us* later."

Indie made a soft whimpering noise. Her eyes were so inviting. When her lips parted slightly, Indie's breath hitched. Even though he enjoyed the unspoken torture of the moment, he bent down, his mouth hovering over hers for barely a breath before it slipped past her waiting lips. He gave Kit a quick peck on the cheek, along with an evil grin. Without looking back, he walked purposefully towards the soldiers, his shoulders back, his head lifted.

Runt and Lump stared up at Kit and whined.

"The dogs need to come, too," one of the guards added. "The captain wants all three."

Both boys looked expectantly at Kit, their eyes bright and pleading.

"Go with Indie," she said and shook her head. "I'll be fine on my own for a few days." Whatever their training was, the boys clearly enjoyed it. Their eyes lit up when Kit gave them permission to join in. As Kit watched them head off, her breath hitched as she clutched her hand to her breast.

I guess I'll have breakfast with the others.

CHAPTER THREE

FOLLOWERS OF ARACHNIELLE

The aroma of coffee, freshly baked bread, cooked meats, and spiced oatmeal greeted Kit as she stepped into the dining hall. Her mouth immediately watered, forcing her to wipe the corner of her lips with the back of her hand before it ran down to her chin. Her friends were nowhere in sight, so she continued on through to the back of the hall. Several times, she paused to look longingly at the food her brethren were enjoying. Her stomach growled as she left through the back of the hall and began her descent to the kitchens.

Sometimes Sister Miyuki had special treats set aside for those who joined her and her staff in the kitchens for breakfast. With hopeful anticipation, Kit strode into the kitchen's dining area. She frowned slightly when she realized that her friends weren't there either.

"Happy birthday, Sister," Sister Miyuki called out from across the room. She was sitting with several others of her kitchen staff, enjoying a quiet breakfast together. Sister Miyuki's eyes were sparkling as she beckoned Kit to come join her.

"Happy birthday, Sister," the others at the table with Miyuki called out. Kit waved feebly in return. The attention from strangers was making her uncomfortable. She really didn't enjoy having them make a fuss over her. Her friends always found a way to celebrate her birthday, which was great, but having strangers knowing about her birthday just didn't sit well with her.

"If you're looking for some breakfast, I've got a nice batch of eggs and sausage on the griddle." Sister Miyuki said as she waddled across the room towards Kit.

She was, as usual, dressed in her priestly robes with a huge white apron that covered her from neck to toe. And, as usual, that apron was covered with stains from neck to toe. The head chef really did get into her work.

"That would be great, Sister. Thank you." Kit's stomach rumbled at the notion of a nice, big greasy breakfast.

Miyuki nodded, pulled up her sleeves to her elbows, and trotted off towards the kitchens. As she headed off, she hummed *Titan Will Hold Me Fast*, eliciting the kitchen staff to join along with her.

Kit took another look around the room and frowned. There were no signs of her friends anywhere. "I guess they didn't expect me to come back so soon," she mused out loud as she took a seat at one of the empty tables.

Her mouth started watering again when Sister Miyuki returned with a plate overflowing with eggs, sausage, roasted potatoes and toasted wintergrain bread. Everything was just the way she liked it. The sausage was cooked near black; the potatoes were crispy on the outside and soft on the inside, and her eggs were scrambled and fluffy. And, as if everything else wasn't enough, Sister Miyuki had spread a generous dollop of prickle-berry honey on her toast.

"Here you go, sweetie," she said with a big, motherly smile. "You're welcome to join us at our table, so you don't have to eat alone."

"Thanks, Miyuki, but I don't mind a bit of time to myself. It's been pretty hectic lately." Kit didn't actually know if she *wanted* to be alone, but the kitchen staff was looking at her like she was some kind of superhero, and Kit definitely didn't want to endure their adulations.

"Okay, sweetie. As you wish. Would you like some coffee? We just brewed a fresh pot."

As Kit nodded frantically at the offer, Miyuki's eyes were drawn to the entrance.

"I'll get two cups. You've got company."

Kit took a peek over her shoulder to see Lin practically sprinting towards her. She groaned inwardly and desperately hoped that it didn't show on her face. The woman was dressed in traveling clothes rather than her acolyte's robes.

"Hey, Kit!" Lin was in her typical, overly enthusiastic mood. "Father Hoarfrost is sending me to Ashcroft to investigate rumors of Arachnielle worshippers there. Apparently, they're trying to convert the townsfolk."

"Why would followers of the spider god be this far north? They typically prefer to stay on the southern continent, don't they?"

The question seemed to make Lin even more bubbly. She was pressing her lips tightly together, obviously trying to stop herself from smiling too broadly. What her mouth tried to hide, her eyes could not. "I guess that's why I'm being sent there. He wants details on what's happening rather than rumors. I can't believe that Father is trusting me with such an important mission."

"Well, that sounds interesting, I guess. How long until you get back?" Kit popped a sausage into her mouth. She barely bothered to chew it before swallowing. It seemed lately that she found chewing her food only slowed her down.

Lin's face was absolutely beaming. "You mean, how long until *we* get back?"

"Father Hoarfrost wants me to go with you? Why didn't he just tell me himself?"

Lin's face went slack. Sweet Titan, it was like she had just kicked a puppy. Lin stared at her for several seconds before she crossed her arms over her chest and drew her mouth up into a tight bow.

"I don't know, but you can go ask him yourself if you'd like. If you do though, it's just going to make me look foolish; like you don't believe me."

"Whoa, relax, Lin!" Kit held her hands up in a defensive pose. "It was just a question."

"Well," Lin said as she closed her eyes and pouted, "you made it sound like you didn't believe me."

"Lin, it was just a question. I didn't mean anything by it." Kit stared at her, waiting for a more positive reaction of some sort. Instead, Lin just glared at her. There was only one way to fix this.

Kit gave Lin a coy look as the corners of her mouth turned upward ever so slightly. "When do we leave?"

The acolyte's eyes popped wide open, and a tiny squeal escaped her lips. Kit groaned to herself when Lin started swinging her arms by her side.

"Well, it's only a few hours away," Lin said as she stepped a bit closer still. Her words came out in bright, bubbly bursts. "We can be there and back before sundown if we leave now. Well, after you finish your breakfast." Lin was practically hopping from foot to foot. "Should we go get Indie?" she continued, waggling her eyebrows.

Kit sighed heavily and pushed another sausage into her mouth. "Nah, he's busy with field training. He's going to be gone for a few days at least."

"Okay then," Lin gave Kit an enthusiastic wink. "It's just us girls then."

"I guess." Kit hadn't been friends with Lin for long, but something in her behavior seemed a bit off to her. "Is everything okay?"

"Okay? Everything's amazing. I get to go on a mission with Sister Kit Standing Bear!"

Kit huffed and glared at her. "Don't do that. Don't act like I'm something other than just another priest."

"But you're not *just another priest*. Outside of Father Hoarfrost, you're the only priest in the Temple who's been acknowledged by Titan."

Kit dropped her fork, sending it clattering across the stone floor. Her eyes never left Lin's.

"What? You can't be serious." She cocked an eyebrow at her friend. Her stomach roiled at the thought.

"Of course, I'm serious. It's all everybody's talking about lately. Don't you pay attention to what's going on around you?" Lin leaned in so close that her nose practically touched Kit's. She dropped her voice low into a husky whisper. "I just need to get my gear from my room and then we can get going."

Kit wolfed down the rest of her breakfast so fast that she barely even tasted it. She said a quick thank you to Miyuki before following Lin to her room. The pair walked up the stairs toward the acolyte's dormitory. As they exited the stairwell, there was a hallway that ran perpendicular to the floor's entrance, connecting to three other hallways. The center hallway led to interior rooms that enjoyed no windows. The two outer hallways led to rooms that all had windows, even if they were barely more than a slit in the wall. The acolytes, especially those who lived in rooms without windows, often referred to their quarters as 'cells,' because they didn't seem to afford any more luxury than the dungeons did. Without really thinking about it, Kit headed off to the hall where her old quarters used to be.

"Wrong way," Lin said with a hint of shame in her voice. A deep blush crossed her face. She lowered her eyes, hoping Kit wouldn't notice. "I'm in this section."

"You're in *wash-out alley*?" Kit's shoulders slumped, and she clamped her hand over her mouth. Wash-out alley was a term reserved for where the Temple housed overaged acolytes; those who repeatedly failed the Rite of Abandonment. A sudden pang ripped through Kit's chest. This was also to where the Temple had moved Danny on his sixteenth birthday, after he'd failed to pass the Rite.

Lin simply bowed her head and walked down the hallway. Her room was the first one on the left. Just before opening the door, she turned to Kit. She was gripping the handle on her door so tightly that her knuckles were turning white. Her eyes became glassy, and she dropped her chin to her chest.

"Don't judge me, okay? You're the only person I've ever let into my cell."

Kit took her by the elbow and gave her an empathetic frown. "Lin, I'm really sorry for the wash-out comment. I didn't mean anything by it."

Lin disregarded Kit's remark and opened the door to her room. A waft of spicy, aromatic smells came rushing out into the hallway. Lin lit the lantern hanging on the wall just inside the door. With no windows, or even window slits in the room, it was pitch black inside. As the flame ignited, Kit's jaw practically hit the floor. Every wall, from floor to ceiling, was lined with shelves and every shelf was jam-packed with bottles, jars, and vials.

"Titan's snowballs, Lin. It looks like you've got your own apothecary in here."

Lin's face heated. She was both ashamed and proud of her room and its impressive array of herbs, potions, and reagents.

"It's kind of a hobby of mine," she said with a sheepish grin. She pulled her shoulders up until they were practically touching her ears. "You're the first person to ever visit my cell. Please don't tell anyone what you've seen. Please!"

Kit's mouth was still agape. She walked into Lin's room letting her eyes run over the array of supplies. Her head was shaking involuntarily as she examined the contents of each shelf.

"Um, wow." Kit said. She didn't really know how to react to this. "That's an impressive, no, very impressive collection. I think even Brother Powder would be astounded with this."

"He helps me from time to time," Lin offered. "If something I'm missing comes in, he lets me know."

Kit immediately thought back to when Brother Powder gave her the two rejuvenation potions, and how much trouble he got into for doing that. "Don't ever tell anybody else that Powder is feeding your collection addiction. I've already gotten him into enough trouble, all by myself. He doesn't need any more grief."

"I heard about that," Lin admitted. "It's why I knew I could trust you with *all this*. Powder's your friend, too, and you'd never intentionally hurt him."

Kit was still examining the contents of the shelves. Her mind was not fully engaged in the conversation.

"Are you sure you're cut out for the priesthood? I mean, you've never had a chance to bond with Titan, even after so many devoted cycles."

Lin's eyes immediately went huge and glassy, giving Kit a sudden knot in her stomach. Yet again, it was like she had just kicked a puppy.

"Sweet Titan, Lin, I'm so sorry. My mouth, well, it's not attached to my brain, and I say the stupidest things."

Lin cast her eyes downward. She paused for a while, obviously trying to find the right words. "My grandmother was a priest of Titan. She made it sound as though it was the best thing on Orth. I tried. Honestly, I did! Every day, I tried to hear the call of Titan, but I never did." Lin raised her head and clutched her hand over her heart. "I'd much rather study spells and potions and enchantments. Oh, to be an enchanter or an alchemist! I'd make the most powerful weapon ever seen! But that's not what I'm meant to be. I'm meant to serve Titan, and that's what I'll do."

"Lin," Kit moved in closer so that she could hear her whisper. "Serve Titan however you wish. Devote your love to him, but don't forsake who you are for it. If you seek to bend items to your will for the glory of Titan, that's what you should be doing!"

Tears spilled down Lin's cheeks while her lower lip quivered. "You wouldn't think less of me? My grandmother would hate me!"

Kit wrapped her arms around the young woman and gave her a deep hug. Then pulling away, she grasped Lin by her arms, forcing her to look directly into her dark brown eyes. The flickering torchlight reflected the gold rings, making them dazzle brightly.

"Your grandmother loves you and she would want you to be happy. Titan seeks those who would help him. How you do that doesn't matter, only that you do."

Lin pulled away and wiped the tears from her cheeks. "Are you sure?"

Kit nodded her head adamantly and Lin stood up straighter and jutted her chin out.

"I will serve Titan in my own way. If my grandmother loves me, and if she loves Titan, she'll understand and support me." Lin paused briefly. "But what about you? Will you think less of me if I choose not to continue as an acolyte?"

Kit gave Lin a broad smile and pulled her in for another deep hug. She put her mouth very close to Lin's ear and whispered, "I don't think I could ever think less of you!"

Lin, too, had smiled before her expression turned into outrage. She forcibly pushed Kit away from herself. "And just what do you mean by that?"

Kit stood there stoned face as Lin's cheeks reddened. Unable to maintain her own composure, Kit laughed deeply and buckled at the waist.

"I like you, Lin. You don't let things slip past you." Kit headed for the door. "Get your gear together and let's get going."

Lin quickly slipped on her acolyte's light leather armor. She sneered at it, knowing it was only the simplest of armors except for the symbol of Titan embossed over the left breast. "Will this do?"

"I don't see why not." Kit gave her a bit of a wink. "You're not expecting trouble in Ashcroft, are you?"

The possibility there would be no trouble seemed disappointing to her. "If the rumors are true, there might be followers of Arachnielle there. That's the sort of thing that could lead to trouble, isn't it?"

"I suppose. I've never met any before, so I can't say for sure." Kit suddenly remembered that she had a spare set of armor in her quarters. "I've a spare suit of studded leather armor that Harding gave me. You can have it if you want."

Lin examined Kit's wolf-hide armor that she was wearing. It truly was a masterful work of art. The way the leather had been cured made it tough as steel but soft like butter. The thick fur collar and trim gave it an extremely rich look. Lin could only dream of placing enchantments on such wondrous equipment. "If you don't need it anymore, I'd be *honored* to wear it." The way she said 'honored' made Kit cringe inside. "And I've got a birthday present for you. I was going to wait until we got to Ashcroft but... I'm sure my grandmother won't mind."

Kit held up her hands and shook her head vigorously. "I don't need a present, Lin. Really." But truth be told, Lin's last statement piqued Kit's curiosity. "Why would your grandmother care if you gave me a present?"

Without a response, Lin reached under her bed and pulled out something wrapped in a deep blue linen. She thrust it out at Kit.

"Open it up and I'll tell you." The acolyte was practically vibrating with excitement.

Kit took the present and raised an eyebrow at her. She pulled back the linen covering revealing an ornate double-headed battle hammer. It glistened in the torchlight. Intricate patterns and runes had been engraved over the entire hammer head. Each groove seemed to have a slight glow, giving it a truly *magical* appearance. Kit ran her fingers over the hammer's cool, silver metal. Her hand paused for a moment at Titan's symbol, a circle with two crossed hammers. A shiver ran up her arm.

"Is this mithril?" Kit asked as she tested the weight and balance of the weapon. Her eyes went wide as she remembered the first time she'd met Lin, right after her Rite of Acknowledgement. This was the very same battle hammer strapped to her back.

"It used to be my grandmother's. She gave it to me on the anniversary of my fifteenth cycle. I believe she had hoped it would – incentivize me – into becoming a priest." She shrugged and gave Kit a bit of a playful sneer. "I've never been particularly skilled with a hammer, so I'm giving it to you. You know, to do Titan's will."

Kit pushed the hammer back toward Lin and shook her head. "I can't take this. I just can't. It's too much. Your grandmother gave this to you!"

Lin pushed the hammer back toward Kit. "And now I'm giving it to you. I'm sure she'd be okay with it... I think."

"I can't, Lin. It's very generous of you to offer it to me, but it's an extremely expensive weapon. Outside the dwarven kingdom of Miran Knott, mithril weapons are incredibly rare."

"This one is even more rare." Lin said, her eyes twinkling with glee. "It has a feather-light enchantment, plus three levels of sun enchantments on it, too. When my grandmother gave it to me, I could barely lift it, let alone swing it. It seems dwarves like their weapons incredibly heavy."

Kit spun the hammer in her hands. Its head was enormous, but it was significantly lighter than her iron hammer. It was perfectly balanced. "Did you enchant this yourself?"

"I put the feather-light enchantment, plus the first two sun enchantments on it. I had to cash in a favor to get the third sun enchantment added. It's going to be really effective if you ever face another vampire."

"Indie told me that vampires being hurt by the sun is a myth." Kit hated getting conflicting information. It made it extremely difficult to know which was correct.

"He's partially right," Lin said as she pulled a bow and quiver out from under her bed. Kit was starting to think she had a full arsenal of weapons under there. "Sunshine doesn't hurt them, but it does weaken them if they stay in it for too long. Sun enchantments are like being hit with concentrated sunlight. In the right conditions it can practically roast them."

"How do you know this stuff? They don't teach this as a part of the Temple curriculum." Kit was suddenly afraid that she had been taught this but had slept through the class. She never really understood why, but as soon as enchantment classes began, she simply couldn't keep her eyes open.

Lin shrugged. "It's been quite a few cycles since I had to attend classes. When I'm not running errands for Father Hoarfrost, I read. I read a lot." She pulled on one of the shelves. It swung out like a door, exposing yet another set of shelves behind it. These shelves were crammed full of books and scrolls of various sizes and colors. Their dusky aroma wafted out with the swing of the shelf.

"You've read all of these?" Kit tried to scan the titles on the spines of the books, but she couldn't make out very many of them.

"This is just one of my book collections." Lin had a huge smile on her face. "There are three more just like it," she said as she pointed to three other shelves.

"How long has it been since you last attended classes here?" Kit had expected that Lin was a cycle or two older than her, but now she wasn't so sure.

"Well, I turn twenty-two on my next birthday," Lin answered. She crinkled her nose as she tried to do the math. "So almost six cycles."

Kit very nearly made a snide remark but somehow managed to rein in her tongue for once. "Thank you," she said instead, motioning to the hammer in her hand. "If you change your mind and you want this back, just say the word and it's yours."

Lin laughed, reached under her bed again and produced a pair of blessed longswords. Blessed weapons were an enigma that no enchanter really understood. During the forging process the smith would quench the steel in ice stolen from Titan's ice statue. Typically, putting forge-hot metal into cold water would make the steel brittle, but the ice from Titan's statue reacted differently. It hardened the steel and, at the same time, imbued it with magic that made the weapon particularly useful against netherworld creatures and animated corpses. Even though blessed weapons were incredibly powerful, the Temple frowned on them because they deemed the use of Titan's statue for such endeavors as blasphemous. Lin didn't seem to care one bit. Now that Titan's ice statue was gone, these blessed weapons would never again be created.

"Swords and bows are more my style," Lin said as she gazed down at her twin long swords. "Even without a feather-light enchantment, these are less than a tenth of the weight of that hammer." She put on a small display of her swordsmanship before strapping them to her hips. "C'mon, let's get going."

The two headed up a flight of stairs to the priests' quarters. There was only one hallway here running down the middle of the dormitory. Kit's room was at the far end of the hall.

"My new room," Kit said as she opened the door, revealing a room that resembled a hallway with a window at the end of it. Like the acolytes' rooms there was a stone bed with a thin straw mattress on it. Beside the bed was a small wooden writing desk that also served as a night table. A tall, simply carved wardrobe, which many acolytes considered as a luxury item, was wide enough to hang eight robes. Near the end of the room, with a view out the window to where Titan's statue used to be, was an iron kneeler, a piece of furniture that resembled a torture device.

Lin stepped into the room and frowned heavily. "It's not much of an upgrade from the cells, is it," she said as she examined the interior. "At least you get a window and a wardrobe though. That's a huge step up from what we acolytes get." Lin chuckled as she took a closer look at the kneeler. Her gaze lingered on the iron grate that the priest was expected to kneel on while in prayer. It looked like it could slice open your knees if you weren't careful. "Maybe I'm glad not to have been promoted to priest. I don't think I could stand having to pray on this. The cold stone floor in my cell looks considerably more... comfortable than this contraption."

Kit shrugged. "I think it's intended to prepare the priest for the Rite of Acknowledgement. The altar steps at the foot of Titan's statue were just as uncomfortable – more so, really, because they're also freezing cold."

Lin just shook her head at the kneeler and stared out the window.

"Without the statue glaring down at us, Mount Toka looks really beautiful." Lin sighed and let her hands run over the window's thick stone ledge. "The world is changing, Kit. Can't you feel it?"

Kit just shrugged and opened up the wardrobe. She removed the studded leather armor. She wasn't sure why, but she felt a sentimental attachment to it. Kit shook off the feeling and held the armor out for Lin.

"Here you go. It's worn, but it's still functional. It barely weighs any more than the light leather you've got on now."

Lin slipped off her leather armor and pulled on the studded leather armor Kit had handed her. She shrugged her shoulders a few times as she tried to get a feel for it. "It's a bit heavier, but it's still pretty comfortable." Lin ran her fingers over the rounded steel studs that adorned the armor's breast plate and pauldrons. "Thank you!"

"Don't mention it," Kit said as she slipped out of her robe. She padded across the room to her wardrobe and pulled out a pair of thin, loose-fitting leather trousers and a linen tunic. She was just about to pull on the trousers when she noticed Lin staring at her. Kit suddenly became uncomfortable standing nude in front of the woman.

"What's up?" Kit asked. The question seemed to have surprised Lin, causing her to practically yelp. Lin immediately blushed scarlet and turned away.

Kit just shook her head, pulled up her pants and slipped into her linen tunic. She pulled out the wolf-skin armor that Fenrir had made for her and slipped it on. She ran her fingers over the thick wolf-fur collar. It drew up the memory of the dire wolf that she had been forced to kill. Even though some time had passed, Kit still maintained the connection to the animal's spirit.

She had just finished clipping up the last of her buckles when Lin handed Kit the chainmail gloves Captain Harding had given her. Lin's face was still bright red.

"We really should get going. We've spent too much time talking as it is." Kit was already out the door and heading for the stairs by the time she'd finished the sentence.

Standing in Kit's room by herself, Lin fanned her face with her hand and gave a long, slow whistle before she bolted out of the room and slammed the door closed behind her.

As they headed down the stairwell, Kit couldn't resist prying a bit into Lin's personal life.

"I've got to ask; how can you possibly afford these weapons? Are your parents rich?" There were several moments of silence as they continued down the stairs to the main floor of the Temple. "Lin?"

"Yes, my parents are rich, but they don't buy me anything, well not weapons anyway. My mother is forever sending me clothes. She hates that I wear *Temple rags* as she calls them." She tugged on the sleeve of the rough-spun tunic she was wearing as if to make a point. "But I have to say some of the stuff she sends me is really nice."

As they stepped out the Temple's main door, a gust of wind bit lightly at Kit's skin. She shielded her face for a moment while her eyes adjusted to the morning's brilliant light. The sky was so clear and bright it was more white than blue. The bite of the wind welcomed them like a familiar friend.

"So where do you get the weapons from, then?" Kit asked while she strode across the expansive stone landing at the top of the formidable staircase leading down from the Temple.

Lin quickly stole a glance over her shoulder as though checking to see if somebody might be close enough to listen in on their conversation. She moved her mouth uncomfortably close to Kit's ear.

"I trade for them," she whispered. "Sometimes for services, sometimes for information."

Kit pulled away. Her eyes bulged and her mouth dropped open. "You trade your *services*?" The words came out much louder than Kit had intended. Lin's head quickly swiveled about before she glared at Kit.

"Not like *that*!" Lin practically screamed. Her voice suddenly dropped back down to a hoarse whisper. "I put enchantments on weapons, and in return,... I get to keep one or two pieces. I enchant those and trade them up for better ones."

By the time they made it to the bottom of the Temple's staircase, Lin was puffing heavily, and her forehead was wet with perspiration. Tiny rivulets were pouring down from her temples. Kit, on the other hand, was barely even breathing hard.

"You also said you trade information," Kit whispered, her head tilted slightly to the side. She couldn't help wanting to know what sort of information the woman might trade on. "I trust it's not the sort of information you might acquire hanging outside Hoarfrost's office door?"

Lin's face immediately turned beet red.

"Lin, tell me you're not doing that. Are you?"

"I don't sell anything important," she said as her shoulders hunched forward. A pained expression crossed Lin's face as her head spun left and right, again looking to see who might be listening.

"I sit in on budget and planning meetings. I take notes and distribute them to the senior priests." Lin rolled her eyes. "Sometimes I let vendors know if they are planning any major expenditures. That way they can make sure they have enough supply on hand to sell to the Temple. In particular, I like to share news of bulk purchases of weapons, you know, to the weapon smiths. In return they give me access to some of their nicer pieces." Lin pulled out a jet-black, narrow-bladed dagger that she had strapped to her thigh.

"Is that obsidian?"

Lin nodded and pushed the dagger back into its sheath. "Next time I can pick one up for you – if you'd like."

Kit just patted her fancy new hammer and gave Lin a lopsided grin. "No need, I already have more weapon here than I'd have ever expected in my entire life."

The conversation had completely distracted Kit. She was so intent on learning more about Lin that she had completely forgotten that she had intended to head for the stables.

"Do you want to ride to Ashcroft?" Kit asked. She really wanted to take Angel out again.

Lin shook her head and crinkled her nose. "Nah. I'm not much of a rider. Besides, it's a nice walk to the village and it will give us time to chat."

Lin's fingers were twiddling uncontrollably as she waited for Kit's response. When she gave Kit a tiny pout, the young priest chuckled and pursed her lips. "Sure, it's a nice day for a walk."

Lin squealed and clapped her hands together. She practically skipped down the street.

CHAPTER FOUR

TASEKO

Danny's arms, or wings, or whatever they should be called were nearly ready to fall off his body as the city of Taseko came into view. Like most Berrat communities its tiny clay huts were arranged in concentric circles spreading out from its heart. The center would be reserved for community buildings, a central gathering place, plus the homes of the elders. He had little recollection of his village but from high above the city the configuration of the buildings appeared *magical*.

He had been flying for more than a full day without any rest and without any food. He hated the idea of leaving Kit behind, especially without saying goodbye. Somehow leaving a letter for her felt... cowardly. He knew she'd have wanted to come and help and that she'd have only slowed him down. When their mutual friend, Slate, had told him about the problems at his home in northern Berrathia, he had no choice but to leave immediately.

It had barely been a week since Danny discovered that he could shift into a phoenix. The last thing he remembered before turning into this firebird *thing* was Eris, one of the five Fates terrorizing Orth, throwing him off the side of a mountain. He remembered falling, the cliff face passing in front of his eyes in a blur of ice and snow and rock. He remembered thinking he had failed Kit, that he had let his love for her get in the way of his helping her. He remembered the searing pain he experienced the moment his body plunged upon the rocks hundreds of feet below from where he had started his rapid descent. There was a brilliant flash of light when his spirit left his body. Something was trying to pull him away from his ruined corpse. A great force tugged at his soul, but he was somehow tethered, preventing the indomitable force from having him. He remembered the feeling of life flowing back into his body as flames licked up around him, weaving their way through his broken frame, mending it, and rebinding it to his soul.

Flying over the city, watching its people going about their lives, Danny realized that he had no clue what he was going to do. He came to find his family, to free the people and to destroy the slavers. But he had no plan, not even an inkling, about how he was going to go about doing any of that. He was reacting, driven by instinct and a burning need to know his family was safe.

Danny's home, the village he was born in, was not far from Taseko but he was only six cycles when his parents took him to Aarall. They had left him at the Temple of the Fist, the seat of Titan's high priest. They had instructed him to learn as much as he could about Titan and his worshippers. Twelve summers had passed since he'd last been home.

With only a vague notion that his village was near the city, Danny flew in ever-widening circles, hoping beyond hope that he would recognize the village when he flew over it.

His heart sank when the sole village he flew over was nothing more than a pile of ash and rubble. It was the only community within walking distance to Taseko, the only real fact he remembered from his childhood. Circling downward, hoping to get a better look, he spotted a group of Berrat being set upon by, of all things, a Gigas.

Why would he be attacking them? The Gigas are pacifistic by nature. It's almost impossible to make them become aggressive.

This was something Danny had learned from his Gigas friend, Amara, an acolyte at the Temple. Even though she did enjoy using her size and strength to inflict pain upon him, it was always in good natured fun, never intending to cause any serious harm. Roughhousing with family and friends was a favorite pastime of the Gigas.

This particular giant was not pacifistic, not at all. Danny watched in horror as the big man grabbed one of the Berrat, ripping his arm from his body like he was pulling a wing from a fly. The only conclusion Danny could come to, the only logical conclusion based on the circumstances unfolding before him, this Gigas was a slaver.

Not today.

Remembering back to the first time Danny had changed into his firebird form, he had killed a shadow demon by flying himself through its back like a bird-shaped fireball.

It worked before.

Using the Berrats as a diversion, he flew to the back of the marauding Gigas before sending himself into a dive, picking up speed at a terrifying rate. Just before making contact Danny unleashed his firebird screech, a high-pitched battle cry, filling himself with resolve.

This was a mistake.

With catlike reflexes the giant spun and swatted the firebird from the air, extinguished his flames and slammed him into the branches of nearby evergreens.

"You've got a new weapon, I see," the Gigas said with a wicked smile, striding towards the Berrat as they fanned out around him. The man was huge. He was bare-chested, showing off his near-black, abnormally muscled body. "Throw whatever you've got at me, there will not be a single slaver alive by the time I am finished with you."

Were they attacking him? It would explain his fighting. The Gigas could be pacifists, but they wouldn't allow themselves to be openly attacked.

"We could ask for a mountain of gold for you, Ulip," one of the Berrat said, as he shook out his black-feathered cloak. He was dragging a weighted net behind him. "But, after the trouble you've caused us, I think *The Claw* would rather keep you for a plaything."

"The Beak, The Wing, The Claw; they'll all fall to my blade. We will put an end to your ways. We will reclaim the north." The Gigas' voice was full of defiant confidence. There was no bravado to his words or to his voice. He was simply stating facts. A point he made abundantly clear when he hacked the net-wielding Berrat in two with his enormous black-iron blade.

Danny now understood that he had attacked the wrong side. Even though the Gigas was certainly capable of defending himself, he wasn't going to let him fight alone. Once he managed to free himself from the bows of the giant pine, he leapt from the branches, immediately igniting into bright red flames. Flying barely a foot off the ground, he sped towards the Berrat as they closed in on the Gigas. One by one, he flew headlong into them, bursting through their bodies, setting each of them ablaze.

The look on the Gigas' face was a mixture of surprise and glee as he walked among the burning bodies of the fallen slavers. There was a look of utter satisfaction as he stomped upon them, extinguishing their flames and any hope that one or more might survive the firebird's attack.

"Why did you kill them, slaver?" the giant man boomed out, his voice a terrible baritone. "Why would you kill your own?"

Danny changed back to his Berrat form just before landing, crashing rather, in a heap on the ground. He managed to keep a good number of paces between himself and the giant just in case the big guy was considering ripping him into tiny pieces like he did the others.

"I'm no slaver," Danny said, keeping his distance as the Gigas moved towards him. "I thought you were attacking these Berrat. I didn't know they were slavers."

"How could you not know?" Ulip asked, continuing to move on Danny while the red-headed Berrat back peddled as fast as he could. "They are wearing Split Crows clothing. How could you not see their black feathered capes?"

"I am from Aarall," Danny sputtered out as though the declaration would explain everything. The way the Gigas continued to bear down on him, it obviously didn't explain anything. "My family is from this village. I was told they were attacked."

"That attack took place nearly two moons ago," Ulip declared. He was drawing his blade back, ready to bring it to bear. He did not believe anything Danny was saying.

"I only found out yesterday. I came immediately." Danny continued to retreat but not quickly enough to maintain his distance. "I was born here. I left when I was barely six."

"What is your name?" the giant asked, finally stopping his progress. He rolled his bare shoulders. The muscles across his upper body rippled. His heavy brow hung low over his nose, almost entirely hiding his beady black eyes.

"My name's Danny."

"What is your full name?" the giant asked again, his eyes narrowing. He seemed to be looking at the young Berrat in a new light.

"Danny Fox-Dancing."

"What were your parents' names?" The edge was now gone from the big man's voice, but it was still filled with distrust. He slowly moved forward, his hand flexing as he renewed his grip on the handle of his colossal sword.

"What do you mean, were?" Suddenly Danny was no longer back peddling; he was now striding towards the giant. His hands were clenched by his side while flames licked from the corners of his eyes. "What happened to my parents?"

"Show me your mark," Ulip said, holding out the point of his giant sword to keep Danny from getting any closer.

"What mark?"

"If you do not bear the mark, you are not who you say you are." Danny held out his hands, turning them over, looking for whatever mark the man was asking about. "The mark is not on your hands or your arms."

"Then where is it?" Danny was becoming frustrated at this point, his anger building enough that he was ready to either try to finish off this giant oaf or he would just fly away. But the man had information about what had happened here at his family's village. He wasn't giving up until he got it.

"The mark is on the back of your neck, if you have it."

"How could I know about a mark that I can't see?" The frustration in Danny was now coming out in his voice. The height difference forced him to crane his neck to look up at the giant that was now only a few feet away. "How can you ask me about something that I would have no way of knowing anything about?" The question caused the Gigas to pause, unsure of how to proceed. His indecision made Danny groan. "Will you abide by the laws of your people, by not attacking an unarmed person, somebody who poses you no threat?"

"You've already attacked me," Ulip said, bending over top of the Berrat who was barely more than half his size. He bared his teeth and seethed. "I am within my rights to kill you. It is the law of my fire drake clan and every other clan, alive or since passed."

"Will you accept my offer of peace?" Danny asked, holding out his hands in front of himself, showing he held no weapon.

"If I do, how do I know you won't attack me?" This conversation was forcing Ulip to think things through and he was clearly not enjoying it.

"Are you actually afraid that I might attack you?" Danny asked, continuing to hold out his hands. "I just watched you rip these slavers apart like they were nothing. Does my physique make you tremble?"

The giant's growl sounded like a great bear. "I accept your offer of peace. I will not act against you unless you dishonor yourself and attempt to harm me." Following Danny's gesture, the giant pushed the tip of his blade into the soft ground and held out his empty hands. "Now, lift your hair and let me look at the back of your neck."

"Keep your distance," Danny said as he pulled his long red hair up over his head. He suddenly had an irresistible urge to pretend he was a dancing girl holding his hair in a provocative pose. He considered swinging his hips in slow, rhythmic circles but Ulip didn't appear to be the *humorous* type.

"Huh," the giant declared before picking up his blade and jamming it into its scabbard. "Welcome home, Danny Fox-Dancing."

"Do I have the mark or is whatever it was you were looking for back there?"

"It is," Ulip declared, a hint of admiration in his voice. "You are Dannith, son of Paylor and Dyanna Fox-Dancing. You bear your father's mark."

"Where are my parents? What happened to my village? Who are the Split Crows?"

"Follow me," Ulip said. "I'm going to introduce you to some folks."

Chapter Five

ASHCROFT

When Kit and Lin arrived at Ashcroft, Lin was practically dragging Kit through the streets. The village was quite pretty with small brightly colored stone and wood houses with well-tended gardens out front. The streets were packed dirt and clay. Tall wooden poles, with oil lanterns dangling down from them, stood at regular intervals along the roadway.

"Good day to you, Lin!" a Berrat couple called out, as they collected eggs from a chicken coup in their front yard. Lin smiled and waved back to them. No sooner had they passed the couple, their voices dropped to low whispers, and they hurried back into their tiny, bright red home.

"How do they know you?" Kit asked as she surveyed the area. Several Berrat families were walking along the street in open, animated conversation with Nomad families. The children, who had been pushing barrel bands with a small stick, stopped their play and stared at Lin. They gave her a small wave before racing off to catch up with the barrel hoops that were rolling away from them.

"I come here often to visit my grandmother," Lin replied with a shrug. "She's the village elder. She took up the mantle after she retired from the Temple a few cycles ago. The previous elder passed away and the man who was next in succession, Byrnard Whiting, is not well liked by the community. Truth is, I don't think anybody trusted that he'd have the villagers' best interests at heart."

"Why's that?" Kit asked while she surveyed the people, looking for any signs of unrest. Surely something had to be going on here to warrant Father Hoarfrost sending them to investigate. But, as far as Kit could tell, the village was quiet and peaceful, and everyone seemed content.

"According to my grandmother, Elder Byrnard would only advocate for the rich, even if it meant the poorer members of the community suffered." Lin turned away like she couldn't bear to have Kit see her face. "I'm ashamed to say it but my parents were some of those who benefited significantly from his actions."

"Your parents live here, too?" Kit was suddenly much more attentive to what Lin was saying.

"No, not anymore. They moved to Two Peaks, the kingdom capital, almost seven cycles ago, pretty much right after I failed my Rite of Abandonment for the third time." Lin's face crumpled. "They said it was for *business reasons*, but really, I just think I was an embarrassment to them."

Kit took Lin's hand and squeezed it hard. She stared up at Lin until her friend looked her square in the eye. "If you were an embarrassment to them, then your parents are morons." Once again, Kit failed to filter the words that came out of her mouth. Before she even had a chance to apologize, Lin nodded.

"I couldn't have said it better myself." Lin chuckled a little and gave Kit a crooked smile. "That's not the first time I've heard that. My grandmother tells me that all the time." Lin pulled her hand away from Kit's and continued walking up the street. "My grandmother loves my mother, with all her heart, but she was never happy with her taste in men. She refers to my father as *that man your mother married.*"

Lin suddenly became aware that she was spilling too many family secrets, but when she noticed Kit listening intently, she pressed forward. "My father, Lord Arthure, as he likes to refer to himself, is from an incredibly old family of mages. He and Lady Jaquine, my mother, are forever traveling across Arnnor doing Titan knows what. They left me with my grandmother more often than not. I guess that, since I was at the Temple all the time anyway, my grandmother had me join classes with the other novices. When my grandmother told them that I was doing very well in my studies they just... left me there."

"Your grandmother just enrolled you as a novice at the Temple while your parents were gone?" Kit's eyes were wide in disbelief. "They must have been furious with her."

Lin shook her head. "You'd think so, but according to my grandmother, they seemed more relieved than anything else. I guess I was just a burden on them. I haven't seen them in a long time now. My mother sends me expensive gifts from time to time. I think she's just trying to buy my love, but I don't care anymore. I've got my grandmother, the Temple, and my friends." She gave Kit a wink when she said *friends*.

The two girls walked in silence for several minutes. People continued to greet Lin as they turned down a rundown side street that led them to a seemingly poorer part of the village. The street there was much narrower than the others. There were no oil lanterns to light the way at night and the homes had little space for a front garden. They stopped at a simple house made of rough-cut logs, chinked with mud. It was a rather cheery shade of yellow with bright green moss growing out of the mud chinking. It made the house look like it had green and yellow stripes.

"This is my grandmother's house," Lin said. She rocked up onto the balls of her toes and her chest noticeably puffed out.

Kit involuntarily cocked an eyebrow. "Don't the village elders usually live in much fancier homes? The Lord of Templeton lives in a grand mansion."

"There is an exceptionally large house that was built by the community for the head elder to live in, but my grandmother refused to use it. Instead, she turned it into an orphanage." Lin was beginning to laugh. "You should have seen the uproar that came from the wealthy community. Their homes practically surround the orphanage. They were outraged, having to live so close to the *dirty little children nobody wanted.* I was never prouder of my grandmother."

At that moment an old nomad woman stepped out the front door. Her hair was white as snow and it was tied in a loose braid that hung over her shoulder, down past her waist. Her dark brown eyes were sunk deep into her face but still sparkled with vitality. There were a number of other people with her. They all appeared distraught.

"Lin!" the old woman practically screamed. The wrinkles that covered the woman's face seemed to get even deeper when she gave Lin a broad toothless smile. "I'm so glad you've come, and you've brought Sister Standing Bear with you. Titan be praised!"

Kit couldn't understand how this woman could know her. She didn't recall ever seeing her at the Temple.

"Pleased to meet you,..." it was only at that moment that Kit realized she didn't know the woman's name. Lin had only ever referred to her as her grand-mother.

"Call me Grams, everybody else does." For a retired priest of Titan and a village elder, Grams was very informal. Kit took an instant liking to her. She simply had that, certain something, that told you she cared.

The people who had come out with Grams jostled each other to get closer to Kit. "The Savior of Aarall," they kept saying as they reached out to touch her. Perhaps they believed that doing so would give them good luck.

While Kit tried to avoid their grasping hands, they talked over one another, each of them trying to tell their story to the famous young priest. Unfortunately, there was so much commotion and so many voices, Kit couldn't make out a word they were saying.

"Hush!" Grams' sudden harsh voice cut through the din instantly. Her guests immediately clamped their mouths shut and took a step away from Kit.

There's the priest of Titan.

Kit looked upon the old woman in a new light. This frail, hunched over elder, could command people around her with the same authority as Father Hoarfrost.

"I'm assuming you two are here to help with our *problem*?" Grams focused her eyes squarely on Kit when she asked the question.

Kit dipped her head slightly. "I will do what I can, but – I'm not exactly sure what the problem is. I serve my lord, Titan, but if I can render aid to the community, I will do so willingly."

Grams laughed, perhaps despite the seriousness of the situation. "Relax, Sister, I'm no longer a member of the Temple. There's no need to impress me with the traditional responses."

Kit's face reddened slightly as she gave the old woman a tiny smile.

Grams shooed away the people who had been in her home. "Off with you now. As you can see, we've got the situation under control."

As the people left, they bowed deeply to Kit, repeating, "We are saved. Titan has heard our prayers. We are saved."

Grams hitched her arms with Kit's and Lin's and led them briskly into her house. Kit had never been more relieved to be dragged away from a situation.

The interior of the home was painted the same cheery yellow as the outside. There was practically no furniture in the room, save for a large rectangular wooden table surrounded by chairs and a single comfy looking sofa beside a deep stone fireplace. The walls were completely bare except for a symbol of Titan that was likely made of brass.

Grams motioned to the heavy wooden chairs that surrounded the table. "Please, sit. Would you like something to eat or drink? You must be hungry after your journey here?"

Kit was about to decline but Lin beat her to the punch. "Yes, please, Grams. Do you have..." Lin pursed her lips waiting for her grandmother to finish the sentence.

"Fresh goat's milk and winterberry biscuits?" A warm smile split Grams' face when Lin's eyes sparkled. She licked her lips as she remembered the biscuits' fabulous flavors. "Of course, I do."

Lin started doing a happy dance in her chair as her grandmother hobbled into the kitchen. A few moments later she returned with a tray of food and drink. As Grams poured the fresh milk into the earthenware mugs, she told Kit about the problems they'd been having.

"Nearly a moon ago two strangers came to our village." Grams' lip curled up and her eyes went dead. "With their oil-slicked hair and sallow skin, ugh, they made my flesh crawl." Grams feigned a shiver.

"They gathered the young and told them of the power and the glory of following Arachnielle, the spider god." Grams flopped into one of the chairs across from Kit.

"They were very convincing. Many of the children fell into their web of deceit." The old woman blinked several times, trying hard to hold back tears that threatened to spring from her eyes. "We tried to make these strangers leave. We tried to convince the children not to listen to them. My grandson, Treedale, attacked one of the two men. All he wanted to do was scare him off, but the stranger was very strong. He toyed with my grandson like a cat with a mouse. When Treedale managed to get a lick in, the man struck him so hard that he knocked the boy unconscious. The children scattered when they saw it happen."

Grams was trembling badly. Kit locked her unblinking gaze on the old woman. The story had totally mesmerized her.

Grams swallowed hard. "He scooped up my grandson and threw him over his shoulder. They just... disappeared into the night. Nobody has seen either of them since.

Lin gasped and covered her hand over her mouth. She made a weak strangled noise and buried her face into her hands. Her shoulders heaved heavily.

"Lin?" Kit asked, placing her hand gently on the woman's shoulder. Kit could feel waves of distress pouring off her. When Lin lifted her head, tears were streaming down her face.

"Grandmother, how could you let them take him. How could you let them take my brother? He's just a skinny little kid. He had no business trying to defend the village. That's your job!" Lin was practically screaming as the last few words fell from her mouth.

The old woman stammered; her bottom lip quivered as she tried to find an answer for Lin. "I... I wanted to stop them but... I couldn't." At that point despair completely overtook her as well, and she, too, wept openly as she collapsed onto the table.

Kit tried to console the women, but their spirits were crushed. She pushed herself away from the table and placed her hand on her battle hammer.

"Is the second stranger still in the village?" Kit asked Grams, her voice hard as steel.

Lin's grandmother raised her head up and nodded. Her shoulders slumped like she was carrying the weight of the world on herself. With a heavy sigh she picked herself up and moved next to Lin. The old woman wrapped her weary arms around her granddaughter and drew her in. The two of them clutched onto each other as a drowning man might clutch a broken plank in rough seas. With their faces buried in each other's shoulders they wailed uncontrollably.

Kit pushed her chair in, slamming it against the table a little harder than intended. Her fury was getting the better of her and she desperately wanted a place to unleash it.

"I will speak to the stranger and show him the error of his ways. The only true path to righteousness is through Titan." Kit didn't bother waiting for a response. The two women were still clutching tightly to each other. She strode across the room, slamming the front door as she exited.

The people she'd met earlier were standing on the street in front of Grams' home. They all jumped at the sound of Kit slamming the door.

"Where is he?" She growled at the onlookers as she pulled on her chainmail gloves. "Where is this *stranger*?"

"He's at the orphanage," one of the women replied as she straightened her pale green dress. She pointed her long bony finger toward the large house at the top of a hill overlooking the village. The house was more of a mansion really, with tall pillars supporting a balcony that overlooked the front gardens. Even from a distance it was extremely impressive.

CHAPTER SIX

THE MAN IN BLACK

Without so much as another word Kit broke into a run. Her boots kicked up clods of dirt as she ran along the street that led up towards the mansion. Her blood was pumping hard, making her ears ring as she turned onto the cobbled street that passed through a set of heavy, wrought-iron gates. There were four unkempt armed guards at the entrance, dressed in ragged armor. They scrambled frantically about as the young woman raced past them.

At the entrance to the orphanage an even taller, more ornate set of wrought-iron gates blocked the entrance to the mansion. Well, they would have if they weren't already open and covered in a thick layer of rust. Heavy vines wound their way through their twisted, black iron bars, adding to their austere appearance. Beyond the gates, up a winding cobble stone walkway, stood a majestic building constructed of red brick and gleaming white stone. Grand fluted pillars held up an ostentatious second-floor balcony that overlooked the mansion's dilapidated front gardens.

Kit lowered her head and redoubled her efforts as she bolted up the walkway, her arms pumping hard at her side. As she crested the hill a small theater of sorts came into view. It had a low dome with a series of benches that rose up, allowing those present to have a clear view of the venue. A tall, thin man with sallow skin and slicked back white hair sat at the edge of the stage. His feet dangled off the edge. He wore fine black silk clothing that covered him from neck to boot. There was a large gathering of children sitting on the benches at the man's feet. They sat in rapture of the man as he wove his tale, speaking of the glory and the power of Arachnielle. As Kit approached, a wicked smile crossed his face.

"Arachnielle is the one true god! To follow any other is to waste your life." His voice dripped with magic. He was clearly an orator of significant skill, perhaps a *bard* of some sort. Kit had never met a bard before, but she had heard tales of their magic-infused voices and how they could ensnare weak minded individuals through words or song. She had even heard a tale about a bard who had enchanted the children of a village and had coaxed them into willingly leaving their homes and family.

The bard's magic had no effect on Kit. She cocked an eyebrow and drew her battle hammer. She let it swing menacingly at her hip as she took longer, more purposeful strides towards the man.

"You are mistaken," Kit called out. The children all turned to see who had spoken. Their eyes were wide, glassy, and glazed over. They were either in awe of this man or they were utterly terrified of him. Either way, Kit was going to break his hold over them.

Kit's voice boomed out as she stormed down the steps of the theater towards the stage.

"Titan is the true path to justice and righteousness. Only through *him* will your life have meaning!"

The man's sallow skin went even paler. His neck tipped back slightly, and he brought his hands slowly up to his cheeks. He stared at Kit, unblinking. Whatever spell this man had woven over the children was immediately broken. Perhaps Kit's faith was an inspiration to those gathered, helping to free them from their rapture. They scampered up from their benches and moved behind Kit like she was a shield protecting them from the stranger.

"Never before have I felt such power and devotion to one's god!" The wide-eyed stranger's hands dropped limp at his sides as he hopped down from the stage. He reached out for a moment, then retracted his hand. His shoulders crumpled inwards as he stared down at his shiny, black boots. "How could I have been so blinded?"

"Where is the boy, Treedale? The one your cohort took prisoner." Kit softened her tone slightly after the man's act of contrition.

As he explained where to find their camp, a small group of villagers gathered at the top of the stairs that led down to the stage. Most of them had armed themselves with farm implements and assorted crude weapons but there was also a handful of them, the guards who had been at the main gate, who were dressed in proper armor, carrying broadswords and shields. Based on their angry tones, Kit assumed they were there to lynch the man in black.

Kit shook her head and stepped between the stranger and the mob. "This man has seen the error in his ways," she called out to them. "He will atone for the crimes he has committed."

The stranger's eyes narrowed, as he laughed, a shrill, cackling sort of laugh. "They're not here for me, you silly little girl. They're here for you!"

A shiver ran up Kit's back at the sound of the man's laughter. The similarity to the vampire Pental's insidious laugh was uncanny. This man was a zealot and yet he had convinced Kit of his repentance as easily as he had manipulated the children. Whether he had power over her or whether it was just her nature to believe in the goodness of mankind, it was not a mistake she would make a second time.

Kit became suddenly aware that she had an enemy at her back and another at her front. The villagers, for the most part, didn't appear to be a major threat, but even weak opponents could overwhelm a trained fighter if they were to come in enough numbers – and there were more than enough villagers here to bury Kit in a wave of bodies.

Not wasting a second, Kit threw her foot backward in a donkey-kick, catching the stranger squarely in the chest. He flew hard against the front of the stage with a sickening *crack*.

Still facing the advancing crowd, Kit held out the head of her battle hammer.

"Titan, hear me," she uttered and unleashed a cold attack at them. She expected a single frost-bolt but instead her attack was more like she had hurled a giant ice storm toward the group. Snow and fist-sized hail issued forth from her hammer, spurned forward by a heavy gust of frost-filled wind. The young priest didn't understand why her standard spell had changed but she was glad for it, nonetheless.

The villagers screamed in pain and dismay as the storm knocked them off their feet. The hail smashed into them, cutting them open wherever it struck unprotected skin. Those who were able bolted down the hill while the others curled up into small balls in an attempt to shield themselves from the frozen onslaught. Those who had shields set their feet and held them in front of their bodies while the hail rang off their iron bindings.

Kit turned back to the stranger and found him standing in a low crouch. In his hands were two deep-bellied drop-tip short swords. The stranger shook the blades, and they immediately ignited into bright orange flames. The steel seemed to turn black as the fire licked the swords' cutting edges.

The man slowly opened his mouth and sung. His voice was sweet like honey and as the melody continued, he grew in stature. With each passing moment he grew more and more ominous as he glowered over Kit. By the time he'd stopped singing he was nearly eight feet tall, the size of a large Gigas. His crazy, high-pitched laugh turned into a deep baritone.

"Behold the power of Arachnielle! Know now your folly. Learn the truth the Temple has never taught you."

Kit's legs buckled beneath her as the man towered high above. She had hoped her opponent hadn't noticed, but the evil grin on his face said otherwise.

This is no different from fighting Amara. Remember your sparring matches with her. Remember how she moved and how you moved. Remember how badly the giant had thrashed you. Don't let that happen now.

The giant-sized bard slashed out with his fat-bellied sword.

Stay inside his guard.

Kit stepped towards the man and ducked under his attack. Kit watched as the blade swept over her head. She didn't see the knee that followed it. The impact knocked her off her feet, sending her flying towards the stands. Her body slammed against the first row of seating.

"Now do you see, priest, that you are no match for the power of my god?" The giant stood over Kit and laughed. He motioned to Kit to stand up, and he took a step back, giving her some space.

Kit's eyes flicked to her left. The children stood dumbfounded. Several of them moved towards the stranger, their eyes filled with awe and adoration. A pain ripped through the middle of her back, right where the bench had struck her.

"Get away from him," Kit growled as she picked herself up off the ground. A new, more intense shot of pain blossomed across her back.

Sister Gale's lessons came flooding back. Kit could hear her voice in her head telling her how she was unprepared, telling her how she was not being mindful of her surroundings. Like when she sparred with Amara, speed was her best weapon. There was no way that Kit could compete using her strength.

"Titan, hear me," Kit whispered as she gripped the handle of her battle hammer. A surge of warmth coursed through her tiny body. Her muscles became looser. Her nerves were suddenly set ablaze.

Kit twirled her hammer in her hand. She set her feet, ready to make a counter strike.

The giant lifted his foot and brought it down with a thundering crash. A shock wave flew outwards, knocking Kit and all the children off their feet. The giant laughed as he stepped closer and pointed the tip of his sword at Kit's face.

"How many times must I prove that you have chosen the wrong side?"

Kit grimaced as the children picked themselves up off the ground and ran to stand behind the giant. Kit's brain went foggy. She couldn't fail. If these children abandoned their faith in Titan, they could be lost forever.

Kit picked herself up off the ground and twirled her hammer in her hand. "You will prove it to me when I no longer draw breath." She swung her hammer by her side and beckoned the giant to continue.

The giant shook his head. "It's a shame you're forcing me to destroy you. But, then again, I've never seen the insides of a priest before."

With surprising speed, he thrust forward with his blade.

Again, Kit stepped inside his guard and again the giant countered, bringing his knee up as a follow-up attack. Kit ducked under his leg and spun to her left, landing the hammer on the inside of his knee.

The giant bellowed out and spun around, sweeping low with his blade, intent on cutting Kit down at the waist.

She dove over the blade and smoothly rolled over her shoulder. She let her momentum carry through to her battle hammer, delivering another solid blow to the inside of the giant's knee. She figured that if he couldn't stand up, he wouldn't be quite so tall.

Again, the giant bellowed out, more out of frustration than from the considerable pain he must have felt.

Before he had a chance to set himself, Kit lashed out with a kick, catching him in the same spot she had hit him with her hammer. The giant wobbled and swung his blades wildly. She avoided the first strike and used her hammer to block the second. The impact sent her skidding on her back, slamming her into the front of the stage. Dark spots danced before her eyes. She tried blinking to clear her vision. Everything was in shadows, like she was looking through a dense fog. Through the mist, a silhouette moved towards her.

"Warrior of the north, my strength is your strength. My heart is your heart." The familiar voice of Amaruq, the wolf spirit, came bursting through her mind.

Kit's vision cleared just as the giant's blade came arcing towards her head. She threw up her hammer to deflect the blow. Laying prone, if the hammer took the full force of the attack, it would surely shatter its handle. Just before the sword made contact, she angled the hammer. The blade glanced off the edge of its head and bit deeply into her shoulder. She screamed out as blood sprayed across her face. The taste of copper filled her mouth.

"Where is your god now, you foolish little girl?" The stranger's voice had a lilting, musical tone to it. The pain was blinding but the fever-pitched battle dulled it enough to continue.

The young priest lashed out with another kick, catching the giant in the shin of his weakened leg. As his body lurched forward, she rolled to her side, away from where the giant was about to fall. She popped to her feet and readied herself for another attack.

"I am Kit Standing Bear, *acknowledged* Priest of Titan. My god is with me now and always." Kit was practically spitting the words out. "There is only one fool here today, and he's about to feel the full wrath of Titan." The pain in her shoulder blossomed anew as blood poured down from the gaping wound.

"Wrath of Titan!" the children chanted out in response.

Kit's gut twisted into a knot. In the heat of the battle, she had completely forgotten that there were a good number of children present. But there was no turning back now.

Kit tried to bring her hammer up in a defensive position, but her arm wouldn't obey. She scowled as it hung limp at her side. Her grip on the handle was beginning to falter. She set her jaw and took a deep breath.

"Titan, hear me." Kit called on her healing powers and a pale-yellow aura surrounded her body. The feeling in her shoulder returned with an intense blast of pain. Kit flexed her arm and brought her hammer up to her chest. The pain was still there, but it was manageable. At least she had full function of her arm again.

"Get up," Kit said as she twirled her battle hammer in her hand. "I will now deliver Titan's justice upon you this day."

The children scrambled to stand behind Kit. They all screamed out, "Justice, justice, justice!"

A hint of a smile crossed Kit's face. This time the children's words gave her extra resolve. She was not about to let them see anything other than an absolute, dominating victory.

As the giant hobbled to his feet, Kit sprung forward. In a heartbeat she closed the distance and swung her hammer in a sideways stroke, hoping to catch the giant-sized man in the ribs. In one smooth motion he stepped back. The hammer passed harmlessly in front of him. As the hammer's head missed, Kit let her body spin, and she brought her heel around, slamming it into his belly. A great whoosh of air escaped the man's mouth. His face turned purple as he struggled to catch his breath.

Kit raised her hammer for an overhand swing. As she did, the stranger took a defensive pose, raising both of his blades high to block the impending attack. In doing so he opened himself to a low strike. With all her might she placed an expert kick into his nether regions. The man's eyes bulged out from his face. He stood motionless as a high-pitched whine escaped his lips. His weapons clattered on the ground as he reached to cradle his man-parts in his hands. He gasped for air before he dropped to his knees and then onto his face.

Not giving him a chance to recover, Kit took her hammer in a two-handed grip. She raised it over her head and brought it down onto the top of his head. On contact, an intense flash of light burst out, blinding Kit and everyone within several paces.

When Kit's vision cleared, the stranger was lying dead on the ground in a puddle of his own blood, his hands still firmly grasping his private parts.

The children were now cheering wildly. Kit didn't want them to see such a gruesome sight, but they learned the power of Titan this day. She hoped that the bright flash of light from her hammer had also blinded them from the worst of the gruesome spectacle.

CHAPTER SEVEN

THE NORTHERN RESISTANCE

Ulip's fast-paced strides practically forced Danny into a dead run to keep up with him. Despite his size, the giant barely left any sign of his movement through the forest. He seemed to instinctively avoid branches as he deftly wove his way through the thick underbrush. "You know, my legs are less than half the length of yours, and I'm tall for a Berrat." Danny's breaths were starting to become labored. They had been keeping this pace for several hours and the big guy showed no sign of letting up.

"You need more exercise," the Gigas replied, not really caring much about Danny's discomfort.

"I've been flying for the better part of a day. I get plenty of exercise."

"Then a little more won't hurt you."

"Easy for you to say," Danny retorted. "Maybe you should try keeping up with me while I'm flying. It would be interesting to see you try to follow me."

"I have no interest in following you."

"That's not the point," Danny yelled. His face was turning red, and not just from overexerting himself. "Your legs are twice as long as mine. You're barely walking and I'm having to run to keep up."

"You can stop complaining now."

"I'll stop complaining when you slow down!" Danny yelled again. The Gigas stopped dead in his tracks, causing Danny to run into his tree-trunk sized legs. "You didn't need to stop," he said, picking himself up off the ground, rubbing his cheek where he slammed into the giant. "I just wanted you to slow down."

"I needed to stop."

"Because you're tired?" The giant's scowl cut Danny's laughter short. Sweet Titan, the man could scare a dragon with that look.

"No, I am not tired. I stopped because we have reached our destination."

Just then a great white bear came barrelling out from the trees, growling out a challenge. It pulled back his lips, exposing his massive teeth. With the animal less than ten paces away, Danny morphed into his firebird form and took flight. As soon as he was high enough to be clear of the animal's weaponry, he circled, looking for an opening to attack it.

Sweet Titan, what is going on? The encounter was not playing out how he might have expected.

The Gigas showed no sign of fear at the sight of the animal, even though the bear might have weighed as much as he did. From the trees behind the great white beast a band of Berrat came pouring out, yipping, and carrying on like puppies greeting their parents. None of them appeared to be concerned about the marauding creature as it watched the firebird circle the clearing. When the bear shifted into Berrat form, Danny understood why.

"What magic is this?" the bear turned Berrat yelled up at the firebird. "Phoenix have been extinct for ages."

Danny, unable to speak in his firebird form, landed a good distance away from the group, shifting back to his natural state. "It's a long story," he offered, his eyes shifting towards the Gigas. "Are these the *folks* you wanted me to meet?"

"Ryn," Ulip said. "This is Danny Fox-Dancing. Danny, this is Ryn, my second in command."

"Second in command?" Danny scoffed. He clamped his lips tight for fear of laughing out loud. "Are you some sort of military group?"

"No. We are not," Ulip boomed. "We follow a hierarchy to keep order, to be disciplined, so we know who to listen to when the fighting begins."

"That pretty much sounds like the definition of a military group," Danny said, as he rolled his eyes. His cocky smirk following shortly thereafter. "All you're missing are the uniforms."

"Why did you bring this jester?" Ryn asked. "Why should we believe you are a Fox-Dancing and how is it that you can take the shape of a phoenix?"

"He bears the mark," Ulip said, answering at least one of Ryn's questions. There was an unexpected amount of reverence in his voice.

"Do you have any food?" Danny asked, flashing his infectious grin at Ryn. "I've been flying for over a full day, and I can't recall the last time I've eaten." As Ryn scowled, Danny's grin got wider. "Maybe I can tell you my story over a nice bit of roasted boar, or elk, or even some good cheese?"

"Give him some food and we'll listen to what he has to tell," Ulip said. "If we don't like his story, we can use him as bait. Red-haired Berrat are rare, and the Split Crows will jump at a chance to take him."

His eyes widened at the giant's incredulous comment. "I am not bait!" Danny said shaking his head.

Ryn grinned up at Ulip, perhaps liking the notion that they could use him to draw out the Split Crows. The man was barely four feet tall, average height for a Berrat. "If Ulip says you're bait, then you're bait. Follow us, we'll take you to our camp." And with that, he and the other Berrat started heading back into the forest.

Danny could feel the Gigas on his heels as they walked through the thick evergreens, but he couldn't hear a single noise coming from the big man as he pushed through the forest. "I'm not bait," he muttered.

They continued to walk for some time but at a pace that Danny could more easily manage. The heady scent of the evergreens, the ceaseless chittering of tiny songbirds, the way the tree-sap clung to his fingers as he ran his hands over the bows, transported Danny back to his youth, to a time when he was but a child still living in Taseko.

⚬⚬⚭✦⚮⚬⚬

"Put the vole down and let's get moving," Danny's mother gently scolded. "We've got a long trip ahead of us, and we need to get going." Dyanna tossed her flame-red hair over her shoulder and flashed a smile at her son. Her eyes widened slightly, "Adventure awaits."

"But I don't want to go," Danny whined. "I like it here, with you and Ataata."

"Your father is coming too, sweetness," she said, holding out her hand, coaxing her son to follow. "It will be a wonderful journey, filled with sights and sounds that you have never experienced before."

"No!" the child exclaimed, stomping his foot onto the soft ground. He stared down at his bare foot, annoyed that stamping it didn't have the desired sound effect.

"You'll do as your mother says," Paylor said in his deep honey baritone voice. "No son of mine will ever disrespect his parents."

"Yes, Ataata," the boy replied, letting his head hang in shame. "Can I bring my pet?" he asked, his eyes suddenly brightening while he grinned widely at his parents. He held out a small vole, letting the animal run around on his hand and up his wrist. "Please?"

"The creatures of the wild are not pets," his father scolded. "But if he joins with you willingly…"

"He can leave anytime he wants," Danny said, petting the silky fur of the tiny rodent. "But he won't. He likes me."

<hr />

"We're here," Ulip said, bringing Danny back to the present. His heart ached for his parents. Not knowing if they were okay was killing him.

Danny's mouth dropped open as he surveyed the camp. Had he come through on his own, he never would have known that people lived there. The huts blended seamlessly with the trees and the hillside. An irregularly shaped opening was visible where the ground jutted up in a shear-faced wall. There were so many vines covering the cliff that the entrance was barely visible. Small children were running about, chasing each other, squealing with delight. Berrat adults, seated in small circles, were busy working leather while others were fashioning bows from supple yew branches. Nobody seemed to notice or care that he was there. All except for a woman with fire-red hair, braided into many long tails. She crossed the compound like a thunderstorm, pretty from a distance but capable of wreaking havoc upon arrival. She held her hands by her side, clenched into tight fists. Her dark gray eyes swirled with destructive force.

"What is this man doing here?" she growled at Ryn. "We can't take in any more strays. Feeding and housing the ones we have has already stretched us too thin."

"But honey badger," Ryn squeaked out.

"Don't you honey badger me," the woman continued until she was nose-to-nose with him. "I don't care."

"This is Danny Fox-Dancing," Ulip declared, drawing the woman's ire away from Ryn.

The woman's head spun from Ryn to Danny, her long braids swirling around her neck. She was practically a blur as she advanced on Danny. Giving him no time to react, she grabbed him by the wrist, and spun it behind his back. Intense pain burst forth in his shoulder. Dark spots danced before his eyes. Even with all his years in hand-to-hand combat training at the Temple, this woman's attack broke through his defenses like he was a fresh-faced novice. A moment later the taste of soft earth and fallen evergreen needles filled his mouth as she pressed his face into the ground. Warm spittle splashed on the back of his neck, followed immediately by brisk scrubbing.

"I don't know what you're doing," Danny muffled out, getting more soil and pine needles in his mouth as he spoke. "But I would let you look without all... this."

"Welcome home, cousin," the woman said when she finally pulled her knee out of the middle of his back, releasing her death-grip on his wrist.

"We're related?" Danny asked, rolling over onto his back, his bright red hair strewn across his face. "Too bad. I'd have liked a chance to roll around with me on top of you."

"That's my mate," Ryn threatened. "Speak like that to her again, and I'll..."

"Whoa, friend," Danny said, holding up his hands, even though his shoulder was screaming in pain. "I'm just having some fun with my cousin, a woman I've never met before and is one of the most beautiful creatures I've ever seen in my life." He grinned and popped back up to his feet. He rolled his shoulder a few times, trying to help the blood flow back into his arm.

"Why are you here?" Ryn's mate asked, cutting through the tension. "You've been gone forever. Why did you pick now to return?"

"It seems that everybody is looking for me to tell them stories," he replied, keeping his eyes locked on the beautiful Berrat woman. "I was brought here for some food, and in return, I'll tell you everything I can."

"We barely have enough food to feed our own," the woman replied shaking her head. "But if you'll tell us why you're here, we can spare you some bread."

"Are your food stores truly that low?" Danny asked, his playful demeanor replaced with real concern. "When I lived here, there was never a shortage of food – at least, not that I remember."

"The Split Crows follow the game trails," Ryn interjected, his voice full of spite. "They sit in wait for us. When we hunt the animals, the Split Crows hunt us."

Danny rubbed the back of his neck, thinking about the implications of the problem. He mustered what strength he could and blew out a breath. "Make ready your weapons," he declared just before morphing into his firebird form. With a few quick flaps of his wings, he lifted off the ground. The collective sound of gasps spread through the compound.

"Gaia, protect us," the woman screamed, staggering a few steps away from where Danny had been just a moment ago. "He melded with a phoenix?"

"I don't know, Breayn," Ryn said, taking his mate's hand. "I'm hoping he'll tell us how he came to host such a spirit."

⸎⸎⸎

Time passed slowly as they awaited Danny's return. While some got bored and wandered off, others gathered into small groups, chatting amongst themselves. Nobody was prepared for the crashing of trees under the thundering hooves of a herd heading their way. They scrabbled about, trying to ready their weapons when the first of the animals broke into the clearing. A great elk stag with a massive set of vorpal antlers bellowed, his eyes wild with fear. Several Berrat dove out of its way before the animal's razor-tipped rack eviscerated them. His sudden appearance caught even those who had their weapons at the ready flatfooted. A few of the Berrat launched arrows at the elk but their aim was off the mark, sailing harmlessly over the animal's back. Moments later, several more bucks came crashing through the trees. This time, everybody was ready, and they quickly brought three of them down.

Danny arrived a few moments later, bursting out from the trees where the first buck had disappeared. "You missed the big one," he said with a big, arrogant smile. "I looked after him for you. He's about two hundred paces that way," he said, pointing into the forest. "It's going to take quite a few of you to haul him back here though."

Ulip scoffed before heading off in the direction Danny had pointed.

"You are reckless," Breayn yelled. "You'll bring the Crow down on us!"

"Not today," Danny said, strutting around like he'd just won first prize at the most wonderful person contest. "I took care of the bad guys before I herded the animals this way."

"You fool," Ryn cursed at him. "You've brought them all down on us."

"They will tell no tale," Danny replied, screwing up his face as he considered the man's overreaction. "I left none standing."

"When they don't return," Breayn said, speaking to Danny like he was a child, enunciating each word slowly, to ensure he understood, "they'll send others to investigate, many others. They're divided up into small bands spread across Taseko. Each band is responsible for a region, and they don't ever leave that area. If they're killed, the Crow know where to look, where to find *us*."

"How many did you kill?" Ryn asked.

"I didn't really stop to count," Danny shrugged. He mumbled to himself, counting on his fingers. "There were seven loners, and six that were gathered together."

"There were thirteen. Are you sure?" Breayn's jaw jutted out, daring him to lie to her.

"You killed six? All at once? All by yourself?" Ryn asked, rolling his eyes. Danny got the distinct impression that he didn't believe his recounting of the story.

"They were lined up," Danny said, shrugging again, thinking that he had adequately explained how he had killed six people without any help. "I flew through them. They just stood there, staring at me when I attacked. Their black cloaks lit up like dry kindling." His voice cracked slightly. He dipped his head low as his shoulders hunched. He had never killed a person before. In the heat of combat he hadn't given it a second thought. But while recounting the tale, the screams of those he had set ablaze, they came crashing back. He would have these deaths on his soul for the rest of his days.

"Is that how you killed all of them?" Breayn asked, looking a little less concerned than she had a moment ago. When Danny nodded, she laughed deeply. A look of extreme relief crossed her face. "They're going to think it was fire drakes. Setting people on fire isn't our style, but it is what the drakes do – and the drakes have as much reason to hate the Crows as we do."

"The Split Crows wiped out Ulip's clan," Ryn offered. "The Fire Drake Clan, and the drakes they're named after, lived in symbiosis, in perfect harmony."

"That is not your tale to tell," Ulip bellowed out, walking into the clearing with the great elk over his shoulders. The animal must have weighed over a thousand pounds, but the Gigas carried him as easily as a shepherd carries a lamb. With surprising gentleness, he laid the carcass on the ground, bowing his head to the animal as he did.

"Since you delivered us enough meat to last a good long while, why don't you make yourself comfortable while Ryn fetches you some food," Breayn said with a wink at her mate. "After you've had your fill, you can tell us your story."

CHAPTER EIGHT

THE SEARCH FOR TREEDALE

Kit stared down at the spider god's follower. A silence had fallen in the theater, like the whole world was holding its breath.

"Sister, behind you!" one of the children screamed.

Kit spun around to see that the five well-armed guards were closing in on her. One of them spat at her feet. He slowly raised his sword in a shaky hand.

Kit's hammer crackled as bolts of lightning jumped across the mithril head. The bolts traveled up the handle to her hand. A wicked grin split her lips. The grin quickly turned into a menacing grimace.

"Back off!" she snarled through clenched teeth. Kit took a threatening step towards the guards. They all took a step backwards, their eyes now glued onto her crackling hammer.

"Do you really want to die today, to rejoin the Great Cycle?" Kit asked. She kept her voice calm and threatening. "Do you think the spider god will help you any more than it helped... him?"

"We are five," one of the men retorted. He was tall and lean with a wild scruffy brown beard. The other four men, emboldened by his words, took a step forward. The lightning that wreathed Kit's hammer burst forth, its bolts slammed into the ground and scorched the stones.

"Be at peace and return to your families," said a voice from behind the guards.

Grams and Lin were standing behind the men. Grams was decked out in brilliant white armor, the holy symbol of Titan emblazoned on her breastplate. She held out an enormous battle hammer. Lin stood at her side, her long swords drawn and at the ready. Her hands were flexing on the handles as she readied herself to strike.

"Be at peace," Grams said again, this time with a powerful, threatening tone to her words.

There was indecision on the faces of several of the guards. One of them pointed his broad sword toward his cohorts. "We're done here. The community is safe. We can go home."

"No," replied one of the other guards, a chubby man with long, greasy, black hair. He glared back at his counterpart. "We have Arachnielle behind us. She will not let us fail."

The tall, bearded guard slashed at the chubby man's sword and knocked it from his hand. He slowly shook his head at him. "The spider god does not care about us. Titan is our savior. It's over. Go home."

Grams and Lin stepped to the side, allowing the guards to pass. They climbed the stairs out from the theater and disappeared from sight on their way to the front gate.

"Why in Helja would you just let them leave?" Kit asked, her outrage burning out of control.

"The stranger's words were compelling," Grams replied calmly, like she was simply talking about the weather. "We are simple people, Kit; some of us are easily swayed by those promising a better life, even if those promises are entirely empty."

The lightning bolts on Kit's hammer died out. Her chest was still heaving as her wrath continued to course through her veins. She furrowed her brow and scowled at the old woman.

"They were trying to kill me!" she yelled in an uncharacteristically high-pitched voice. Even though Kit heard what Grams was saying, she was not able, or willing, to accept it.

"Child," Grams said with a knowing smile. "You're young and you have much to learn. It was not the time to deal with them, not when tempers were raised, and children were present." Grams motioned to the children who had surrounded them. They were staring up at Kit with wide-eyed wonder.

With the dead body of the Arachnielle worshipper laying in a pool of his own blood and too many children about, something needed to be done to sever the moment. Grams quickly clapped her hands together and several of the children jumped. The old woman's face became bright and cheery. "Okay, inside with you. All of you!" She motioned to Lin, instructing her to take the children back into the orphanage.

"Alright, children, who wants a snack?" The children met Lin's offer with cheers, as they raced to the mansion's front door. She gave Kit a smile and a quick wink. "I'll be right back."

As Lin headed off to finish herding the children into the orphanage, Grams stared down at Kit's bloodstained sleeve. She pulled back the tear in it to reveal a fully healed shoulder. The old woman's eyebrows raised as she gave a grunt of approval.

"Your healing skills are impressive for someone so young. I'd like to know how you called upon that lightning."

"I seem to have a knack for healing," Kit replied as she poked at her skin.

"And what of the lightning?" Grams pressed.

"I don't know," Kit said as she stared at her hammer. "I thought about casting an earthquake spell, and the lightning just... came."

Grams chuckled and nodded. "I knew I chose wisely," she said to herself.

"What? What do you mean, you chose wisely?"

The old woman waved her hand dismissively. "So, will you take up the search for my grandson, Treedale? Will you attempt to return him to me?"

Kit stared at Grams' glassy eyes. She inclined her head lightly to her. "I will do what I can, but I don't even really know where to start looking. That Arachnielle fool told me where their camp was, but I have little faith that what he said was true." Kit blanched at the sight of the dead man with a crushed head, lying in a pool of thick blood.

"Don't worry about him, child," Grams said as she gently turned Kit's face away from the man she had killed. "I will ensure he gets a proper burial."

Kit glanced down at the battle hammer the old woman was carrying. "Why didn't you just deal with him yourself? Why did you wait for Father Hoarfrost to send someone to investigate?"

Grams gave her a sad smile, recalling a time in her youth when she would have dealt with these men herself. "My days of combat have long passed. If Lin hadn't enchanted this for me, I wouldn't even be able to lift my old friend here, let alone swing her."

"You certainly fooled me – and the guards," Kit laughed as she twirled her own weapon in her hand. "I hope you're okay with Lin giving me this hammer. She told me it was a gift from you."

Grams examined the mithril weapon and then smiled warmly at Kit. "I see that she's placed sun enchantments on it. I think it's only fitting that you wield it, since you are destined to bring light into what will surely be a time of total darkness."

"What do you mean by that?" Kit asked. A shiver ran up her spine at Grams' choice of words.

"Oh, don't mind this old woman," she said as she glanced up towards the mansion. "I have seen too many winters and I tend to imagine the worst. But to answer your question more plainly, if Lin deemed you worthy to wield my hammer, then I trust her decision. Use it well and bring glory and honor to Titan and the Temple of the Fist."

"Thank you, I will do my very best." Kit's eyes followed Grams back to the mansion's entrance. "I suppose we could head to where the stranger said their camp was. I don't have much else to go on, so I might as well give it a try."

"I can show you where that is," said a voice from behind Kit. It caused her to practically jump out of her skin. She spun around to see a Berrat, perhaps two or three cycles older than her. His brilliant white hair was braided into multiple rows across the top of his head. Shots of red strands stood out in stark contrast. He was shorter than most male Berrat, easily under four feet tall. He was dressed in light leather armor dyed a deep forest green. He seemed pleased that he was able to surprise her.

Kit was considerably less pleased, displaying a deep frown and a skeptical eye.

"I am Mukale. I am not of this tribe, but they are my people. They saved me when I was young, and I would like to repay that kindness now. I think I know where the kidnapper has taken Treedale."

"Titan's peace upon you, Mukale. I didn't see you there." Kit's heart was still pounding up in her throat. Even though she didn't doubt what he said, she looked to Grams for confirmation of his words.

Grams laughed and waved the boy over to her. "He's got a bit of a knack for sneaking up on people," she said with a hint of a scolding tone. "If you're willing to let him go with you, he will make an excellent guide."

Mukale stood a bit taller at Grams' words. "I know these lands and I am a good hunter. I can stalk prey without them knowing. I must pay back the debt I owe to the community. Helping to rescue Treedale is how I'll do it."

Kit suddenly found herself torn. She recognized Mukale's desire to repay his life-debt, but she'd much rather go back to Aarall and get Indie to help track the kidnapper. Then again, Indie was going to be in training for at least another few days. That was time she didn't have. If Treedale had been kidnapped, time was of the essence. She bowed slightly in response.

"Thank you, Mukale. I would be happy to have you as my guide."

Mukale's face lit up. His dark brown eyes twinkled with joy. He immediately ran off to gather up his belongings.

"Men!" Kit said as she gave Grams a weak half-smile.

The old woman smiled broadly back at Kit, but the smile quickly faded away. "Find my grandson. Take care of Mukale and my granddaughter."

The young Berrat returned in just a few minutes. His belongings were few, but he seemed ready and eager to travel. "We need to head north, toward the spires of Silverhawk. I'll be able to pick up the trail along the way."

Suddenly, Mukale's eyes went wide, and his mouth dropped open. His bronze skin darkened as he became visibly agitated. Even his breathing became erratic.

Kit stole a glance over her shoulder. Lin was striding down the steps from the mansion, her twin long swords swaying with her hips as she took each step. Kit turned back toward Mukale. His mouth was still agape as his eyes followed the woman's seductive walk.

"So, what did I miss?" Lin said as she approached the group. When she caught sight of Mukale standing behind Kit she stammered. "Oh... um... hi... Mukale. Nice to see you."

"I am going to help Sister Kit look for your brother. I will show her the way to the camp." The small man's chest was puffed out. He was standing on his tiptoes and lifting his chin, trying to add a bit of height to his tiny frame.

Lin turned to Kit and gave her a death-stare. Kit grimaced back and shrugged. She wasn't sure what was causing Lin to be so upset. However, judging by the way Mukale continued to ogle Lin, maybe she could come up with a reasonably good guess. A tight-lipped grin appeared on Kit's face.

"You will need a good guide if you're going to find your brother," Grams chimed in. "There is no one better than Mukale."

"Grams...," Lin's voice was part panic, part pleading.

"Do you want to find your brother or not?" Grams' voice had a no-nonsense, threating tone to it. Lin immediately recoiled and lowered her eyes. She stole a quick glance up at Kit and grumbled.

"We're not provisioned for a trip to Silverhawk," Kit said, knowing that it was at least a week's travel from Ashcroft to Silverhawk by foot.

"Travel light, travel fast," Mukale said, his eyes never leaving Lin's.

"He's got a point." Lin said reluctantly. She stole one last glance at her grandmother, desperately hoping for some support.

Kit shrugged at Lin, "Lead the way then, Mukale. If you know where to go, take us there."

Lin groaned again, resigned to having Mukale with them.

Grams slid her hammer into its holster and followed the trio up the stairs leading out of the theater.

"Bring back my grandson. Keep my family safe."

Chapter Nine

Two Girls and a Horse

The trio pushed themselves for a couple of hours before Kit called out to Mukale to slow down. Lin was sucking wind so hard that Kit feared she was about to pass out. The temperature continued to climb as the midday sun beat mercilessly down from the cloudless sky. Waves of heat rose from the barren countryside while tiny insects scurried about over the dry, cracked ground. Lin dropped to her hands and knees, looking like she was about to puke.

"You don't train as much as you should," Kit chided, knowing she was too winded to offer any sort of comeback. Lin did manage a scowl between wheezing breaths, but that was about it.

"I'm sorry for pushing so hard," Mukale said as he came jogging back. Outside of small pit stains in his leather vest, he seemed fresh and ready to continue. "If you'd like to run up front with me, I'll make sure to keep at a pace you're comfortable with."

Lin's face wasn't quite as bright red as it had been a few minutes ago, but she clearly hadn't fully gotten her breath back. She managed to shake her head and wave off Mukale's offer, but no comprehensible words managed to come out of her mouth.

"Here, this will help." Mukale held out a small water-skin. Lin waved off the offer, but Mukale ignored her protest and pushed it closer to her.

Lin grudgingly accepted the waterskin and took a small sip from it. Her eyes brightened noticeably, and she took another pull on the refreshment, this time significantly deeper.

"Wow," she said as she handed it back to the tracker. Just that small bit of acknowledgement made his face light up. Lin gave Kit a sideways look as Kit tried to stifle a snigger.

"Maybe a spell on your boots to improve your speed might help?" Mukale rubbed the small amount of hair growing on his chin.

"I don't have the necessary reagents to do that," Lin said, shaking her head. "Besides, I'm already so slow that I don't think it would help me much. Speed enchantments only increase the wearer's speed by a percentage of their normal pace. So, in my case, twenty percent faster than slow is still... slow."

Lin popped up to her feet and winced slightly. The look of exhaustion was gone but the muscles in her legs were cramped, and she struggled to maintain her balance.

"I could catch a mount for you to ride." Mukale tilted his head skyward and sniffed at the air. He turned around and tried again. "There is a herd of horses nearby. I can easily get one for the two of us to ride on."

"Can't I just ride it by myself?" Lin asked. The idea of riding double with Mukale was not something she was ready to entertain.

"Can you ride without saddle or bridle?" Mukale asked, his eyebrows raised.

"You can?" retorted Lin.

"If I bind with the animal, it will follow my commands without the aid of a bridle, and I've never in my life used a saddle; its easier on the mount that way."

"You mean like Indie did when he went through that *binding* thing with his charger?" Kit could still see how Indie had tamed the huge horse, how he somehow created a connection with it. "I thought that was a Nomad thing."

"I don't know this Indie person, but I grew up in a Nomad village. I was taught many of their ways, including how to bind with animals. It's not that different from our spirit binding, but it's not as deep a connection." Mukale's eyes suddenly went wide.

"I could spirit bind with one, then you could ride me when I shift into horse form."

The look on Lin's face was indescribable, somewhere between repulsion and disbelief. The reaction was not lost on Mukale; his face crumpled as Lin crushed his heart.

"Can you do that Mukale, spirit bind with a horse?" Kit completely disregarded Lin's reaction. When Mukale nodded, Lin shook her head vehemently.

"Absolutely not!" she barked out. "I am not going to *ride* Mukale."

"Listen, Lin, we're here to save your brother. If you can't keep up, we're going to leave you behind. Whatever your issue is, you need to get past it." Kit wasn't holding back at this point. She didn't know how fast the kidnapper was able to move with Treedale in tow, but every minute they wasted here was making finding him that much harder. "Well?"

Lin glared at Kit. She fully understood that she was right, but Lin had been holding off Mukale's *advances* for more cycles than she cared to admit. No matter how hard she'd tried, how much she'd ignored him, or how she'd acted, he simply would not give up whatever infatuation he had for her.

"Fine!" Lin screamed, throwing up her arms in defeat.

Mukale's face lit up like a lantern and he immediately ran off across the broken ground and into a swath of the tall grasses. In mere minutes, he was so far away that Kit couldn't see him anymore.

"Do you have any clue how humiliating this is going to be? Do you?" Lin was furious. She stomped about. She crushed small clumps of dirt and ground crawling insects beneath her boot. She found a small, bright blue flower. She was about to kick at it, but she held back and spared the tiny plant's life.

"I don't get it, Lin. He clearly likes you." Kit's voice was playful. When Lin wasn't taking the bait, she turned it up a notch. "C'mon Lin, he's a fine young man. Surely it would be okay for you to wrap your legs around his waist and ride him like a pony!"

Lin's head practically exploded, causing Kit to fall down from laughing so hard. Lin picked up a clump of dried mud and tossed it at Kit, striking her cleanly on the side of her head.

"Hey!" she screeched out, putting her hand to the spot where the mud-clump had struck her. When Kit pulled her hand away, she gaped at her fingers. "There was a rock in that clump. I'm bleeding!"

"Oh, Kit, I'm so sorry!" Lin came running over to inspect the wound which made Kit start laughing even harder.

"You didn't actually hurt me, but you did manage to mess up my already messed up hair." Kit's laughing died down, but her eyes were still full of mirth.

"It was a nice throw though," she added as she pulled more bits of dried mud out of her long, black hair. "What's your deal with Mukale, anyway? He's cute."

Lin turned red; her eyes darted about like she was trying to find some place to hide. "I'm just not into him," she said finally.

"Because he's Berrat? If you've never been with a Berrat, you should know that height is the *only* place that they're short." Kit had a wicked gleam in her eye. She waggled her eyebrows and smirked.

"It's not because he's a Berrat." Lin stared down at her feet and mumbled, "It's because he's a boy."

"He's not that young, Lin. Besides, Berrat mature much quicker than us Nomads."

"No, not because he's a *boy*." Lin's eyes went wide. She hated having to explain it – out loud. "Because he's not a *girl*."

"Oh," Kit's eyes also went wide as what Lin was saying finally became clear to her. She covered her mouth in an attempt to hide her grin. "Just tell him. Then he'll back off."

"I can't tell him. I can't tell anybody. You're the only person I've ever shared that with." Suddenly Lin's voice became fearful. "You can't tell anybody else I told you that."

"No worries, Lin. I won't tell, but if you don't tell Mukale, he's going to keep making cow-eyes at you for the rest of this journey."

Lin's expression suddenly changed. Her eyes danced with mischief. "And how exactly is it that you know that Berrat men are..."

"Well endowed?" Kit finished her sentence for her. "Do you know Danny Fox-Dancing?"

"Sure," Lin replied with a good amount of disdain in her voice. "Everybody knows that arrogant little jerk."

"Well, that arrogant little jerk is my best friend," Kit retorted. She crossed her arms over her chest, almost daring Lin to say something else bad about her friend.

"Oh, sorry, I didn't know." Kit's expression softened with Lin's apology, leaving the door open for more questions. "You were *with* Danny?"

Suddenly it was Kit's turn to blush scarlet. Words came pouring out of Kit's face faster than her brain could consider them.

"Sweet Titan, no. Never. I mean, I've seen him naked more times than I'd care to admit, but we're just friends – best friends, and that's all we'll ever be to each other. He's like a big brother... who's not afraid to be naked in front of his sister."

Just as Kit was trying to find a way to change the conversation, a great stallion came trotting up.

"Hey!" the big gray horse said as he approached. Mukale had picked out a magnificent stallion. He was a bit leggier than a standard horse, with a dappled black and white hind end and obsidian-black mane and tail.

"Mukale?" Kit asked, as she drew back her head. "Is that you?"

The horse huffed and pawed at the dry ground.

"You killed this horse so that you could assume his shape?"

The horse shimmered and its form melted away before it transformed into Mukale.

"Killed him? I did no such thing." Mukale snorted loudly, appalled by the suggestion that he had killed the animal.

"Then... how? I've always been taught that a Berrat must defeat an animal in single handed combat to take their spirit."

Mukale shook his head. "I've never had to perform that barbaric ritual to gain an animal's spirit. If they will not willingly offer me a piece of themselves, I leave them be."

"I've never heard of such a thing," Kit said. She could somehow tell he was speaking true, but this went against everything she'd ever been taught about how spirit binding worked. No Berrat from Lilloet could do that, not even Old Sky Eyes.

"We should get going," Mukale said as he shifted back into his horse form. "Hop on!"

"I like girls!" Lin blurted out. Her face practically turned purple as the words flew from her lips. She clamped her hands over her mouth as her eyes bulged. She had said it. Out loud.

"What?" Mukale instantly shifted back to his natural Berrat form. "I don't understand."

"I like *girls*," Lin repeated, this time with a lot more emphasis on the word girls. "It's nothing personal Mukale. You're a great guy and you've been a good friend to me, but I prefer the company of women."

"Oh," Mukale replied. If there were any hurt feelings, or any other negative emotions, there was absolutely no sign of it. His eyes swung from Lin to Kit, and he waggled his eyebrows.

"Sweet Titan, Mukale," Lin groaned. "She's got a boyfriend."

"No, I don't!" Kit protested. Lin's eyes bulged out yet again, and she shook her head slightly at her. She had given Kit an out, a way to keep Mukale at bay, but she had totally missed the opportunity. When Kit finally caught on, her mouth formed into a large 'oh' shape and she nodded back.

"I mean, I do, but it's not formal or anything." Kit shuffled her feet, her hands fidgeting uncontrollably. Admitting Indie was her boyfriend wasn't as personal as Lin admitting her preference for women, but she'd never had a boyfriend before. She wasn't even sure if she had one now. She was unfamiliar with games of the heart. Just thinking about it caused her pulse to start racing.

Sweet Titan, what is wrong with me?

"Oh," Mukale replied again. His chin dipped down to his chest. It seemed that being turned down twice in as many seconds was enough to crush his spirit. However, the darkness that had consumed his face disappeared, quickly replaced by his bright smile.

"No worries," Mukale said with a happy shrug. "Plenty of fish in the sea. Hop on, let's get going." These were his last words before changing back into his stallion form. It would seem the young man had no trouble moving past his crushes.

Both girls clambered up onto his back. Kit took the front and Lin took her place behind the young priest. She wrapped her arms around Kit's waist and gave her a gentle squeeze.

"You know I have a boyfriend, right?" Kit said over her shoulder.

"I don't care," Lin said as she tightened her grip on Kit's waist a bit more. "He's not here right now."

"I like boys, Lin." Kit said, with zero hint of joking in her voice. "Just so you know."

Lin scooched up even closer, pressing her body tightly against Kit's back.

"That's okay," Lin replied. "I'm just holding tight so that I don't fall off."

"I can tell that you're lying, Lin."

"I can tell that I'm lying, too." Lin leaned the side of her face against Kit's back and practically snuggled herself against her long black hair.

"You know I can hear you two, right?" Mukale laughed as he leapt forward into a full gallop, nearly throwing the girls off his back.

⚬⚬⚬⚭⚬⚬⚬

After having traveled for over an hour across open planes of grass and small rolling hills, Mukale suddenly changed direction and headed due east. "The terrain is getting rougher. If you want me to keep up this pace, you'll need to hold on tight."

Kit took the horse's mane in her hands and weaved it through her fingers for a better grip. Lin took advantage of the opportunity and tightened her hold around her friend's waist. Kit peered over her shoulder and gave her a low growl. Lin completely ignored Kit's objections and snuggled up closer to her until their bodies were completely mashed together. Lin leaned her head against Kit's shoulder and let out a happy sigh.

Even with the two riders, Mukale nimbly picked his way across the countryside. He easily avoided rocks and ditches, but after an hour of running cross-country, Kit's backside had become unbearably sore.

"Do you think we could take a break?" she asked Mukale, unwittingly stroking his neck as she asked the question. When her brain finally told her that she was caressing a man, and not a traditional horse, she snapped her hand back.

Mukale slowed to an easy trot before coming to a stop. The two women slid down off his back before he switched into his natural Berrat form.

"I don't think I can ride any further; the insides of my thighs are killing me." Kit doubled over and tried to rub some feeling back into her legs.

"No need to keep riding," Mukale said as his eyes scanned the area. "If the stranger's directions were true, the camp is just past that treeline."

Chapter Ten

Midnight

The area Mukale was pointing to appeared to be a small forest of thick-branched evergreens.

"The trees provide excellent cover for a camp, and with everything else so wide open, it's where I would be if I was trying to hide." There was a note of approval in Mukale's voice. If the kidnapper had selected the forest to make camp, the location suggested he was not stupid.

As they jogged towards the treeline, Kit struggled to keep her lead-filled legs pumping. A feeling of dread pressed down on her. She had never seen either Mukale or Lin in combat. She had no sense of their skill level at all. She guessed that Mukale could likely handle himself well enough, based on how comfortable he seemed to be in the wilderness, but Lin was a complete unknown. Sure, she had trained at the Temple just like Kit had, but the woman preferred blades and bows over hammers and shields.

When they reached the outer edges of the treeline, Kit motioned the group to come to a stop.

"I'm going to go on ahead, on my own." Kit watched her two cohorts, trying to gauge their reaction to her suggestion. "I'll scout the camp first. If I can deal with the situation on my own, I'll do it immediately. Otherwise, I'll come back for you two."

"You're going to do the scouting?" Mukale asked, one eyebrow cocked in disbelief. "I've watched how you move. You're a fighter, not a scout."

Kit knew he was right, but she wasn't willing to let either of them face any trouble; not if she could help it.

Mukale watched Kit carefully as she considered what to do next. "Can you smell that?" he finally asked, growing tired of waiting for Kit's response.

"Smell what?" she asked. Kit's head swiveled about, wondering what the man was referring to. "I smell the evergreens."

"You are not a good scout," Mukale retorted. His voice indicated that he was stating it as a simple truth and not as a matter of opinion.

"What do *you* smell then?" Lin chimed in, coming to Kit's defense.

"Well," Mukale said as his eyes switched back and forth between the two ladies. "I can smell that Kit hasn't had a bath in a few days. I can smell that you bathed in lavender and raspberry salts just this morning. But more importantly, I can smell the smudge coming off a campfire that was extinguished within the last twenty minutes."

"I stink?" Kit was horrified by Mukale's comment.

"A bit musky, perhaps," the Berrat replied. He took another sniff. "But not bad. You smell of sweat, horse and... wolf."

Kit's stomach clenched. She was aware hygiene was never her strong suit, but she had no idea that she actually *stunk*. She resisted the urge to give her pits a quick sniff.

"If you've finished smelling us, maybe we can move in to check out the camp." Lin's voice had an uncharacteristic edge to it. "I'm the only one with a bow here, so I'm coming."

A reasonably silent argument broke out among the three of them as they tried to decide who was going to do what, when Kit finally gave in. She shook her head at the other two.

"You're both putting me in a difficult spot here. I've never fought with you. I don't know what you know and what you don't know."

"I was trained at the Temple, just like you were, *Sister* Kit Standing Bear. I can fight as well as the next person." There was steel in Lin's voice, like she needed to prove a point.

"We are taught the ways of the hammer, ax, and shield," Kit replied, raising her eyebrows at her friend. "And yet, you choose to fight with bow and sword."

Lin shook her head, knowing that she had no strong defense against Kit's accusations. "He is my brother. I'm coming. End of discussion."

"We're both coming, Kit. End of discussion." Mukale's voice had the same steely determination as Lin's. The three stared silently at each other for several seconds.

"Fine," Kit sighed. "Then lead the way, scout."

A few minutes later, the three of them were through the thin line of pine trees, looking out at the small camp. Kit rubbed herself several times against the resin-filled pine needles, hoping to transfer some of their scent to her clothing. It would badly stain her clothes, but maybe it would help to mask her musky aroma.

"It's a strange campsite," Kit whispered as she surveyed the site. "There's only a firepit, and no shelter built." She was about to continue her assessment, but it was cut short when the cold tip of a steel blade pressed against the back of her neck.

A small reedy voice with a hint of a whistle to it threatened her. "Speak quickly and true, or today you will have seen your last sunrise."

Kit slowly turned to get a look at the person behind the voice. A dark blue rabbit stared back at her. His pink eyes held her gaze. He wore a chainmail shirt and wielded a bone-white fourteen-inch blade. A gust of wind ruffled the feathers of his fluffy, white wings.

He has wings. He's a rabbit – with wings.

A smirk broke across Kit's face, much to her chagrin. Sweet Titan, why can't she control her mouth?

"You find me amusing, do you? Perhaps you'd like to test your mettle against my steel?" With that, the rabbit made a series of complex moves, his blade flashing in the dappled sunlight. He completed his movements with a lunge, leaving his blade less than an inch from Kit's throat. His nose twitched. He cocked an eyebrow. His nose twitched yet again. When Kit didn't react, he gave a small harrumph and sheathed his blade and rounded on Mukale.

"What about you, horse-man? You think you're clever, but I heard you coming from a great distance."

Kit shuffled her feet, and once again the rabbit unsheathed his blade and held it firmly against her chest. The tip threatened to cut through her armor's hard leather shell.

Kit held her hands up, showing she held no weapon or ill intent. "Whoa, small friend. We are only seeking the man who stays at this camp and the prisoner he holds."

The rabbit retracted his blade slightly, offering a skeptical look. His nose twitched heavily as he scrutinized the girl standing before him. "There is no *man* at my camp. This is my home and I protect it like a she-wolf protects her cubs. But I believe I know the *man* to whom you are referring." The winged rabbit's eyes narrowed as he raised his blade towards Kit's face. "Are you in league with him?"

Kit's face turned purple, and her hands clenched into tight fists. The rabbit took a step back when she snarled at him. "In league with him? Titan, give me strength! I seek this man to free his prisoner and bring justice upon his body."

"Titan?" the rabbit exclaimed. "Titan?" He shook his head and sat himself down on the edge of a small stump. "You're another one of those fools who worships a god who brought nothing but pain and suffering to our land. But, if you are looking to bring retribution to this *man*, then you may not be all bad." The rabbit thumbed the edge of his blade. "But hear these words. Followers of that false god are to blame for the mess our world is in. It has been countless cycles since he's arrived, and he brought nothing but despair and hardship to these lands. My kind used to be numerous, but we have been all but wiped out by what he considers to be a Game! A Game!" The rabbit tramped about, flailing his arms over his head. "Oh, what good fun, kill the inhabitants of this world and see what new things we can create!"

Kit couldn't help but notice that this rabbit-thing's ranting closely resembled the words from the strange book contained within the box Father Hoarfrost had given her. It spoke of a game, the creation, and the extinction of many races. It couldn't be a coincidence. There had to be some merit, some truth behind what he was saying – unless it was all a conspiracy of some sort to sully the good name of Titan.

The rabbit continued rambling on and on. He was practically foaming at the mouth when he stopped and stared up at Kit. "If you can talk to your god, tell him to bring peace upon this land." With his head hung low, the rabbit walked back towards his camp, his white cotton tail bobbing side to side. "The *man* you seek was never here, but you can likely pick up his trail on the road to Cormorant. I saw him only yesterday, heading in that direction. I did not see any prisoner with him though."

"How do you know who I'm talking about?" Kit called out, hoping the rabbit was willing to give her more information. If he wasn't willing, she'd have to find another way to squeeze the knowledge out of him.

"Because he came through here nearly a moon ago. He was with another man who worked in the slave trade. We scared them off and told them the next time they came through here, they'd not see another sunrise." And with that, the rabbit popped down a hole near the ashes of the campfire.

"We?" Kit asked, turning back to her cohorts. "There are more than one of... him?"

Kit's friends stared back at her and offered nothing.

The rabbit had certainly spun an interesting tale. If what he said was true, Kit was going to be facing a difficult decision. Seek the stranger who kidnapped Treedale or seek Treedale himself. If the stranger was heading for the port city of Cormorant, he was likely going to hop on a boat and disappear for good.

"We need to hunt the kidnapper," Kit declared as she turned toward the northwest, the direction of Cormorant. "If we don't stop him, he'll continue catching and selling people. The choice is clear."

"The choice *is* clear," Lin said. She wrapped her arms around her waist. Her stomach-muscles clenched. "But it's not to hunt the kidnapper. We have to find Treedale. We need to rescue my brother."

When Kit didn't respond, Lin grabbed her firmly by the shoulder and spun her around. Kit stared blankly up at Lin. Lin glared down at Kit.

"We need to rescue my brother. There is no other option."

Kit's hackles raised. "As a priest of Titan, my duty is to justice."

"And, as a priest of Titan, your duty is to uphold your word. You told Grams you'd find Treedale."

"But that was when I thought they were together. I thought..." The conviction in Kit's voice wavered.

"I don't care what you thought. I care about what you said, and what you said was that you would find Treedale. If you're not going to be true to your word, then I'm done with you and the Temple."

Kit's chest was heaving badly. Not from Lin's aggressive posture, but from the realization that life outside the Temple was far more complex and nuanced than she could have ever imagined. Her head was swimming. The decision was overwhelming her.

If I look for Treedale, I'll lose the kidnapper. If I continue the search for the kidnapper, I will have sealed Treedale's fate.

Lin's fiery eyes and her ever deepening scowl clearly displayed her feelings on the matter.

Titan may be a god of justice, but I cannot allow a child to suffer or perish because of my inaction.

"We'll continue the search for Treedale," Kit said. The words washed over Lin. Her death-stare didn't waver. Moments passed. Lin blinked several times before her face finally softened.

"Thank you," Lin said. "Thank you for staying true to your word."

Kit's shoulders slumped. "You understand that by choosing this path the stranger will surely get away."

Lin nodded her agreement. She didn't like the possibility of the kidnapper escaping, but her duty was to her family – above all else.

Mukale cleared his throat and offered his own words of wisdom. His voice was even and measured. "Find the boy, the kidnapper is not important. There are hundreds of kidnappers, but there is only one Treedale, and I swore to Grams that I'd bring him back. After he's home we can hunt the kidnappers at our leisure."

Kit clenched her hands into tight fists. Even though she had already made her decision, she still hated the idea of letting the kidnapper go. She knew in her heart that Mukale was right but letting the wicked run free gnawed at her. Kit stormed over to the winged rabbit's hole and screamed for him to come out. She waited barely three seconds before she thrusted her hand inside, hoping to catch a hold of him. She called down the hole again, threatening to strangle the life from him if he didn't come out. She suddenly stopped groping inside the hole and groaned.

"You got a death-wish, girl?" Midnight asked, sticking the point of his blade hard against her neck.

Kit sighed and slowly turned to face the rabbit. "We just want to know if you can tell us any more about Treedale, the boy the man kidnapped. Can you tell me where you think he might be?"

"I couldn't care less where that man-whelp is," the rabbit raged. "But, if it will get you to leave, I'll tell you where to start looking." In a flash, the rabbit scooted past Kit and disappeared down his hole again, only to return a few moments later. He held out a shiny bit of jewelry in his fur-covered hand.

"Here. Take this amulet. It belongs to a friend of mine. His name's Feigh. Go to where the grass tastes the best. Not by the old tree though – go to where the really big rock is." The rabbit blinked at Kit's blank face. "Damn, girl, do you know nothing? Here, give me your map and I'll mark on it where you should go. Feigh isn't friendly like me. You'd better show him the amulet fast-like. Tell him Midnight sent you. He'll be able to tell you where to look."

Kit stared at the map to see where the rabbit was sending them. She rolled her eyes when she saw the location of the mark he left.

"You could have just said, go to Silverhawk!"

The rabbit had already disappeared again. The young priest growled, more than a little frustrated at how this little creature vanished before answering all her questions.

"It's the better part of two days to Silverhawk from here," Mukale said as he surveyed the darkening sky. "We should camp here and head out at first light. If I'm going to carry you two the whole way there, I need some rest."

Kit was just starting to get feeling back in her legs, so she nodded her agreement. Lin didn't seem so sure of the decision though. "The longer we wait, the more likely things will go badly for Treedale. We have no time for rest. We need to leave. Now!" She strode over to Mukale and glared down at him. She was well over a head taller than him, and she used her height to her advantage. "If you can't carry us, then we'll head out on foot."

"Lin," Kit was about to put Lin in her place when the woman spun around and glared at Kit. Her eyes were wide and glassy, but her hands were clenched into tight little balls. A tiny tremor crossed her bottom lip.

Kit closed her eyes and nodded. "What's the fastest way to Silverhawk?" she asked Mukale. "Looking at my map, it seems like it's due north of us. There are no roads this way though. Do we head back to the road, or do we go cross country?"

"Cross country is about half the distance, but the terrain here is difficult, especially by night."

"Kit's hammer can supply us with enough light to move safely," Lin said, motioning to the weapon at Kit's side. "The sun enchantments on it cast a glow in the dark."

Kit took a quick look at it and even though it wasn't dark yet, she could see a faint glow coming off it. "Hopefully, it will be enough. If you twist an ankle in the dark, I can heal you."

"As can I," Lin added. "I've never been particularly good with the priestly miracles, but I'm rather good at casting spells. Healing is one of the ones I'm better at."

Mukale pulled his water-skin off his belt. "If you want to ride me, I'll drink the rest of my water. It should give me enough energy to get me through the night."

"What's in that?" Lin asked. "I felt so much better after just a few sips."

"A rejuvenation potion, perhaps?" Kit asked. There was an accusatory tone to the question. She remembered the feeling of euphoria and limitless energy after having drunk the potion Brother Powder had given her. She hadn't slept in over a day, but the potion completely masked her exhaustion. But therein lies the problem with the potion. It doesn't actually fix tiredness; it only masks it. When the potion wore off, it was like being run over by an ox – repeatedly.

Mukale shrugged and grinned at Kit. "Secret family recipe."

Kit rolled her eyes at him. "Do what you need to do so that we can get out of here."

Mukale quickly downed the contents of his water-skin. His face flushed as the *water* took effect. He was practically hopping on the balls of his feet. "Do either of you have rope with you?"

Lin shook her head. "What do we need rope for?" she asked, narrowing her eyes. Whatever the Berrat was up to, she wanted no part of it. Feeling her distrust, he shook his head and blew out a long breath.

"It's to tie yourselves to my back," Mukale replied. "I have a small rope, but it's not long enough for the two of you. If you can bind yourselves to me, you can sleep while I travel."

Kit took the short length of rope from the Berrat. "We'll make do with this. Time to make like a horse." A moment later, the large stallion was standing before the two ladies. His withers shuddered, and he pawed at the soft, loose ground. The big gray stallion's muscles were quivering, desperate to be put to task.

Kit quickly tied the rope into a loop and placed it over the horse's head. She hopped up onto his back and wrapped her wrists into the rope. She had to hunch over his neck to get a good grip, but she figured she'd need to do that anyway if she was going to rest while riding. Kit freed one of her hands and offered it to Lin to help her up. Holding Kit's wrist, the woman leapt up and threw her leg over the horse. After a few moments the two had settled themselves into place.

Kit patted the horse's neck, Mukale's neck. "We can rest when the sun goes down, but for now, let's get as close to Silverhawk as we can before nightfall."

Mukale whinnied in response and started off at a slow canter. The ground there was uneven, so he didn't want to risk moving too quickly. Fortunately, the uneven ground gave way to open meadows that glowed golden in the dying light of the day. Mukale broke into a full gallop. The tall grasses tickled his underside as he thundered along, rapidly closing the distance on their destination.

Chapter Eleven

Bow, Fish, Blade

They had been riding hard for nearly an hour when, over their left shoulders, the sun was barely kissing the horizon. The pain in Kit's thighs was back with a vengeance. The possibility of putting up with it through the night made her cringe internally. Her mind was drawn back to the night of her Rite of Acknowledgement and the pain she endured kneeling on the rough stone before the altar of Titan's statue.

I offer my suffering unto you, Titan. May it help bring me closer to your glory.

The setting sun touched the rolling hills to the west, igniting the sky in a blaze of glorious oranges and reds. Wisps of clouds reflected the dying light of the sun, turning them from white to deep shades of lavender and purple.

"It's a beautiful sight," Lin whispered into Kit's ear as the two of them watched the natural beauty unfold. "I don't think I'll ever get tired of watching sunsets. It's a shame the beauty only lasts a few minutes."

"Like our time here, before we join the Great Cycle," Kit replied. "Our lives are so short. We need to make sure we live them well." Lin tightened her hold on Kit's waist. She was about to object but Lin wasn't doing any harm, and she actually welcomed the extra body heat.

A moment later, the last of the sun dipped below the horizon, leaving only a pale orange glow in the distance. High above, in the ever-darkening sky, stars started to make their appearance.

Mukale slowed to a walk. "You'd better pull out that hammer of yours, Kit; my night-vision isn't great in horse form."

Kit pulled the weapon from its holster. The hammer's head was definitely glowing, but it was not a significant source of light. "Does this help much?" she asked.

"Not really," Mukale replied, disappointment carrying through in his voice, despite his being a horse.

"You need to call on the light, Kit," Lin whispered in her ear. "Let yourself connect with the weapon, feel for its power."

Kit didn't bother to question Lin. Instead, she took a firm grip of the hammer and reached out with her senses, trying to feel the weapon's magic.

Lin whispered again, "Don't force it, just let it come."

Kit again reached out to the weapon's power, but when she felt nothing, she let go of her emotions and opened herself up to the magic. She imagined it to be a tiny spark floating just out of reach. As she relaxed, the spark grew closer, hovering tantalizingly just beyond her grasp. In her mind's eye she took a deep cleansing breath and the spark lowered until she was able to wrap her tiny hand around it. Like a jolt of lightning the hammer's power surged through her as though it was speaking to her very soul.

"Light!" she commanded to the weapon and its magic immediately surged, casting a bright-yellow glow all around them. The light extended out for about ten paces in all directions. The young priest's heart surged. She had never commanded a magical object before.

Titan's snowballs! Fury!

Kit had completely forgotten about her dragon-bone cane. She had left it in her cell. Why in the name of Titan was she so absentminded? She quickly shook it off, returning to the here and now.

"How's that?" she asked Mukale. There was a hint of pride in Kit's voice. The feeling of calling forth the magic of a non-sentient object exhilarated her.

"Impressive," he responded as he broke into a canter. As Mukale became more comfortable with the lighting, his speed increased. In the silence of the night, his hooves resembled the rhythmic beat of war-drums as they pounded across the grass covered countryside.

After only a few minutes of riding, Kit found herself struggling to find a comfortable way to hold the hammer. She could continue to hold it out by her side, but she would never be able to sleep while doing so.

"Hang the hammer from your back," Lin said as she watched Kit fidget. "The holster is designed to be a back-strap. Just move it up from your waist to over your shoulders."

It took them a short while to work things out without falling off the running horse but, eventually, they managed to get the holster situated so that the hammer's head was sticking out over Kit's left shoulder.

Kit wrapped her wrists into the rope around the horse's neck and rested her body against Mukale. Mukale managed to adjust his gait so that his head stayed reasonably stationary. Lin wrapped her arms a bit tighter around Kit's waist and laid her head on her shoulder. After only a few minutes she was snoring gently.

Between the rhythmic pace of Mukale's gait and Lin's gentle snoring, Kit couldn't help but let sleep take her. She rested her head on the horse's withers and slipped into a deep sleep.

⚬⚬⚬◈⚬⚬⚬

The icy spray of water jolted through Kit. It was so cold that her joints were seizing up. With each wave that broke over the great turtle, his shell became more and more slick. A thick layer of ice was building up and Kit wasn't sure how much longer she could maintain her balance.

Another wave approached. Kit had to crane her neck up to see its crest. If she didn't do something, and fast, it would sweep her away. Kit dropped down to her hands and knees, desperately trying to find a hold for her frozen fingers to grip onto. She tried to dig her nails into a seam between the turtle's shell-plates, but ice clogged them, leaving no room for purchase.

"Burn," Kit screamed out. Her hands were immediately wreathed in bright red flames. The wave of heat warmed the shell, and the ice poured out of the crevasses, leaving room for Kit's fingers to sink in. She hoped that she wasn't hurting the creature that had willingly offered itself to carry her across the northern strait.

The wave crashed down upon her. The water roiled and churned as the surge threated to sweep her away. She dug in with all her might and somehow maintained her grip. Kit held her breath and waited for the great turtle to resurface. Her lungs were beginning to burn. They craved life giving air. If she didn't get it, and fast, she would take her last breath beneath the frozen surface of the great North Sea.

The turtle belched. A great bubble emerged from its hard beak-like mouth. It clung to the turtle's head and extended back to engulf Kit as well. Unable to hold her breath any longer, Kit gasped and sucked in the somewhat fresh air that surrounded her. She waited a moment, checking to see if there were any ill effects. She waited another moment while she allowed her gaze to search out into the sea's inky darkness.

Kit gasped again, and again, sucking in more and more air until her breathing finally settled into slow, easy breaths.

Encased in the giant bubble, the young priest could easily see into the sea's dark waters. The water was remarkably clear, but it was so dark that visibility was somewhat limited.

A shadow passed by the turtle's side. Even against the sea's blackness, the shadow stood out like an enormous void in the night sky.

"Light," Kit commanded, holding her hammer high over her head. Its light burst forth, illuminating the water. A great eye came into sight. Its pupil contracted suddenly at the brilliance of the hammer's glow. Whatever this creature was, it appeared that it could swallow Kit and the great turtle in a single bite.

The creature turned towards Kit. A great spiral horn which protruded from the animal's head burst the air bubble. Frigid water crashed down, the weight of the sea above crushing Kit onto the shell. Biting, searing pain stabbed Kit's inner ears as the water pressure threatened to burst her eardrums. With a flap of the turtle's long, scaled flippers, they were thrust upwards, and in moments burst through the surface of the sea's turbid waters.

The great horned creature surfaced near the side of the turtle; its blue gray back rising some twenty feet out of the water. Kit instinctively knew there was much more beneath the breaking waves. Like a giant iceberg the animal only showed a small part of its greater bulk.

The great turtle turned to face the creature as though preparing for its imminent attack. It opened its enormous beak and bellowed. The vibrations that ran through his shell nearly knocked Kit off her feet.

The blue-gray creature circled the turtle once. The amphibian spun helplessly in the creature's spiral wake. With nary a splash, the creature exposed its great forked tail before slipping down beneath the waves.

Kit's heart hammered in her chest. She waited. She trembled. She anticipated the great beast's attack from deep below. She expected the great horned creature to swallow both her and the turtle - whole.

The attack never came.

⤙⤙⤙⤙◈⤚⤚⤚⤚

When Kit woke, the warmth of the morning sun beat down on the side of her face. A streak of drool had dried and stuck to her cheek. Her mouth was dry and sticky. She pulled great strands of Mukale's long black mane from her lips.

"Good morning," Lin said. She still had her arms wound around Kit's waist and she gave the young priest a gentle squeeze.

"If you two are well rested, you need to get off me." Mukale managed to get the words out mid yawn. His facial expression, while simultaneously talking and yawning, gave the horse a comical appearance.

Lin jumped off Mukale's back and held her hand out to Kit. The young priest pushed Lin's hand aside and slid off the horse's back. Her legs wobbled badly, and she keeled over, rather ungracefully, and disappeared into the tall, scraggly grasses. She had expected to be unsteady on her numb legs, but she hadn't expected to lose all feeling in them.

Lin had a playful look on her face. She pursed her lips and stared down at her friend. She reached out, offering to help her. When Kit reached out to take hold, Lin pulled her hand away and laughed.

"Fine. I'll just rest here until the feeling in my thighs comes back."

"Would you like me to, umm... rub them for you?"

"No, Lin, I wouldn't." Kit rolled her eyes and rolled over onto her stomach. She got up on all fours and slowly pressed herself up into a standing position. Her left knee buckled slightly, but she managed to not fall on her face a second time.

"Um, Mukale, you don't look so good," Lin said, drawing Kit's attention.

He was back in Berrat form, and he really didn't look well, not well at all. His skin was pallid and clammy. His eyes had deep purple circles under them. He wavered slightly. His chin dipped involuntarily to his chest several times. "I can go no further. By foot, Silverhawk is about two hours straight north of here." He pointed off across the grassy field. His eyes rolled back in his head. He dropped heavily to his knees before keeling over onto his side.

Kit immediately dropped down beside him. She checked his breathing. It was shallow and rapid, but he didn't appear to be in immediate distress.

"He's exhausted," she said, as she carefully checked him over. "He must have run non-stop all night." She pressed her lips together and shook her head. "Secret family recipe? Titan's snowballs, that water-skin held rejuvenation potion, sure as I'm drawing breath right now."

"He just needs sleep," Lin said, placing her hand on Kit's shoulder. "He gave us everything he had to get us this close. We need to keep going. He'll be fine after he gets some much-deserved rest."

"We can't just leave him here," Kit protested.

Lin scanned the area. "There's nobody around, and he's hidden in the tall grasses. He'll be fine. We need to keep going. We need to find Treedale. He ran himself ragged to get us here. We have to continue."

Kit nodded and bowed down over the man. "Thank you," she said and placed a soft kiss on his cheek. "If we succeed, Treedale will owe you his life." She brushed his hair out of his face and ran her fingers across his brow. "May Titan keep you safe. Sleep well, my friend. Sleep well."

Kit picked herself up off the ground, her legs still unsteady beneath her.

"Okay then, let's get going." Kit hated leaving Mukale behind, but she knew in her heart it was the right thing to do.

Lin bent down next to the sleeping Berrat and gave him a gentle kiss on the cheek. "Thank you, Mukale. Grams would be proud of you this day. I am proud of you, too. You're a good friend."

The pair jogged at a decent pace but not so fast that Lin couldn't manage. Kit's feet were pins and needles with each step shooting a sharp pain up through her shins. She was thankful to move at a slower pace, at least until the strength in her legs returned.

"I'm going to need some food," Lin said between labored breaths. "It feels like it's been a week since I last ate."

"With all the noise we're making running, we're never going to spot any game." Kit's stomach rumbled at the mention of food. "Maybe we'll be lucky enough to..."

"Is that a river up ahead?" Lin asked, cutting Kit off. "Maybe there are fish in it."

The two girls stopped at the edge of the fast-flowing river. Except for white caps and eddies created by rocks poking up through the surface, it was crystal clear. Large, silver and red-spotted trout were resting in the small back-currents provided by the eddies. Other smaller trout were fighting to stay in the middle of the river, scooping up bits of food supplied by the swift current.

"Titan shall provide," Kit said with a smile. Without breaking stride, she leapt into the river and tried to grab one of the fish with her bare hands. The fish easily avoided her grasp and swam away. Another, much larger fish swam up right next to her, as though taunting her to try to capture it.

Kit threw herself face first into the water, her arms thrashing about as she tried to grasp onto the fish's thick, slippery frame. She managed to clamp onto one for barely a second before the fish flexed its muscular body and escaped her grasp. It leapt briefly from the water before darting off with the current.

Yet another fish came into view, barely a foot away upstream from her. Once again, she threw herself at the fish and, once again, she came up empty handed. The girl was now on her knees, waist deep in the frigid, fast-flowing river. She was soaked from head to toe and shivering badly.

"Are you going to keep splashing about in the river, or are we going to eat?"

Fury ripped through Kit at her friend's taunting. She spun about, her hands curled into tight, shivering fists. Her jaw went slack while her bright-blue lips trembled. Lin was standing on the riverbank, dry as a bone, holding up a large brown trout, an arrow through its head.

"Oh. Nice." Kit said by way of response as she pulled her freezing, water-logged body out of the icy waters.

"Since you're already wet, why not carry me across the river?" Lin said with a broad smile on her face. "No sense in both of us catching our death from sickness."

Kit groaned and shook her head while shivers continued to wrack her entire body. She bent over slightly, offering Lin to climb up on her back.

"Too bad you can't switch into a horse," she said as she wrapped her arms around Kit's neck, the mostly dead trout still flapping about. As Kit climbed down from the bank and into the shallow river, Lin wrapped her legs around Kit's waist, trying to keep her boots from dipping into the water.

When they got to the far side, Lin hopped down from Kit's back and searched for wood suitable for building a campfire. Lin couldn't help but start laughing as she watched Kit shake herself like a dog, trying to rid herself of the ice-cold river water.

"We don't have time for a fire, Lin. We'll eat it raw and get moving." Kit had stopped shivering, and she was holding up the fish like she was about to bite into it.

"Raw? Gross!"

Kit rolled her eyes and took a big bite out of the back of the trout. "It's delicious," she said before even trying to swallow. Bits of fish flew from her mouth with each disgusting word she spoke.

"Give me that!" Lin grabbed the now mutilated fish from Kit's hand. She dropped on her knees, pulled out her dagger and cleaned the fish. With just a few quick slices, she removed the head and all the entrails. She then ran the blade down the back of the fish, from head to tail, splitting into two equal pieces – except for where Kit had already taken a massive bite of it. She handed the bigger piece to Kit and eyed the raw meat apprehensively. She looked up to find that Kit had already taken another bite and was wiping fish-bits off her face with the back of her hand. Not wanting to look weak in front of her friend, Lin also took a huge bite of the fish. Her eyes went wide, and she immediately spat it out, scraping her dirt-filled nails across her tongue, trying to rid her mouth of the slimy, raw fish taste.

"Nope, can't do it," she said as she continued trying to spit the rest of the fish out of her mouth. "I don't care if it costs us a few minutes, I need to eat and if I'm going to eat fish, it's going to be cooked."

"Can you cast a fire spell of any kind?" Kit asked as she took another bite of fish. Lin practically gagged as Kit ripped a massive chunk off the trout. She had to keep poking the food back into her overstuffed mouth as she chewed.

"Don't need fire spells when I've got these with me." Lin drew one of her longswords and gave it a shake. Bright red flames ignited along the cutting edge of the blade. She jabbed it into the fish, skewering it from front to back. The flames continued to burn brightly and quickly charred the flesh. Using her sword like a giant kabob, she took a delicate bite from the end of the fish. She closed her eyes and savored each morsel, letting the flaky white meat fall apart on her tongue. A small whimper interrupted her blissful moment.

Kit stood eyeing Lin's nicely cooked filet of trout. She had bits of raw fish and tiny pin bones stuck to her cheeks and chin. Kit wiped a bit of drool that was beginning to pool at the corner of her lips.

"Let me guess, still hungry?"

Kit nodded enthusiastically in response.

"Do you want mine, or would you like me to catch you another one?"

Kit gave her friend a sheepish grin.

Lin handed Kit her fish-kabob and nocked another arrow.

There were a good number of trout swimming near the river's edge. Apparently, without Kit splashing around in the water, they were much easier to see. Lin calmly drew back the bow and released the arrow. There was a satisfying thud as the arrow struck the back of an exceptionally large trout, pinning it to the riverbed. It was a bit further away from shore than Lin had expected, forcing her to wade into the water to retrieve it. The rush of icy water over the top of her boot made the woman squeal. Not wanting to be in the water any longer than necessary, Lin bolted through the current to retrieve her fish. She turned her ankle on a loose stone and toppled over, the rush of the current swept her several dozen feet down stream before she was able to regain her footing.

When she finally climbed out, Lin held up her prize, displaying it proudly for Kit. "Here you go," she said just before her jaw flopped open. "You ate my fish! What the Helja?"

Kit had a sheepish look on her face while she continued to lick the fish-juice from her fingers. "Sorry."

"Can I cook this one for me, or do you want some of it, too?"

"You can cook it for yourself," Kit said, but her eyes told a different story.

In just a few moments, Lin butchered the fish and sliced it into two large filets. She slid them onto her swords and ignited their flames. She handed one to Kit and kept the other for herself. Lin nibbled at the outer edges where the skin had been roasted to crispy perfection. She let out a small moan as she worked her way up the skewer until she had finished, perhaps, one third of the fish.

"There's no way I can eat all of this," Lin said, still in a state of rapture over the taste of the freshly cooked trout.

"I'll have it," Kit muffled out. She held out Lin's longsword, which was now devoid of fish.

"How can such a tiny girl eat so much food and still look as... amazing as you do?"

Kit shrugged and accepted the rest of Lin's fish and immediately took an enormous bite of it.

"I don't know," she said as she finally swallowed her mouthful. "Lately, I've had a crazy-big appetite. Besides, we don't know the next time we'll get to eat. It's something I was taught by my guide that led me out from Berrathia."

Kit hadn't thought of Jeger, the Berrat hunter who had accompanied her from Lilloet to the border of Arnnor. In the short time they had spent together, he had taught her a good deal about how to live with the land. If only Brother Rime had been able to teach in a similar fashion. Maybe she'd have done better in his classes and maybe he wouldn't have hated her so much.

RISE OF THE PHOENIX

"Where do I begin?" Danny asked, holding out his empty plate in one hand, accepting a full plate in the other. "I was very small when I left Berrathia, less than six cycles if I remember correctly."

"Yes, we know that." Breayn was becoming more and more irritated with Danny with each bite of food he shoveled into his mouth. "The deal was we feed you and you tell us your story. So far, you've eaten three plates of food and not said anything meaningful."

Danny grinned, his mouth, cheeks, and chin glistening with elk juices. "But did you know that my parents told me to never take the final rite to become an actual priest of Titan?"

Breayn raised her eyebrows and shook her head. "No, I suppose that is something. But what does it mean? Why take you to the Temple if they didn't want you to become a priest?"

"I wondered that the whole time I was in Aarall," Danny said, ripping off another strip of meat with his teeth. "I could have passed the challenge to become a priest had I tried harder. But as for why they took me to the Temple, I can only guess that they felt the High Priest, Father Hoarfrost, would keep my presence secret; that he would keep me safe."

"You failed because you didn't try? If you weren't going to try, why bother taking the test at all?"

"My friend, Kit. She insisted and she's ridiculously hard to refuse. When I got to the mountain, it fought against me. It was unnatural, like it was telling me I didn't belong. My first night the winds howled so strongly I thought they were going to pick me up and throw me off." Not wanting to talk about it further, he stretched his arms over his head and yawned widely. Doing so lifted his tunic, exposing his washboard abs. He scratched them absentmindedly, drawing a growl from Ryn. The man's reaction was too perfect, and he couldn't let it go. He gave him a wink and whispered, "And I don't even exercise."

"How is it that you can transform into a phoenix?" Breayn asked, shaking her head at her mate. "That animal has been extinct for hundreds of years."

"This is going to get weird," Danny said, leaning forward, "and I swear that what I'm about to tell you is all true."

Now that he had everyone's undivided attention, he began.

"My friend, Kit, an actual priest of Titan, showed me a box that Father Hoarfrost had given her. It appeared to be solid wood, no hinges, no opening of any kind." Danny rubbed the back of his neck again. It seemed that ever since Ulip told him there was a mark there, it itched. "I don't know how, or why, but Kit believed it was old magic. She addressed the box like it was a living thing. She spoke words that I've never heard before. Even though I couldn't understand her, the words were beautiful, rhythmic. Suddenly, the box unsealed and opened towards me."

Danny's eyes moved to every person in the group, resting for a moment or two on each, examining their reactions to his story. When his eyes fell on Ryn, he paused. "It was full of bones and papers and a small book. The words on the papers, and in the book, well, neither Kit nor I could read them. The words were nothing more than pure gibberish." Ryn leaned in a little closer, mesmerized by the tale. Danny's eyes widened, and he continued addressing each person individually, drawing them in as he did. "One of the bones was fashioned into a flute. The flute was no longer than a cat's forearm, but it was intricately carved, a sight to behold. I once got some lessons from a pretty girl named SouSou, well, after I taught her a thing or two about Berrat physiology," Danny said, pausing again, waggling his eyebrows, with a grin so wide that it made his face look unnatural.

"We neither need nor want to hear of your *exploits*," Ryn growled. "Just get on with your story."

"Of course," Danny replied with a mock bow, still grinning from ear to ear. "When I played the flute, the words changed. The music made them readable. While I continued to play, Kit read the pages aloud. It was the strangest thing. She was speaking in a foreign tongue, but I understood it. I understood every word of what she said, even though the sounds she was making made no sense to me."

"What language was she speaking?" Ulip asked, speaking for the first time since he sat down.

"I am not certain, but I think it was Berrabbithi."

"The tongue of the ancients?" Breayn asked, a mix of awe and skepticism in her tone. "They were the true Berrat, the pure bloods. Do you have the book, the papers?" When Danny shook his head, Breayn pressed on. "What did the papers contain?"

As he considered the contents of the writings, Danny's face became solemn. "Based on the teachings of the Temple, and the stories of Titan and his followers, the words were pure blasphemy. They spoke of a time when gods walked the lands, the creation and destruction of races, a time before the coming of the Travelers."

"The Travelers?" Ryn asked, fidgeting slightly. His eyes snapped to Breayn. The reaction wasn't lost on Danny. He quickly lowered his voice to hushed tones.

"The Travelers came here, to Orth, back when Pele and Medeina presided over us, when Gaia watched and cared for us as a mother would care for her children. The Travelers were brought here by the Fates, to play games."

"You speak of children's bedtime stories," Ulip said, getting up from his place on the ground. He waved his hand dismissively and walked away. "You speak of nonsense."

"These were the stories in the box?" Breayn asked, ignoring Ulip's protestations.

"No," Danny said, his mind suddenly going foggy. "Not from the box." Whatever it was he was talking about was slipping from his memories, becoming almost dreamlike. "From the library!" he blurted out, as though the words were somehow being suppressed from his consciousness.

"The library?" Breayn asked.

"Tyr told Kit about it, and she let me come with her to see it." Thinking back to the early morning excursion up Titan's Trail made Danny laugh. "It was in the frozen butt of Titan's ice statue, the same one that is now a lake outside the walls of Aarall." Ulip had wandered back, his gigantic frame catching Danny's eye. The Gigas was standing a few feet away with his arms crossed over his massive chest. Danny beckoned him over, but the big man just scowled. "When we neared the entrance, Eris tried to stop us. She set creatures upon us. They were bizarre, horrible things. They didn't belong on the mountain. Some didn't belong on Orth."

"Who are Tyr and Eris?" Ryn interrupted. "How did Tyr know about the library and why did Eris want to stop you from getting into it?"

"They are Fates," Ulip responded before Danny had a chance to. He had quietly moved in closer. "They are all characters in fairy tales parents tell their children. Stories the elders passed down through the generations. And that's all they were – stories."

"Wait," Ryn said, perhaps even more intrigued by Danny's tale. "What happened with the box and the flute?"

"Well," Danny said, again scratching at the unseen mark on his neck. "The papers had drawings of creatures, both wonderful and grotesque. They told of how the Travelers created these creatures from nothing and how they wiped them out of existence when they finished playing their game."

"Why would they do that?" Breayn asked. "Create these creatures, just to destroy them."

"It wasn't like that," Danny continued, trying hard to remember what Kit had said. "They were created to fight against each other, or something like that. Whichever creature won the game was allowed to continue into the next cycle. Every other creature, the Travelers wiped out, or decimated them so badly that they just expected them to die off on their own. Whoever authored the stories found the bones, cataloged them, and he was killed for it."

Danny glanced down at his hands to find they were shaking badly. Grasping them together, he continued. "After Kit finished reading the stories, I tried to give the flute back to her, so she could return it to the box." He pried his hands apart and gawked at the palm of his right hand, examining the tiny scar on his skin. "But the bone flute – it disappeared into my hand before I could give it to her. It just slipped through my skin. I felt it travel into my arm." Danny showed his forearm to the group, even though there was nothing to see. "After that happened, I could still play the flute's music with my voice."

Danny closed his eyes and pictured his parents as best he could remember them. He started singing a soft, sweet tune. He didn't know where the melody came from, but it was like it had always been there, kept safe within his heart. Memories of his family, long since forgotten, poured out of him.

Chapter Thirteen

The Rift

Kit and Lin were about thirty minutes outside of Silverhawk when the city came into view. Even though it was considerably smaller than Aarall, Silverhawk was a beautiful city – from a distance. Its walls were a brilliant white, and from within the fortifications, a single, blue-topped spire stretched up skyward. Around the spire were a series of platforms which formed the city's rookery. The City Watch reserved the uppermost level for griffons, with the lower levels reserved for the city's substantial great-hawk population.

A *flight* of six hawk-riders trailing long red banners flew overhead. Their great brown wings flapped slowly, with each beat raising the bird higher into the crisp, clear morning sky. In perfect unison, the riders banked south, bringing them on a direct path towards the girls.

"Have you ever been to Silverhawk?" Lin asked as she watched the riders fly over them.

"No," Kit replied as she spun around to gawp at the riders as they continued past. "When I came through northern Arnnor last, I never came this far east."

"The red banners identify those riders as members of the warrior caste." Lin said, as though she was offering a lesson in Silverhawk's traditions. "White are healers, green are diplomats, and gold are the royal guards, but they typically fly griffons."

"Uh huh," Kit's eyes continued to track the flight until they were nothing more than dark specks in the vastness of the endless blue sky. "I would give anything to be able to fly like that."

"Who wouldn't?" Lin gave Kit a bit of a shove to knock her out of whatever daydream she was enjoying. "Maybe you can use your connection with Hard-ass to get us into the rookery."

"Who? What?" Kit finally returned to the conversation.

"Hard-ass Harding; you know, the Captain of the Guard; the guy who seems to give you so much of his time."

Kit sucked in a sharp breath. "Why would you say something like that? I don't need any more stupid rumors started. I do work for him, and that's it." Kit's chest heaved. She clenched her jaw, hard, while she tried to regain her composure. "And don't call him that name. He's a good guy. He's hard on his soldiers because he doesn't want them to die."

"Okay," Lin laughed. "If you say so. But there is no denying... he gives you way more attention than any other member of the Temple." The sing-song way she added the last part made Kit flinch. He did, in fact, give her a good deal of personal attention. He even remembered it was her birthday, and he gave her gifts; really, amazing gifts. Kit grimaced as she considered the pair of chainmail gauntlets tucked into her belt. The young priest thrashed wildly, waving her hands about her head like she was trying to chase the idea out of her head. When Lin giggled at her antics, Kit stormed off towards the city.

"Let's find the place where the *grass is the best*," Kit screamed out as she stomped through the tall grasses. She held her hands out to her side, letting them graze the top of the grasses and tickle her palms.

"Tastes the best," Lin corrected. "Midnight told us to go where the grass tastes the best."

"Whatever! It's grass. How can it be that much different wherever it is? It's near a big rock or something."

"A really big rock," Lin corrected again. "We have no clue what we're looking for, so if we're going to find this place, the details matter."

Kit scoffed and waved her hand at Lin, totally dismissing what she had to say.

The two continued their walk toward Silverhawk. As they neared, brightly colored tents outside the city walls came into view. They could only assume that, like Aarall, the market district was outside the main gate.

"Kit, look at that." Lin pointed to a massive tree off to the left of the city. It had to be hundreds of feet tall, with branches spanning out nearly as far. Beneath its gold-green canopy, there were thousands of wooly haired cattle spread out in every direction. A brief shift in the wind carried the pungent scent of manure. It was thick on the wind, having an almost tangy quality to it.

"If that's the tree Midnight was talking about, I can see why the grass there wouldn't taste so good." Kit scrunched up her face and pinched her nostrils to help make the point.

As they continued toward the city, the girls stopped at the edge of a ravine. Kit picked up a small stone and tossed it over the edge. She watched with detached amusement as the stone bounced and skipped down the side. Each time it struck the ground, it dislodged more small rocks, creating a small avalanche of gravel. The stones slowed as they neared the bottom, with several rolling into the coal-black river running through the bottom of it.

"Is this a moat?" Kit asked as she peered over the edge. "It's got to be a few hundred feet down to the river."

"It's no moat," Lin said with a small whistle. "But it doesn't look natural. It almost looks like a giant scar across the land, like a great claw had rent Orth open." Her eyes scanned left and right. "I don't see any bridges nearby either. We should head east. The north road out of Two Peaks should only be a few hours from here. It's probably faster than trying to get across this river."

"I think we need to head down into the moat," Kit said, motioning with her head to the left. "Do you see what I see?"

"What? Do you mean the small animals down there?" Lin groaned and rolled her eyes. "Don't tell me you're hungry again!"

"Look higher up the bank – and no, I'm not hungry again." But now that Lin mentioned it, she could eat if there was food available. Her stomach rumbled as if to affirm her relentless hunger.

Why am I always so hungry lately?

Lin's eyes went wide. "Do you think that's Midnight's really big rock?"

"Well," Kit replied as though she was thinking out loud. "The way the rock is sticking out of the moat like that, it makes a lot of shade, and the animals all seem to be congregated there."

"It's not a moat," Lin said in a similar, far-off kind of voice. "But that is a really big rock and there is a lot of grass below it."

"Well then, let's not waste any more time thinking about it." Kit took off west until she was pretty much even with where the rock was. "Follow me!"

Lin watched as Kit skid down the side of the cliff. It was incredibly steep, but the young priest showed no fear as she slid down the bank. Not wanting Kit to leave her behind, or for the young priest to think less of her, Lin took a careful step to check the footing before committing herself to going over the edge. As soon as she put weight onto her lead foot, the loose gravel gave away, throwing her off balance. She scrambled for purchase, but the more she moved, the faster the cliff-side crumbled beneath her feet. Her hands flailed about as she tried to find something, anything, to latch onto. In a heartbeat, she was careening down the side of the steep cliff, tumbling completely out of control.

Kit managed to turn, just in time, as Lin's flailing limbs came within reach. She tried her best to solidify her stance before grabbing onto Lin's leg. It wasn't like Kit had much time to plan this, but she quickly discovered that it was a terrible idea, as the full weight of Lin's body slammed into her. The momentum of the woman's fall swept the feet out from under Kit, causing them both to start tumbling down the embankment.

Kit miraculously maintained her grip on Lin's leg while she desperately grasped for purchase with her free hand. The face of the cliff was mostly loose dirt and gravel, and there was nothing solid to grab onto. Kit's fingers were starting to feel like they were going to break when her fall came to a sudden, bone-shattering halt. Lin's screams of agony pealed through the canyon when they landed, hard, on a large rock that was jutting out from the cliff's face. Lin seemed to have taken the brunt of the impact, with Kit splayed across her body.

Kit rolled off her friend and gasped. Lin's right leg was in a very unnatural position and her shattered thigh bone was sticking out through her blood-soaked breaches.

Lin's wails of agony echoed off the cliff face, driving Kit into a frenzy. She clutched at her breast while she watched her friend's lifeblood pour from the wound.

"Sweet Titan..."

Kit had never seen this sort of injury before. She didn't know if her healing powers could fix a compound fracture. She found it difficult to breathe as her chest tightened, like a vice was squeezing her heart. She had only ever healed cuts, poisonings, and other similar afflictions. Broken bones protruding from the skin were a completely different story. Kit had not used her healing powers this day, but she feared her skill wouldn't be enough to mend the shattered bone.

"Lin, can you hear me? Lin?" Kit bellowed at her friend. Lin's own screams of pain drowned out her words.

Kit tilted Lin's face toward her, desperate to get her attention. Lin's eyes were wide and wild. Her pupils were drastically dilated. The skin of her cheeks was pale, cold, and clammy. The woman's breaths were shallow and rapid. The vice that held Kit's heart turned, tightening its grip further.

"Help me," Lin cried. Her face contorted in pain as she screamed out again. She clutched at the stone beneath her, shattering her fingernails in the process. "For the love of Titan, make the pain stop!"

Kit gripped Lin's hand. She squeezed it with all her might, hoping to find a way through the woman's suffering. All she could see in her eyes was agony and fear.

"Lin, I am going to try to set the bone. This is going to hurt. It's going to really, really hurt." Tears flowed down Kit's cheeks. Her heart seized in her chest.

Lin's eyes were still wild, but she managed to nod with enough force that she was able to convey her understanding of the situation. Kit quickly pulled one of the straps off from her holster and held it in front of Lin's mouth. "When I say so, bite down on this, as hard as you can."

Lin nodded and Kit stuffed the leather strap into her mouth.

The young priest moved around so that she was standing below Lin's legs. She braced her foot against the stone as best she could, before gently grasping

Lin's right foot in her hand. As soon as her fingers touched Lin's boot, she screamed out in agony again.

Not wanting to waste any more time, Kit yelled at the top of her lungs. "Lin, now! Bite down as hard as you can!"

Lin's screams immediately switched to muffled cries as she bit down on the leather strap in her mouth. With all her might, Kit yanked Lin's foot towards herself, hoping to reset the broken bone. There was a tremendous, muffled yelp before Lin fell silent.

Kit quickly moved up to Lin's head to check her breathing. It was ragged and labored, but as long as she was breathing, Kit figured it was a good thing.

Thank Titan. She must have passed out from the pain.

Not wanting to wait until Lin woke up, Kit jumped down to inspect her leg. The bone was no longer protruding through her thigh, but there was a huge pool of blood beneath the woman, and it was spreading out fast; much too fast. Setting the bone had likely severed one of her arteries, meaning she had less than a minute before she would completely bleed out.

The priest turned her face to the heavens. "Titan, hear me."

She placed her hands over the gushing wound as she called out to her god. As she continued her prayer, her hands took on the familiar soft yellow glow. As the glow spread out across Lin's wound it changed from soft yellow to a deep, rich gold. An intense pain stabbed in her left arm and her right leg. Her lungs seized up. Her head swam. Refusing to stop, she gutted through the agony and continued her prayers. Kit's body was trembling badly, but she maintained her prayer until they were both enveloped in the golden aura. When the wracking pain finally ceased, Kit removed her hands to have a look.

She swayed as she tried to focus on the wound. A sudden heat washed over Kit and her vision blurred. She renewed her grip on Lin's leg, trying to steady herself.

Don't pass out. Don't pass out.

The world was swimming. Kit's brain couldn't seem to function. Thoughts were coming in slow bursts.

What is happening to me?

She leaned her head against Lin's waist and took slow, deep breaths. She was unconsciously stroking Lin's leg. Her fingers sought out any more damage, finding nothing but soft smooth skin.

"You can rub my leg all day," Lin said with a coy smile.

Kit's eyes snapped open, and she lifted her head. Her vision suddenly cleared. It was as though Lin's words had pulled a gauzy film from her eyes. Her friend stared up, her eyes still wide and glassy. The tracks of her tears ran over her dust-caked skin.

"You can move your hand up a little higher," Lin continued, raising her eyebrows high up on her forehead.

Kit blinked at her friend. Her hand had slipped beneath the tear in Lin's breeches. She had been caressing the soft, supple skin beneath. Kit snatched her hand back and reddened.

"The wound looks completely healed," she said, her face still burning. "Can you move your leg?"

Lin winced before even trying. But as she pulled her knee towards her chest, the wince changed to a cheery smile.

"It's completely better," she said as she flexed her knee a few more times. She also checked her left arm. At some point during her fall, she had felt it snap. Like her leg, it too was in perfect condition.

"You? Are you okay?" Lin sat up and blanched at the pool of blood on the ground beneath her. "Holy Helja, is that mine?"

"I'm a bit tired, but otherwise I'm fine – and yes, that's all yours."

"What happened to me? All I remember is falling down the hill and feeling unbearable pain in my arm and leg." Lin rotated her left shoulder. She gave Kit a nod of approval. There wasn't the slightest hint of pain.

"It doesn't matter," Kit replied, not wanting to tell Lin how serious the wound was, and how fearful she had been that she couldn't heal it. "Are you ready to continue?"

Lin gingerly got up onto her feet, testing the strength of her leg as she did. "Everything seems to be in tip-top working condition." She quickly reached out her hand to help Kit off the ground. "What about you? Are you good to continue?"

Kit wobbled slightly and grasped onto Lin's arm. "Yaa, I'm okay. Let's keep going."

"Are you sure? You don't look too steady right now."

"I'm fine. Really. I just need a moment to get my balance." Truth was, Kit wasn't sure how she felt. Healing people never used to cause her any pain, but today it seemed the healing process nearly killed her. The pain in her shoulder and leg, the same places where Lin had been injured, hurt worse than anything she'd ever experienced before. When she considered the number of beatings she'd taken at the hands of Sister Gale at the Temple, that was saying a lot.

The pair were about twenty feet from the bottom of the ravine. The giant rock and the tasty grass were now above them, on the far side of the river. The last bit of the climb down would be easier. The slope there was gentle and grass-covered, not like the loose gravel higher up.

"Do we swim across?" Lin asked. She peered down at the coal-colored water below. "It's a pretty fast current, but it's not too far to the other side. We can probably make it before it sweeps us too far downstream."

"I wouldn't do that, if I were you," suggested an unfamiliar, high-pitched voice.

CHAPTER FOURTEEN

FEIGH

A large mouse-like creature with gray-brown fur, gigantic mouse ears, and fluffy white wings was staring down at Kit and Lin from the bank on the far side of the river. His wings were almost identical to Midnight's. In his hand he held a gnarled green walking stick. It had a twisted wooden top that resembled a candle flame.

"Why not?" Kit asked. Like Lin had said, she thought they would be able to cross it easily enough.

"Kappa!" the mouse called back.

"What?" the two women replied in unison.

"Kappa! River monsters. They live in this river. You're standing too close to the bank as it is." The mouse took a few steps away from the bank himself as he studied the surface of the black, rippling water.

"They're real?" Lin asked. There was more than a hint of disbelief in her voice. "They're not just fairy tales told to children, to keep them from playing by the water?"

The mouse shrugged his tiny shoulders at them. "If you don't believe me, you're likely going to die. They're much faster than they look."

"Is there a bridge, or another way across?" Lin called out. She was looking up and down the river, but there appeared to be no natural crossing.

"There are bridges in either direction. They're both about two hours away, but you'll need to climb back up top to get there. If you follow the river, you'll get eaten for sure!" The mouse scampered back up the hill towards the great rock.

"Wait," Kit called out. "Are those bridges the only way across?"

The mouse stopped and turned back to Kit. He stared at her for a few seconds before responding. "Who are you, and why are you here?"

"My name is Sister Kit Standing Bear, and this is my friend, Lin. We're looking for the place where the good grass is."

"Where the grass tastes best," Lin interjected. "A winged rabbit named Midnight sent us here to find someone."

The mouse's ears perked up at the mention of Midnight's name.

"This is my patch of grass," the mouse replied. His eyes narrowed. "You'll need to find your own if you can. Why did Midnight send you here? Who are you looking for?"

"He sent us to return something to someone named Feigh." Kit didn't want to give out any more information than she absolutely had to.

The mouse took a few steps closer to the river's edge, his hands convulsing like he was desperately clutching for something. "Could this *something* be an amulet? Show it to me."

"Is there another way across?" Lin asked. "We can't show it to you if we're on this side of the river." The last comment made Kit snicker slightly. Lin was smart, and she really liked that about her.

"Hold it up so I can see it!" the mouse yelled back. "I'll show you the way if it's my amulet. I can tell from here."

"You're Feigh?" Kit asked as she reached into her pocket to retrieve the tiny medallion. The mouse nodded adamantly. She unfurled the fine golden chain to reveal the tiny heart shaped amulet with a gemstone in the middle of it. The smooth silver surface reflected the sun, creating a dazzling display of colors.

The mouse's eyes became the size of small saucers. His free hand convulsed repeatedly. He coveted the amulet, and he was doing a terrible job of hiding that bit of information.

"The way across is to your left." The mouse held out a tiny staff, closed his eyes, and muttered a short phrase. A wide log that crossed the river materialized out of thin air. "The way is safe. It's too high for the Kappa to jump."

The two girls clawed their way up the side of the embankment, about fifteen feet, to get to where the giant log hung. A large mass of tangled roots held it tightly in place. There was an abundance of thick, sturdy branches sticking out from it, providing handles that they could easily hold on to as they crossed over the water. The footing on the log was slick and treacherous, but the twisted branches provided good foot holds. The longer branches, which crisscrossed the fallen tree, made the travel difficult in spots as they forced the girls to duck under and hop over them to continue forward.

It took them several minutes to traverse the bridge. Feigh called for them to follow as he scampered up the side of the ravine, sending rocks and loose debris tumbling down the hill. He paused when he crested the ridge just below the great rock.

Lin's face was bright red, and she was breathing heavily when the pair caught up with the winged mouse.

"Show me! Give it to me!" Feigh's voice was practically frantic. He held out his hands to Kit. They were convulsing again, clutching at the air as he awaited his prize.

"Not so fast," Kit said as she patted the pocket holding the amulet. "Midnight said you could give us some information."

The mouse's eyes went dark. His demeanor changed completely. His hands flowed in front of him while his fingers wove intricate patterns, obviously preparing to cast a spell.

"You know she's a priest of Titan, right?" Lin muffled out as though she was talking with her mouth full. Kit turned her head, only to find that Lin had grass sticking out of her mouth and she had another handful ready to stuff into her face.

"What?" she sullenly protested. "It really is delicious! It's remarkably sweet and tender."

The mouse's expression changed immediately to outrage. He raced over to Lin, knocking the grass from her hand. He leaped up on her chest, his tiny paws probing at her face as he tried to pry the food out of her mouth. "That's my grass. Get your own. This is mine."

Kit grabbed Feigh by one of his ears and dragged him away from her friend. "Are you going to help us or not?"

Feigh's eyes narrowed as he continued to glare at Lin. "The amulet is mine, and I want it now!"

Kit gave the mouse her absolute best smile. "It may be yours," she responded coolly, "but I'm delivering it, and for that, there is a charge."

"Fine, fine. What information do you seek?" The mouse's hands were convulsing again, albeit slower than they had before. His body relaxed slightly.

"We're looking for a kidnapped boy. His name is Treedale. A man took him from a village outside of Aarall and the village elder has sent us to find him. On Titan's name, I have sworn to complete this mission."

"Alright!" the mouse shouted. It seemed he really didn't have any interest in listening to Kit rail on about her god.

"I know of Treedale. Grams, the elder you speak of, is kind to us Sprites. I'll help you find him." As soon as he uttered the words, his eyes bulged out again and his hands convulsed at a frantic pace. "Now, give me what's mine."

Kit tossed him the amulet, which he quickly snatched up. He stared at it through glassy eyes for a few moments, before bolting for a hole under the rock. Kit attempted to stop him, but he was just too fast. A tiny wooden door slammed shut, shaking loose earth from below the great stone above.

"Miserable creature! By Titan's honor I will end your life." Kit stood before the hole trying to come up with just the right curse to hurl at the treacherous little mouse. She paused for a moment. There was a tiny garden on either side of the door. Colorful mushrooms and ferns peaked out from between tiny flat slabs of stone. Thin branches, painted white, formed a perfect little fence around what appeared to be a bed of radishes.

"You don't trust my word?" asked the mouse from behind her.

This was the same trick the rabbit had pulled on them earlier. Kit turned to the hole and then back to the mouse.

"How did you do that?" The mouse didn't seem overly interested in the question, as he waved his hand dismissively.

"Treedale is being held inside the city. There is a place behind the tavern called the *Crimson Ale*. They hold prisoners there until they have enough to take them to market."

"To market? You mean they're going to be sold as slaves?" Lin's blood boiled as she pictured slavers carting off her brother and selling him as they would cattle.

"Hush!" the mouse fumed at her. "Stop talking and start listening." He reached into his pocket and pulled out his amulet. "I know why Midnight returned this to me now. He wants me to use it to free Treedale." The mouse stared longingly at the amulet, while his tiny hands continued to tremble violently. He clearly had other plans for this piece of jewelry, but it appeared he was deeply indebted to Treedale's grandmother.

"I will help you, if you ask me to," he relented, his tiny face lowered. "But there is another way, a dangerous way." He looked back up at Lin, his eyes were wide and glassy. His whiskers twitched.

"Why take the dangerous way, if you can free Treedale easily?" Lin asked, shaking her head.

"My amulet will only let me save one person, and they have my wife as well." The mouse waited a moment, the fur on his chest twitched with each beat of his heart. "If I save Treedale, my wife will die."

Kit glanced over at Lin. It was her brother they were here to save. She was going to leave the decision up to her.

"Tell me about the dangerous plan," Lin said. She moved closer to Feigh, sidling up next to him.

Feigh's voice dropped down a bit lower as he conveyed his proposal. "The place where Treedale is being held is behind the Crimson Ale. It's kind of like a jail room. There's only one door in and there are no windows. It's at the very back of the tavern and it's heavily guarded."

Kit's hand instinctively moved to her weapon. "By the strength of Titan, I will kill those guards and free Treedale!"

Feigh slapped his forehead. He stared at Kit like she was a total idiot. "Rave on, priest. The establishment is not filled with random thugs. Did you not catch the name of the tavern? The Crimson Ale?"

Kit and Lin shared a brief glance at each other. Neither of them said a word in response.

The mouse huffed and shook his head. "Blood suckers? Undead? Vampires? Any of this getting through to you? These folks are seriously dangerous. You can't beat them in a straight-up fight. You've got to come at them sideways."

Kit's face dropped as his meaning sunk in. She swallowed hard. Lin's face turned white. If only Indie and the boys were with them now. Their anti-vampire training would really come in handy.

"Seriously? Vampires?"

"Well, not usually." Feigh scrubbed the back of his neck. "It's usually just their mules, but sometimes they're there. They keep a pretty low profile because they don't want their presence to be known, but I've seen them drain a body and leave an empty husk on the ground."

"Mules?" Kit asked. Her face screwed up as she considered Feigh's words. "Do you mean, like barnyard animals?"

Feigh glared at Kit. "Are you dim or did the Temple just... you're a new priest, aren't you? Is this... you're first mission?"

Kit's face reddened. She stole a sideways glance at Lin again who still had her hand pressed hard over her mouth. Her shoulders were shaking. She slammed her eyes shut, unable to look back at Kit.

"Mother Gaia, save us all," Feigh said as he pulled his great, round ears over his eyes. After a moment of swearing under his breath, he released his ears, and they popped back up.

"How are we supposed to fight vampires?" Kit asked. "We have no blessed weapons and..." She wanted to throw up. Her one and only encounter with a vampire led to the deaths of hundreds of innocents. She had witnessed firsthand a vampire's powers. She still carried the weight of those deaths on her soul.

"We need to get you a disguise," Feigh said, nodding his head slowly. A plan, of sorts, was forming in the winged mouse's brain. "If you walk into the tavern looking like you do, you had might as well slit your wrist and let them drink you dry right off."

He tapped his fingers on his nose and his eyes lit up. "I've got it! There are some gang members who like to strong-arm the local merchants. You know, shake them down for whatever coin they might have. If you hang out inside one of their stalls, you can catch a couple of them in the act."

Kit stared at the mouse, as though trying to determine if he made any sense at all. "You want us to hide in a merchant's stall and catch vampires when they come to shake down the shopkeeper."

"They wouldn't be vampires. No, not vampires at all. These guys will be thugs, well, less than thugs, really. They're just dumb muscle that the Scarlet Tide sends out to do these dirty tasks. Nobody usually gives them a hard time because of whom they represent." Kit continued to stare at the mouse. Whether she understood what he was saying, the mouse continued. "While you do that, I'm going to get just what you need to have the guards let you in."

"What are mules, if they're not barnyard animals?" Kit asked.

"It's just a term, a phrase, a nickname given to vampire wannabes who act as a beast of burden, doing whatever the Scarlet Tide tells them to do."

"Scarlet Tide?"

Feigh sighed. Kit's questions were sidetracking him, and he really wanted to move on. "They're a group of vampires. They buy people to use them as blood slaves – food for King Faol's vampire horde. Please, can we just focus on my plan. Every second we waste is an opportunity for those... people to do harm to Treedale – and my wife."

Kit's mind was reeling. Information was coming too fast, and she couldn't process it. She nodded slowly as her brain went numb.

"Okay then, we need to find some of these thugs." Kit stared up the side of the cliff. "But first we need to climb out of here."

Feigh smiled and tapped his staff on the ground twice. He muttered something under his breath. Behind him, just above the great rock, a set of stairs carved into the face of the cliff materialized. They were very narrow, and they twisted back and forth up the cliff face. Even though they seemed to be natural, they appeared to be expertly crafted.

"Well then, let's get climbing," Kit said brightly. "Today, we bring justice to the merchants of Silverhawk." As usual, she was full of enthusiasm, but in the pit of her stomach she dreaded the possibility of facing vampires. It was only a remote chance at best, but still, the thought of it made her blood run cold.

CHAPTER FIFTEEN

GIGAS, BERRAT, AND YETIS

Following Feigh's advice, Kit and Lin entered the marketplace outside the city's walls. The bright colors and the never-ending calls of merchants hawking their wares reminded Kit of the marketplace back home. It was not quite as large as Aarall's market, but it was still a vibrant, bustling area. There were more Gigas here than Kit had ever seen in a single location.

Two Gigas men were knee deep in a group of four Berrat men. The Berrat were dressed and painted as warriors, with rows of long white braids filled with eagle and hawk feathers. Each of them had a vast array of teeth and claws dangling from necklaces that hung upon their bare, well-muscled chests. The Gigas seemed to be trying to sell grizzly bear skins to the group of warriors. With the Gigas men being nearly eight feet tall, and the Berrat barely more than four, the scene looked more like a group of adults trying to sell to children.

"Perhaps we can lower the price?" one of the Gigas asked his partner, in his deep baritone voice. They were speaking in their native tongue, but Kit had no difficulty understanding them. Apparently, the book of languages that she'd read in Titan's secret library had truly taught her to understand the various languages and dialects of the north.

The thick-set brow of the other Gigas became covered in deep wrinkles. His scowl hid the way he was grinding his teeth, but the way his jaw tensed told the true story. "We hunted for nearly a full moon to catch these animals." He bowed his head in respect for the lives they had taken. "The price we're asking is fair. If they won't pay it, somebody else will."

"They think we're stupid because we're small," one of the Berrat ground out, also in his native tongue. "They're overpricing the hides because they know we're desperate." The small man's hands were flailing about as he railed on. The other three warriors with him seemed unsure, but they were nodding slowly in agreement.

"Peace unto you," Kit offered to both the Gigas and the Berrat. "Peace." The eyes of the Gigas and the Berrat all turned to Kit. The Berrat eyed her suspiciously as they wondered why she was inserting herself into their negotiations. She smiled sweetly and bowed slightly to them.

"My name is Sister Kit Standing Bear, a priest of Titan. If you would allow me, I might be able to help."

The Gigas men, with their dark brown skin and their heavily muscled bodies, nodded and smiled politely back at Kit. The Berrat spoke with each other at a feverish pace, again in their native language.

"They do not believe they are treating you unfairly," Kit said to the Berrat, also in their native language. The Berrat immediately stopped talking and stared blankly at the young priest. Her ability to speak their language had caught them completely off guard. "Just tell them your concerns, in the common tongue. If you only whisper your fears to each other, there is no way for these gentle giants to help you out."

"Likewise, to you, too," Kit said to the hulking men in their native tongue. "Tell them why you are charging the price you are. If they are not hunters, they cannot possibly understand what you have to go through to secure your catch."

The taller of the two Gigas, with short, cropped hair, a huge brow, and boar tusks for earrings nodded. He crossed his arms over his massive chest in the traditional sign of respect. "Peace unto you, little human. Thank you for your time and your words of wisdom."

Kit couldn't help but smile at the gentle manner in which these gargantuan men spoke. Their monumental appearance was absolutely intimidating, but their manners and their speech were so calm and polite.

"My family hunted nearly a full moon to capture these three great bears," the second Gigas said as he took a knee in front of the Berrat and leaned back onto his heel. He wasn't quite as tall as his partner, but his shoulders were more heavily muscled and substantially broader. Even crouched and on one knee, he was still a full head taller than his customers. "These animals are difficult to track and dangerous to hunt. These particular bears are much larger than most." As he said this, he held out the pelt to illustrate just how big it was. "What we ask is a fair price."

"But we cannot afford those prices," one of the Berrat replied. His voice was now calm and measured, but the tension in his body said differently. These Berrat were desperate for the pelts. "But we'll need them if we are to make our hunt on the ice fields."

"You're going to the Ice Fields of Kylee?" Kit asked, unable to hide her disbelief of the comment. Even the Gigas raised their eyebrows at the Berrat's declaration. The ice fields were a vast expanse of tundra and snow that never seemed to melt. The wind that blew in off the North Sea was relentless and bitter. White-out conditions were normal and winter squalls could appear without warning.

The tallest of the Berrat, who was maybe four and a half feet tall and dressed in bright green leathers, scowled at Kit. He flexed his own considerable muscles. His bronze skin glistened in the late morning sun. "You don't think we can survive the trip? Why? Because we're too little?"

"I do not know you well enough to say if you would or would not survive the trip," Kit responded calmly, "but there is only one reason to go to the ice fields, and that's to hunt Yeti." The Berrat all nodded adamantly, their eyes filled with excitement.

Kit shook her head. "Tell me you are not going on a spirit quest, to merge with one of those beasts."

"We are. All of us," the tallest Berrat replied. He set his jaw, indicating that his decision was final, and they could not be convinced otherwise.

The taller Gigas enquired, "You're planning on hunting four Yetis?" The Berrat men nodded back. "And the bear hides? What are they for?"

"Yetis love the taste of bear," the tallest Berrat responded. "When they catch the scent of the hides upon the winds, they'll come looking for a meal."

"But if there are three bears, the Yeti won't attack. A yeti can kill a single grizzly, but not three at once," the broader, shorter Gigas added. All the Berrat nodded in agreement.

"Have you ever tried to spirit bond with a grizzly bear, or any type of bear?" Kit asked the Berrat. They averted their eyes and shook their heads. "Don't you think that would be a better place to start before trying to defeat a yeti in single-handed combat?"

The Berrat seemed confused by Kit's question, so she pressed forward. "If you defeated the bears, you could switch to bear form." The Berrat continued to stare blankly at Kit. "If you're in bear form, then you'd be the bait."

And just like that, their eyes all lit up when they finally caught on to Kit's meaning.

"That would take too long," the tall Berrat replied, shaking his head adamantly. He turned to the Gigas, his face resolute. "We need to do this before the new moon. Hunting the bears first would take too long."

"What's the rush?" Kit asked.

The Berrat all stared at one another. Their brows became thick with wrinkles as they communicated wordlessly amongst themselves. Perhaps they were trying to decide if they wanted to speak further on the subject. Finally, the tallest Berrat spoke up.

"Our village was raided by slavers last night. They took our families. The black ships will stay in harbor at Cormorant until the next new moon. That's what they do. They will continue to raid our lands until the night sky goes dark. When it does, they'll set sail south and our community will go with them."

"What will you do with the yeti bodies after you've bonded with them?" one of the Gigas asked. It seemed that the possibility of going yeti hunting had piqued his curiosity.

"We'll leave them for the wolves," the tall Berrat replied with a shrug. "We only need the animals' spirits."

"If we help you, can we keep the yetis?" the broad Gigas asked. His partner's eyes were wide, and his head was bobbing. "If this quest will help free your people, then we will help. You are doing a noble thing."

"But we can't afford the bears," the tall Berrat responded, throwing his arms in the air. "Are you offering the bears at a better price? Is that how you'll help us?"

"We will help by joining you on your quest. We will bring the bear skins, but they are still ours. When you kill the yetis, they'll be ours, too. This way, we share the risks and the rewards as well." The Gigas held out his arm to the Berrat. If the Berrat clasped his arm in response, the deal would be set.

The Berrat spoke feverishly amongst themselves, again switching to their native dialect. The Gigas seemed to think they were being disrespectful, but he continued to hold out his hand to them. The muscles in his forearm were rippling as he waited. His patience seemed to be wearing thin. The talking came to an abrupt halt and the tall Berrat firmly grasped his arm. "We accept your offer, but only if we leave right now. The trip to the ice fields is long and dangerous and we need to be back before the new moon. Above all else, we need to return on time."

The Gigas gave the Berrat a wide grin. "We can leave immediately. My name is Teelar of the Bear Clan. This is my brother, Pan." And with that, the unlikely group started off on their journey together. For each step the Gigas took, the Berrat took a dozen. The Berrat warriors scurried about the feet of their giant-sized partners, again looking like children running alongside their parents.

"You did a good thing, Kit." Lin said as she playfully nudged Kit in the ribs with her elbow. "Except, well, I'm not sure if you noticed, but those Berrat didn't seem too bright. I wonder if they'll survive their spirit quest."

"I'm hoping that Pan and Teelar will be able to protect them if things go badly." Kit chuckled to herself. "The Gigas might be pacifists, but they're incredibly talented hunters. These two were surprisingly good negotiators as well."

"What do you mean?" Lin asked, not really sure how Kit could say that. "They didn't even make a sale."

"No, they didn't, but they are going to get four yeti hides out of this, and they get to keep their bear-skins."

Lin shook her head. "It was the Berrat who got the better part of the deal. They got the hides they wanted, and two giants are going to provide the muscle, and they paid nothing."

"Were both sides happy at the end of the deal?" Kit asked, raising her eyebrows.

"I suppose," Lin said with a shrug.

"Then it was a good deal," Kit said with a bright smile. "How can it be any better than everyone being happy with the outcome?"

Lin shook her head. She might have understood what Kit was saying, but she was still convinced that the Berrat got the better part of the exchange.

CHAPTER SIXTEEN

THE SPLIT CROWS

"Danny?" The voice sounded far away, pulling him from the warmth of a cozy embrace. Whoever was speaking to him was ruining everything. He tried his best to ignore the voice, focusing on the comfort wrapping around him, protecting him from the elements. Just when it seemed his efforts were about to pay off, the heavenly aroma of coffee broke through, rousing him from what had been a deep and peaceful sleep. When he opened his eyes, Breayn was standing over him, holding an earthen mug of steaming hot coffee. Pushing off the mound of furs covering him, he reached out to accept the gift. He winced slightly at the bright morning sun. From the looks of it, it was perhaps an hour past sunrise.

"I guess I fell asleep," he said, taking a sip. His eyes brightened immediately as a look of ecstasy spread across his face.

"We all did," his cousin laughed nervously. "Whatever spell you weaved, it put us all in a trance."

"I don't do spells," Danny said, flashing his teeth in a bright smile. "What happened?"

"You started singing. When you did, images formed in front of you, images of your parents." Breayn's gray eyes immediately welled up, turning them a pale blue. "It was like they were standing right before us. They were so young, so sad. They were leaving you at the Temple. They spoke of their love for you and how this was the only way to keep you safe."

"Safe from what?"

"The Split Crows, I'm guessing. Even before they took over Taseko, they were a menace." Breayn quickly wiped an errant tear from her cheek. "They've been trying to catch or kill our family off since as long as I can remember. After your parents, my aunt and uncle, spirited you away, my mother took me into hiding. Seeing how much your mother looks like my mother, it broke my heart."

"Our mothers are sisters?" Danny asked, carefully taking another sip from his mug. The hot, bitter drink chased away the morning's chill, but it did nothing to alleviate his growing sense of dread.

"Twins." Breayn sat beside Danny, pulling some of his furs over her legs. "I haven't seen my parents in many years."

"What about my parents?" Danny asked, a lump forming in his throat. Breayn's eyes became even bluer.

"I don't know. There were rumors they were captured by the Crows when they were returning home from Aarall, but nobody has ever seen them since they left with you."

"And what of your parents?"

"I haven't seen them since I was a small girl. They were searching for your parents, chasing the rumors. My mother never gave up hope her sister was out there. She said she knew that she was alive, that she could *feel* her."

"There have been stranger tales than of twins who can feel each other's presence," Ulip said. Something in his deep voice made what he said have a ring of truth to it. "It's time to hunt."

Danny laughed and patted his belly. "Didn't I bring enough meat last night? Don't tell me you ate it all."

"We hunt Crow." Ulip flexed his massive muscles, the fibers of his bare, copper-skinned chest rippling like waves across the sea. "Select some weapons," he said, pointing to one of the huts. "We're leaving shortly."

"I am a weapon," Danny laughed, pulling himself from the furs, tossing them over Breayn's head. "I just need to... you know, take care of some *personal business.*"

A deep rumble came from Ulip as he shook his head. "You can't do that firebird thing. If anybody sees it, and lives to tell the tale, will know it was us who killed the scouting party." The big man held his nose and pointed to the forest. "You can take care of other things... that way."

"What's the matter, big-guy," Danny teased. "Everybody poops."

"But we don't talk about it," the giant growled. It was a surprisingly menacing sound. "Do what you need to, get your weapons, and let's get going."

⬥

Danny cinched up the buckles on his breeches as he walked into the weapons hut. His eyebrows raised at the surprisingly large array of weapons. A young woman testing out a small wooden shield caught his attention, earning her a subtle wink. Even in the dim light, the reddening in her cheeks was obvious. She quickly lowered her eyes and turned away. "Oh, little sun, don't hide your light from me."

"Let me guess," Ryn said as he followed Danny inside. He pulled a torch from its sconce and used it to light several more torches in the room. "You're an ax or hammer kind of guy. Something that shows off all those bulky muscles of yours." Even though Danny was wearing a rather loose-fitting tunic, his well muscled body had no trouble revealing itself through the fabric.

"That is what we're taught to fight with at the Temple," Danny said, grinning as usual. "But I actually prefer a longsword and a bow." He pulled a bright silver blade from one of the racks, testing its weight and balance. "In the hands of a human, this would be a short sword, but it's plenty long enough for me." He continued to scan the room until he found a plain leather scabbard suitable for the blade. He quickly strapped it to his waist and holstered the weapon. When he came to a rack full of bows, he moved to take one of the heavy hunting bows.

"The draw on that dragonwood weapon is too heavy," Ryn said, pulling out a thin yew bow. "These let you fire more quickly."

Danny took a heavy, braided bowstring from a pile on a table. He ran his fingers over its length, nodding approvingly. He methodically hooked one end of the string to the notched end of the hunting bow before hooking the bow with his leg, bending it heavily with his free arm. After hooking the string over the other end of the bow, he slowly released the tension until the string became taut, taking up the weight of the bow's flex. He flashed Ryn another grin before easily drawing it back, testing its draw-weight.

"If I'm going to shoot something, I want it to go down and stay down." Danny gave the young woman a wink, causing Ryn to frown. He then grabbed two quivers of arrows and hoisted them over his shoulder. "I want to try this marvelous weapon, and if I like it, I'll be ready to head out."

"Extinguish the torches," Ryn said to the young woman who was now openly gaping as Danny exited. "And stop looking at him like that. He's just another Berrat, just like the rest of us."

There were multiple hunting parties waiting as Danny emerged from the weapons hut. Their hushed silence made him uneasy for a moment. "Who's ready to see some crazy-good bowmanship?" he clucked, strutting about like a cock in a henhouse. "Somebody, point out a target for me."

The women, young and old, chittered with one other, pointing out many different targets. Each one of them desperately hoping that he would select their choice.

"All excellent suggestions," Danny said, blowing a kiss to a particularly beautiful and deadly looking young woman. "Do none of the men have a suggested target for me?" Danny's eyes went wide, raising his eyebrows as they did. "Surely, one of you handsome men have a suggestion for me."

"Okay, big shooter. How's about you hit that pinecone, the one hanging off that lone branch."

"That's a pretty small target, Ryn." Danny said with a grin. "You aren't trying to embarrass me, are you?"

"You're doing that all on your own," Ryn replied, planting his fists on his hips. "We don't have all day."

Danny shook out his long red hair, nocked an arrow, and drew back the bowstring. He momentarily held his aim at the target, before swinging away, releasing the arrow well above the mark. The arrow neatly struck a branch, much higher in the tree, cutting it from the trunk. As the severed bough fell, it struck the branch holding the intended target, sending the pinecone tumbling through the air. Danny gave Ryn a quick smile, nocked a second arrow, and released it. When the arrow struck the falling target, it exploded into tiny pieces, showering down upon the cheering crowd of onlookers.

"You're an ass," Ryn said, walking through the crowd of Berrat rushing to congratulate Danny.

"Enough," Ulip bellowed out, scattering the crowd. "Ready yourselves. We leave now." Breayn scoffed as she approached.

"How'd you learn to shoot like that, cousin?"

"I read about archery in the library." The memory of reading the book was disappearing almost as quickly as it popped into his head. It became hazy. He wasn't even sure if what he was saying was true. "I don't think we're meant to remember the library," he offered, the memory of the book now completely gone. "It's like trying to recall a dream. For a moment, it's there, clear as day. A moment later, it's gone."

"You can't learn to be a marksman from a book," Ulip objected. "You learn by being taught, and by practicing."

Danny shrugged. "I've always liked using a bow," he said, still trying to recall the contents of the archery book he had read. "I've always been good with one, but it's only since my trip inside the library that I've been *that good*."

The trio moved on in silence for several minutes before Danny broke the quiet. "Ryn doesn't like me very much, does he cousin. I'm not used to people not liking me." Breayn huffed and shook her head.

"And that's why he doesn't like you," Ulip offered. "I don't care how you behave, as long as you get the job done. But not everyone is wise like me."

"That's the truth," Breayn replied with a grin that looked an awful lot like Danny's when he was buttering someone up. "You see things from a whole different perspective... from way up there, high above us." She patted him on the thigh, as though she was patting a tree trunk. Like Danny, she was taller than most Berrat, but she still resembled a toddler when standing next to the Gigas.

"I see many things," the giant said, scrubbing his chin with his meaty hand. "Much more than you might expect."

"Okay," Danny said, pulling the topic away from the giant's point of view. "Why are we hunting Crow? You said we're not supposed to be killing them, and that attacking them will tell the Crows where our location is."

"Every day we hunt, drawing them away from our home," Breayn said, picking up a stick. She cleared the leaf litter, exposing the soft, moist soil beneath. She poked a hole in the ground. "This is Taseko." She poked another hole in the ground, several paces from the first. "This is our home." She poked holes in the ground well away from both of them, forming a rough circle. "This is where we hunt them. Each one of these spots are places we return to, killing off the Crows when we find them."

"What's in the middle of that circle?" Danny asked.

"A fake camp," Ulip said with pride in his voice. "We make them think it's where we live. It makes them think we fan out from there, looking for Crows to hunt."

Danny considered where the fake camp was in relation to the city. "I flew right over that area. I never saw anything."

"It needs to look like it's well hidden," Ulip replied. If it wasn't, they wouldn't believe it was real.

"The Crows send their own hunters there, mostly humans," Breayn said. "They are vicious killers, each and every one of them. But they don't know our lands like we do. They don't know how to hide where they can't be found. They rarely see us when we strike."

"But all you're doing is killing people. You're not stopping the slave trade." Danny wiped the map with his foot, clearing any sign they'd been there. "We need to bring the fight directly to the Crows."

"That's not possible," Breayn said. "The Claw's men are well trained. They know our ways. They know our tricks. They are many and we are few. If we openly attacked..."

"Who's *The Claw*?" Danny asked, picking up a stick of his own.

"The Split Crows are run by three Berrat known as The Beak, The Wing, and The Claw," Ulip answered in his matter-of-fact kind of way. "The Beak is the mouth of the house. She speaks for them and when she does, people listen. The

Wing is a master spy and assassin. His network spreads across most of northern Berrathia. People who act against the Crows are dead before the next morning. Sometimes the Crows kill them in a horrible way. Sometimes they die quietly for reasons unknown, and sometimes," the big man paused, taking a deep breath to steady himself. His mouth turned to a disgusted frown, like even thinking the words left a horrid taste in his mouth. "Sometimes they publicly mutilate the people, for all to watch, so that those watching will be afraid. I am not afraid."

Danny suddenly got the feeling there was much more to this story. The giant was clearly speaking from personal experience as he described The Wing. "What of the Claw?" he asked.

"He is a dark sorcerer, and the most powerful warrior Berrathia has ever seen," Breayn answered while Ulip toed the ground. "His warriors are well trained and well disciplined. They are skilled sorcerers in their own right."

"A dark sorcerer?" Danny asked, his eyes still on the brooding giant.

"A necromancer," Ulip answered, his mind returning from wherever it had gone. "He uses the fear and blood of those he captures to raise the dead. He is an abomination."

"Um, okay then," Danny said as his hand moved to the mark on his neck. "If they are so powerful, why isn't Taseko still the capital city of Berrathia? Why did it fall to Ravenlord? Why would it fall to a human city of all things?" When his two cohorts rolled their eyes at him, Danny cocked an eyebrow. "What?"

"The city's name is Ravenlord. Does that not tell you something?" Breayn crossed her arms waiting for Danny to catch on. "Ah, c'mon. Even this towering hunk of muscle can figure this out."

"I explained it to you," Ulip said, crossing his arms in the same manner as Breayn. "You didn't get it then either."

"You do know that ravens and crows are not the same bird, right?" Danny raised his eyebrows at the others. "You know that, right?" He chuckled at the confused look on their faces. "They are similar looking, and they share similar feeding habits, but they are completely different birds. Ravens are nearly twice the size of crows. One thing they do have in common though, they equally hate each other."

"So?" Ulip asked, not following where Danny was going with his bird-talk.

"So, nothing," he said, shaking his head. "I'm just saying that the city of Ravenlord isn't connected to the Split Crows, at least not by name. But if the Split Crows and House Nobilis hate each other, like real crows and ravens do, we could use that to our advantage."

"How do we do that?" Ulip asked, the plan to use Ravenlord against Taseko was making his head hurt.

"By making them think the attacks are coming from whoever runs the slavers in Ravenlord," Danny answered with a smile.

"How do we do that?" Ulip asked again, scrunching his hands into gigantic fists. Danny couldn't tell if that was for his benefit, or if perhaps the big guy was just looking forward to crunching some Crows' heads.

"Ravenlord is run by Jingen Nobilis, the Black Grimhold," Breayn said, checking over her shoulder like just mentioning his name might invoke him. "But he's been missing for over a cycle, replaced pro tempore by his lady, Aleksandra Nobilis."

"Pro tempore?" Danny asked, wondering what his cousin was getting at.

"Temporary replacement," she said with a grin. "I thought you priestly types were well read, scholarly."

"And I thought you would know the difference between a crow and a raven." The gray of Breayn's eyes got darker, like a storm was brewing behind them. He quickly flashed a grin, hoping to quell the tempest before it was unleashed. "So, what's up with this Aleksandra person. Is she as scary as her missing husband?"

"Much worse," Ulip interjected, shuddering as he did. "News of her cruelty travels fast."

"So does her willingness to spend her husband's gold on art and other fineries." The woman rolled her eyes, as though the arts were a waste of resources. "Don't get me wrong," she corrected when Danny gave her a scolding look. "I love the arts, but what she apparently spends on the *pieces* she buys, it could supply enough food to feed the city for an entire cycle."

"We need more information, current information on Ravenlord and these Nobilis people," Danny said, his eyes getting a far-off look to them. "We need to find a way to make an attack look like it was done by…"

"House Nobilis," Ulip said, finishing Danny's sentence. "They go by the name House Nobilis." The giant glowered at the two overly talkative Berrat. He rolled his massive shoulders and huffed loudly. "Are we going to go hunting, or not? Too much talk, not enough action."

"Today," Danny said with a smile, "we hunt. Tomorrow, we plan." Ulip smiled back, flexing his massive arm muscles, pounding his fist into his open hand. The thought of being pulverized by Ulip's knuckles made Danny wince.

CHAPTER SEVENTEEN

THE SCARLET DISGUISES

Lin motioned to the large tent behind Kit. Its owner had decorated it with bright red and white stripes, making it somewhat less ostentatious than the other merchant tents covered in brilliant blues, pinks, and purples. The front flap was tied back, but it still fluttered in the breeze. It almost seemed to beckon passersby to step inside.

"It's as good as any," Kit said. "Feigh didn't really give us any direction as to which merchants were being harassed by these vampire mules."

The tent's flap continued to flutter and snap in the breeze.

Kit took a tentative step inside, finding the merchant standing against the back wall. He was a wispy looking fellow with ebony skin and a long slender face that gave him a horsey appearance. He had shoulder length, wavey black hair and a beard that draped down to the middle of his chest. Judging by the way they both hung in long tangled clumps, he had not bathed in many days. A small red and white pillbox hat sat slightly askew on his head. His large gray eyes shifted left and right, as though he was searching for an escape route.

Kit stepped a bit further inside with Lin directly behind her. A delicate scent of spices mixed with the more pungent aroma of incense gave the room an exotic feel. Perhaps they were designed to mask the merchant's personal aroma.

There were tables set up in rows along the perimeter of the tent. Each table was covered with what appeared to be inexpensive jewelry and other similar sundry items. Kit let her fingers run aimlessly over some of the pieces, pausing when her hand fell upon a small parchment. The artist had intricately painted an image of a lone wolf standing in the snow. It was remarkably lifelike in its details. The merchant cleared his throat, drawing Kit's attention away from the tiny painting.

"Titan's greetings unto you," Kit offered the merchant, her finger still tracing the outline of the wolf. The man's long, thin fingers were fidgeting badly while his eyes continued to dart about. "Good merchant, is everything okay?"

"You shouldn't be here right now. I have... customers coming here soon." Beads of sweat were beginning to gather on his forehead and cheeks. "I watched you outside, dealing with those people. I know you are kind and honest but, please, you should leave. Now."

Just as he was finishing his warning, three rough looking customers came strutting into the tent. As they did, one of them pulled down the entrance flap of the tent, casting the room in muted pinks and deeper shadows. The only woman in the trio pushed Kit out of the way as she strode up to the merchant. She had a scowl on her face and a look that dared the merchant to challenge her.

"Time to make your *offering*," the woman hissed at him. She turned toward Kit and Lin. Her eyes were such a pale blue that they appeared silver. She had a long, thin scar that ran from ear to ear, directly across her nose. There was a sizable chunk missing, which helped her appear all the more threatening.

The woman turned towards Kit and glided over to her. She wore something resembling a smirk as she stared down at the young priest. "Time for you two to leave." As she said the words, she pointed to the blood-red patch on her chainmail armor. The patch depicted two crescent opposing moons, bisected by a dagger. She had the same symbol tattooed on her neck, marking her as a member of the Scarlet Tide.

Kit pursed her lips, as though she was considering her options. She gave the nasty woman a wink and shook her head. "Nah, I think we'll stay. I am the Hand of Titan, and your days of harassing merchants has come to an end."

A baritone voice from behind Kit threatened, "You, little lady, are dead and you don't even know it yet."

With surprising speed, Lin drew her obsidian dagger and threw it at the thug who threatened Kit. The blade caught the bald-headed southerner just below his left ear. Blood spurted across the room, spraying deep crimson over the jewelry laden tables. The man's hand went to where the shaft of the dagger protruded below his jaw. A sad gurgling noise escaped his thick, ruby lips. He blinked several times as though trying to process what had just happened. He slumped down to his knees before keeling over onto his face.

It seemed that neither of the two remaining thugs had expected any resistance. They hadn't even bothered to draw their weapons. They just stared blankly at their comrade lying in a pool of his own blood as it slowly seeped into the dirt floor. They gaped at each other, dumbfounded by the strange turn of events.

Lin, in one smooth motion, stepped over the dead body, drew one of her two long swords, and stabbed the thug guarding the entrance. He was a large, bulky man, a westerner most likely. If he was muscular, it was well hidden under the layers of fat that enveloped his frame. Lin's rapier-thin blade slid effortlessly into his throat. He grasped the sword with both of his hands, trying desperately to pull it out. The razor-sharp steel bit deeply into them and blood immediately poured out and ran down his wrists to his elbows. It pooled there and dripped onto to his worn leather boots. His bulky body swayed before he stumbled over a table. Lin retracted her blade just before he toppled over, scattering cheap jewelry and miscellaneous bits of artwork across the ground.

The horribly scarred woman was a bit faster to react. She had managed to draw her dagger as Kit took a sideways swing at her with her hammer. The woman barely escaped the impact as she backed into a table, sending it over onto its side. She managed to get her blade up into a defensive position as Kit brought her hammer around in a second attempt. Unable to block the strike with her small weapon, she stepped away again, tripping over the upended table, landing hard on her back, her head pressed against the canvas wall of the tent. It left her in a precarious position, unable to move with speed in any direction.

"Yield," she called out, tossing her dagger to the side. "I yield."

Kit withdrew her attack, holding her hammer down by her side. She renewed her grip on the handle. The long lithe muscles in her arm rippled as she tensed, ready to strike at a moment's notice.

The scared woman held out her left hand, displaying its emptiness as she pushed herself up with her right hand. A flicker of malice crossed her face just before she attempted to pull a second dagger from her knee-high black leather boot. The woman's fingers had barely touched the weapon's hilt when Kit's hammer arced upwards, catching her squarely in the jaw with a resounding crack. The woman bounced off the canvas wall and landed across the fallen table. Based on the unnatural position of her head, Kit assumed that the strike had broken her neck, likely killing her instantly. Concerned that it might potentially be yet another feint, Kit slammed her hammer into the side of the woman's head, showering herself and everything else in a ten-foot radius with a grotesque spray of blood.

Kit's stomach roiled for a moment before she regained her composure. Using her foot, she rolled the woman over onto her back, revealing her patch and matching tattoo. She also had a black leather band strapped to her wrist bearing the same dagger and crescents emblem. Kit slipped it from her wrist and held it up to the merchant.

"What is this?"

The black-skinned merchant was trembling uncontrollably. He was shaking his head and stammering desperately. The southerner moaned something that was completely incomprehensible. He dropped his head down and wrapped his hands over it, as though shielding himself from an attack from above.

"Be at peace," Kit said, using the most reassuring voice she could muster. "We are only here to help."

The man peeked up from beneath his arms. "You're not here to rob me?"

"Sweet Titan, no!" Kit exclaimed.

"We were here for them," Lin added.

The southerner furrowed his brow and gave his bushy eyebrows a good scrubbing. "Why?"

Kit and Lin shared a quick glance. Kit wrinkled her nose at the man. Her voice dropped down to a low whisper. "We need a disguise. We need to look like members of the Scarlet Tide. We'd really rather not say why."

"No need," the merchant said. "The less I know, the safer I'll be."

Kit held up the small band she had taken off the scarred woman. "Can you tell me what this is?"

The merchant craned his neck to get a closer look. "It's a rank badge. That woman you took it off. She is a second level mule. Well, she was."

"Second level mule?" Kit asked as she held the band in front of her. She slid her hammer back into its holster and examined the badge more closely. She cocked an eyebrow at the merchant, inviting him to continue.

"Scarlet Tide mules, they're vampire wannabes. If a mule makes it to first level, they have a chance of being turned. You know, as a reward for their service." The merchant's eyes were glued to the tent flap, seemingly afraid that other Scarlet Tide members might be outside. His thrumming pulse was visible in the large artery that ran up the man's long skinny neck.

"Why don't they just turn them all? Aren't vampires really powerful? It would make their collectors that much stronger." Lin was busy pulling the patch off the armor of one of the men she'd killed. The stitching that held it in place was shoddy at best, making the task easier than it should have been. She quickly slid her dagger's point between the threads and severed them with a flick of her wrist. She rolled the patch over in her hand. It was poorly applied, but the embroidery on the patch itself was of the highest quality.

"They only turn a small number of the mules; those they think will survive the transformation without turning into blood-fiends."

Kit's face was blank. Her lips parted slightly as though she was going to speak, but nothing came out. When the merchant saw that Kit didn't understand, he continued. "The transformation process is hard to control. Some of the vampires go crazy because of the bloodlust. They start killing everybody they see, sucking them dry or just plain mutilating them. When that happens, they have to destroy the vampire."

"You seem to know an awful lot about the Scarlet Tide and vampires," Lin said as she closed the distance between herself and the merchant. As she stepped over the mutilated remains of the woman, she turned away so as to not have to witness the carnage. She purposefully adjusted the grip on one of her swords, trying to make her point that the merchant had better keep talking.

"Everybody up north is harassed by the Scarlet Tide on a regular basis. If you don't know who you're dealing with, you end up dead. There likely isn't a merchant in Silverhawk who hasn't had to deal with them." The merchant plopped himself onto a lone rickety chair. "It's hard enough to make a living as it is. Having these thugs come and take your earnings every day doesn't make it any easier."

"Where's the City Watch? Why don't they intervene?" Lin asked as she put her swords away. The merchant just shook his head without saying a word. Lin was aware that there were corrupt members in Aarall's City Watch, but the problem wasn't as systemic as it appeared to be here in Silverhawk.

"They're in on it?" Kit asked, her voice dropping to barely more than a whisper. The merchant simply shrugged his shoulders while continuing to shake his head.

Kit's face went dark, as though a great shadow had just fallen upon it. Even though the merchant wasn't confirming that the Silverhawk Watch was a part of the shakedown, he certainly didn't say they weren't. "What else, besides this patch and the wristband, marks these people as Scarlet Tide members?"

The merchant tapped his neck. "The tattoo. That's the true symbol of their membership."

Kit tipped the dead woman's body over, revealing the blood-red tattoo just below her chin. It was the exact same symbol as the one on her patch. "Are there any merchants who sell dye this color?" Kit asked.

"I do," smiled the merchant. "I sell just about anything you might want. If you can't see it, just ask for it." He pulled a trunk out from under a table covered with a multi-colored cloth. He opened it up, revealing a small artist's supply shop. "Take whatever you need."

"We will pay for what we take," Lin said as she reached for a pouch at her hip.

The merchant eyed another chest at the back of the tent. "No payment necessary. You saved me a fortune already. I had a particularly good morning, and my coin-chest is nearly full. If these thugs had opened it, they'd have taken most of it. If you'd like, I can even paint it myself."

"You can reproduce this image on my neck?" Kit asked. "It looks pretty intricate."

"I would be happy to do it for you," the merchant offered. His chest puffed out with pride as he tapped it with his hand. "I make all of this jewelry, as well as the finer pieces that I don't leave out in the open."

"Titan provides," Kit said with a smile. "We appreciate the offer. Thank you."

Lin took up a position at the tent's entrance. "I'll wait outside and make sure nobody comes in." Scanning the dead bodies on the floor she added, "We're going to need to do something with them, too."

"You stand guard," the merchant replied. "I'll paint up your necks and take care of the bodies after I'm done. My cart is behind my tent." Kit nodded her assent and Lin slipped out the door.

⋘⋙

It took the merchant nearly an hour to paint the fake tattoos on the girls' necks, but the workmanship was pristine, absolutely perfect. The two women helped the man wrap the bodies up in tarps and carried them out the back of the tent to his cart.

Inviting them back into the tent, the man held up his hand. "I have something else for you. One moment." Kit was trying to object, but he disregarded her words and rummaged through another chest. He pulled out a pair of silvered bracers, both with the symbol of Titan etched into the metal.

"Here," he said, holding them out to Kit. "I bought these off a widower several months ago. He said his wife died while trying to save a group of children from slavers." He ran his fingers over the engraving, a circle with two crossed hammers. "I don't deal in this sort of merchandise, but the man said it was all he had, and he needed money to buy food for his children."

With a broad, white-toothed smile, he handed the bracers to Kit. "I want you to have them. My gift to you. May they serve you well."

"You're a good man," Kit said as she accepted the offering. "May Titan's light shine upon you all the days of your life."

Lin nudged Kit and motioned to the exit with her head. "We had better go. We've already taken much longer than we should have."

CHAPTER EIGHTEEN

BERRABBITHI

"We gave up too quickly," Ulip complained.

The sun had set by the time they had returned to camp. The Gigas was in a foul mood. It was the first time he had spoken since they had abandoned the Crow hunt. There were a few small campfires dotting the compound. The fires were kept low, to make sure they didn't give their presence away. This far north, it was common for the temperature to dip below freezing, even this late into the spring.

"There were no Crows today, big guy. Maybe we're making a difference." Breayn tried to sooth the angry giant, but he just stormed off into the cave.

"For a pacifist," Danny said with wide eyes and a small laugh, "he sure does enjoy bringing violence to the Crows."

"The Gigas are slow to anger, but even slower to forgive." Breayn's eyes lit up when she caught sight of Ryn. "I pity the soul who raises the ire of the giants."

"You're well?" Ryn asked, touching his forehead to his mate. "This fool didn't bring the Crows down on you?"

"We saw no Crows today," Breayn said gently, taking her mate's face in her hands. "There were none at their usual locations."

"Probably because you scared them off," Ryn scoffed at Danny. "Ulip has never failed on a hunt before, so it must be your fault. No?" When Breayn growled at his behavior, Ryn pushed her away and followed Ulip into the cave.

"What is his problem?" Danny asked, while winking at a pretty Berrat girl showing him some attention from across the clearing.

"You were the reason our village was destroyed," his cousin replied, pulling his attention away from his admirer.

"What? Why would you say such a thing?"

"The Crows wanted you. They came to our village every new moon, seeking information on where you were." Breayn's eyes went dark as she recalled the events of cycles past. "Every moon they came, asking the same questions. Every moon they selected someone from the community. They made an example of the person. They tortured the poor soul until their life left them. They forced everyone to watch. If someone turned away or even just averted their eyes, they selected another. They were indiscriminate with their choices. They killed elders, men, women, and even children. Despite all that, nobody would betray you to them. Nobody would betray your parents."

"Why?" Danny was horrified at this revelation. "Why would they care about me? Up until recently, I was just another acolyte at the Temple."

"Because our bloodline is nearly pure Berrabbithi."

"We're not Berrat?"

"Yes, and no," Breayn replied. "The Berrat are born of Berrabbithi, but their bloodline has been so watered down, there's barely anything left that makes us, us." Danny scrunched his brow trying to figure out what his cousin was telling him. "We Berrabbithi have strong *urges*," the statement made the woman blush slightly. "Until we pair-bond, we will seek out a mate at all costs. By our nature, we are not discriminant about who we choose. When the first Nomads came to our lands, we welcomed them with open arms and open beds."

Danny got a sly look on his face. "Well, that does explain a lot about me. But it doesn't explain Ryn."

"He's jealous," Breayn replied simply. "He thinks I will want to mate with you, to further our bloodline." Danny held up his hands, like he was suddenly fearful that she'd try to jump his bones.

"Okay, that's nuts!" he screeched, putting a little extra distance between him and his cousin as he did. "You're, well, gorgeous, but you're my family. That is just so wrong, on so many levels."

"Ryn has nothing to worry about there," she said with a small laugh, the redness in her cheeks deepening. "But even brothers and sisters will mate if necessary. It is the way of our people, well, it was." The horrified look on Danny's face made Breayn laugh. "I have bonded with Ryn, a deep connection that cannot be broken by anything. He knows this, but he's never seen another of our kind. He knows I would never, but..."

"But I'm amazingly handsome, remarkably rugged, marvelously muscled," Danny said, flexing his considerable biceps. It didn't take him long to recover from his uncomfortable surprise.

"And you've bonded with someone!"

Danny lowered his eyes and shook his head. "No, I never. Not really."

"Does this woman know?"

"She's my best friend," he replied, shaking his head. "It's not like that with us. I can be myself with her, share things with her. I would willingly die for her, in fact, I kind of did." Danny's brow suddenly furrowed, like he was trying to solve an unsolvable puzzle.

"Why did you say they were after me? If we are both Berrabbithi, then so are our parents. Why would I be special?" The question made Breayn pause. Her brow furrowed in an identical fashion to her cousin's.

Three scantily clad Berrat girls approached, each of them giggling uncontrollably. Their fawning presence brought an abrupt end to the conversation. "We have prepared your bed," the first one said, rubbing her hands together. "There is no fire in your hut, so we'll keep you warm." The remaining two nodded in agreement. While Danny's eyes were lighting up, Breayn was audibly groaning.

"Sorry, girls," Breayn said, clucking her tongue at them. "He's taken."

"But you have Ryn," one of them protested. "You can't have all the best men."

"Apparently she can have whomever she chooses," Ryn said, his fists in tight balls at his side.

"You, sit," Breayn growled at her mate. "You, shoo!" she growled at the girls. "You, cousin, get some sleep. We've got a lot to do tomorrow." When Ryn sat next to her, she pursed her lips and shook her head. "Have you lost your mind? Do you really think... that?"

"No," Ryn sulked. "Never, but..."

"But what, my love?"

"You are supposed to be the phoenix, not him."

"You two need to make up," Danny called from just outside his hut, the three girls clinging to his arms, still giggling wildly. "But don't stay up too late. Big day tomorrow!" He flashed his infamous grin and disappeared into the hut, drawing its curtain door as he did.

Chapter Nineteen

The Crimson Ale

As Lin and Kit worked their way through the merchant district to the front gate, Lin tied her patch to her forearm.

"Do you have any more of those leather straps?" Kit asked. "I know the merchant said we don't need these patches, but maybe I could cover Titan's symbol with one of them. I'm guessing the Scarlet Tide are not Titan worshippers."

"Sure," Lin said as she tied off the last of her straps. "Hold out your arm and I'll tie yours over your bracer." Kit followed Lin's instructions and in just a few quick moments her patch was in place, hiding the holy symbol on her bracer.

The guards at the city gate were not paying any attention to the comings and goings of the people. They seemed more intent on their private conversations. Kit watched with disdain as more than a few of them seemed to be sleeping at their post. Their body posture suggested they may have been well into their cups.

Harding would skin them alive if he saw this.

The main gate to the city opened to a large courtyard with the rookery spire in the middle of it. Kit craned her head back to watch several hawk-riders circling high above. They were either on patrol or waiting for their turn to land.

The courtyard's dark gray cobblestone stood in stark contrast to the spire's vivid white bricks. Its base was at least one hundred paces across, and the courtyard encircled the entire structure. Women in elaborate hats and finery sat up on their gilded open carriages, looking down upon the commoners. Their drivers made no attempt to slow down when a woman and her two raggedy children crossed the street in front of them. In fact, if Kit didn't know better, she'd have guessed they had urged the horses to move faster. The beauty of this city was a façade, covering over something much uglier. Aarall had its problems, but the nobles there at least feigned their respect for the lower classes.

Lin gave Kit a nudge and motioned to a sign hanging off a building to their right. It was shaped like a shield with a beer-mug carved into it. The mug's contents were painted red with a bright pink foam on top. Below the mug were the words, "Crimson Ale."

"Do we go inside?" Lin asked, "or just wait out front for Feigh to show up?"

Kit stared up at the sign. She had never been to a place like this before and she had no clue what to expect inside. Moments passed like hours as she continued with her internal debate, *should we stay here or should we go inside?* The point of a blade digging into her upper thigh cut her musings short.

"Are you ever going to start paying attention to your surroundings? I could have killed you three times before you even knew I was here."

Kit looked down to find Feigh staring back up at her with a hint of a grin on his smug little mousey face. His whiskers twitched while the corners of his mouth pulled up, ever so slightly.

"You got your disguises, I see." He gave Kit's neck a close inspection as he tucked his dagger into his belt. "Those tattoos look real!" Suddenly he grasped the sides of his head, and his breathing got uncontrollably faster. "You didn't actually join them, did you?"

"By Titan's eyes, are you really so blind? I could never leave the service of my god, especially not for the likes of the Scarlet Tide." Kit's snarl lightened up slightly as a slight grin on Feigh's face grew into a huge smile.

"You're incorrigible!" She shook off the desire to throttle the mouse when he gave her a deep, theatrical bow. "What was it that you needed to get to help free Treedale? We did our part."

Feigh brandished a set of playing cards. "These! You'll use them to get the guards to give Treedale to you."

Kit blinked at him a few times and gave him a dubious look.

Feigh blew out a deep sigh and shook his head. "Oh, ye of little faith. These cards are kind of *enchanted*. If you bring them to a betting table, you will always win. You're going to gamble for Treedale's freedom."

Kit did not like this plan. No, not one iota. She couldn't help but think Feigh was insane. "You think that I'm going to gamble for him? First, I don't know how to gamble and second, I don't have any money to gamble with!"

"At these games you don't need money. You need a prisoner." Feigh dangled a set of cuffs in front of his face. "I'm going to be your stake in this game."

Kit furrowed her brow and shook her head. "There's got to be a better way. Let's just break in and take him!"

Feigh was already putting on the shackles. "Trust me. This is the only way. Drag me into the tavern and say you're looking to play high stakes. They're going to wager just about anything to try to win me." Feigh gave her a bit of a sheepish grin. "I'm a bit of a local legend with these guys. I've been robbing them blind for the last two cycles. Tell them you want two Nomad boys and one female Sprite. They only have two nomad boys in the cells, so we're sure to get Treedale. The female Sprite is my wife, Triss."

"But I don't know how to gamble!" Kit hissed at the mouse. "They won't believe me."

"Hand me the cards," Lin said, rolling her eyes. "I've played in a few games of chance over the past few cycles."

Kit sucked in a deep breath. "But you're an acolyte. Gambling is outlawed by the Temple."

"Maybe that's why I never received Titan's graces," Lin replied with a bit of a nervous laugh. "Gambling helps me keep my supplies up." She bent down to face Feigh. "I'll win your wife back for you. You've done your part, now it's our turn to do ours."

Kit's mouth was still wide open as she handed over the deck of cards.

"Drag me inside," Feigh said to Kit, holding out his shackled hands. "Be as rough as you need to be to make it look real." When Kit just stared blankly at him, the mouse jumped up and smashed Kit across the face with his manacles, splitting her lip in the process.

Unbridled fury ripped through Kit as she glared down at the mouse. With her left hand she wrapped her fingers around his throat while she pulled back her right, ready to break his face.

"Good," Feigh said as he raised his chin, ready to take the punch. "That's the girl I need when you take me into the tavern."

The muscles in her arm relaxed as she took a slow, deep breath. She gave the mouse a bloody smile. He was clearly willing to go to any length to save his wife and rescue Treedale in the process.

"You're a lucky mouse to have someone you love that much. We'll get Treedale out, as well as your wife, Triss. But before we go inside, I need your weapons – all of them."

The mouse stared up at Kit, his face completely deadpan. With his hands still in manacles, he reached into his pocket and pulled out the dagger he had jabbed into her leg. He bent over and pulled a second dagger from his boot. Both knives, if you could call them that, had blades that were no more than four inches in length. After he finished handing them to Kit, he gave her a weak grin.

"And what about your staff?" Kit asked, eying the small staff that he was still grasping.

"It's just a walking stick," he replied quickly, pretending to use it to hold his weight. "It's of no consequence."

"Hand it over."

"Fine," the mouse grumbled. He reluctantly held it out. As Kit reached for it, it vanished in a puff of white smoke. "Oh, that's weird," Feigh said, innocently holding up his now empty hands.

"If you're so good with magic, why do you even need us?" Lin asked. She was looking about now, wondering who might be watching their conversation. Despite there being a good number of people out and about, nobody appeared to be paying them any mind.

"My magic is weak," Feigh said with complete seriousness. "I can perform a small set of illusions, like making things appear or disappear. Without my staff, what little magic I have is completely useless."

"So, where's your staff now? Where did it disappear to?"

"It's still in my hand," Feigh replied. He rapped Kit across the shins with it to prove his point.

"Fine, keep that one with you," Kit growled out. She grabbed the mouse by the ear and dragged him through the front door of the tavern with Lin following close behind her. A long counter with rough stools occupied the right side of the room. Small, battered tables with rickety looking chairs filled the left. Towards the back, the tavern fell into deep shadow. The barkeep's brown eyes fell on them, his expression flat. He was mostly bald, and a filthy white apron covered most of his ample belly. Kit twisted the mouse's ear, causing him to squeal out in pain.

"You'll pay for that, you raven haired bitch!" Feigh screamed out. "I'll gut you, like the pig you are."

Lin spun around and cracked the mouse across the jaw with the back of her hand. "Which way to the *tables*?" she asked the barkeep, using a rather unexpectedly pleasant voice. The thin smile on her face matched the voice but the shadow over her eyes was less inviting.

"Who's asking?" the barkeep snarled as six thugs stood up from the tables around the rescuers. What few teeth the barkeep had were badly rotted. Even from a distance, the stench of his breath cut through the thick cloud of stale ale and vomit.

"I am," Kit snarled back, exposing the tattoo on her neck.

The six thugs took a step back, unsure of how to proceed. One of the bolder or perhaps less bright thugs spoke up. He was dressed in ragtag armor but the sword at his hip was of a high quality. "So what? You ain't no vampire. Our boss is a member of the Tide as well, and by looking at you, I'm guessing he outranks you. Carver asked who you are."

"I'm the one holding the cards," Kit said as she brought Feigh out in front of her. She flashed her forearm to show the black leather band she took from the second level mule she'd killed earlier. As she held it out, the straps holding her badge let go, revealing the holy symbol on her bracer.

"She's a bloody priest!" one of the men screamed out. All six of the thugs drew their weapons.

Without missing a beat, Kit shook the exposed bracer at the thug and laughed. "Well, these did belong to a priest a week ago. Right up until I gutted the fool right on the steps of the Temple of the Fist." She quickly pulled out her battle hammer. "Took this from the mewling moron, as well." She spun the weapon a few times before putting it back in its holster. "Don't care much for hammers, but it's shiny. I like shiny things." She leaned in towards the thug closest to her, staring at his mouth. "Got any gold fillings in there?" The thug quickly slammed his mouth shut and took a few steps away from her, knocking over a chair in the process.

"No gold," he said with a toothless smile. "Barely got teeth at all."

Lin turned slowly, holding her arms out at her sides, and called out a challenge. "Anybody got anything worth gambling for? I expect this little feller is going to fetch a pretty price at the *market*."

Chapter Twenty

OVERCARD

A man, western human most likely, came walking out of the shadows from the depths of the tavern. He had shaggy brown hair and striking blue eyes. He was of average height and build, but there was a certain air to him that made the hair on the back of Kit's neck stand up. "Somebody finally caught that little thief. I'll play you for him."

"What you got to play for?" Kit growled. "You're going to need at least three, no four, Nomads as a stake."

"Four nomads?" the man laughed and spat at the floor. "Never going to happen." He turned and melted back into the shadows.

"Let's go," Kit said as she dragged Feigh towards the exit. "He's probably enough as it is to get me to first level."

"How's about two nomads and another Sprite?" the man said. He was shrouded in darkness. The shadows hid his facial expression, but there was something in his voice that gave Kit a reason to pause. He was offering her exactly what she wanted, but for some reason that bothered her. Their plan was working too well. Perhaps there were more enemies in the back, hidden within the shadows. Perhaps the plan was to just lure them deeper into the tavern, making it impossible to escape.

Perhaps you're overthinking this. Perhaps he's just desperate to win the winged mouse.

"You buy the drinks while we play, and you've got yourself a deal." Lin called out, obliterating any chance of Kit changing things up. When there was no response, she expected that the fellow agreed. With Lin leading the way, Kit dragged Feigh into the darkness. It seemed every patron in the tavern wanted to watch as they all clambered over each other to make it to the back of the room.

"Light a fire and bring me three ales," Lin called out. It's too dark in here and I'm much too sober to play cards.

"You," the man said, pointing his stubby finger at Kit. "I'm playing you."

"I don't play cards," Kit said shaking her head. "My girl here will be playing."

"Dice then?" the man offered. "I don't care what the game is, but I'm only playing against you."

"I don't play *games*, not like that anyway." Kit rested her elbow on the table and placed her chin in her hand. She batted her eyes and gave him a coy grin. "Do you know daggers and hammers?"

The man shook his head, but based on his reaction, he liked the sound of the game.

"It's pretty easy," Kit said with an evil grin. "I draw my hammer and my dagger, and you draw whatever you like; whoever is still standing at the end, wins." Kit's suggestion drew hoots and hollers from the crowd at her back. Apparently, they would also enjoy watching this sort of game.

Lin, not seeming to like the direction this was going, blurted out. "Before we play any games, you're going to need to show us your stake; two Nomads and a Sprite if I recall."

The man sneered at Lin like she was a bit of dung stuck to the bottom of his shoe. "Do you always let your *help* talk for you? I'm thinking you're too young and too naïve to be in this business."

The sweet demeanor that Kit had been using on him vanished, immediately replaced with an unexpected darkness. Her eyes narrowed into thin slits as her upper lip curled up. The split in it, supplied by Feigh when he had smacked her with his manacles, helped sell the look. Her otherwise sweet-sounding voice turned into a deep, visceral growl. "And I think you're too stupid to run this operation. Instead of playing for these broken souls, how's about we play for leadership. I've been looking to branch out."

The room went silent while everyone held their breath, waiting for the man's reaction. She could feel the weight of the crowd pressing in on her. She may have overplayed her hand before a single card was dealt.

"Hammers and daggers it is," Kit said, quickly standing from her chair. The surrounding crowd all took two steps backward. It seemed that they were not going to interfere in a power struggle. As best as Kit could tell, the man sitting in front of her was the only other person here with the Scarlet Tide tattoo on his neck.

The man didn't move a muscle, other than to roll his eyes. "Yes, yes. You're very tough, even if you are a child. Sit down and let's play."

"And when do you plan on showing my mistress your stake in this game?" Lin continued. She scratched at the painted-on tattoo, just to make sure everybody saw that she too was a member of the Scarlet Tide.

The man never took his eyes off Kit. He simply motioned to the door behind him. It was an iron-bound, solid wooden door with a small, barred window near the top.

There were more than a few patrons who seemed to be quietly showing their support for Kit as she walked over to the door to have a look inside. When she stood before the great door she growled as she considered the window which was a good foot higher than the top of her head, making it impossible for her to peer inside. When she stood on her tippytoes the small crowd roared with laughter.

"Maybe I'll just stack up some dead bodies for me to stand on," she screamed at the room of thugs. "I wonder how many of you will be laughing then?" Her statement didn't quite have the intended effect, as the entire group cheered again, yelling out, "*Daggers and Hammers, Daggers and Hammers.*"

Before things got out of hand, Lin quickly dragged a chair over for Kit to stand on, her lips pressed tightly together, trying to stifle a grin. Kit promptly cuffed her across the side of the face, knocking her back a few paces. "What took you so long?" The words came out as a snarl. "Maybe I should be standing on *your* dead body?"

"Sorry, Mistress," Lin said as she lowered her head and pushed the chair to the door. Several drops of blood from her nose landed on the chair as she positioned it under the window. Kit turned her ire to those thugs who stood nearest to her. The mirth on their faces immediately disappeared. Many of them decided it was a good time to either examine their boots or beat a hasty retreat. Those who stayed bowed respectfully to the small woman, perhaps hoping to gain her favor.

Kit stepped up on the chair and peered through the bars. The stench of mold, urine, and fear wafted over her, making her want to gag. Moldy hay covered most of the room's muddy floor. As expected, there were two Nomad boys and another mouse-sprite. One of the boys was likely near death. The left side of his face was badly swollen, his eye a purple mass of pain. His lower lip was split open. Dried blood was caked on his chin and neck. Kit's stomach dropped, fearing it was Treedale who was in rough shape. The Sprite was sitting on the lap of the broken boy. She had tucked her face away, hiding it from Kit's view. She was singing softly as she gently caressed the boy's hand. The second Nomad boy was sitting by himself against the room's heavy stone wall. His eyes met Kit's and a sneer immediately twisted his mouth. He slowly shook his head at her, his eyes filled with loathing.

"I can't use a slave who's practically dead," Kit snapped as she stepped off the chair and kicked it across the room. "Are you trying to cheat me?"

Kit was doing her level best to play up the part, but the man showed no sign of fear whatsoever.

"He'll live," he said with a shrug. "He got uppity, and I was bored..."

Lin quietly took a seat at the table and pulled out her deck of enchanted cards. She started shuffling them but not too deftly. Several times a card fell onto the table as she manipulated the deck. "Are we going to play or not?" she asked. Her face was devoid of expression. She feigned stifling a yawn, like the whole ordeal was becoming tedious.

The man motioned to the door and raised a questioning eyebrow to Kit, as though to ask if his stakes were sufficient. Kit gave him a curt nod. The man turned his attention back to Lin. He splayed his hands across the table and drummed his fingers, his nails clacking on the hard wood surface. "I'm not playing you," he said. "I'm playing your boss, or we have no deal."

Kit shook her head and pushed Lin from her seat. Taking Lin's place, she gave the man her very best smile, even if it was clearly forced. "I don't play cards. You're going to have to tell me the rules. Maybe you can tell me your name, so that I don't have to keep calling you, *you.*"

"Jailer," he said with a thin-lipped smile. "Yours?"

"My friends call me Kit. People looking for a quick trip to the Great Cycle call me *Kitten.*"

"You've never played cards?" Jailer asked.

"Nope. Not once. Not ever." Kit replied with a shrug. "I have more interesting ways of entertaining myself." The tiniest hint of a grin pulled a one corner of her mouth.

"Okay then, we'll play a game called *Overcard.* It's remarkably simple to learn, even for a little girl such as yourself."

Kit wanted to reach across the table and throttle the man, but instead, raised an eyebrow at Lin, who nodded back at her. It bothered her that she knew this game. The Temple forbade its members from gambling. It seemed this woman had no respect for rules.

"Take that deck of cards there," Jailer said with a flat tone, "and give us each six cards." Kit was about to deal but he stopped her before she even started. "Shuffle them for me first. I don't trust that one." He gave Lin a sneer and a foul wink as he said it.

Kit started trying to shuffle the cards but only managed to repeatedly drop most of them on the table and a few more on the floor. She smiled up at Jailer and gathered the cards together. After another weak attempt to sufficiently mix up the cards, the man cleared his throat and pursed his lips.

"If you're play-acting, little girl, you're a master at it."

"I wish," Kit said, flashing her best smile at him. "If you'd prefer, you're welcome to do the dealing. If I deal, we'll be here all day."

"You have to take turns dealing," Lin said in Kit's ear. "Who's dealing makes a difference in the game."

"Don't you worry, sweet thing," Jailer said, his voice dripping with disdain. "I'll make sure we take turns with who plays first."

"Why does it matter who plays first?" Kit said to Lin over her shoulder. A good-sized stone was now sitting uncomfortably in the pit of her stomach. She was gambling for the lives of people, and she had no idea what she was doing. Having enchanted cards meant little if she didn't have a clue how to play.

Not giving Lin a chance to reply, Jailer piped up. "Because we're going to take turns playing first, and the dealer always plays the first card. The object of the game is to take the other person's card. The highest card played - wins. If you play a card I can't beat, I'm going to play the lowest card in my hand. If you play a card I can beat, I'm going to play the lowest card I have that can still beat your card."

Kit screwed up her face. She understood the rules, but the game sounded like something children would play. "Okay, that sounds easy enough. How do we score points?"

"You get one point for each card you win. After we finish playing our six cards, whoever has won the most cards, gets an extra point. First player to fifteen points, wins."

Kit shifted herself in her chair and sat up straighter. She might not have ever gambled before, but this game was so simple that she assumed she'd have no trouble mastering it. "So, after I get fifteen points, your prisoners are mine?"

Jailer laughed, perhaps louder than he intended. "Sure thing, sweetie. But, if I get to fifteen points first, I get to cut the ears off your prisoner before I sell him on the market." Feigh, who had been standing quietly beside Lin, spat at Jailer's feet. He quickly received a cuff in the face from Kit for his efforts.

Jailer blew Kit a kiss and took the deck of cards from her. He let his fingers linger against her hand long enough that it made the girl uncomfortable. "I'll deal, but you're playing first this hand."

"If you're going to be handling the cards for the whole game, you should be playing first," Lin barked at him. "You're stacking everything in your favor."

"And I'm betting three prisoners against your one," he replied with a scowl. The man's mouth narrowed slightly as he leaned forward.

Up until this point, Jailer had appeared to be nothing more than your average thug. In a heartbeat, his true evil nature surfaced. The man's eyes narrowed and turned fully black. His skin paled, making his eyes appear even more sinister. "And if you can't keep your pet quiet, *Kitten*, I'm going to have my men here gut you here and now, and I'll still get your prisoner."

Kit's body tensed as she witnessed the man's transformation. She pulled her hands from atop the table and moved them to her lap where they fidgeted uncontrollably. Based on his smug look of satisfaction, her response was exactly what Jailer had hoped for.

"Save your weak illusions and parlor tricks for those who can't see through them," Feigh said. Kit didn't know how illusion magic worked, but as soon as Feigh spoke, Jailer's appearance immediately returned to normal.

Kit closed her eyes and took a deep breath. "Just deal. I'll play first."

As Jailer passed each of them six cards, he continued with the rules. "The cards are numbered one to ten. There are four types of picture cards, the prince, the queen, the king, and the castle. They are higher than a ten and their value is the same order I described them. A prince beats a ten, a queen beats a prince, a king beats a queen, and the castle is the highest card in the game."

The man gave Kit a condescending look. "Am I saying this too fast for you? I hope this isn't too complicated."

Kit held his gaze and set her jaw. "No, you're doing fine. But what if we both play the same card?"

"In the case of a tie, we each get to pick a card from the opponent's hand. Whoever picks the best card, wins them all."

"What if we match the last card in our hands?" Kit pushed, figuring this might be important.

"Then we each draw one card from the deck. The highest card wins both cards." Jailer gave Kit a bit of a sideways glance. "Are you sure you've never played?"

"I've never played cards in my life." She rolled her eyes and blew out her cheeks. "If you'd rather play against my girl here, she's welcome to take my seat."

"She speaks the truth," whispered a man with pale skin, an enormous nose, and straight snow-white hair dipping down to his waist. His voice was raspy, like his throat was filled with rust.

"Apparently some pets are allowed to speak," Kit said, narrowing her eyes. "You threaten my girl again for talking, and I'll gut this one standing beside you."

Her threat made Jailer burst out with laughter. "I wish that we could be friends, Kitten. I really do."

She leaned forward and let her lips part slightly. "If you let me win, maybe we will be." Her eyes widened slightly as she waggled her eyebrows at him.

"Sorry, Kitten, but as much as I like you, I'm not willing to trade three prisoners for a toss in the hay with you." Jailer dealt the cards, continuing to chuckle lightly as he did.

When he had finished dealing, Kit gathered up her cards and fanned them out in her tiny hands. She had a castle, a king, a queen, a six, a five and a two. She smiled brightly and played her castle. Lin groaned in response to her choice of cards.

"What?" Kit asked. "It's my best card and he can't beat it, so why not play it?"

Before Lin had a chance to answer, Jailer tossed a two out and pushed the cards towards Kit. "Because all you managed to do was capture my deuce. You're better off leading midland cards, forcing me to overplay them with something bigger. Save your best cards for the end."

Kit frowned and stared down at her hand. "That makes no sense. I won your card and now I've got a point. That means I'm winning and you're losing."

Jailer shrugged his shoulders at Kit's comment, the smallest hint of a smile pulled at the corners of his mouth.

"Play however you like, sweetie. It's my turn to lead." As he said the words, he tossed a seven onto the table. Kit glared at the card and frowned. She pulled out a queen and tossed it out before dragging the cards to her pile. She quickly followed it up with her six.

Jailer played another seven and raked in the cards before tossing an eight out. Kit growled slightly looking at the card and played her king. As she did, Jailer carefully examined the face card. She dragged in the cards and played her five. Jailer kept his face completely stern as he played a five, matching Kit's.

"Now we each draw from the other's hand," he said with a smile. "You can have my three here. What are you holding?"

Kit stared down at the three. She blinked at it a few times while she tried to process what was happening. A moment later, she pursed her lips and gave Jailer a coy smile. "Well now, if that card's mine, and this one's yours, then I guess I win. I've got a two here." She tossed the two out and gathered up the cards. "I won four times and I have the most cards, so I get five points."

She again cocked an eyebrow up at Lin, who smiled brightly and nodded.

Jailer's hands balled up into tight fists. "Where's my ale?" he screamed out to the bartender. A moment later, a tall, scantily clad woman with yellow hair placed three tall mugs of ale on the side of the table. Her eyes lingered on Kit for several seconds before she slunk off into the crowd.

Jailer snatched up one of the mugs and immediately downed it. He pushed one over to Kit, spilling some foam and amber liquid onto the table.

"Drink!" he commanded as he drained the second mug.

Kit sniffed the ale in front of her and took a small sip. Her eyes lit up, and she downed the entire contents in one, noisy gulp.

"That was delicious!" she exclaimed, just before shouting out for another round. She followed it up with a massive belch. The gathered crowd, which had grown considerably, cheered at the sound of her thunderous burp.

Not wanting to wait for the next round, Jailer dealt out another six cards. Kit examined her cards, finding four sevens and two sixes. When she raised her head, she saw that Jailer had already played a six. With a smile and a wink, she quickly threw one of her sixes out and proclaimed, "Matchy matchy!"

Lin closed her eyes and groaned. She should have played a seven and taken the easy point. Jailer, reading Lin's reaction, nodded his head.

Disregarding their reactions to her play, Kit laid her cards face down on the table. "Pick whichever one you want." She searched for the barmaid and the magnificent mugs of ale she'd ordered. As Jailer took his card, a new girl arrived with three mugs on a tray. Like the first girl, she was scantily dressed, but she had shoulder-length, mousy brown hair. As she placed the mugs on the table she stared intently at Kit, as though trying to size her up. Tucking her tray under her arm, she curtsied and gave the young priest a wink before disappearing into the crowd.

With wide eyes, Kit held one of the mugs between her small hands. She sniffed the earthy contents and blew the foam off the top. The crowd seemed to lean in, waiting for her to take a drink. Kit waggled her head, licked her lips, and promptly drained the mug of its bitter-sweet contents. Following Jailer's lead, she pushed one of the two remaining mugs to him, and then promptly drained another. The crowd went silent, almost as though they were holding their breath. Kit pursed her lips and raised a finger to them as she gazed upon the crowd. Her eyes went wide for a moment before she let loose another thunderous belch that shook the table – and the crowd went wild.

"Just pick your card," Jailer barked at her before draining his own beer. His eyes went to the gathered crowd, daring them to continue cheering for his opponent. While he glared at the spectators, Kit examined the cards offered to her.

"I don't know which one is best. You pick!" she said to the sweaty fat man standing closest to the table. He trembled as he stared at Jailer with wide eyes, hoping for some sort of direction from him. When his boss nodded, he motioned with his eyes to the leftmost card in his hand. The fat man drew the one next to it and dropped it on the table, revealing an eight. Jailer flipped over the card he had selected, revealing a six. He practically screamed and threw the card at Kit.

"You're either a cheat or the luckiest little bitch to walk the lands." Jailer's face had turned beet red, with veins on his neck and forehead bulging angrily. "Play!" he growled at Kit, spraying spittle on everyone within two paces of him.

Kit tossed one of the four sevens in her hand, but as soon as she revealed it, it turned into a castle.

"How can you possibly be winning? You play terribly!" Jailer screamed as he threw his own castle onto the table. He spread his cards out. "You pick one this time. YOU!"

Kit smiled brightly at him and slowly pulled one of his cards. When she flipped it over, it showed a three. Jailer laughed and selected one of the cards from Kit's remaining hand. When he flipped it over, it was also a three.

"That's impossible," he screamed as he pounded on the table. The force of the blow knocked one of the empty mugs to the floor. With lightning-quick reflexes, Kit snagged the glass before it shattered. With a small shrug, she placed the mug back onto the table and picked another card from his hand. This time she turned over a prince, causing Jailer to practically explode. He was gnashing his teeth together when he reached out and picked one of Kit's two remaining cards.

He grimaced as he flipped it over to reveal yet another prince. Seeing that this was again a tie, his body relaxed dramatically. An evil grin spread across his face as he blew Kit a small, revolting kiss.

"I guess you get my last card, sweetie; it's all yours." He tossed the card toward Kit, revealing a two. Kit smiled sweetly back at him and flipped over her card, revealing yet another two.

Jailer's breath was now coming in ragged whistles. Spittle gathered at the corners of his mouth as his nostrils flared. His jaw was clenched so tightly that his teeth might shatter at any second. A low rumble rolled in his chest as he spread the remaining deck of cards out in front of him. "Point! Don't touch!" He sprayed the words across the table. Kit grinned at him and batted her eyes, completely disregarding the bit of spittle that struck her cheek.

"You pick for me," she offered, as she twisted her hair between her fingers. Her eyes widened and bulged slightly as she motioned to the deck. "I dare you."

The crowd pressed in even closer, threatening to crush the players while they sat at their seats. A low chant of "pick, pick, pick" rippled through the audience.

Jailer held his breath as he picked a card from the middle of the spread and flipped it over – a seven. He groaned audibly knowing that he had a fifty-fifty chance of beating her. He pulled a card out near the top of the deck and flipped it over, revealing another seven. He slammed his fist on the table, causing the cards to bounce up into the air.

"Pick your own damned card this time!" he screamed, again spraying foamy spittle across the table. Holding the man's eyes with her own, Kit calmly reached out to the deck. She let her hand hover lightly over the cards, moving it left and right as though she was trying to feel for just the right card to pick. Finally, she settled on her choice and pointed to a card near the middle of the deck.

"That one," she said brightly.

Jailer flipped over the card she'd picked, revealing a ten. A shocked gasp came from those standing behind the man. Assuming he would lose, he quickly drew a card for himself and flipped it over. When he revealed another ten, the crowd screamed for joy. People jostled for position as they made side bets on who would win the match. Each time someone offered to make a wager, ten of the spectators would scream out, hoping to get in on the action. Before long, the tavern was jam packed, with patrons barely able to make it in the door. It was unclear if they all knew what was going on, but people kept pushing their way in, nonetheless.

There seemed to be two camps forming as the spectators pushed and shoved their way to take up a place near their preferred player. Lin used the point of a dagger to keep anyone from pushing too close to Kit. She feared that they might not be as friendly as they appeared, and she also didn't want them to see Kit's cards. There likely wasn't a single patron who wasn't also a cheat.

Jailer bellowed out for quiet, practically shaking the windows in their panes. In a heartbeat, the place went as silent as a graveyard.

"My turn to pick," he said with a grin on his face. He carefully scrutinized the deck, scanning each card carefully. His grin turned into a toothy smile when he spotted a card with a slight bend at the corner. "There you are," he said with a laugh. He took the card by the bent corner and flipped it up, revealing a king.

Lin leaned across the table with her dagger poised and ready. "You're a cheat," she murmured. "I saw that. Nobody else might have seen it, but I did, and you're a scum-sucking cheat."

Jailer rocked back in his chair and knitted his fingers behind his head. He blinked a few times and yawned. "They're your cards, sweetness. It's not my fault that I noticed one of the cards had a bend in it." His gaze dropped down to Kit. Any hint of amusement vanished. All that remained was vile contempt.

"Pick, girl!"

"That one," Kit said almost immediately, pointing at the third card from the top of the deck.

"Here you go," Jailer replied as he drew the fourth from the deck.

"That's not the card she picked," said the man with long white hair. "She wants the one next to it."

"But this is the card that she's getting," Jailer screamed. "Speak again and I'll have your tongue ripped from your head."

"As you wish," the man said. He bowed his head slightly to Kit before slowly slipping into the crowd. His place was immediately filled as several onlookers pushed their way to the front.

"Flip it! Flip your card!" Jailer had a crazed look in his eyes, his pupils so wide that they almost entirely swallowed up the blue of his irises.

"No, I think you should flip that card. After all, you picked it for me." There was no longer any hint of a smile on Kit's face. Her expression was flat and monotone as she stared down her opponent.

"Flip the card! Flip the card!" the crowd chanted over and over.

With a smug look of superiority, Jailer flipped the card over – revealing a castle.

CHAPTER TWENTY-ONE

A MYSTERIOUS WOMAN

Jailer's smug look of superiority quickly changed to confusion, several beads of sweat appearing along his hairline. He seemed to be having difficulty processing what had just happened. He stood from his chair. Having so many people hovering over him made him suddenly uncomfortable.

"That's not possible. That wasn't the card you chose; you didn't win," he screeched out, banging his fists on the table, toppling over the empty beer mugs.

Sweat continued to gather on his brow and at his temples. His head swiveled from side to side, looking for support from those around him. Based on his widening eyes and trembling hands, he just realized that losing this game of chance may well result in him losing his life. Now terrified that he was in mortal peril, he screamed at those standing around the table. "Take the women! Do what you want with them, but this mouse is mine!"

The crowd seemed somewhat perplexed. If they moved against the women, they were moving against their masters – but if they didn't follow Jailer's orders, well, that could lead to a completely different set of problems.

Kit already had her battle hammer in her hand as the surrounding thugs closed in on them. Lin drew her swords and with the flick of a wrist ignited both blades. She held them in front of her while orange and red flames licked at the steel. Those nearest her eyed the blades carefully, uncertain as to what other magic they could contain. As the patrons backed away, they drew their own weapons. The ringing of steel filled the already crowded room.

Just when Kit was starting to think that this might be her last fight, the crowd parted as a woman dressed in a black cloak, came strolling up between them. She was not tall of stature, but she strode through the group purposefully, her boots clacking on the floorboards with each step. The cloak's hood was up, casting the woman's face in shadows. The only identifiable traits visible were the tip of a longsword that peaked out near her black boots and locks of platinum blonde hair that flowed down over her chest.

"You follow the rules, or you join the ranks of the dead," the mystery woman said in a calm, measured tone.

Jailer blanched at the comment and took his seat. He continued to seek out support but with the arrival of this person, people were treating him like a pariah.

"She's either a sharp, or she's a cheat. Nobody is that lucky." Jailer screeched out.

His eyes continued to scan the surrounding people. These were his people. They reported to him.

"There's only three little girls! What in Helja is wrong with you. Take them!" The man's voice was filled with panic.

There was a flash from under the woman's hood, as light reflected off two golden eyes hidden from within its shadows.

"She never touched the cards," she hissed at him. "You made sure of that. Her friend wanted to play, but you insisted that Kit play against you. She chose her final card, but you chose another."

"How could you know that?" Jailer screamed out. "How?" His eyes continued darting around the room, trying to figure out who was spying on him, watching the game, reporting it to this... woman.

"I'll take my prisoners. Now!" Kit said as she pushed back the few remaining thugs standing near her. While several of them backed off, many more moved in beside her. Their stance, their body language, the hateful way they were staring at Jailer told the story. They were all taking her side.

"Even your own people know that you've lost," the cloaked woman said to Jailer. "Does she need to kill you before you'll accept defeat?" There was a cool sense of satisfaction in the woman's voice, as though this was an outcome long since overdue.

Jailer's gaze returned to Kit. He eyed her up and down, a sneer on his lips. He scoffed, "I've never lost before, and you won't always have *her* looking out for you. You've made some powerful enemies today. You best be watching your back from now on."

"Your words are nothing more than fetid wind. I won, you lost. Now, give me the prisoners," Kit smirked, as a few more of the patrons fell in behind her. Kit motioned to Lin to gather up the cards while she followed Jailer to the cell door.

Using a key from around his neck, he jammed it into the rust-covered lock and gave it a turn. As he did, the door swung open, making a horrible grating noise in the process. The stench of moldy hay and urine followed, forcing Kit to cover her nose.

"Take them," he said, spitting on the ground at Kit's feet. "They're near dead, anyway."

Quick as a viper, Kit struck Jailer in the throat with the side of her hand. A strangled, gurgling sort of noise came from his mouth; his hands grasped at his neck in a reflexive action. The man's face paled as he tried to comprehend what was happening to him. His head snapped back when Kit's right knee came up, crashing into his groin. His strangled noises turned to a moan and a grunt as he dropped to his knees. Jailer was making pathetic whimpering noises, but Kit didn't let up on her attack. She spun in a half circle, using her bodyweight to add speed to a hammer swing. With a sickening thud, it crashed into the middle of Jailer's back, knocking him prone.

The young priest put her foot on the back of Jailer's neck and took stock of the gathered crowd. Her eyes sought out every person within striking distance, gauging their reaction to her attack. None of them, not one, showed any form of hostility towards her; their eyes were firmly locked on their fallen leader. Most of them seemed pleased at the current state of affairs. Satisfied that she was not in immediate danger, Kit pulled the key from the door's lock and called out, "Who is second in command here?"

A woman with short, light brown hair stepped forward. She was perhaps thirty cycles; her face and arms were heavily scarred. She did not have the mark of the Tide on her neck. "That would be me," she said as she strode up to Kit. "They call me Nicks."

"Well, Nicks," Kit said as she tossed her the key. "You're in command here now. Take Jailer's band and do with him as you see fit."

"You don't have the authority to promote me," Nicks said as she eyed the key. "Only the masters can do that."

"I'll deal with the masters," Kit said with a wink. She moved closer to the woman, forcing her to tilt her head backward to look into her eyes. "Are you up to running this group or not?"

"I am."

"Then get horses and provisions for my prisoners. I want them ready for the road immediately and I want them treated respectfully. They're already damaged beyond repair. If any of them die, you'll take their place at market."

"Prepare the prisoners for transport," Nicks said to the men standing nearest her. She gave Kit a curt nod. "And make sure they're treated carefully. The mistress doesn't want any more damage to them before she delivers them to the masters."

Kit gave Nicks a knowing smile. "I'll be back when there is no moon in the sky. I'll want a full report, as well as my share of the gold."

"Absolutely, Mistress. It will be done." Nicks gave Kit a stiff bow. Even though the scarred woman was saying and doing all the right things, there was a hard look in her eyes. Perhaps she and Jailer were more than master and subordinate.

The woman's mannerisms weren't lost on Lin either. With her eyes locked on Nicks, Lin stepped up to Jailer, her swords still ablaze. Still watching for a reaction, she effortlessly slid a sword tip into the fallen man's neck, twisting the blade as she did. A gout of blood sprayed from the wound.

"One less enemy at your back, Mistress Kit."

Nicks' eyes were like steel. They did not betray her. The way the muscles in her jaw jumped, did.

Kit did her best to hide her shock at Lin's action, but her body shuddered, nonetheless. The woman was full of surprises, and most of them were unsavory. It was at moments like this that told Kit she really didn't know Lin at all. The woman existed outside the norm of the Temple, seemingly only following the rules if they suited her needs.

Kit shook off the feeling and returned to the here and now.

"Take Jailer's body out of here. Burn it, grind his bones, and scatter his remains to the wind. Leave no trace of him." Three of the larger thugs grabbed Jailer by the feet and dragged him towards a back door, leaving a thick crimson slick on the tavern's filthy floorboards. Jailer moaned slightly when his head banged off a table leg. One of the thugs used his iron-clad boot to stomp on his head, ending Jailer's moans immediately. He gave Kit a crooked smile and bowed his head to her.

When the three prisoners came out, only one of them was able to stand; the nomad boy who was about the same age as Kit. Judging by how much he resembled Lin, Kit could only assume that he was Treedale. Her suspicion was confirmed when he caught sight of Lin. The look of recognition gave him away, but he quickly dropped his head hoping nobody noticed his reaction.

"I want five horses and supplies for three days," Kit barked to Nicks. "And enough healing potions to enable these two to travel. What good are prisoners who can't be sold?" At her words, a number of the thugs went scurrying off.

"Take this one," Kit said to Lin, pushing Feigh towards her. The mouse's eyes were wet with tears as he beheld his wife's broken body. "I want to inspect my winnings."

Kit looked Treedale in the eyes, "Are you well?"

The young nomad responded by spitting in her face.

"Well enough, then," Kit said with a sneer. "If the others behaved this way, then I guess they deserved what they got. Is that what you want for yourself as well?"

Treedale's eyes stayed locked on Kit's. He never turned away, and he never backed down. Waves of hatred poured off him like the stench that flowed out from the prisoners' cell.

Kit moved over to Feigh's wife. She maintained the same stern appearance, but she fought with a giant boulder that sat on the inside her stomach. Triss, the mouse-sprite, had been horribly beaten. Even through her fur-covered body, gashes and bruises were easily visible. Her left eye was milky-white except for where broken blood-vessels had turned it red. If she hadn't already, she would likely lose the use of it.

"You must have been a pretty little thing," she cooed, stroking the fur on her face with her fingers. "You'll fetch a hefty sack of gold for sure, but only if we can get you fixed up."

The barkeep, Carver, cleared his throat from behind Kit. When she turned, he produced two vials of deep red liquid. Within its scarlet depths, a swirl of orange was visible as well.

"Healing potions," he said as he held them out, "with a complacency chaser. It will keep them... quiet during transport."

Kit took the first of the two vials and held it to Feigh's wife's lips.

"Drink," she said in a soothing voice.

The beaten Sprite shook her head. She weakly held out her hand as though trying to ward off an attack. Her chin dipped slowly down to her chest as her hand fell back to her side.

Sweet Titan, how the sight tore at Kit's heart. "It will take the pain away. Please, don't make me force it on you."

The little mouse blinked slowly at Kit. Somewhere in her broken mind she was able to understand. She opened her mouth, allowing the young priest to pour the liquid in. The potion's honey-sweet flavor induced her to swallow. A tiny pink tongue peeked out from her muzzle to lick her lips. Within seconds, the potion's healing powers began to work, magically knitting the hideous wounds that covered the mouse's body. The milky-white color of her damaged eye returned to its normal shiny black. Any hint of the broken blood vessels also disappeared.

"Thank you," Triss said as she slowly closed her eyes and took a slow, deep breath.

Kit led her to a chair and sat her down on it. "Bring me the boy, the broken one," Kit ordered. Even though his face was bloodied and bruised, his wounds were not as severe as the mouse's. Where his body would quickly heal, the look in his eyes told a different story. Though only barely visible through his swollen eyelids, his eyes were empty and lifeless.

"His name is Ashkey," Triss offered. "He's a good boy. Please be gentle with him."

The compassion in the Sprite's voice surprised Kit, and at the same time made her heart ache. When she offered Ashkey the potion, he opened his mouth immediately. Tears fell down his cheeks as Kit poured the honey-sweet liquid into his mouth. Like the mouse, the potion immediately healed his visible wounds.

"Fixing a broken spirit is beyond the potion's healing power," Triss said as she climbed up onto the boy's lap. She sang softly to him, as she curled up in the cook of his arm.

"Your horses are ready, Mistress," someone said from behind Kit. "They're out front, with saddle bags loaded with five days rations – just in case."

Kit nodded in response. "Help them get saddled up, and remove that one's shackles," she said to Lin.

"Remove the shackles?" Lin asked, a tinge of nervousness in her voice.

"Did I stutter?" Kit hissed. "They have nowhere to run. I want them in their best possible shape when we bring them to market."

Lin immediately bowed to Kit and removed Feigh's shackles. When she had finished, Kit barked at her again.

"I want them mounted up and ready to leave, now. I'll be out in a moment."

As Lin guided the prisoners out the front door, Kit surveyed the scene, desperately hoping to find the blonde woman in the black cloak, but she was nowhere in sight. She turned back to Nicks. "What were my orders?"

"Mistress?" she questioned. "You ordered the prisoners to be put on your horses."

Kit glared back at the woman, wondering if perhaps she had placed the wrong person in charge. It was only when Kit's lip began to curl did Nick's catch on.

"Oh, the orders you gave me. Oh... you will be back when the moon goes dark. You want a full accounting of everything on your return, as well as your share of our take."

"Good," Kit said with a nod. "And I want each and every prisoner treated with care and respect. I want them whole and unharmed. Am I making myself clear?"

"Sure, Mistress, perfectly clear – but what you're asking will cost us."

"If you don't do as I say, it will cost *you* a lot more."

"Sure, Mistress. No problem, Mistress."

Kit wasn't sure if Nicks' responses were out of fear or out of respect. Either way, any prisoners who came through the city wouldn't be treated as badly, which was all Kit cared about at the moment. Without another word, she stepped out the front door to find everyone mounted up and ready to leave. The two mice were on the same horse, easily sitting together, sharing a saddle. Treedale and Ashkey were both on their own horses, but Treedale was holding the reins for the other boy's horse. Lin was on her own mount, holding the reins of Kit's steed, waiting for her to saddle up.

Chapter Twenty-Two

A Choice Made

The group rode in silence until they were a little more than thirty minutes outside the city's gates. "You were amazing," Lin finally said, her eyes wide, beaming with pride. "You freed the prisoners and took control of the Scarlet Tide slaver operation in Silverhawk."

"They're not Scarlet Tide," Feigh spoke up as he continued to hold his wife in his arms. She had her face buried in his chest since they had started the ride. "Most of the thugs there were Auctioneers. Only the ruling body are Scarlet Tide. You actually took control of a small arm of the Auctioneers. They're responsible for delivering slaves to the Tide, as well as to other places all over Orth."

"Who are the Auctioneers?" Lin asked. "If they weren't Scarlet Tide, why did some of them have the tattoos?"

Feigh continued to stroke the fur on his wife's cheek as he considered the question. "The Auctioneers are the actual slavers. They are the ones who rip people from their homes and bring them to market. They are a despicable lot. They used to keep their people-poaching to Berrathia, but it looks like they're spreading out into Arnnor."

Triss shifted in the saddle and took a quick look over at the Nomad boy. He appeared well and healthy, but his eyes were empty, lifeless vessels. His face was devoid of expression of any kind. The small Sprite pressed her cheek against her husband's tunic. She tried to brush away a bit of dried blood that had stained the fabric.

"As for Jailer," Feigh continued, "his was likely a bottom tier member, offered a place in the Tide to give him incentive to tow the line. It's also more likely that he'd turn in anyone who might try to skim some profits for themselves. They say there is honor among thieves, but there is definitely no honor among slavers."

"Then I'm glad I killed him," Lin said. She remembered the thug who had boot-stomped his head into the tavern's filthy floor. "Well, maybe I didn't kill him, but I started him off on his journey."

"Who was that lady?" Kit asked. She wasn't really paying much attention to the conversation. "The one who came to help us."

"I'm not sure," Feigh said as he gently tugged on his wife's muzzle, lifting her chin so that he could look at her eyes. "Have you seen her before Triss, my sweet?"

Triss shook her head and pressed her cheek against Feigh's chest again. She closed her eyes and hummed softly. Her voice was barely a whisper on the breeze, but Kit found it to be remarkably soothing. It reminded her of her mother's gentle touch.

Feigh sighed and shook his head. "Whoever she was though, they were all afraid of her. I think it was her presence that changed the outcome in there. When the Auctioneers saw that she was on your side, they flipped allegiance almost immediately."

The group went silent again, each of them lost in their own thoughts.

"Thank you, Lin," Treedale finally spoke up. "Thank you for finding us."

"I'd travel to the ends of Orth for you, little brother, but in this case, it's Kit here who you need to thank. She's the one who made this happen." Lin rubbed her cheek where Kit smacked her. She couldn't see it, but she knew she had a bruise spreading across the side of her face. "She put on a good show for everybody."

Feigh chuckled as he rubbed the cut on his mouth. He gaped down at his wrists, bloodied where the manacles had dug into his skin. There was almost no fur left where they had bitten into him. He was willing to endure much worse if it meant saving his love. He nodded his appreciation to Kit as well.

Kit found her own fingers tracing the deep cut on her face, where Feigh had struck her with his manacles. It seemed they had all suffered some damage in order to play the part. She had considered healing the wound but chose otherwise. Sister Gale, her Temple combat instructor, viewed wounds as a reminder of a learning opportunity.

A large stallion came across the fields towards the group, clumps of grass and mud flying up from his hooves as he sped towards them. The leggy horse was gray with a dappled black and white hind end and obsidian-black mane and tail. The sight of him barrelling across the landscape brought a smile to Kit's face.

"It looks like Mukale recovered just fine," Kit said to Lin, gesturing towards the speeding horse.

"You left me behind!" the horse screamed as it approached. The talking animal startled Treedale, nearly knocking him from his saddle. Ashkey, the other Nomad boy, showed no reaction to the talking horse's arrival.

"Hey, Mukale," Lin said in an easy tone. "You were in no shape to travel, and we needed to get going. Thanks to you, we saved Treedale, and a few more in the process."

Mukale shifted from horse to Berrat form. "But…" His reaction seemed to be a series of mixed feelings, "I needed to help, to repay my debt to the village." His eyes brightened when they fell onto Treedale. "I'm happy to see you alive and well, my friend."

"You can change into a horse now, too?" Treedale said with a bit of laugh. The look of surprise was still firmly planted on his face. "Not quite as inconspicuous as the titmouse you usually change into."

Mukale's face blanched, and Lin's face turned beet red.

"That's been you, flying into my bedroom at night! You're the little bird that sleeps on my pillow beside me?" Lin nudged her heels into her horse's ribs, urging it to move towards Mukale who was backpedaling fast, trying to keep his distance.

"Let it go, Lin. We need to get Treedale home, and Feigh and Triss as far from Silverhawk as possible." Kit was having a lot of trouble controlling her laughter as she attempted to keep Lin from beating on the Berrat man.

"If Grams will let us, we'd like to stay at her village," Triss said, pulling her face from Feigh's chest for the first time since they'd left the city. "We owe her a great debt, and I think we should start repaying it right now."

Feigh pressed his palm over his heart and nodded in agreement.

"I'm sure Grams would love to have you," Treedale said, tilting his head towards Lin, asking for her approval.

Lin finally pulled away from Mukale and gave her brother a small smile in agreement. She glanced back over her shoulder and glared at the Berrat. "I'll deal with you later, titmouse."

Treedale turned to Feigh and took a deep breath, his eyes blinking rapidly. "Your wife is incredibly brave."

The boy's posture stiffened as a deep, hate-filled scowl crossed his face.

"They tortured her for days, hoping to gain information as to where you were. We were only a few feet away from them when they did it. She never said a thing, except that you'd save her. She never gave up hope."

Triss buried her face in her husband's chest again.

"Why?" Feigh asked, wrapping his arms around his wife, pulling her closer. "I'm so sorry that happened to you. You should have told them. You should have told them, right away. You didn't need to do that for me."

Kit watched their interactions, her heart breaking for the pair of Sprites and the young Nomad. Tears were now streaming down Ashkey's cheeks even though his face was still emotionless. She could only assume that witnessing her torture was what caused his spirit to snap.

The group took the road out of the city until they arrived at the great rift in the land. As they crossed the bridge, several creatures were sunning on the bank. She assumed that these were the river monsters, the Kappa, that Feigh had mentioned when they'd first met. They resembled blue, soft-shelled turtles, with wicked long claws and a mouthful of huge teeth. Their bodies ended in a long, forked tail, somewhat resembling that of a fish. She had never heard of such a creature before and was thankful that the rivers near her home had nothing like them living there.

"They can run down a horse," Feigh said from his saddle. "They're much faster than they look."

Kit's jaw flopped open at the thought of these creatures chasing her. She just turned away and continued along the road. As much as she had traveled across these lands, she knew almost nothing about the kingdom she lived in. The Temple's teachings were narrowly focused, seemingly targeting the faith of priest and their ability to deliver justice upon those who would do evil.

The group traveled in relative silence for another thirty minutes. On occasion, travelers on their way to Silverhawk would pass by. In some instances, they did little more than grunt at the group. Other times they would try to strike up conversations. It was uncommon to see Sprites, let alone see them traveling with a group of Nomads. After the last, particularly nosey group of riders had passed by, Mukale suggested they start heading cross country, away from prying eyes.

The travel across the countryside was slow but pleasant. The mountain ranges to the west made for a pleasant backdrop to the wide fields of grasses and wildflowers. When they reached the small river, the one loaded with trout that Kit and Lin had feasted upon, Mukale recommended they stop and make camp for the night.

Nobody disagreed with the proposal.

⚬⚬⚬⚭⚬⚬⚬

The food provided by the Auctioneers from the Crimson Ale was plentiful, but not of the highest quality. Most of it was either dried, or heavily salted, or both. Seeing the young man sitting alone, Kit joined Treedale by the fire, pretending to warm her hands as she did.

"Attacking the men who came to your village was foolish," Kit said to him. The words were an admonishment, but there was a hint of pride in the statement. The young man took note of the tone in her voice.

"I needed to expose them for what they were. They spoke of Arachnielle, but there was more to them than just faith-peddlers. I wanted Grams to act against them."

"What would you have expected her to do? Bring Titan's wrath upon them?"

"She's not as feeble as she pretends," Treedale replied with a small laugh. "She could have destroyed them with a thought; with a flick of her wrist, she could have annihilated them."

"Perhaps in her youth, but her days as a warrior have long since passed." Kit liked the obvious way the boy respected his grandmother; she had clearly been a source of inspiration to him. She could only surmise that, since he was Lin's brother, his parents must have abandoned him as well. It was odd though that he had not also joined the Temple like his sister.

The Nomad just chuckled to himself. "You don't know her like I do. I think she let them take me because she knew you'd come for me. She risked my life, so you'd have a chance to witness, first-hand, what's been happening. People were being taken across Berrathia, and now Arnnor as well. They are ripped from their homes and sold into slavery."

Kit's eyes danced with mischief. "You believe Grams has prescience; far-sightedness?"

"No, nothing like that. But she did speak to a woman who did; a woman that she said she trusted deeply. This woman spoke of a girl who would change the world. A girl, twice marked by the gods, who would deliver the world from injustice." The boy's words made Kit shiver. This wasn't the first time someone had said she was twice marked. "I'm quite certain that you're the girl she spoke of."

The conversation's direction was making Kit exceedingly uncomfortable, so she quickly tried to change the subject. "What did you learn of the man who kidnapped you, and of the people who held you?"

"Quite a bit, actually," Treedale replied with a grim face, "and none of it's good news." After taking a few moments to gather his thoughts, the young Nomad began. "When they're in their cups, they speak loudly, with almost all of their conversations being at Jailer's table, which was right outside the cell. I guess they figured we were as good as dead anyway, so who cared what we heard. I heard a lot myself, but Triss heard much more."

Treedale seemed to wither under Kit's intense stare. This girl was supposedly destined to change the world, and yet, she was treating the young man as her equal. He could feel his ears beginning to heat.

"There are two more shipments of slaves to be brought into Silverhawk over the next few days. They're going to be coming in from villages around Mooncrest, the city on the shore of the North Sea, a couple days' ride from Silverhawk. After they gather the slaves in Silverhawk, they'll transport them to Cormorant for sale at the market. Apparently, they're branching out from Berrathia, hitting the northern villages in Arnnor."

The dancing flames of the fire illuminated the concern on Kit's face. If the slave trade was infecting Arnnor's north, it could explain why the Berrat were listening to the ravings of people like Pental. "I wonder why they're moving into Arnnor. Surely they know the king will send his troops north to destroy them."

"I don't think they're worried about the king or his army. I think the masters, the real vampires, are directly involved at this point. The Auctioneers fear them far more than the king."

A chill ran up Kit's spine. The thought of dealing with vampires in numbers made her bowels churn.

"From what Triss told me, there's a problem in Cormorant, the port city at the northern tip of the Gaelinora Sea. She didn't know why, but apparently the masters were going to oversee operations there, until the situation was rectified. She also talked about a new *house* that is taking power in the north, a violent bunch of slavers who don't really care what sort of condition their product arrives in."

He paused for a moment, trying to recall any other details.

"What can you tell me about the Scarlet Tide?" Kit asked, her mind racing, trying to process everything Treedale was telling her. "Is Pental a part of that group?"

"I don't know who Pental is," he replied. "His name was never mentioned, but I can tell you that everybody is afraid of the Tide. Whenever Jailer spoke of the masters, his voice would get very quiet, like he was afraid they might be listening in on him." The young man shrugged and shook his head. "Once the whispering began, I wasn't able to hear anything."

Treedale turned his attention back to the fire. His eyes became unfocused, appearing to be in some sort of deep trance. He covered his mouth to stifle a yawn. Kit could only imagine the horrors he had lived through these past few days.

"You should get some sleep. We've got a long way to travel tomorrow if we're going to get you home before night falls again."

Nodding to Kit, Treedale moved away from the fire and slipped into a bedroll. In moments his breathing became deep and steady. It seemed that Kit was the only one not sleeping at this point. Using a long stick, she poked at the fire, sending a burst of sparks skyward. Her eyes followed the tiny embers as they rose into the night sky. As she did, the tapestry of stars caught her attention. She shuddered when she found the Hunter, the Healer, The Wise One and the Warrior. Perhaps this was the spirits' way of telling her it was time to choose a path – to seek out the slavers, or to seek out Pental.

She aimlessly poked at the fire again, releasing another gout of embers into the darkness.

What am I to do, Gaia? Which path is the one I must choose?

Kit suddenly became aware that she was praying to the earth god, and not Titan, the one true god. When she sought guidance, she turned to the earth mother. When she needed strength, she turned to Titan. She hadn't realized this until that moment – or perhaps it was just a convenient excuse for why she felt the need to commune with Gaia. A rustling to her right, away from the dying embers of their campfire, disrupted her train of thought. The shadow of a hare stood at the edge of the grasses and stared intently at her. The hare stood motionless for several seconds. Its whiskers twitched slightly, and its left ear swiveled toward the darkness, beyond the reach of the fire's light. In the span of a heartbeat, it disappeared in a single bound.

Three sets of jade-green eyes emerged, right where the rabbit had vanished. The sight of them warmed Kit's heart. Under any other circumstance, the sight of a wolf-pack appearing in a camp would have been cause for concern, well, complete terror, really. There was no fear. There was no aggression.

"Thank you for watching over us while we sleep," she whispered to the wolves. In response, one of the wolves laid down at the edge of the camp and curled up into a tight ball. The other two moved off in opposite directions, their dark gray fur blending into their surroundings. Like ghosts, they simply vanished.

Knowing that her group could rest safely, Kit moved to her own bedroll and slipped beneath the coverings. She sighed deeply, relieved that she had finally chosen a path for herself. Pental would wait. For now, she was going to deal with the slavers. If that led her to Pental, all the better. Tucking her arm up under her head, she closed her eyes and drifted off into a much-needed sleep.

CHAPTER TWENTY-THREE

CAVE PAINTINGS

Several small cook-fires were burning merrily as Danny came out from his hut, his new braids dangling down his back and over his shoulders. The tiny beads woven into them tickled his skin as he moved. Even though he had barely slept, he felt good and totally rested. The whiff of coffee drew him to one of the fires where two young Berrat tended to an iron pot extended over the flames. They were, at most, in their early teens. Neither wore any embellishments in their hair, nor did they have any painted whorls. As Danny approached, they both lowered their eyes. "Phoenix," one of them said softly, "may we serve you?"

"The name's Danny," he said with an easy smile. "And if you mean, do I want some coffee, then the answer is a resounding, yes." The two young men nodded briefly. One quickly snatched up a mug while the other ladled the coffee out of the pot.

"It smells very good." The boy held the coffee out to Danny, his eyes still downcast, like he was making an offering. "Don't do that," Danny scolded as he accepted the mug. "Whoever it is you think I am, I'm not. I'm just me."

"You are our salvation," the boy who gave him the coffee replied, finally looking up to meet Danny's eyes. "You are the one who will deliver us from the Crows, and free our people from slavery."

"I'm going to try," Danny said with a shrug. "But it will take all of us to make it happen. This cannot be done by one person."

"It will be you," the other said, not making eye contact at all. "You are the phoenix."

"What's your name?" Danny asked, but the boy stayed silent, staring at the ground. His long, pointed ears brightened.

"He's Bay and I'm Kryn," the bolder of the two boys responded. "Would you like us to get you some food, or will you wait until after we greet Pele?"

"Greet Pele?" Danny asked. "Do you mean after the sun comes up?"

"We greet Pele," the shy boy said, now staring intently at Danny. "The sun god chases Medeina away, shows us the way, and lights our path." There was a small smile now on the boy's face. "He delivers unto us, the phoenix, the harbinger of rebirth."

Danny groaned silently. *These people are bigger zealots than the priests of Titan. Out of the pot and into the fire.* He desperately wanted to tell them they were crazy, but instead he took a long, slow sip of his coffee and stayed quiet. Whatever he might think about these Berrat, these two could make a good pot of coffee.

"He'll wait to break his fast, like the rest of us," Breayn said as she joined the group. She peered over the rim of the pot and raised her eyebrows. "Do you have enough for me?"

"Of course," the young men replied together, instantly squabbling over who was going to get to serve the woman her coffee.

"Nice braids," she said to her cousin, the tiniest hint of a grin on her face. "That must have taken a while. They're very elaborate."

"All night," Danny said with a pout. "When they said they'd keep me warm..."

"You were expecting something different? Something *more*?"

"By the time they'd finished, this," he said waving his hands around his head. "I was already asleep. When I woke up, they were all sleeping." A wistful smile tugged at the corner of his mouth. "But it was very pleasant. I feel like I belong here." He got a far-off look in his eyes. "I enjoyed my time at the Temple. I made many friends. But..."

"It didn't feel like home," Breayn finished his thought. She clearly understood the man's feelings.

"Nice braids," Ryn said with a laugh as he helped himself to the pot of coffee. "Not what you were expecting, I'm guessing." Whatever had been causing Ryn to be surly with Danny, now seemed to have passed. Putting his mug on the ground, Ryn gazed off to the east. The sky was lightening by the second. "Pele will be upon us shortly, to chase Medeina from the sky."

"Arise, Pele," Ulip called out, his deep voice penetrating the entire camp.

"Arise, Pele," the others repeated as they emerged from wherever they had been a few seconds earlier.

As the first rays of the sun broke over the horizon, everyone closed their eyes, tilted their head upwards, and welcomed the morning. The ceremony, such as it was, barely lasted a few seconds. No sooner did the moment pass than everybody filed into the cave.

"Where are they all going?" Danny asked as he drained the last of his coffee.

"To break their fast," Breayn replied, holding her hand out to her cousin. "C'mon, I'll show you the way."

"Stay here," Ryn said, pulling his mate's hand away. "I'll bring your breakfast to you."

"Um, okay," Danny said, a puzzled look on his face. "I'll wait here."

"What is wrong with you?" Breayn questioned. The sharpness in her tongue made Danny cringe. Based on the tone, the conversation was likely going to continue on for a while. As they headed toward the cave, Ryn's hands were flailing about, like he was trying to explain himself, but his mate wasn't having it; not any of it. The camp was empty. Danny frowned when he looked around the area. He was the only one not inside the cave. Helping himself to another mug of coffee, he found a comfortable spot next to a tree. The morning air was crisp, and the deep scent of pine filled his nostrils. He was more than happy to enjoy a few moments of silence. As he closed his eyes his mind drifted back to Aarall, to the Temple, to Kit. His heart ached.

I'm sorry I left you behind, Kit. I hope your sixteenth birthday was everything you could have wished for. I miss talking with you, hearing you laugh. You're the only true friend I've ever had.

"Hey, wake up!" Ryn said, kicking Danny's feet. He held out a plate, a look of expectation on his face. "Eat up, I have something to show you."

Danny took the plate of food, inhaling the wonderful aroma of root vegetables and lightly charred meat. Berries and sliced fruit were intermixed with the cooked fare. He gave Ryn a questioning look. "You didn't spit on this, or anything, did you?"

"And have Breayn separate my head from my neck? No. Your food is fine." Ryn plunked himself down beside Danny and chuckled. "I did have to fight off several others who wanted to *personally* deliver this food to you. You're popular with the boys and girls alike." Danny waggled his eyebrows as he tossed a handful of berries into his mouth.

The two men sat in silence as Danny ate his meal. He let out several appreciative noises as he made his way through the pile of food. "If you ever go to Aarall, you must visit the Temple. Sister Miyuki makes the best breads and sweets I've ever tasted," he commented, tearing off a hunk of bread with his teeth. "But to be fair, this is pretty close."

"Bring your plate with you," Ryn suggested, picking himself up off the ground, brushing the evergreen needles from his leather trousers. "Ulip's going to want to head out soon, and apparently I need to show you this."

"What's *this*?" Danny said, using the last of his bread to mop up the meat juice on his plate.

"Just follow me."

They had barely made it to the entrance when two Berrat children crashed into Danny's legs, snatching his plate from his hand. They were fighting over who was going to get to wash it. "Everyone is very kind," he laughed as the children raced off, still having a tug-o-war over the now twisted piece of tin.

"They think you're our savior," Ryn replied, with that familiar twang of jealousy in his voice. "Even if I think they're wrong."

"I'm your what?" The question got stuck in Danny's throat when he caught sight of a giant mural painted on the cave wall. Even though there were fires burning in the cave to cook meals, the cavern itself was brightly lit. Throughout the walls and ceilings, tiny veins glowed a brilliant green, their light softly pulsating. His eyes were slowly drawn back to the painting. The mural depicted dozens of Berrat, their heads raised, and their arms extended upwards towards a firebird, a phoenix. Beside the art were words written in red script.

And they will cleanse the lands with ice and fire. From the ashes a sword will rise. From the wilds a child will seek the passive, a mighty roar unleash. From the heavens a star will fall, to lay waste to the wicked and break the circle.

"We believe it is the phoenix who will rise from the ashes and be the sword that will cut the bonds of our slavery," Ryn said, his eyes focused on the cave painting. "I expected it would be Breayn, but your arrival suggests I was mistaken. The Crows believe you are the phoenix. It's why they destroyed your village. They are becoming increasingly more desperate to find you."

"I hate prophecies," Danny said with a deep sigh. "*Three will try. Eight shall die. Three will go. Two shall grow. One will lose. One will choose.* This is the prophecy of who is to free Titan. At least, that's what everyone believes." Danny laughed lightly, "But the painting is quite nice. You can worship me if you'd like." Danny blew Ryn a kiss.

"Do that again and I'll knock your teeth out," Ryn seethed and stormed away.

"Holy Helja," Breayn said, punching Danny hard in the shoulder, making him yelp. She had slipped in beside him at some point in his conversation with Ryn. Apparently, he had been too engrossed in the mural to notice. "Just when he was warming up to you, and then you had to do that. Are you broken between the ears? Did they beat you about the head and shoulders daily when you were at the Temple?" She stormed off, following her mate, but not before yelling back over her shoulder. "I can't believe we're related. You're an imbecile."

Chapter Twenty-Four

A Broken Mind

The rich, invigorating scent of coffee roused Kit from what had been a wonderful slumber. There was a deep chill in the morning air, and she wrapped her arm a little tighter around her fury companion. She snuggled her face into his thick warm fur and smiled.

"Good morning, Lump," she whispered.

It took her brain several more seconds before it processed the situation.

Lump is in Aarall. How is he here?

She pulled her head away from the warmth of the fur to find a gray wolf laying next to her, under her bedroll. She didn't know when, but apparently at some point during the night, one of the wolves guarding their camp had shared her bed with her. He stirred slightly as she ran her hand over his soft, fluffy ears. A moment later, the wolf climbed out from under the blanket, dragging it off the girl in the process.

"Thank you," Kit whispered. Giving her a quick nod, the wolf disappeared into the tall grasses towards the north.

The rest of the camp was still fast asleep, except for Mukale who was busy cleaning a stack of trout he had beside him. The sky was gloomy and overcast, resembling a vast sheet of gray. A gust of wind raised goosebumps on Kit's arms. Snatching up the bedroll, she quickly wrapped it around her shoulders and padded over to Mukale and the small campfire.

"That was an interesting friend," the Berrat whispered. "Perhaps that's why you smell of wolf?" Kit shrugged in response, so he changed the subject. "Coffee?"

"Please," she replied, as she eyed the fish. "Thank you for catching us some breakfast."

"We have plenty of supplies, but it's all dried and salted. Good for travel, but not as tasty as fresh food." Mukale carved off a strip of trout and popped it into his mouth. When Kit started to drool, he offered her a strip of the raw fish, which she quickly gobbled down. "Not many people like their fish *fresh*," he commented with a wry smile. "You are a mystery to me, Sister Kit. But I feel you are trustworthy. The wolves do, too, it seems."

"Thank you," Kit replied, bowing her head slightly for the complement. "When are you going to start cooking that fish?"

"I could eat," Lin called from beneath her bedroll. "Is it colder than usual this morning, or is it just me?"

"You're always cold," Treedale laughed as he pulled on his breaches. "Who do I thank for making some coffee. It has never smelled so good to me."

"Ashkey," Treedale said as he gently nudged the boy's shoulder with the toe of his boot. "Time to wake up."

When the young Nomad didn't respond, Treedale groaned lightly and took a knee beside him. He didn't like the boy's pallid complexion. Even with his ear over the boy's mouth, Treedale had to strain to hear his breathing. "Lin, come here, quick! Ashkey doesn't look well."

Lin rushed to their side and shouldered Treedale aside to give herself some space. She placed her hand on Ashkey's forehead, checking for any signs of fever. She gently placed her ear over his heart and held it there for several seconds. "Ashkey," she said, gently shaking his shoulder. After several such attempts, Lin rubbed her brow. "The healing potion should have cured him of any physical injuries. I don't see any signs of infection, or any other reason to explain why he won't stir. I'm worried he's lost his will to live. His heartbeat is weak, and he's barely breathing." She looked to Kit, hoping she had some advice on how to proceed.

"I don't know how to help with this," Kit said as she knelt down beside the group. "I only know how to heal injuries. I can't do anything to help his broken spirit."

"Move aside," said a tiny, but very stern voice. Triss pushed her way past the group. "Give the poor boy some space," she said. Her voice was soft and low, yet still commanding. "Give *me* some space," she continued, pushing the others away from the boy.

The little Sprite moved quickly around the boy, inspecting him from several angles. She placed her paw beneath his nose, checking his breathing. "Feigh, can you find me some Sorrowsage?"

Feigh pursed his lips. "It's going to be difficult to find this time of year, but I will try."

"I will help," Mukale offered. "I don't know the herb well, but if Feigh can tell me the type of ground it likes, I can help locate it." Without another word, the two headed due west. A moment later, Mukale was in horse form and Feigh was riding high on his neck.

While the others searched for the herb, Triss climbed up onto Ashkey's chest. She pulled open his jerkin, exposing his smooth, deeply tanned skin. She placed the palm of her hand across his heart and sung softly, a melody that was both haunting and soothing. Using the claw at the tip of her tiny finger, she traced an intricate pattern on his chest. As she did, her voice became stronger. "Let your troubles go, sweet son of the lands. Let them blow across the plains and o'er the mountains until they are no more. Your journey has just begun, and you must return from the realm of shadows. You have friends and family who love you, and they want to be with you again. Turn from the darkness and return to us."

Kit was holding her breath, waiting for a sign, any sign, that the Sprite might bring the boy back from the brink. She sighed heavily when Triss repeated the words to her song for the third time. Unable to watch any further, she moved back to the fire. Even though there was a stack of fresh fish to eat, she no longer had an appetite.

"What will happen to him?" Treedale whispered to Kit. His voice was thick with emotion.

"Time will tell," Kit said. "I've never seen anybody who has given up on life before. The Temple didn't prepare me for this. We have to trust that Triss knows what she's doing and that Mukale and Feigh will find the herb she sent them for, whatever Sorrowsage is."

"It's a versatile herb," Lin said as she joined the pair. She wrapped her arms around Treedale and hugged him deeply. "It can be used as a reagent to make potions, but it can also be used to make tea. If brewed strongly enough, it can help revitalize one's spirit. I'm going to get some water from the stream. I'll start it boiling just in case they find some." She gave her brother a light kiss on the cheek, grabbed an iron pot, and headed toward the water.

"What are we going to do?" Treedale asked Kit. He ran his fingers across his cheek, rubbing the light stubble growing on his face.

"We'll wait, I guess," she replied, staring into the flames. "Not much more we can do until Feigh and Mukale return."

"No," the young man said, shaking his head. "I mean, after we return to Ashcroft. What will we do then? What's the plan?"

"No plan," Kit said, flopping to the ground, sitting cross-legged before the campfire. She rubbed her eyes, trying to chase away the growing dread spreading through her. She eyed the pile of fish once more. "Not yet anyway. First, we're going to eat and then we're going to return to Ashcroft. Maybe Grams can help heal Ashkey."

"Hasn't that been our plan all along?" Treedale asked. He slowly lowered himself down beside Kit and tilted his head in front of her, trying to get her attention.

Kit didn't bother looking at him; she just nodded. "That part of the plan, such as it is, is unchanged. Once I drop you off at Ashcroft, I'll head back to the Temple. I need to speak with Father Hoarfrost and Captain Harding. If they don't know what's going on at Silverhawk, they will."

"What do you mean, drop us off?" Lin asked, sounding something like a hurt child. She placed the pot of water over the flames, starting the boiling process. "We're coming with you."

Triss was still running her fingers over Ashkey's chest when she chimed in. "Now is not the time for this discussion," she said in a calm, soothing voice. She hopped down from the boy's chest and moved between Kit and Treedale. She kept her voice low and threatening, like a mother speaking to her disobedient children. "Discuss your plans on the way to Ashcroft. That much, we all agree on so far."

Lin was still glaring at Kit, appalled by the thought of being left behind. "I'm coming with you," she growled, "and there is nothing you can do to stop me." She waited for Kit to respond and stormed off when she didn't.

The mouse's eyes locked onto Kit's. "Your friends believe in you, Sister Kit. They will follow you to the gates of Helja if you ask them to."

Kit's brow became creased with worry. The memory of Hoarfrost's tale, about how his friends and family died when they joined him on his quest to free Titan. She rubbed her hands on her thighs and blew out her cheeks. "I will not send them to their deaths," she replied to the Sprite. "I don't want to be responsible for that."

The small mouse gave her a half-smile and moved a bit closer to her. "You don't need to send them anywhere. You are a beacon of hope right now, and they are drawn to your light, to your energy." She gave Kit's hand a gentle squeeze and stared up at her with shiny black eyes. "There is so much darkness, so much despair. I am grateful, not just for what you've done for me, but for what you'll do for our world."

Kit's shoulders slumped and her face went slack at her words. Her breathing became heavy, coming in short, shallow breaths. She scrubbed her hands against her thighs again. Without warning, she popped up to her feet, practically knocking Triss off hers. "I'm going to have some breakfast. Can I get you some coffee and fish?"

Triss wrinkled her nose at the offer. "Thank you, but I don't eat meat. Some coffee would be nice, though."

For whatever reason, her response made Kit smile. She pulled out the smallest tin mug from their gear and poured the Sprite some coffee. The simple act of service chased the dark thoughts from her mind.

"Thank you for helping Ashkey," Kit said as she offered the cup of coffee to Triss. "He seems to respond well to your singing."

The little Sprite accepted the mug and blew on the hot liquid. "It's not going to be enough to heal him, but I can ease his worry somewhat. If my husband can find some Sorrowsage, it will help until we can get him a proper bed and care."

As though on queue, Mukale and Feigh came running into the camp. Mukale was holding a small sack in his hand, and they were both wearing a hopeful look on their faces.

"You look like you've had some success," Triss said as she ran to embrace her husband.

"More than I expected," Feigh replied. "Our young friend here is a remarkably good ranger. I told him what type of conditions would be the best place to find the herb, and he took us right to it. We harvested enough to last a good long while."

Triss took the sack from Mukale and peered inside. Her whiskers twitched as she took a deep sniff of the bag's contents. "This is very high quality," she said, raising her eyebrows to the Berrat. The young man practically blushed at the complement.

The Sprite took a quick sip of her coffee before tossing the remainder onto the ground. She dipped it into the pot of water that Lin had set in the fire, which was already in a heavy, rolling boil. She carefully pulled some of the fuzzy green leaves from the sack and crushed them lightly between her fingers, releasing the oils from within. She dropped the leaves into the boiling water and swirled the cup, turning the water to a deep shade of green. She closed her eyes and murmured some words over the tea.

"Sit the boy up," she said as she moved to his side. She blew gently on the hot tea, cooling it slightly so as not to scald the boy's mouth. It was still steaming heavily, so she continued to blow on it.

"I can cool it down," Kit offered. She said a quick prayer to Titan and her hands became covered with a thin layer of frost. With Triss' consent, she took the tin cup in her hands, immediately lowering the tea's temperature.

"Pour it gently into his mouth, just a few drops at a time," Triss said, motioning to Ashkey. "Keep his head tipped back while you do. Just let it trickle down his throat."

While Treedale propped up the stricken boy, Kit carefully brought the tepid tea to his lips. As instructed, she tilted his head back and slowly poured the liquid into his mouth, just a few drops at a time. The seconds dragged on as the young priest administered the tea. At no point did the boy try to swallow, but none of the tea spilled from his mouth.

"Why is it not helping?" Treedale asked. "Should we make some more?"

Kit turned her attention to Triss, waiting for her response.

"He needs to rest," Triss said. "More tea won't help right now. Enjoy your fish breakfast and I'll stay with him."

"I brought us some breakfast too, my love," Feigh said, holding out another small sack. "Our friend Mukale here also found a winterberry bush as well as some sweetgrass. It's not as good as our patch back home, but it's still very good."

"I love you," Triss replied, her black eyes becoming a bit shinier than normal. "You are the joy of my life."

Kit motioned to Treedale to follow her to the campfire. Lin was already there with Mukale, the two of them working together to finish cooking the fish. As Kit approached, Lin held out a tin plate heaped with barely cooked trout. "I'm coming with you, and that's final."

With a large piece of fish already stuffed into her mouth, she mumbled, covering her mouth with her fingers to prevent any food from escaping, "We'll see."

Only when everyone had eaten their fill did Kit suggest they pack up and head out. With Triss curled up on Ashkey, singing softly to him, Lin and Treedale hoisted the catatonic boy onto a horse. They carefully lashed him to the saddle, to prevent him from slipping off while riding.

"Oh, sweet child of the plains," Triss sang as she traced her fingers over his heart. "Free yourself of your burden and return to us. The past is behind you and there is much life to live."

"I'm sorry I couldn't help you." Ashkey spoke for the first time, his voice breaking. "I wish I had been a better man." The boy cradled the Sprite in his arms, his body quaking. His face was still ashen, and his hands were trembling, but he appeared more aware. "I'll make them pay," he continued, "I'll make them all pay."

Triss was about to try to comfort him, to free him of the guilt, but his eyes glazed over before she could. Without speaking a word, Treedale conveyed his concern to the Sprite, his hand gripping the boy's thigh.

"He'll be okay," Triss said. "But it will take a long time for him to learn how to cope with his ordeal. I will ride with him and do what I can until we reach your village."

"What did he mean, he couldn't help you?" Feigh asked as he moved his horse alongside his wife's.

"He tried to protect me when the men came to torture me. He did his best, but they were too many and too strong for him. They beat him mercilessly for what he did – and then they tied him up and forced him to watch while they tried to compel me to say how to find you." Triss' words were crushing Feigh. His emotions were boiling over, like he was about to fly into a rage.

"Jailer paid for his sins with his life," Kit said as she rode up. "Many more will pay as well. I'll burn them all. I'll burn them and their foul operation to the ground."

Chapter Twenty-Five

Return to Ashcroft

It was late afternoon, and the weather continued to be dull and overcast. Light rain fell periodically, dampening everyone's abysmal mood. Ashkey continued to be nonresponsive, despite Triss' best efforts to comfort him. By the grace of the ropes binding him to his saddle, he managed to stay upright. Unfortunately for the group, it forced them all to move at a slow walk. Nobody had any interest in food, so they pressed on since their morning meal. Mukale, in horse form, ranged ahead of the group, scouting for any potential trouble.

Lin's mood was particularly sour. Each time she locked eyes with Kit's, she'd scowl and move away. After the third such incident, Kit had had enough.

"What is your problem?" She asked as she swatted at a group of gnats that were stinging at her ears and neck. The stiffness in her jaw forced her to speak through clenched teeth. "Are you going to be like this for the entire ride to Ashcroft?"

Lin blew out a forceful breath, her eyes locked onto Kit's while a dozen different responses flashed through her head. "You can't be serious about ditching us. We worked as a team to free my brother and, what, now we're not good enough to stay with you to see this through?"

"No, it's not that," Kit tried to answer by way of an explanation.

Lin's nostrils flared. Her mouth opened, closed, and then opened again. "The only way I'm not coming with you, wherever it is you're going, is if I'm chained up behind a locked door."

"I won't ask you to follow me," Kit replied, her shoulders slumping. "I don't want to be responsible for a friend's death."

Lin nudged her horse close enough to Kit's that she could take the girl's hand in her own. "That's the point, Kit. You don't need to ask. We're going to help you do... whatever it is you want to do." She raised and eyebrow and chuckled lightly. "Do you even have any clue what that is; what you're going to do?"

"Not a clue," Kit replied, giving her friend a warm smile. "I rarely have a plan. I just... move forward." For the first time in many hours, the tension between them melted away.

"It's better than doing nothing," Mukale offered as he ran up alongside of Kit. He had just returned from another foray across the countryside; his coat wet from sweat. "If you're going to move forward, you're going to need a scout, someone to tell you what you're heading into."

"I think Indie's got that covered," Lin interrupted. She purposefully made her eyeballs bulge as she waggled her eyebrows at Kit.

"Nobody asked you," Mukale whinnied. "Besides, you can never have too many scouts."

While Lin and Mukale continued their bickering from either side of Kit, she tried to formulate something in the way of a plan. As she considered all the possible directions she could go, anxiety took hold. "Just stop," she scolded, pressing her forehead into the palm of her hand. "I have no idea what I'm doing, where I'm going, or even if I'm going to let you come with me." Her sudden outburst drew the attention of everybody in their party. Everybody, except Ashkey, who was holding Triss in his arms while she continued singing to him.

Treedale fell back from his lead position, until he was only a horse-length in front of Kit. "Grams can help you with a plan," he offered. "But regardless of what you're going to do, you'll be needing help from people you can trust."

The young priest closed her eyes and sagged in her saddle. With each step of her horse, she rocked back and forth, her thoughts awash with doubt. She absentmindedly rubbed the horn on her saddle, trying to polish off water stains from the rain.

"I know I need help," Kit said, after several minutes of silence. "And I trust you all with my life, but... I just... I don't know if I could deal with my causing the death of a friend."

"We're going to continue this fight," Treedale said, raising his eyebrows. "I'm going to guess that we'll be safer with you than on our own. You'll be safer, too."

Kit rubbed her face, dragging her hand from forehead to chin. "Fine. I'll talk to Grams. We'll see what she has to say."

⚬⚬⚬⚬◈⚬⚬⚬⚬

It had been a long, slow journey, having had to spend a second night camping before arriving at Ashcroft. It was midday when they reached the outskirts of the village and for the third day in a row, the sky was a bleak, monotone gray. The brightly colored homes and tidy gardens out front of each stood in stark contrast to the weather, lifting Kit's spirits, if only a little.

The first house they passed, perhaps a thousand paces from the village proper, had been painted lime green with bright white shutters. The owners, an elderly Nomad couple, who were out front tending to their vegetable garden, paused their work to wave hello to the group as they rode past. The woman, with a long, braided ponytail of silver, was the first to see that Treedale was among them. She threw her hoe to the ground and sprinted as best as she could through the freshly tilled soil to welcome him home.

"Titan be praised," the woman screamed. "He has returned the boy to us! Titan be praised!"

Treedale slipped down from his saddle and gave the woman a warm embrace. Her husband, who was not quite as spry, ambled up to greet the boy as well. "Grams knew you'd be safe. She never lost faith, and neither did we." The man clasped Treedale by the forearm. His grip was weak, but his emotions were strong. "Welcome home, son. Titan be praised."

There was talk of celebrations and suggestions of slaughtering a spring calf to honor Treedale's return, but Lin was able to dissuade the couple from pressing the matter by telling them they were exhausted and, above all else, they needed rest. After much more hugging and well wishes, the group finally left the elderly couple's residence and continued on their way into the village.

"We need to head west and avoid coming in through the thoroughfare," Lin said, looking back at the couple who were still waving frantically, while clutching at their breasts. "If we don't take the backstreets, we won't make it to Grams' before sundown."

Following Lin's advice, the group took a little used road that entered the village from the west. The road was uneven and thick with brambles and clinging vines, perhaps the reason for it being hardly used. Mukale had switched to his natural Berrat form and walked ahead of the horses, scouting for holes that one of the animals might trip in.

When they arrived at Grams' house, they found her tending to her small flower garden in the rear yard. She seemed to have a penchant for day lilies. Her entire garden was thick with their bright yellow flowers, practically a perfect match to the cheery yellow paint that covered her house. Even the straw thatching that covered her roof seemed to be the same sprightly color. With the backdrop of the gray sky, the home reminded Kit of a sunrise seeming to chase away the day's gloom.

The old woman moved slowly, methodically through her garden, using a narrow-bladed knife to cut away any dead leaves or spent blooms. The wrinkles of her brow seemed extra deep, her eyes were deep set and lifeless. She was barely more than two paces from her garden's back gate, but she was oblivious to the group's arrival.

"Grams?" Lin asked, her voice soft. "We're back."

The old woman lifted her head from her task and stared at the door to her house. Her gaze lingered there for several seconds before she discovered that the voice had not come from that direction. Turning towards the back gate, she found the source. The pruning blade dropped from her hand at the sight of her grandchildren. Her mouth was drawn into a wide oh as her hands went to her cheeks. Her previously lifeless brown eyes now sparkled as a sheen of tears threatened to spill down her face.

"Titan be praised," she called out as she bustled towards the back gate. "Into his hands I entrusted my family. My faith in him, rewarded."

Treedale had already dismounted and hopped the gate before the woman had taken three steps. They shared a deep hug for several seconds before breaking apart, giving each other a knowing look and a slight smile.

"I knew you'd save him," Grams said to Kit. "We both did."

Kit dismounted, her legs a bit wobbly from the long ride. "It was a group effort," she said. "It wouldn't have been possible without Mukale, Lin and this wonderful Sprite, Feigh. Your granddaughter is an amazing woman."

"A pleasure to meet you again, Grams." Feigh stayed up on his horse, choosing to stay near Triss and Ashkey. "Truth of the matter is that my actions were primarily self serving. I would have done anything to save my wife. Saving your grandson was, for me, a very happy happenstance."

"Whatever the reason," Grams said, bowing her head to the Sprite, "I'm grateful for whatever role you played in freeing my grandson." Her eyebrows knit together when she spied Triss sitting on Ashkey's lap. The boy was sitting upright, but his appearance was still that of a lost soul. His unblinking eyes stared forward, unaware of what was transpiring around him. She stepped over to his horse and watched him carefully.

"Help him off his saddle and get him inside. Quickly now!" Grams strode purposefully to her back door while Lin and Treedale lifted the broken boy from his perch. Mukale was hot on Grams' heels, explaining the situation and the Sorrowsage tea they had been giving him.

⫷⫸

While the rest of the group entered Grams' house, Kit stayed outside and tended to the horses, making sure they were all fed and watered before she joined them. More than anything else, she wanted to give them all a chance to enjoy their reunion before she pressed Grams for answers to her questions.

As she went about her business, several small children that were playing tag on the weed-infested street came running over to see the horses.

"Lady, can we pet your horses?" a small Nomad girl of maybe six or seven cycles asked, her dark skin invisible under a thick coating of dirt and grime. Her dress, which may have once been green, was now a tattered mass of mud and grass stains. The horse Kit was riding willingly lowered his head to the girl, offering to let her touch her muzzle. Kit smiled and raised an eyebrow at her, telling the girl she could proceed, but to do so with caution. As the girl gently rubbed the soft skin around the horse's nostrils she squealed with delight when the horse huffed, its great long lips flapping with its breath.

The other children were about to clamber around the horses when Kit drew their attention away with two simple words. "Anyone hungry?"

The children stopped what they were doing, their eyes flashing to a tall, lanky Nomad boy of perhaps twelve cycles. His long hair was an un-braided, tangled mass of black, reminding Kit of her own hair on most days.

"We could eat," he replied with a shrug and an easy smile. Although he was not unfed, his face said that he could afford to have a few extra-big meals. The children quickly forgot about the horses and gathered around their leader.

There were two saddle bags still bursting with food, plus several more that were at least half full. It was likely too much for the children to carry. "Are you comfortable around horses?" she asked the boy as she moved the saddlebags to the horse she had been riding. He watched her carefully, taking note of the size of the saddlebags. His mouth dropped open when he spied the contents of a bag whose flap had not been secured.

"I sometimes care for the horses at the livery," he said, wiping his mouth with the back of his hand. "But I haven't ridden a horse since..." The boy's expression turned grim, and he stared down at his feet.

"I'm sorry for your loss," Kit offered, recognizing that look, one that she had seen many times when novices and acolytes at the Temple spoke of the families they no longer had. "I want you to lead this horse up to the orphanage. When you get there, take what food you want for yourself and your friends here. Bring everything else inside for the other children."

"Most of us live at the orphanage," he replied, still eying the bags of food that Kit was tying to the horse. "I'll make sure it all goes to them." Several of the smaller children complained, drawing the immediate ire of their leader. Several of the children wilted under his admonishment, but the small girl in the filthy green dress stayed resolute.

"The lady asked us if we were hungry. I assumed we were going to get something to eat." She crossed her skinny little arms over her chest and stamped on the ground. Kit's horse stamped on the ground in response, eliciting yet another squeal of glee from the child. "See! Even horsey wants us to eat."

Kit rummaged through one of the packs, pulling out a handful of sugary treats. Apparently even thugs had a sweet tooth. She showed them to the group's leader and cocked an eyebrow. The boy rolled his eyes and nodded his head.

"This should keep you busy on the way back to the orphanage," Kit said as she handed out the treats. All the children gladly accepted the gifts, but they all waited patiently for the go-ahead from their leader. The boy sniffed the treat and blinked at it, perhaps in disbelief. He eyed the children, smiled, and took a big bite. In barely a heartbeat, the other children followed suit. The small girl in the filthy dress bit off a small piece and spit it into her hand. Kit's heart melted when she offered the treat to the horse. She squealed for the third time as the horse reached out with its lips and gently lifted it from the girl's outstretched arm. It pawed at the ground as it savored the tiny morsel.

"Take the horse to the orphanage," Kit said to the boy. "When you're done, return the horse here and tie him up with the others."

"Thank you," the children called out in unison as they walked away, the small girl skipping merrily as she followed several paces behind the group. Before they had gotten too far away, the little girl turned, waved, and then scampered to the lead of the pack.

Chapter Twenty-Six

A PLAN OF ATTACK

Hushed voices, deep in discussion, were coming from Gram's sitting area. The tiny kitchen, which contained nothing more than a small cookstove, a butcher-block counter and a pantry, was painted the same cheery yellow as outside. Either this was the only paint that Grams had access to, or she just really loved the color yellow. With a smirk on her face, Kit quickly slipped through the kitchen to find the old woman hovering over Ashkey who was propped up in Grams' comfy sofa. Triss was still on the boy's lap. While she continued singing to him, the soft melody washed over the boy, soothing his tortured soul.

"We were about to send out a search party for you," Lin said. She was sitting at the large rectangular table with Mukale, Treedale, and Feigh who was sitting on a small cushion on top of the table. Kit just shrugged at the comment, saying she needed to take care of the horses and the food.

"He's still there," Grams said as she turned to Kit, "but it will be several moons, if ever, before he's back to normal. You did a good thing bringing him here."

"I'm glad you believe he'll recover," Kit offered as she put her hand on Treedale's shoulder, "but I think it's your grandchildren who deserve the credit."

"Yet another reason why we'll follow you, Sister." Treedale clasped Kit's hand in his own. "But we're going to need a plan, a solid plan."

Ah, yes, a plan. Up until now, her only plan was to get everyone here. She had only a vague notion of what she was going to do next, but she at least had an idea of her goals. She pulled out one of the heavy wooden chairs, its feet scraping along the room's rustic floorboards. Looking like she was carrying the weight of the world on her shoulders, Kit plopped herself down and stared up at the ceiling, which, as it turned out, was also painted yellow.

Closing her eyes and blowing out a deep breath, she verbalized her thoughts. "I believed Pental was the greatest threat to our kingdom. I was prepared to hunt him down and put an end to the divisiveness he's spreading across the lands, but now, I believe the slavers are the greater threat. I don't have a single clue as to how we might bring them down."

Lin perked up at the words. "You said we. Does that mean you'll let us come with you?" Kit opened her eyes long enough to glare at her friend.

Grams took a chair at Lin's side, across the table from Kit. She hooked her arm with her granddaughter's. The old woman had deep, dark circles under her eyes. Perhaps the stress of Treedale's kidnapping had taken its toll on her as well. "Taking down the slavers will be like fighting a hydra," she said, staring intently into Kit's eyes. "The slavers have many heads and knowing which head to strike first is the real challenge."

"She's already taken over the Auctioneers' prime operation at Silverhawk," Treedale said. There was no mistaking the awe in his voice. "I couldn't see what was happening, but I heard it all from inside my cell. She was amazing."

Grams' brow furrowed as she turned her gaze from Treedale to Kit. "Tell me more about this."

Kit had a hard time getting a read on Grams' reaction to her grandson's news, so she simply told the whole story, at least, as she saw it.

Feigh pulled his prize amulet from his pocket. He gave it a wistful look and handed it to Kit. "Since I didn't need to use this to free Triss, I want you to have it. And, I have something else for you." Before Kit could object, Feigh took her hand in his paw. "Triss and I are in your debt. We cannot follow where you are going but know this; we will never forget what you've done for us, and we will come to your aid should you ever need us. I am giving you the mark of the Sprite-kind."

Feigh whispered an incantation, his hands glowing a pale purple color. As the glow intensified, a warmth passed through Kit's body, giving her a pleasant feeling, reminiscent of a hug. When Feigh removed his paws, a light purple insignia was left on the back of Kit's hand. Moments later, it faded away. She didn't fully understand the significance of the act, but it was clearly a gift of great importance.

"Offer your hand to any of my kind. We can see this mark, even if you cannot. You will forever be known as Sprite Friend."

Kit simply blinked at the mouse-sprite. She had no idea how to react to such a gift. "I will do my best to live up to the trust that you have in me."

The little Sprite's eyes went solemn. "I know how much pain you felt, when you struck me – all to save Treedale, my wife, and this young man here. We Sprites, we're deeply sensitive to the emotions of those around us."

The room had fallen silent after the exchange between Feigh and Kit, save for Triss' gentle melody. Grams had carefully watched the interaction; she was stroking Lin's arm while a grin pulled at the corners of her mouth. "You are everything I had hoped you would be and more," she declared. "Walk with me if you will. I have need of some air."

Treedale and Lin quickly stood but Grams slowly shook her head at them. For a moment they both behaved like petulant children denied a desire, but they quietly returned to their places and didn't speak a word. They both drummed their fingers on the table and hung their heads.

<hr />

No sooner had Kit closed the front door, the raised voices of Lin and Treedale could be heard from inside the house. The look of exhaustion on Grams' face had disappeared, replaced with a healthy glow. Her brown eyes were twinkling. "They haven't changed a bit, not in the nearly fifteen cycles they've been in my care. I hope they never change."

"They are good people," Kit replied. "Lin's a bit of a mystery to me if I can be so bold. There is so much more to her than what she shows the world."

"You don't know the half of it, but I trust Lin will share her tale with you, when she's ready to do so." This comment piqued Kit's curiosity, making her desperately want to press the woman for more details.

The two ladies headed through Grams' gardens and out past the front gate. They talked at length, discussing various options Kit might have for approaching the problem set before her. She was reluctant to agree to any plan that might put her friends at risk, but she understood that she was going to need help if she had any chance of achieving her goal. The pair walked aimlessly through the streets; their conversation interrupted repeatedly by villagers offering their sympathy for Treedale's disappearance. At no point did Grams speak of his safe return, fearing they'd monopolize all of their time. They eventually found their way back to Grams' house.

As they walked through the door, Triss was still sitting on Ashkey's lap, singing softly to him. Treedale, Lin, Mukale, and Feigh were all at the table discussing plans of their own. Their voices were raised with excitement, each one shouting over the others as they tried to explain their plan. Finally, Treedale managed to get the point across.

"We need to split up," he practically screamed. The others all nodded their enthusiastic agreement.

Kit gave Grams a knowing smile. "It seems you think exactly the same way as your grandmother." Apparently, her words were a huge compliment; Treedale's face beamed while his chest practically puffed out. "How do you think we should split up?"

Mukale took the opportunity to speak up. "Treedale and I will head for Cormorant. We will gather as much information as we can on the slave trade there. You and Lin will return to Aarall to gather up your friends and supplies. Once you do, head back to Silverhawk. You need to solidify your rule over that group."

Kit and Grams shared a look with each other, as though comparing plans. When Grams nodded to her, Kit turned to Lin. "And you're in agreement with this?"

Lin paused, biting her lip. After a couple of seconds of sitting motionless, she turned her eyes to the ceiling and blew out her cheeks. "It's what makes the most sense. Treedale can't return to Silverhawk, otherwise they'll know something is up. If Cormorant is the hub where the slavers are running their operation, then we've got to know more about what's going on there." Her hand absentmindedly went to her neck. "If we're going to be fighting vampires, we're going to need Indie and the boys."

"I guess we didn't need to make plans of our own," Kit said to Grams with a laugh. "We basically fell on the same decisions."

"Except, this was their decision – not yours," Grams responded, cocking her head to the side. "What perils may befall them will be a result of their choices, not yours." Kit's expression turned flat; her lips drawn into a tight line.

"You took me away so that I wouldn't be a part of the planning. You expected they'd do this, come up with something similar to our own plans." Grams blinked slowly, her eyebrows lifting ever so slightly.

"I have no clue what you mean." She turned her palms upward; her eyes widening. "It does look like it turned out well though. They made a plan, on their own, relieving you of the burden of asking them to help you."

"She would never need to ask for our help," Lin added, her eyes were shinier than usual.

Mukale tapped his finger on the map they had spread out across the table. "This is where we will rendezvous in seven days' time. We will look for you at sunset."

Kit contemplated the timeline. Seven days didn't provide much in the way of wiggle room, especially if things went sideways on them. Everyone, Grams included, seemed to be holding their collective breaths, waiting for the young priest's reaction. Finally, she clasped her hands together and nodded in agreement.

"We have no time to lose then. Lin, I'll get our horses ready to go. You can say bye to your family."

"Before you leave, I should explain how my pendant works." Feigh stretched out his hands, waiting for Kit to return it to him. Just as when he wanted to use it to free Triss, his hands were convulsing, waiting the return of the amulet.

Kit reached into her pocket and pulled out the tiny necklace. "No need," she said with a wry smile. "I want you to take it back." The little Sprite wrung his hands together, a tiny twitch in his right eye. Whatever his connection was to this amulet, it ran deep. "You said that if I need your help, you'll come." Feigh was now nodding furiously. "So, if I need you, can you use this to come find me?" Feigh continued to nod, his eyes never leaving the amulet. "Then it's settled," Kit declared as she tossed the amulet back to him.

As soon as the amulet was in his hands, Feigh laughed weakly. Even beneath his fur, his face and neck visibly reddened. He gawped down at the delicate piece of jewelry in his hands. His body slumped. "I... I don't know what just came over me. As soon as you offered it, something inside, something I can't explain, cried out to me, telling me to take it."

"No explanation necessary," Kit said with a warm smile. "I am in your debt. What you did for us in Silverhawk, well, may have been to help free Triss, but by your actions, you also ensured that many more will never *need* to be freed." Kit's smile broadened even further. "Proving that you don't need to be big to do great things."

Mukale's chest puffed out as he considered her words.

Not wanting to get caught up in further conversation, Kit nodded briskly and headed for the back door. Grams, showing surprising speed, cut her off and wrapped her arms around the girl. The old woman had a musky fragrance, with a hint of winterberry, the same scent that Sister Miyuki liked to wear.

"You will succeed," the old woman whispered. "In my heart, I know you will. Your journey may be fraught with danger but know this; I trust you are on the right path. Evil times lie ahead. I only hope that I will live long enough to see the woman you will become."

A weight suddenly grew in the pit of Kit's stomach. She tried to pull away from the woman's embrace, but she tightened her grip all the more. "Go now,"

Grams whispered, "lay waste to the wicked, bring your judgment upon the world."

The weight in her belly only got worse.

"Lin, I'll meet you out back. Take as much time as you need." Kit averted her eyes as she sped out the back door and through the garden. The horses, including the one she had given to the orphan boy, were tied up where she had left them. She didn't really have anything to do, to prepare to leave, but she busied herself with her horse's tack until Lin joined her.

"Grams can be a bit... intense," Lin offered as she stepped through the gate. "She believes in you, and so do I."

"Please, don't," Kit said, dipping her chin to her chest. "I would do anything to not have this burden. I didn't ask for it."

"It might be your burden to bear, but you have friends to help lighten the load." Kit nodded weakly. She set her foot in her stirrup and lifted herself into her saddle.

"Very soon, the sun is going to set on this day. What do you say we start heading back?" Kit dug her heels into her horse's ribs and started the journey back to Aarall at a light canter. The wind in her hair brightened her mood slightly.

CHAPTER TWENTY-SEVEN

THE NOBILIS AFFAIR

"House Nobilis uniforms," Danny declared. "We get some of their uniforms, kill some Crows, and plant some evidence that they were killed by the Ravenlord people."

"House Nobilis is made up of humans," Ryn replied, continuing his objections to Danny's plans. "They'll be too big for any of us to wear." He cocked his thumb towards Ulip. "And much too small for the big guy here."

"We don't need people to be wearing the uniforms," Breayn replied, scratching out a map of the area with a stick. "We just need to leave pieces of the uniforms. Enough that the Crows will think they were killed by Nobilis soldiers."

"Dead bodies would be better," Ulip said in his sonorous voice, clearly not liking the subtle approach.

"Humans, even Nomads, are hard to find this far north," Ryn offered, "unless we go to Mishal Crags."

"Dragon country?" Breayn raised her eyebrows at her mate's suggestion.

"The only humans there are dragon-hearts, those loyal to the Dragon Lords," Ulip growled. "Crossing them will only serve to make enemies of them. We do not need another enemy."

"Lilloet is too far away," Ryn said. "The journey would take too long."

"Lilloet?" Danny asked. "That's a Berrat city. My friend Kit is from there. Why are there humans there?"

"It was a Berrat city until six moons ago," Ryn shot back, happy to rub his knowledge of the kingdom in Danny's face. "Lord Damil Byssus used to be the ruler of Wantage, but his cruelty to the slaves was too much, even for the Auctioneers. But he had provided so much wealth to the city that they chose to exile him, rather than kill him outright. When he left, he took much of his personal wealth, and his army, to Lilloet. He overran the city is less than a day."

Not good. Not good at all. I promise, Kit, once I deal with the Crows, I'll find a way to return Lilloet to its people.

"Danny?" Breayn asked. "You have a strange look on your face."

"Sorry, I was just making a promise to a friend." When he saw how they were all staring at him, he waved it away. "Who are the Auctioneers?" The question drew a dumbfounded look from the entire lot, Ryn in particular.

"The Auctioneer houses run the slave trade across all of Berrathia. Gaia save us, they practically run the entire kingdom." He ran his hand over his bone-white braids. "How can you possibly not know this?" Danny wanted to try to defend his ignorance, but he feared he would only make matters worse. The Temple didn't teach them much about the other kingdoms. In fact, the Temple practically never mentioned Berrathia at all, other than to say it was the birthplace of Fenrir and Ymir.

"So, we want people in uniforms, and not just empty uniforms." He gave them all a weak grin and a shrug.

"Maybe we're going about this backwards," Breayn suggested, a hint of optimism in her voice. "We've got the right idea, but instead of making the Crows think Nobilis is attacking them, we turn it around. Make Nobilis think the Crows are attempting a coup, like they are trying to seize power for themselves."

"We can get plenty of Crow uniforms," Ryn chuckled, "but we're too far away from Ravenlord. It will take many days for us to walk there."

"What about Lilloet?" Danny asked. "How long to travel there?"

"On foot?" Ryn asked. "About the same. It's closer, but the terrain is much more difficult."

"We could fly to Ravenlord in a few hours," Breayn said cautiously, knowing that Ryn was going to object.

"That would leave Ulip behind," Ryn said. He did object but the quizzical look on Breayn's face suggested he was taking a sideways approach.

"You two can shift into something big enough to carry people while flying?" Danny asked, unable to mask his surprise.

Ryn's face turned beet red as his shoulders crept up towards his ears. He was about to explode until Breayn took his hand, the calming effect instantaneous.

"Ryn has bound with the spirit of a great hawk," Breayn said, a loving smile on her face. "I have bound with an air elemental." Danny's jaw popped open. "But to fully take its form is... taxing on me."

"It wasn't just *any* air elemental," Ryn said, his eyes never leaving Breayn's.

"She bound with Boreas," Ulip stated, "the north wind."

"Yes, my loving mate bound herself to the north wind, and now she spends every moment of her life keeping the retched creature from consuming her."

"You would have died," Breayn said, her eyes still locked on Ryn's. "If you had, I'd have died, too."

"He tried to steal you from me!" Ryn pulled his hand away. The two glared at each other for several moments before Ulip broke the stalemate.

"Boreas wanted Breayn for his mate," Ulip gave Ryn a nod of approval. "And this skinny little guy challenged him to a duel, to the death. Before Boreas could accept the challenge, Breayn bound herself to him."

"Holy Helja!" Danny exclaimed, his jaw dropping a little further. "You bound yourself to a full elemental, the actual North Wind? Are you completely insane?"

"I have him under control," Breayn said, trying her best to appear confident. "He will never take control of me." When Ryn walked away, Breayn gave chase, grabbing him by the arm. "You can bear me to Lilloet. I won't take his form."

"I will see if a fire drake will bear me," Ulip said. "Go ahead without me. If I can make it there, I will."

"His clan lived with the fire drakes," Ryn interjected, seeing the look of confusion on Danny's face. "But they don't ride them."

"One of them might be willing to bear me," Ulip said, his voice a bit sullen. "After what the slavers did to our clan, they may be willing to help."

"So, we're all good with this plan?" Breayn asked.

"How are we going to bring the humans back?" Danny asked, not exactly clear on what they were hoping to accomplish.

"We don't need to," Breayn said. "We go in with Crow uniforms, kill off as many scout forces as we can. But we need to make sure some escape, to tell the tale of how the Crows attacked them."

"Time to hunt some Crow?" Danny asked, eliciting a wide smile from Ulip.

"Hunting Crows always cheers me up," the giant said. The glee on his face fell away when Danny shook his head, his braids jangling about as he did.

"Don't you need to get yourself a mount?" Ulip's face crumpled at the question.

"He can visit the fire drakes after we get enough Crow uniforms," Breayn suggested. "Just make sure you don't hack their cloaks in two. We need them for our plan." A deep, throaty chuckle rolled out of Ulip's chest. For a pacifist, he sure did enjoy killing Crow.

CHAPTER TWENTY-EIGHT

HIGHWAYMEN

The sky, which had been a solid mass of gray for the past few days, was showing signs of worsening. Dark clouds were coming in from the east. They hung thick and gray over Two Peaks, Arnnor's capital city. With any luck, the fell weather would cling to the mountaintops long enough for the pair to make the journey home without getting soaked. By the time they had reached the king's road that would take them to Aarall, Lin seemed to be forever tugging at her hair, her head on a swivel as she struggled to find a comfortable position in her saddle.

"If we stick to the roads, we should be back at the city before dark," she offered. There was something odd in her voice. She cleared her throat, trying to mask her worry. "If we hurry, we can make sure we're not out after nightfall."

"It's not really a big deal," Kit said with a grin, patting her battle hammer. "You've given me an ever-lasting lantern." Lin pursed her lips. Her shoulders seemed to be creeping up to the bottoms of her ears. Her behavior was perplexing.

"You know, you've got me to protect you – not that you really need it. I've seen you using those enchanted swords of yours."

When the look of concern on Lin's face didn't disappear, Kit shrugged and urged her horse into a full gallop. Within a few minutes, they were outside the village's perimeter and on their way home.

As they headed northwest towards Aarall, Lin's eyes were forever darting about, scanning the countryside. Her normally bubbly personality and incessant questions were nowhere to be seen. The way she was fidgeting, her pants may have been filled with fire-ants.

"What's up with you, Lin?" Kit asked. She had never seen Lin like this before. Lin practically jumped out of her saddle.

"Nothing," she said, her head snapping back. "It's just, well, you know... highwaymen."

"Highwaymen?" Kit practically snorted as she laughed out the word. "Where did you ever hear such a thing?"

Lin slowed her horse down to a walk. "The quartermaster had mentioned it. Apparently, bandits have been raiding caravans along these southern roads." Kit shook her head and dug her heels into her horse.

"I doubt there are bandits," she called out over her shoulder, "but those clouds are real enough, and I don't want to ride in the rain."

The skies continued to darken, and a brisk wind blew at their backs. After about a half hour the road entered into a section of heavy forest. The sun, what little there was of it, was now low in the sky, casting heavy shadows across the road as they entered the trees. It was considerably darker there, under the canopy of great oaks and tall, white-barked aspens. Lin's eyes continued to dart about as she hunkered low in her saddle. Kit smiled inwardly, finding Lin's apprehension more than a little amusing.

The amusement ended abruptly when they came upon the remains of a battle. Kit pulled hard on the reins, slowing her horse to a walk.

"Sweet Titan," she exclaimed as she hopped down from her saddle, rushing to the side of a soldier laying face down on the road. He was wearing a surcoat of green and gold, with an emblem depicting a single golden shield. The decorative embellishment did little to stop the two arrows that protruded from the middle of his back. A third arrow was embedded at the base of his skull. Several feet away another man dressed in the same green and gold had met with a similar fate. The dead soldier's skin still had a hint of warmth to it, even though he had already passed to the Great Cycle.

"I told you," Lin said, her voice shaky. "I told you there were highwaymen, but you wouldn't believe me. Do you believe me now?"

Kit glared back at Lin who was still mounted on her horse. Even in the dim light of the forest Kit could see that her face was ashen. "Lin!" she barked at her. "Get over here and help me check out these soldiers." Lin's eyes went vacant as she shook her head.

"Lin!" Kit screamed this time. "Get over here! Now!"

As Lin slowly dismounted, a man lying off to the side of the road, partially covered in leaf-litter, moaned out. Forgetting about Lin and her worries, Kit rushed to the side of the injured soldier. He had a gaping wound in his belly, visible through his chainmail shirt. As Kit approached, the man coughed, spraying blood in all directions. She placed her hands across the wound in an attempt to slow the bleeding. Like the others, he too was dressed in green and gold.

"Martelle!" Lin shrieked as she hovered over Kit's shoulder. "Kit, we can't let him die!" The woman's voice was frantic as she knelt down beside the man. She took his hand in hers as she started muttering a spell. She spoke the words so low that Kit couldn't hear them, but she was stuttering badly, her body trembling. She seemed to have restarted several times before she finally gave Kit a pathetic, pleading look.

Understanding, Kit gently pushed her out of the way and called upon Titan's grace.

"Titan, hear me!"

Before she even had a chance to say her prayer to call for her god's help, Kit's hands took on a pale golden aura. The aura spread from her hands across the soldier's abdomen, radiating outward until the dull, golden haze engulfed his body entirely. The light around Kit's hands and the man's wounds pulsated, the color becoming a brighter, more intense shade of gold. A sharp, stabbing pain ripped through Kit's stomach, causing her to buckle over. At no point, however, did she break contact with the man. Sweat dripped down the nape of her neck. She squeezed her eyes tight, trying to maintain consciousness as a sharp pain ripped through her.

Sweet Titan, what are you doing to me?

Just when she thought she could bear no more, the pain subsided.

The man's eyes fluttered open. He seemed to have trouble focusing. He did not look like a soldier. His face, even though it was filthy, was full and clean shaven. His long black hair was oiled and braided with precision. A well-practiced smile appeared. "I've been saved by an angel," he said, his voice smooth and resonant.

Kit shook her head and glared at him. "I am no angel, nor did I save you. It was the will of Titan that you were to return to the land of the living. Today was not your day to die." The man turned his gaze away from Kit.

"Is it you I have to thank, Sister Lin?" Kit's eyebrows shot skyward as she gazed at her cohort. She couldn't get a read on Lin's reaction. Her frozen expression seemed to be a mixture of fear and relief.

"Martelle, what are you doing here?" her voice cracked as she asked the question. "Why aren't you in Two Peaks?"

"You two can catch up with each other later," Kit growled. "How long ago were you attacked?"

Martelle shook his head, "Not long, I don't think." His hands were searching for the rent in his armor, his fingers probing through the splintered rings of chainmail, looking for the grievous wound he had suffered.

"Can you travel?" Kit asked.

As Martelle was about to move, Lin pressed her hand across his chest, pushing him back down to the ground. "No, he can't!" Her voice came out shrill, panicked. Her breaths were coming too quickly, her eyes clenched tight. "He's not well enough to travel."

"Sister Lin," Martelle objected. "You have healed me fully. I'm okay." Martelle pushed her aside and hopped to his feet, as though to prove the point. All the while Kit stared at Lin; her head tilted to the side as she tried to figure out what had gotten into her friend.

"I don't know what's up with you, Lin, but we need to catch up with whoever did this to him." Kit was saddled up by the time she finished the sentence. Not even bothering to wait for a reply, she pushed her horse into a hard gallop. The attack had happened recently, and the culprits might be nearby.

As Kit drove her horse along the ever-darkening road, she spied a group of soldiers on horseback ahead in the distance. They, too, were running, but they weren't pushing their horses nearly as hard. As she neared, eight riders came into view. Even from a distance, in the dying light of the day, she could see they were well armed and armored. Unlike Martelle and the other dead soldiers, they wore dark surcoats which helped them blend in with the ever-deepening shadows.

I shouldn't have left the others behind.

She quickly shook off the idea. Even if they were with her, they wouldn't be able to take on such a large contingent of soldiers, but... her ruminations were cut off when a caravan of wagons came into view further up the road.

The caravan had six guards around it: two were up front, two more were behind and one flanked each side. They wore the same green and gold surcoats as Martelle and the other fallen soldiers. As the riders approached, the caravan slowed to a halt. The soldiers from both parties seemed to know one another. The caravan guards greeted the newcomers enthusiastically.

Not wanting to give herself away, Kit guided her horse off the road and into the trees. After quickly looping the reins over a low branch, she crept through the forest's shadows, trying desperately not to signal her position by stepping on fallen, brittle branches. From her new vantage point, she could see little of what was transpiring, but based on the voices, their mood was jovial. A fallen tree, it's girth nearly as wide as Kit was tall, blocked her progress. She feared she would expose herself, should she climb over it, but there didn't appear to be enough room to squeeze under it. It was at least one hundred feet in length, which would take her too far from her quarry. With no better option, she took hold of the tree's thickly scaled bark and clambered up the trunk. Keeping her tiny body as low as possible, she climbed to the top of the log. From this position, she had an excellent vantage point from which to observe the goings on. She was less than a stone's throw away from the caravan now, and even in the failing light, she had a decent view. Her eyes widened as the jovial conversations changed to angry shouts. The caravan guards became suddenly uneasy in their saddles. While their horses retreated their eyes searched the treeline. Kit's heart rate increased rapidly as she pressed her body low against the tree, fearful that, somehow, the guards had spotted her. She struggled to keep her breathing under control.

The twang of bowstrings broke the uneasy silence. Screams of pain and panic echoed through the forest. Several of the caravan guards fell from their horses while others threw themselves to the ground in an attempt to find cover. The wagon driver was the next to fall. Arrows sank into his body with sickening wet thuds. The draft horses whinnied and reared, perhaps sensing the death of the man controlling them. A soldier quickly grabbed the reins of the wagon-team before they could bolt.

Shouts were now coming from all directions. The soldiers in black waved their swords over their heads and yelled into the surrounding forest. In the mayhem, Kit couldn't make out what they were saying, but the missile attacks died off immediately. With deadly intent, the soldiers slipped down from their mounts and made their way to the guards cowering beneath the wagon. When one of those hiding was dragged out and executed, the others scrambled to escape out the other side of the wagon, only to meet a similar fate. The soldiers then methodically worked their way through the guards that had been felled by arrows. Without remorse, they slid their longswords into the throat of each guard, ensuring a speedy journey to the Great Cycle.

Bile rose up in Kit's throat. These poor people were being massacred and there was little she could do about it.

"We had an agreement!" a woman shouted, as she stepped from a fine carriage at the front of the caravan. She was dressed in a ridiculous, yellow ballgown covered in white lace. Her bearing and mannerisms identified her as a woman of significant means, comfortable speaking down to those around her.

"What are you doing? Have you completely lost your minds?" screamed a second woman, dressed identically to the first. Her arms flailed about as she gaped at the mass of dead bodies that surrounded their wagon. She wheeled around to the largest of the soldiers, pointing her condescending finger at his face. "You've been paid in full. We were guaranteed safe passage!"

The soldier simply laughed at the women's outrage. With his bloodied sword in hand, he strode over to her. He was head and shoulders taller than the woman, but she didn't flinch. With her nose turned up and her chin jutted out she continued to challenge him. She was about to berate him again, when a swift swing of the man's blade abruptly ended the conversation. Her head fell to the ground while her still standing body wobbled. A moment later, it fell in a heap next to her severed pate. The first woman, her eyes wide and her hands clamped over her mouth, stared down at the carnage in disbelief. She never had a chance to speak. The same soldier smoothly ran his blade through her chest. The woman stared up at the man with unseeing eyes, perhaps wondering how her well-to-do life had taken such a turn.

"Not the way you expected this to go," he laughed. He put his meaty hand over her face and pushed her away. Her body slid from his blade, falling on top of the headless woman's corpse.

Kit shuddered. The callous cruelty of the soldier reminded her of the disconnected coldness Pental had displayed at Templeton. This man's utter disregard for the lives he had taken made Kit want to retch. Her hands quaked as her fingers dug into the bark.

Using the skirt of a dead woman, the butcher wiped his blade clean and slid his sword into its scabbard. While the other soldiers gathered the dead, he stalked to the front of the women's carriage and calmly unhitched the horses. He displayed far more concern for the beasts than he had for the people who'd been with them.

"Lieutenant," one of the men called out. "What do we do with the bodies?"

"Leave them," he responded with a dismissive wave, "the wolves will look after them for us. But strip them first." The lieutenant cast a spell, hurling a fireball at the carriage. It immediately burst into flames, lighting the area with dancing orange and yellow light. "Throw the street rats' uniforms onto the fire!"

A shiver ran up Kit's spine. That phrase. The man's voice seemed so familiar to her. He pulled off his dark surcoat and tossed it onto the burning carriage, exposing the City Watch armor he was wearing. As he turned, a burst of flames lit up his face. Kit sucked in a gasp. *Karr!*

For the next few minutes Kit's brain raced as she tried to process everything she had just witnessed. A half dozen hard-faced archers emerged from the forest.

They too were wearing City Watch uniforms. From their place of cover, they had no need to hide their allegiance. With military precision, they joined their cohorts, took control of the wagons, and quickly started making their way towards Aarall.

No longer concerned about making noise, Kit leapt down from her roost and bolted through the forest to where she had tied up her horse. Her fingers fumbled as she tried to quickly free the reins and mount up. She was about to kick the horse into a run when a thought struck her. What if there were more archers hiding in the woods, ready to eliminate anybody who happened to wander too close?

As she contemplated her next move, the forest was steadily getting darker. The clopping of hooves along the road forced her back into the trees. She silently pulled her hammer from its sheath and made ready for battle. From the relative safety of her position, she watched as a single horse with two riders passed by.

"Lin!" she called out, trying to be loud enough to be heard, while still keeping her voice hushed. When Lin continued down the road, she had no choice but to come out of hiding. As soon as her horse broke out of the forest, Lin and Martelle both dismounted and drew their weapons.

"Are you planning on using those on me?" Kit asked, her voice a deadly threat, as she slid down from her saddle. "You two have a lot of explaining to do."

Lin immediately sheathed her longsword. "Give me that," she said to Martelle, demanding the return of her second blade.

"What just happened?" Kit asked as she ignited the light of her battle hammer. With her horse in tow, she marched steadily towards the pair, the light from her hammer illuminating the lethal scowl on her face.

"It was a double-cross!" Martelle blurted out as he moved behind Lin. He was no soldier. Based on his willingness to use a woman as a shield, he was also a poor excuse of a man. "Nobody was supposed to die!" he wailed, clutching onto Lin's shoulder.

Lin dropped to her knees, sat back on her heels, and buried her face in her hands. Martelle, now fully exposed, seemed unsure of what to do. His eyes darted to the forest, ready to make a run for the trees.

"Explain!" Kit snarled, as her eyes flashed golden. Martelle took several steps backward, trying to put some distance between himself and Kit. As he did, he caught his heel and fell hard onto his backside. He immediately started crab-walking, using both his hands and feet in an attempt to move away from the hammer-wielding woman bearing down on him.

"Explain!" Kit snarled again, her voice reverberating off the trees, making it seem like the entire forest was making the same demand.

"It's my fault," Lin choked out. "The shipment is from my parents."

Kit wheeled away from Martelle, focusing her ire on the woman she considered to be her friend.

"Explain!" Kit screamed at her.

"The Moreden twins," Lin screamed back in response, as though invoking their name would have some meaning to Kit. The name did in fact sound familiar, but Kit didn't take any time to consider it.

"Explain!" she demanded, yet again. As she screamed the word, the light from her battle hammer erupted so brightly that it illuminated the entire area. The trees seemed to close in on the group, their branches looming overhead. Kit's face appeared pale in the hammer's luminescence, her eyes alight with fury, the red streak in her hair ablaze.

Lin pulled her face from her hands, her eyes glassy and red. She wrapped her arms tightly around her chest. "The shipment is from my parents. They're undercutting all the local merchants. The Moreden twins are the primary supplier of weapons to the Watch. I told them that my parents had a shipment coming in and if it arrived at the city, the Watch would likely cease dealing with them. My parents sell quality equipment, but their prices are so low – they have to be getting them illegally." As soon as she finished speaking, Lin buried her face in her hands once more.

"What happened?" Kit screamed at Martelle, causing him to curl into a fetal position. "Tell me everything you know, or, so help me, Titan, I'll send you to the Great Cycle right now."

"They double crossed us!" the man whimpered, still curled up in a ball. "They were to come in a show of force, and just take the weapons. But when the Moreden sisters showed up, their men killed everyone."

"I don't understand," Kit stammered. What appeared to be outright murder was much more complicated.

Hearing Kit's voice waver, Martelle finally pulled his arms away from covering his face. "Lin told the Moreden twins when we'd arrive. They were just supposed to show up with a large number of soldiers, and we'd surrender. I'm no soldier, I'm just one of Lin's friends. Her father is a greedy monster, and she didn't want him to profit from Aarall's problems."

"He wasn't supposed to be here." Lin finally spoke up. "Father's guards are as horrible and cruel as he is. I didn't care if they were murdered, but none of this was supposed to happen." Lin picked herself up off the ground and walked over to Kit, her eyes never leaving her feet. "The Moreden twins said they'd give me everything they took from my father's shipment. With it, I'd finally be able to open my own shop. I could be a full-time enchanter."

Kit's head snapped back, as her eyebrows shot up. She rubbed her eyes and shook her head, as she wondered who this person was; the girl she believed to be her friend.

"You did this for gold?" the words came out like an accusation.

"No!" Lin screeched back. Her hands were clenched into tight fists by her side. She stood, staring, for several moments before her shoulders slumped. "Well, not exactly." Her mouth opened and closed soundlessly, like a fish out of water. She threw her hands in the air, exasperated as her words failed her.

"I was never going to be a priest. I couldn't stay at the Temple any longer. When I found out my father was sending a shipment to Aarall, I thought I could use it to get out of the situation I am in. Pretending to be something I'm not." Lin's face crumpled, and she quickly averted her eyes. "It was crushing my soul."

"You were already out," Kit said shaking her head. "I was going to take you with me."

"This plan was in motion long before I met you, Kit. There was no way for me to stop it. Nobody was supposed to get hurt." Lin's eyes were again wide and glassy. "Please, forgive me, Sister."

The information was coming faster than Kit could process it. The tormented look on her friend's face was breaking her heart. She could *feel* that she was telling her the truth; there was no attempt at deception in her words. Kit didn't understand how she knew that, but every ounce of her being was telling her that Lin was speaking true.

"I don't know what to do," Kit mumbled, shaking her head. "I'm taking you both to see Father Hoarfrost. He will decide your fate."

"You're not taking us to see Captain Harding?" Lin asked. The way she posed the question, Kit couldn't tell if she was happy or disappointed with her decision.

"Give me your weapons, all of them," Kit demanded, holding out her empty hand. When Lin gave her a questioning look, Kit's face hardened. "Now!" she growled. "Don't make me ask again."

The tiny muscles in Lin's jaw twitched, her eyes hardened. Whatever internal conflict she was having with Kit's order fell away. Her face went slack, her eyes vacant. She slowly unbuckled her twin scabbards and let her swords fall to the ground at her feet. She then pulled her dagger from her hip, flipped it in her hand so that she was holding the blade by its tip, and presented the handle to Kit.

Kit's gaze never left Lin's eyes. She accepted the dagger and sheathed it in her belt. "Your blades," she demanded, her eyebrows raised. "Pick them up by the belt and hand them to me." When Lin complied, Kit threw the belt over her shoulder. "Now, saddle up and let's get going. If you travel at anything faster than a steady canter, your lives are forfeit."

Tears were flowing freely down Lin's cheeks. "I'm sorry I disappointed you, Kit. I swear on Grams' life that I did not intend for this to happen. Not like this." Kit simply stared at the woman, letting her words wash over her. "We'll go straight to see Father Hoarfrost. I will accept his judgment, whatever that might be." Martelle, who was still lying in a cowering ball on the road, nodded at Lin's words.

Chapter Twenty-Nine

The Bastard Son

The three rode in silence until they reached the outskirts of Aarall. Not wanting to draw attention to themselves, Kit extinguished the light of her hammer. With the sky shrouded by a heavy bank of angry clouds, the party fell into darkness. The tiny lights of torches lit the ramparts of the city's great gray-green walls, although, with the absence of light, they appeared as pitch black. A series of braziers marked the entrance to the city's main gate. The silhouettes of guards ambled about, while many more bodies remained unseen in the deep shadows.

There was little in the way of activity in the marketplace, other than a few remaining vendors who were buckling down their tents and packing up their wagons for their return home. Outside of a wary eye, the vendors paid them little heed. They were intent on packing up and heading home, knowing they'd have scant few hours to sleep and spend time with their families before loading up and heading back for the morning shoppers.

"Why did you call Lin, *Sister*?" Kit finally asked Martelle. Lin groaned loudly, dipping her chin to her chest.

"Because that's what she is, a priest of Titan," he replied, looking at Kit like she had lost her mind.

Kit was about to speak again, but Lin interrupted. "My parents have been telling everyone that I am a full priest. They can't bear the reality of their daughter being a wash-out."

"You're not a priest?" Martelle asked, seeming more than a little shocked at the revelation. "Your parents held a huge celebration five cycles ago, announcing your position in the Temple."

"I know," Lin practically screamed at her friend. "I didn't ask for it and I can't undo it."

"You could have set the record straight," Kit admonished her. It seemed that with every passing minute, something new and disturbing about her friend was coming to light. Life in the Temple was hard, but real life, the things that happened outside its granite walls, were complicated. Kit preferred hard to complicated.

"And how would you propose I should have done that?" Lin's voice was full of sarcasm. "Should I have told Hoarfrost that I needed some personal leave to travel to Two Peaks, so that I could say I'm a failure, that I'm not a priest like my parents had said."

Kit stared at Lin, wondering how to respond to what she'd said. Her ruminations were disturbed when one of the guards at the gate questioned who they were, and what business they had in the city at this late hour. His questioning came to an abrupt halt when Kit glared at him, looking like she was ready to remove his head from his shoulders.

"What's the problem, Corporal?" asked the lanky guard with short-cropped blonde hair.

"This person doesn't like that I asked her to state her business in the city," the guard said, snapping to attention.

"Do you always make a habit of questioning priests when they return to the city?"

"Priests?" The guard took a step back and lowered his eyes. "I'm sorry, Sister, I..."

"Be at peace," Kit responded, giving the corporal's superior a curt nod. "I am on my way to the Temple. My business there is my own. I plan to stop by the Watch barracks to speak with your captain. Do you have any *additional* questions for me?"

The guard made a weak, squeaking sort of noise, before waving the party through.

As they entered the city, Kit steered her horse towards the Watch barracks. There were four guards posted outside the compound. They were dressed in heavy plate armor, carrying long spears. They all snapped to attention in perfect unison as Kit approached. "No entry after sundown," one of the guards declared. At his words, six more guards appeared on the ramparts at either side of the gate, arrows nocked and drawn.

"Idiot," another guard whispered to the man blocking Kit's approach. "That's Sister Standing Bear."

"Sorry, Sister, I didn't recognize you," the first blurted out, trying to recant his original protestations. "How can we serve you?"

This would have been the sort of thing that would have made Kit laugh out loud, but instead she just scowled at the guard. "I want this man held until I return."

"Take him to the dungeon," the first guard said quickly as two others moved to take Martelle down from his horse. Lin's friend gripped the horn of his saddle, his eyes darting about. There was no escape for him. He whimpered yet again as the guards pulled him from his perch. The man was pathetic.

"Just keep him in the gatehouse for now. His fate has not yet been determined." Kit smiled inwardly as she pictured him being thrown in the dungeon, but she needed time to think about what to do next.

"As you wish," the guard nodded. He motioned for the other three guards to take Martelle into custody. The man's eyes locked on to Lin's, pleading for her to help him. She flinched slightly and turned away.

Without another word, Kit wheeled her horse around and trotted off toward the Temple. She did a quick shoulder check to make sure Lin was following. The two ladies rode in silence for several minutes. The only sound was the clip-clop of their horses' hooves on the cobblestoned main street. Those people who were out and about moved briskly, not wanting to be out after dark any longer than was necessary. Even with the Watch's strong presence, crime was a problem, and it was not uncommon for lawbreakers to drag unwary folks into an ally for nefarious purposes.

"Kit," Lin called out, finally breaking the silence. "If you believe I meant for people to die, cast judgment on me here and now; end my life."

"Get off your horse," Kit growled, as she slid down from her own mount. Lin's face went slack at the sight of Kit drawing her weapon, the one she had given her just days earlier. With a shake of her hand, Kit ignited the light of her hammer, creating an ominous glow on her face. Her eyes flashed golden.

Swallowing hard, Lin stepped up to Kit and took a knee in front of her. She craned her neck to look into Kit's brown and gold eyes. "If you believe that I am *that person*, then take my life." There was an unbearable pause as time inched along at a snail's pace. Neither woman showed a hint of expression.

"Get up!" Kit shook her head and walked away. She took a seat at the edge of a small fountain, the water gurgling gently as it poured out from three small cherubs holding tiny bows. She set the still-lit hammer next to her and crossed her arms. "Please, explain to me what just happened."

Lin took a deep breath and slowly released it, her fingers fidgeting as she tried to figure out where to start. "Do you remember when I told you that sometimes I sell... information?" When Kit just stared at her, she pressed on. "Well, I had heard about the City Watch buying up obsidian weapons to fight the firebugs and whatever else is running around below ground. I had let the Moreden twins know about that so they could start finding smiths who specialized in that type of equipment. In return for sharing the information, they said they'd give me some of the weapons when they came in, so that I could enchant them and resell them."

Again, Lin looked to Kit for some sort of acknowledgement of what she was saying, but Kit's face remained stoic. "They had secured several suppliers, but I guess, somehow my parents heard that the Watch was looking for weapon dealers, so they were going to send a shipment. You know, to show the Watch that they could supply quality weapons at below average cost." Lin's face suddenly turned sour; her lower lip quivered. "If my parents supplied the weapons, I'd lose my connections with the local merchants, and I'd be sunk."

"You mean, you'd have to stay at the Temple." Kit's eyes narrowed and her nostrils flared. Lin didn't flinch.

"You're the one who said I was not cut out to be a priest," Lin protested, thinking that using Kit's own words against her would garner some sympathy. The muscles in Kit's jaw tensed. This time, Lin did flinch. There was no sympathy in the young priest's eyes, only steel. Lin's voice raised an octave. "I had to find a way out of the Temple. My only option was to tell the twins that the shipment was coming in, so they could waylay it. In return, I'd get to keep my parents' weapons and the Moreden twins could continue to sell their obsidian gear to the Watch."

"And you didn't expect any bloodshed? Did you really not expect the guards to fight to protect the shipment? You do understand that was their job, right? They're paid to protect their charge, even if it means giving up their lives in the process?" The words were falling out of Kit's mouth faster than she could consider them.

Lin plopped down on the fountain's edge next to Kit. "The guards were in on it," she said, her eyes back on her fidgeting fingers. "I had instructed Martelle to pay the guards to let the caravan be robbed. He was supposed to get green soldiers who would be more interested in gold than in their reputation as guards. My father insisted on sending his own, personal guard." Lin's emotions bubbled over, her voice hitching as she continued. "The Moreden twins knew that. They were supposed to show up with more than enough soldiers to guarantee that the guards would back down. No matter how cruel, guards will choose life over protecting a shipment. Nobody was supposed to get hurt."

"It would have hurt your parents," Kit corrected her.

Lin raised her eyes to Kit, an angry gleam to them. "Who cares! They'd have lost a bit of gold, that's it. It's not like they couldn't afford it."

"So then, why did it all go so badly?" Kit questioned, still waiting to hear something that would explain why everything happened the way it did.

"I don't know," Lin dropped her chin to her chest. "I swear on my Grams' life, I don't know what happened."

Kit sat motionless for a few minutes, contemplating everything Lin had just told her. If only Father Hoarfrost was there, to offer her advice on how to proceed. He dealt with problems like this on a daily basis. She was still wet behind the ears, with no experience in dealing with people's internal struggles.

A bear moth lit upon the head of her hammer, its light shining through the fluffy moth's otherwise dull gray exterior, giving it a golden hue. Its wings slowly opened and closed before leaping up and flitting away.

"How did you know they were coming in tonight? You said this has been in motion since before we met."

Without saying a word, Lin reached into her pocket and pulled out a small blue orb. A soft light emanated from it, illuminating the swirling blue and white patterns within.

"What's that?"

"It's a seers' crystal. Martelle has its mate." Lin answered Kit's question flatly, as though seers' crystals were common items that everyone knew about. Kit stared blankly back at the woman for several moments before cocking an eyebrow. "Seers' crystals allow people to communicate over long distances. One of the two people must invoke its power to initiate the connection. If the other person is holding theirs, they'll see the reflection of the person trying to communicate with them. Once they do, the people holding the orbs can talk with each other."

"And where would you have gotten such a *thing*?" Kit's curiosity was now taking over, pushing aside her anger with Lin.

"My parents," Lin replied weakly. "They used to use them to talk with each other when I was little. My father was away more than he was home. After they shipped me off to live with my grandmother, they didn't need them anymore because they always traveled together." Kit sat motionless, waiting for more details. "Martelle got them for me when I was a young acolyte. He brought them along with a shipment of clothes that my mother sent me."

Kit continued listening patiently to Lin's tale, trying to find ways to tear her story apart. "Who is he, Martelle? How could he get something so valuable from your parents without them knowing?"

"I was told that he's my cousin," Lin said as she stared down at her fidgeting fingers. "But I think he's a bastard son of my father." Lin finally stared Kit directly in the eyes. "I don't know why for sure, but Grams doesn't like him, and she finds the good in everyone. I think she doesn't like him because... of my father. Martelle has only ever been good to me."

The pieces all seemed to be coming together in Kit's mind, well, most of them anyway. She assumed that Lin and Martelle were in communication with each other while they were all at Grams' house, and that's why Lin had been so edgy when they were heading home. Lin knew what was happening, and she didn't want to be near it when the *robbery* took place.

"You said you couldn't stop the shipment. If you could speak with Martelle, why couldn't you call if off?"

"Neither Martelle nor I had any control over the shipment. That was my father's doing. I was..."

"Just trying to steal it?"

Lin nodded while her fingers continued to fidget.

"I'm not sure what to do," Kit finally said after staring at Lin for several moments. "I disagree with almost everything you did, and how you were involved in it, but..." She held out her hand, "In the meantime, give me that orb." Without any hesitation, Lin handed Kit the seers' crystal. It was cool to the touch and unnaturally smooth. She was rolling it about in her palm when the colors swirled more quickly, its light becoming brighter. It was practically humming, calling Kit to stare into it.

"Put it away!" Lin cried; her voice panicked. "Somebody is looking into the other crystal!" Kit quickly pocketed the crystal, raising an eyebrow at Lin. "The power in them upsets people," she said, wrinkling her nose. "They think it's dark magic."

"Is it?" Kit asked, her eyes widening.

"No, it's dragon magic." Lin went back to staring at her hands again. Kit's brow furrowed. A strong urge to take the orb from her pocket pulled at her. Her mind immediately went to Fury, the dragon bone staff she had left in her cell.

"I have no clue what that means," she said, her voice strained. "You're going to have to explain that to me later." Lin nodded her head, without looking up. *Who are you?* She could somehow feel that Lin was speaking the truth, at least to the best of her ability. And even if she disagreed with how Lin had conducted herself, she could see no real crime. She wasn't sure if stealing from your own family was actually stealing, at least in the eyes of Titan.

"I need to sleep on this," Kit finally declared. "Take the horses to the stables and make sure they're cared for. Afterwards, get to your cell. Stay there until I come for you."

"What about Martelle?" Lin asked, exhaling loudly. She wiped the back of her hand across her brow.

"He's going to spend the night at the barracks. I'll get the other crystal from him before something unfortunate happens. After that, I don't know."

Lin gave Kit a weak smile. "Thank you for believing me. I'm sorry I let you down. Of all people, you are the last person I'd ever want to hurt."

For some reason Lin's words made Kit's heart ache for her. Even though Lin had spent most of her life at the Temple, just as Kit had, her life had been far more complicated and far less fulfilling.

"Get some sleep, we'll talk tomorrow." Kit didn't bother to linger, she simply walked away, heading back to the barracks.

"Why don't you keep your horse?" Lin called out. "It would be faster than walking."

"I need time. Time to think and pray."

CHAPTER THIRTY

DRAGON TEARS

"He's going to spend the night at the barracks," Kit said to the guard sitting outside the tiny cell Martelle had been stuffed into. He had immediately whined when she'd arrived, complaining about how badly they were treating him.

"Empty your pockets and give it all to me," Kit said, holding out her hand.

"They already took everything I had," Martelle screeched out. "They threatened to beat me if I didn't."

Kit tilted her head from side to side, examining the man's face. "Not too surprising. It looks like you complied immediately." This comment made the guard laugh. It came to an abrupt halt when Kit turned on him, holding out her hand for whatever he had taken from the prisoner. The man folded his arms across his chest and frowned.

"We did no such thing," answered a sergeant, as he entered the already cramped room with two more guards in tow.

For a brief moment Kit didn't think the guards were going to give up Martelle's possessions, including the seers' crystal. When Kit threatened to march the entire lot of them to the captain's office, strip them naked, and *deliver justice* to whomever was lying to her... well, the sergeant, who had the crystal in his pocket, quickly gave it up. Kit was too tired, too stressed, and too confused to deal with anybody's nonsense. The guards had assured her that Martelle would be properly cared for, fed, and given a bed for the night.

Kit's head was pounding by the time she opened the door to her cell, wanting nothing more than to fall onto her bed, and get some sleep. Between Lin's behavior and dealing with the guards at the City Watch, she was utterly spent.

"I'm not just some child's plaything, to be left in the corner and forgotten about." Kit groaned at the sound of Fury's voice. The last thing she wanted was to get into a fight with a petulant dragon-bone cane.

"Not now," Kit snarled.

"Yes, now!" Fury snarled back. "If you're not going to take advantage of having me, send me back to Tyr. At least he's entertaining."

"I can't deal with you now, Fury," Kit responded dismissively as she placed the seers' crystals on the desk next to her bed. She was about to peel off her armor when Fury whistled. "Don't be crass," she scolded.

"What? Don't flatter yourself. I was whistling at the dragon tears you have." Fury snickered at Kit's reddening face. "How did you manage to come by those?"

"They're not dragon tears," Kit replied as she finished pulling off her armor. She used her toe to pull off one of her boots, just before she kicked it across the room at Fury, missing him by a few inches. "They're seers' crystals." Fury, while trying to refute Kit's claim, was struck by her second boot, sending him skittering across the floor and under Kit's wardrobe.

"Did that make you feel better," came a perturbed voice from beneath the cabinet.

"A little," Kit said with a smirk as she pulled off the rest of her sweat-fouled clothes before slipping into her nightgown. Once she was *presentable*, she reached under and pulled out the cane. Fury's eyes were practically twirling.

"Have you gotten it all out of your system, little Sister?" he asked, blowing a gout of blue flame just beside her head. Even though the heat from the fire was intense, Kit didn't flinch. "Those orbs, little girl with much to learn, are dragon tears. And before you disagree, I can tell you that it's what they are, because I created them."

"Okay then, if you created them, what do they do?" Kit asked. Since she already knew the answer, she figured she could catch the smug piece of bone in a lie.

"It depends on who's holding them and whether they are being used separately or together." The carved dragonhead gave Kit a smug look when her jaw dropped open. "If they are held separately, they can be used to communicate over a long distance. If they are held together, they can be peered into, to see almost anywhere on Orth; the only caveat being that you need friendly eyes at the location you're looking at. It lets you see through their eyes. You cannot communicate with the person, only see what they're seeing."

"You're not telling me everything," Kit said, narrowing her eyes. "What are you leaving out?"

Fury's mouth suddenly clamped shut. "You've changed again," he said, changing the subject.

"What are you not telling me?" Kit repeated, her voice low and steady.

"That's very impressive," Fury chuckled. "You're full of surprises." He laughed, like he was the only one who got his joke. "I've changed my mind. I'd much rather hang out with you than go back to Tyr."

"Why?" Kit demanded. Her grip on the cane tightened, making Fury laugh all the more.

"Oh, nothing I want to speak of," he replied gleefully. "You can't make me tell you anything more about the tears and you can't make me tell you why I find you entertaining, but you're welcome to continue trying."

"Go back to Tyr. I'm not dragging you around with me, even if you are helpful at times." Kit was just too tired to argue with him any further. "When it's important, I'm kind of busy with my hammer. I don't have a free hand to hold on to you as well."

She was just about to put him back into the corner of her cell when Fury cleared his throat. "You know, you don't need a third hand to bring me with you. You could replace your hammer's handle with me."

"What do you mean by that?" Kit asked. The death-grip she had on the cane loosened.

"Your hammer, as nice as it is, has an oak shaft for a handle. If it were Dragonwood, or even Amberwood, I'd say that it was an exceptional hammer, but – oak – makes for a boring handle." Fury's eyes twirled slowly again as he watched Kit's reaction to his words. "If you were to replace the oak handle with... me, well then, you'd have a wondrous hammer, indeed."

"You'd let me do that to you? You'd be willing to suffer the indignation of being a simple tool?" Kit was now giving Fury a coy grin.

"If you pledge to keep me with you whenever possible, then I would gladly accept the indignation." Fury batted his eyes back at Kit, enjoying the banter a little more than he might have expected.

Kit continued her smile, but her curiosity changed into skepticism. "Why would I want to do this? This hammer is a gift from a friend."

Fury blew another gout of blue flame past Kit's face, this time close enough to singe some of the hair on her head. "Who doesn't want a dragon as a cohort? Or in my case, a partial dragon?"

"Where's the rest of you?" Kit queried. It was a question that had nagged at her, ever since she'd met him.

"I wish I knew. You could ask Tyr, but I expect he won't tell you any more than he's told me." Fury shook his head, like he was trying to chase a memory away. "So, do you agree to let me meld with your hammer?"

"What do you mean, meld?" Kit demanded. Something in the way Fury had said the word made Kit nervous.

"Meld, merge, be a part of, be joined with, attached to... pick whichever phrasing you like best. Considering you're turning into a living lie-detector, you'd think you'd become more trusting of people." Kit gave a small yelp at his assertion, making Fury chuckle yet again. "You've been testing me this whole time. Do you think I couldn't tell? Like I said, Kitten, you've changed. You can tell when I'm lying or telling the truth. You can even tell when I'm being evasive."

She bit her lip and turned away. "So, how do I attach you to the hammer?"

Fury couldn't hide the smile on his face, especially since he had no hands to do so. "You'll need a master smith to start with, and a furnace hot enough to forge my body to your hammer's mithril head."

"And where exactly am I to find such a master, and the gold to pay him?" Kit tossed Fury onto her bed as she walked over to her mirror. The red stripe in her hair had gotten considerably wider and the gold ring in her eyes has gotten noticeably thicker. She absentmindedly let her fingers run through her hair.

"It's a good look on you, Kitten," Fury said solemnly. "But, to answer your question, I am both a master smith and a furnace hot enough to forge myself to your hammer's head. We can do it now if you'd like."

Kit yawned widely, giving her butt-cheek a scratch as she did. "No way," she yawned again. "I need sleep," she said as she flopped onto her bed, knocking Fury to the floor. She didn't even bother to pull a blanket over herself. Just before sleep took her, her mind drifted to Indie and the boys. She wondered how their training was going. She hoped they were okay, while her heart ached for their company. She tried to remember how many days it had been since she'd last seen them. The mental exercise put her instantly into a deep sleep.

CHAPTER THIRTY-ONE

THE TRIAL OF ON'NAK

Kit was shivering badly when she opened her eyes. She tried to pull her blanket up over herself, only to find it unyielding. The morning sun was already peaking over Mount Toka, casting a cool yellow light across the wall of her cell. She raised her head to see why she couldn't move her blanket, only to find Runt sprawled out across the foot of her bed and Lump with his head on her pillow. Kit squealed at the sight of her two buddies. She quickly wrapped her arms around Lump and tucked her feet under Runt's neck ruff. In just a few minutes, she was fast asleep again.

"Kit. Wake up!" screamed a voice from outside her cell door. "He's being tried this morning!"

She squinted as she opened her eyes. The room was much brighter than it had been just a few moments ago. She propped herself up on her elbows and gazed around the room, yawning loudly. Neither Runt nor Lump were there with her. Had she dreamed it? Was somebody pounding on her door? She was too groggy to form a coherent thought. She was about to curl back up in bed when the pounding on her door resumed.

"Kit! You need to get dressed and get to the courthouse. He's being brought in front of the magistrate right now!"

"Who's being brought in front of the magistrate?" Kit demanded as she opened the door to her room, only to find Lin staring at her, panic in her eyes. "I thought I told you to stay in your cell until I came to get you."

"They're bringing On'nak in for his trial. If you don't hurry, you're going to miss it." Lin bolted off down the hall, not bothering to wait for Kit's response.

Still trying to clear the cobwebs from her head, Kit quickly got dressed. As she was heading for the door, someone cleared his throat from inside her room. She quickly spun around, finding herself alone in her cell. "Hello?" she called out as her eyes searched for whoever had made the noise.

"Under the bed," Fury responded. "You're not leaving without me." Kit shook her head as she ran out of her room, slamming the door shut behind her as she did. "I am not a child's plaything to be left behind." Fury's screams of protest made her smile as she headed down the hall.

Fortunately for Kit, the courthouse was across the square from the Temple. As she flew down the Temple stairs, she practically bowled over an old woman trying to scale her way to the top. She yelled a quick apology over her shoulder as she continued on her way to the courthouse. She didn't even bother to slow down as she reached the entrance of the grand dark-gray stone edifice. Instead, she simply dropped her shoulder and crashed into the doors, causing them to burst open as she came barging through.

"He's not guilty," she screamed out before she even has a chance to survey the room. Six guards immediately fell on her, dragging her screaming little body to the ground. She tried, somewhat ineffectually, to resist their containment, but instead she decided that submission was the best course of action.

"Who is not guilty?" asked a high-pitched voice from somewhere in the room beyond the mass of bodies holding her to the ground.

"Let her up," the voice continued, still high-pitched but there was a definite air of command to it. The guards immediately backed off, with one of them extending a hand to help her off the black marble floor.

The courtroom was packed with spectators and each one of them was gawking at her. Whispers and murmurs spread through the room. As the moments passed, the whispers turned to sniggers, and the sniggers turned to cruel taunts. Perhaps she'd have received a better reception had she been dressed in her priest robes rather than yesterday's filthy trousers and tunic. When she bolted from her room, she hadn't really considered where she was going.

Repeated blows of the magistrate's gavel brought the courtroom to an uncomfortable silence. The little man peered over his massive black-oak desk from atop a raised dais. His eyes seemed too large for his powdered wig covered head. His face was flat and bright red. As his too-large eyes locked onto Kit's, he made it crystal clear that he was not a happy man.

"I will ask you again, young lady, who is it that you believe is not guilty?" The magistrate was a good ten feet higher up than Kit, preventing her from seeing anything other than his head and the front of his massive, ornately carved desk. He was slowly drumming his fingers on that very same desk as he waited impatiently for her to respond. His white mustache was so long and so thick that it completely covered his mouth. With each breath that mustache billowed out like the branches of a weeping willow.

"Your Grace," Kit said, stalling, as she tried to find the words.

"Honor," the magistrate interrupted.

"I'm honored to meet you, too, Your Grace. I just..."

"You may refer to me as Magistrate or Your Honor. I am not the Father of the Temple, so you will not refer to me as Your Grace." The scowl on the magistrate's face deepened as he explained how he was to be addressed. His grand white mustache twitched, perhaps from the sneer that was creeping across his lips.

"I'm sorry, Your Grace. I don't understand." Kit was slowly making her way towards the front of the courtroom, causing the magistrate to have to lean out over the front of his desk in order to see her.

He made an exasperated sound before leaving his position to come around to the side of his desk. The man was dressed in a black robe with gold trim everywhere. He wasn't much taller than Kit, but he was considerably rounder. Nevertheless, the scowl on the magistrate's face was even deeper than it was before, his too-large eyes narrowed to barely more than a slit. The redness in his face now had a tinge of purple in it. "I will ask you one last time before I toss you in the dungeons. Who are you saying is not guilty?"

"On'nak, Magistrate, Your Grace, Sir." Kit wasn't fearful of the man, not in the slightest, but she was concerned that her inappropriate actions might somehow lead to the execution of the boy.

"Who is On'nak?" the magistrate asked, his eyes ranging over to the small group of people standing accused of one crime or another. They all immediately lowered their gaze, not wanting to taste his growing ire; all except for On'nak who raised his chin and stepped forward. Growing murmurs in the crowd were immediately silenced by the magistrate's stern look.

"If I may, Your Honor," Father Hoarfrost stepped up from his place to the right of the magistrate. "On'nak is the young Berrat boy who stands trial for sedition and murder. The young woman standing before you is Sister Kit Standing Bear, acknowledged priest of Titan, the Savior of Aarall."

The magistrate harrumphed, causing his mustache to blow out in front of his face. Kit anxiously tried to hide a grin that was desperately pulling at the corner of her mouth. "That's a lot of titles for someone so young," he said, the look of annoyance melting away from the man's face. "I have not yet begun to hear that matter, but since you are the *Savior of Aarall*, I am willing to hear his case first."

"Your Honor," a tall, extremely thin man with a nose so large that several children could stand beneath it, called out with an irritatingly nasal voice. "The matter of the Berrat boy is without defense. He murdered four children, attempted to murder five more, and he even attempted to kill Sister Standing Bear, the woman now seeking to have him released."

The magistrate frowned heavily as he listened to the charges being brought against the young Berrat. "Are these accusations true," he asked On'nak. "Did you do what the prosecution alleges?"

"Don't answer that!" Kit yelled, as she moved towards the boy.

"Excuse me?" the magistrate bellowed at Kit. "If you ever try to countermand me again inside my courthouse, I will have you executed where you stand. I don't care who you are or who your friends are. Do I make myself clear, young lady?"

"Yes, Your Honor, I did the things I am being accused of." On'nak's voice was clear, and strong, and proud. The way he continued to jut his chin out, he was all but challenging the magistrate to sentence him to death.

"Please, Your Honor," Kit implored. "There is more to this than what has been said."

"What more is there to hear?" the magistrate blustered at Kit. He took a few more steps down from his dais until he was standing near eye level with Kit. "He murdered four and tried to kill others, including you."

"Does it not even matter as to why he did what he did?" Kit was desperately trying to keep her emotions under control, but she was on the verge of tears. Her emotions were getting the better of her, but she was going to need to rein them in if she was to have any hope of helping the boy.

"The reason why is not germane to these proceedings, child," the prosecutor droned out in his nasally voice, looking down his enormous hawknose at Kit. She desperately wanted to slap that arrogant look of superiority off his face.

"Really?" Kit asked as her anger pushed away any fear that tears might leak from her eyes. "So, let's say, a man is trying to kill your wife, or your mother, or some other person you love, and you protect them. In doing so, you take the life of the assailant. Are you guilty of murder?" The magistrate harrumphed again. The prosecutor sneered down at the little spec of a girl that would dare challenge him.

"Of course not, you impudent little child. I would be honored for being a rescuer, not executed for being a murderer." A smug look of satisfaction crossed the man's face as he folded his long, gangly arms in front of his chest. He clearly believed that Kit was no match for his massive intellect.

"Really?" Kit said, as she strode closer to him. "What if you were brought before the magistrate, but you are unable to explain why you killed them? What if some pompous, self-important moron stood before the magistrate and didn't give you an opportunity to speak in your own defense? What would happen to you then, I wonder. Well, I'll tell you what – you'd be summarily executed as a murderer."

The prosecutor's face immediately became a comical series of facial expressions as he tried to find a rebuttal to Kit's hypothetical situation. "And what defense does this young man have for his actions?" the magistrate finally asked, relieving the prosecutor from having to deal with the young woman standing before him.

On'nak replied to the magistrate's question, his tone accusatory. "My people are being stolen from their families, from their homes. They're being ripped from the hands of dead loved ones, and then they're sold off as blood slaves, servants, or playthings for rich humans' amusement. Lord Pental has tried to make you hear the truth, to listen to his wisdom, to help stem the flow of hatred and death, but you do not heed his words. You stay safe and warm behind your stone walls, safe and warm inside your stone homes, safe and warm inside cozy rooms, far away from the reality of what we Berrat must endure." Kit watched as the same zealous fervor shone in the boy's eyes, as it had the first time she'd met him.

"The horrors your people have endured in their kingdom is no reason to behave the way you have," the magistrate interrupted, seemingly disregarding everything the boy had just said. "We are not in Berrathia. We are in Arnnor, where, like us, you are safe and warm in your stone house. Whatever hatred this Pental person is fomenting, it is completely false."

"That is not entirely true, Your Honor," Kit interrupted. Murmurs again rippled through the crowd. "The slavers are raiding villages in Arnnor, in Aarall even. Just yesterday I returned from rescuing three people from these raiders. At least one of them was taken from Ashcroft, no less than a week ago."

"Slavers in Aarall? That's preposterous," the prosecutor declared, puffing out his chest and waving his arms about in an over-the-top display of showmanship. Just who was he trying to convince of his assertion? Her desire to slap this man hard grew in her belly. Her jaw practically fell open when the magistrate nodded his head in agreement.

"Do you doubt the veracity of my claim?" Kit asked the hawknosed man, her voice becoming a bit more menacing than intended. She barely took a step toward him, but even that slight movement carried the desired effect. "I sincerely hope that you're not calling me a liar."

The prosecutor babbled as he tried to recant his statement. "I never said any such thing," he managed to burble out, sweat suddenly appearing on his brow and cheeks. "I merely stated that there are no known cases of slave rings in our kingdom."

"That still sounds like you're calling me a liar. As though the people I rescued from the Scarlet Tide is something I'm making up. Is that what you're saying?" Kit had continued making her way toward the man. She was now standing a mere foot away from the prosecutor, forcing him to try to retreat. As he backed up into a railing, unable to go any further, he called out for guards to protect him. When he started whimpering, Kit laughed at him and walked away, preparing to address the magistrate again.

"Sister Standing Bear," the magistrate intoned, causing his mustache to again flail about on his face, "this young man was under no pressure or threat. Nobody's life was in imminent danger. He acted out of malice, hate for citizens who were not involved in the crimes against his people, innocent individuals, children. The actions he took were his own, not forced upon him by anyone, and now he will pay the price for his crimes."

Kit's mouth went dry as a lump grew in her throat. She was quickly running out of arguments. On'nak was not resigned to the outcome. Instead, he appeared to be proud that he was about to receive a death sentence. Kit's eyes quickly moved to Father Hoarfrost, imploring him to speak on the boy's behalf. He slowly shook his head, letting Kit know that there were no other avenues to explore.

"He's only a child," Kit finally screamed out, utterly frustrated with herself that she lacked the skills necessary to argue for this boy's life. "He doesn't deserve to die. His mind was entirely poisoned by the rantings of a madman," she cried out weakly, as the prospect of On'nak being executed consumed her. "He's just a child."

"I'm sorry, Sister," the magistrate said as he took the last few steps down from his raised dais. "Our laws are clear on the matter. The boy shows no remorse for his actions. He understands what he's done, and if I'm being honest, I believe he'd be willing to do it again. It's not my job to make up the law. It's my job to apply it."

Without another word, Kit turned away from the magistrate and addressed On'nak. "I'm sorry that I could not have you set free, but know this, I will put an end to the oppression of your people, or I will die trying."

On'nak stood stoic and bowed his head to Kit. "I know you will, and for that, I am grateful. And, for what it's worth, I'm sorry that I tried to hurt you. You are a good person, and you were following your heart – just like I was following my own."

"Magistrate," Father Hoarfrost interrupted. "The boy has now shown remorse for his actions, true remorse." The old priest took a deep breath, as though weighing what he was about to say. "Would it be within your power to place him under the care of the Temple? I will see to it that he pays for his crime, through community service and by teaching my priests and my acolytes how we can better serve the Berrat population."

"I do not want what you're offering," On'nak said, not waiting for the magistrate to weigh in. "I am not sorry for taking those lives. The lives of those children will mean more to my people's plight against slavery than anything I might do in the Temple. I will happily give my life if it saves just one Berrat family."

Kit was suddenly overwhelmed with mixed feelings. She understood the plight On'nak was fighting against. But he just proudly admitted to killing innocent children. Against all odds, Kit wanted to believe that the children's deaths were accidental. How had this boy's earlier words swayed her from the path of righteousness? But he was just a boy, perhaps too young to understand the harm he had caused.

Kit stared at On'nak, unblinking. She was unsure of how to process the flood of emotions coursing through her. This boy was a murderer of children and would be executed for his crimes before the sun set. It would surely be a spectacle that would likely serve to create an even greater divide within the population. Maybe it would galvanize the people, drawing them to work together so that this sort of behavior would never happen again. She wanted to go back to bed and sleep for eternity. She had not been trained for this sort of dilemma, or if she had been, she had slept through that class.

"May Gaia guide you to the Great Cycle," Kit said as she shook her head at On'nak. "I disagree with your methods, wholeheartedly disagree with them, but I understand why you did what you did, even if it was morally reprehensible."

"May Titan's light shine upon you, Sister Kit," On'nak replied with a weak smile. "May the warrior spirit guide you and protect you on your journeys."

Kit nodded to the boy and headed out the door. From the entrance to the courthouse, she regarded the massive set of stairs leading to the Temple. She was about to take a step in that direction when a familiar voice spoke from behind her.

"I'm still going to kill you," she whispered.

Kit spun around to see Iba, the disgraced, excommunicated acolyte, standing in the doorway of the courthouse. Her horns had grown some since the last time she'd seen her, but the girl still had the same burning hatred in her eyes. The glint of a dagger caught Kit's attention.

"I know what you did to help restore my father's name. I watched how you tried to protect that boy. Nothing of what you've done matters. I'm still going to kill you."

"I don't know what I did to you. I have never understood why you hate me, but if you think killing me is going to fix whatever it is that's broken inside of you, get it over with."

Iba paused for a moment, her eyes searching Kit's, looking for – something. The two girls stood unnaturally still for several moments. She slowly slipped her dagger into her pocket and walked across the square, heading towards the city's main gate. Kit turned to look up the Temple's imposing staircase. The notion of climbing the stairs made her mind go numb. She turned back to watch Iba, but she was nowhere to be seen. Kit blew out a deep breath and made her way past the square's statue of Titan until she stood at the base of the ascent. She squared her shoulders and bounded up the stairs. Something inside told her this was the last time she'd make this climb.

CHAPTER THIRTY-TWO

SECRETS REVEALED

Kit walked into the nave, intent on parking herself at the foot of Titan's statue. Penitents were loosely gathered around the god's likeness, but she wended her way through them until she stood before the statue. If she had her way, she would just curl up there and sleep until the problems of the world had passed, and she could just wake up to a land of peace and happiness. She was weary. Not just down to her bones, but to the very fiber of her being. While the others knelt in prayer, she sat at Titan's foot.

Kit tucked her knees to her chest and watched the people as they came and went from the Temple. She watched those before her as they prayed fervently to their god, for whatever purpose suited them. She watched as acolytes went about their business, whatever that might be. She watched the world go on around her, while she wallowed in self pity.

I am not that girl.

She had only six days now to meet her cohorts in Cormorant. The moon would be gone in just five. Even if she ran Angel hard, it might take three days to get to Silverhawk. If she didn't leave by tomorrow morning, at the very latest, her plans would quickly start falling apart. A sense of purpose filled her soul, her righteous fires once again ignited. The haze of uncertainty burned away in the crucible of her fervor. She was just about to move into action when Brother Rimes came striding across the nave. Her righteous fury quickly turned into a knot in her stomach.

What's his problem with me?

From the first day of her arrival at the Temple, Brother Rimes seemed to have had it in for Kit. He seemed to have made it his mission to make Kit's life as miserable as possible. On the mountain during her rite of abandonment, he had seemed intent on killing her. When Iba attacked her with a vorpal blade, he had defended the Tahr's actions, leveling the blame on Kit as the instigator of the altercation. When Kit brought Runt into the Temple, he had only seen the dire wolf. According to Fenrir, only enemies, those who wished to cause Kit harm, would see him in his true state.

Enemy! The voice was not her own. The spirit of Amaruq bubbled up from within. Kit curled her lips back into a snarl.

The man's beady black eyes were set on his destination. His chestnut hair flowed behind him as he sped purposefully across the floor. His smug look of self importance was only intensified as he tugged on his spindly goatee with his long boney fingers. She would have loved the opportunity to smack that arrogant look off his face.

Before she had even realized it, Kit had bounced to her feet and was stalking across the room towards the man. "A word," she declared. The brother's eyes narrowed as Kit marched towards him. As soon as she was within an arm's length of him, she growled out, "Do you have a problem with me?"

"Whatever do you mean, Sister?" he replied, his voice dripping with sarcasm.

Kit's fist struck out, catching the much taller man in the stomach, causing him to buckle over, leaving him gasping for air. Kit used the back of her hand to assault him a second time, catching him in the side of the head, sending him sprawling across the polished stone floor.

"Answer me!" Kit's voice was now a deadly whisper.

"You do not belong here," the brother ground out as he tried to pick himself up off the floor. "You're an abomination that should have been sent to the Great Cycle at birth." Rime spun around, trying to punch Kit in the face, but his aim was well off the mark, earning him another solid punch to the stomach, sending him once again to the floor. That name he'd used, abomination, was the same word used by the villagers where she had been raised. Why would he use that word? A flood of hate suddenly filled Kit's body, all the insults and injuries she had endured as a child suddenly surfaced in a surge of resentment. She wanted to crush this man's head under her heel.

"Sister!" a stern voice, a female voice, called out from across the hall. "Stand down this instant!" she screamed. Every eye in the Temple was fixed on Kit. Some gathered closer to witness the spectacle. Others moved away; fearful they might get caught up in the crossfire. Most of those present stood transfixed, unable to avert their gaze.

Kit hovered over the brother lying on the floor in front of her, her leg raised over him, ready to crush his head with her boot. It took Kit a moment to return to her senses. She looked across the room from where the voice had come, to see Sister Miyuki's face, her eyes wide with horror.

"We're not finished talking," she snarled at Rime. "I will find you and I will get to the bottom of, whatever your problem is with me." Kit immediately stormed off towards the hallway leading to Father Hoarfrost's office. Four priests came running past her on their way to the disturbance. None questioned why she was heading in the opposite direction.

"Stop right there, young lady," Miyuki screamed as she tried to catch up with Kit. Her footfalls echoed off the walls as she clomped towards her. Her face was purple. Her body undulated with each stride she took. "Sister Standing Bear, you will stop where you are and face the consequences of your actions."

"Stand and be judged," Rimes pronounced from his place on the stone floor, his voice labored.

Kit ignored the words of those around her and stomped down the hallway to Father Hoarfrost's office. When she arrived, she burst inside and slammed the door behind her so hard that the doorframe cracked. She screamed hysterically at the empty room and out the window that looked out at Mount Toka where Titan's ice statue used to stand. Something dark had exploded in her mind. Could it have been the spirit of Amaruq? She didn't think so. He didn't feel like, whatever that was, even when he was urging her on to avenge the life of his mate, Polaris.

"Brother Rimes has been taken into custody," a calm voice said from behind Kit. She turned to find Sister Miyuki standing in the doorway, looking at the large crack running down the door's wooden frame. "I don't know what he did to warrant the beating you gave him, but I can only assume he deserved it."

"He did, but I don't know why," Kit responded as she wiped an errant tear that had fallen down her cheek. "He is my enemy, for no reason that I am aware of. He called me an abomination, without cause." Kit stared intently into Miyuki's eyes while her lower lip quivered uncontrollably. "Am I an abomination? I've been called that since my birth."

The young priest's shoulders slumped as the dam that had held back her tears burst.

"Oh sweetie," Miyuki cried out as she raced across the room and took Kit in a deep hug. "I love you with my whole heart. You are different in ways that I cannot describe, but they are wonderful, beautiful ways. Never in my life have I met anyone with your capacity for love and devotion. You give of yourself freely and ask for nothing in return. If your mother were here, she'd tell you the exact same thing."

"But she's not here," Kit said, pulling away from Sister Miyuki. "And I have no clue where Riva is. I don't even know if she's alive."

The portly priest pulled Kit close to her again, whispering in her ear. "Riva is likely in Cormorant, with your mother."

Kit pushed Miyuki back, her eyes wide in disbelief. "Riva? My mother? They're in Cormorant? How do you know? Why am I only being told this now?"

"You weren't ready to know," Miyuki said with a warm smile. "But I believe you are now."

"I don't understand," Kit declared, blinking away tears. "How can you know that? I haven't seen Riva since I left my home over five cycles ago. I've never met my birthmother or been told anything about her. Well, not much anyway."

"Riva has been here, at the Temple mostly, ever since you arrived." Tears welled up in Miyuki's eyes. She had hated keeping this secret from Kit, but it was not her place to tell. "She's been watching over you since the day you left your village."

Kit just stood there, her mouth agape. Riva had been here with her at the Temple all this time, never once revealing herself. Her birthmother was in Cormorant, doing Titan knows what, and Sister Miyuki was aware of this, the whole time. As Kit's knees weakened, she clutched onto her friend and buried her face into her ample bosoms.

"How will I find her?" Kit asked, her voice muffled by Miyuki's clothing.

"I suspect that Riva will find you," Miyuki laughed. "She's had a lifetime of experience watching you and not being seen."

"Have you met my mother, I mean, my birthmother?" Her eyes were pleading as she waited for a response. Sister Miyuki shook her head, dashing Kit's hopes.

"Sorry, sweetie, but she's never come to Aarall, at least, not that I'm aware of. Riva won't say anything about her, other than that she, too, has never stopped watching you." Sister Miyuki took Kit's face in her hands and stared deeply into her eyes. "Even though I've never met her, I'm guessing that you're looking more and more like your mother every day."

"I wonder if I'll ever meet her," Kit sighed. "I wonder if I'll ever know who my father is." Kit's last statement made Miyuki wince. "What? Do you know who my father is?" Miyuki clenched her jaw and shook her head. "Miyuki, you're lying to me. Why are you lying?"

"I cannot answer your question, so please Kit, please don't press me on it." Miyuki pushed Kit away, putting some distance between them. "I don't want to lie to you. I love you with all my heart and I would die for you, but that is not something I can share – with anybody."

"How can you not tell me? I have a father whom I've never known anything about, and you know who he is, and you won't tell me about him?" Kit's eyes flashed with anger, but before it got out of control, she took a deep breath and centered herself.

"Sweetie," Miyuki said, the pain in her voice was obvious. "All will be made known to you when the time is right. It's all I can tell you."

"I trust you, Miyuki. I know you are doing what you believe is right." Kit brushed her hand on Miyuki's cheek. "I'm going to miss you."

"When will you leave for Silverhawk?" Miyuki enquired, happy to change the subject.

How do you know I'm leaving for Silverhawk?

Miyuki chuckled lightly when she saw the screwed up look on Kit's face. "Rare is the priest who does anything without the rest of us knowing." Miyuki's face suddenly went pale. "Don't you dare leave for Silverhawk without saying bye to me," she said as she waddled to the door at top speed. "I have to speak with Brother Rime."

The room felt inexplicably empty when Sister Miyuki left her alone with her thoughts. Her mother, Riva, had been at the Temple since her arrival, but nobody had ever told her. She had since left the Temple to travel to Cormorant to meet with her birthmother, perhaps. Kit slowly moved behind Father Hoarfrost's heavy, wooden, impeccably crafted desk. Her mind was racing at the possibility of being reunited with her mother, Riva, as well as her birthmother.

Who is my father? Why has he hidden himself from me? Why has my past been kept secret?

"Do you find my chair comfortable?" Father Hoarfrost asked, shocking Kit back to reality. Her face quickly reddened. She was indeed sitting in the high priest's chair. She was about to leap up and beg forgiveness, but he waved at her to remain seated. He had a curious grin on his face as he took a seat in one of his guest chairs. "I have a problem that I'd like to discuss with you, *Mother Standing Bear.*"

"What?" Kit squeaked back in response, causing Father Hoarfrost to chuckle.

"The chair suits you. When you take my place as high priest, you'll be inundated with people who will seek your guidance. They will come to you, day and night, asking for solutions to their problems. You will bear the weight of all the Temple's members." The old priest inclined his head slightly, "And you will do it with distinction."

"I don't want to be high priest," Kit said, her voice a few octaves higher than normal. The look of abject terror on her face made the high priest chuckle all the more.

"I know, little Sister, but when I am gone, the task will need to be passed on to someone I can trust." The old man's face continued to brighten, seemingly enjoying watching Kit squirm. "Despite all of your *shortcomings*, I've never met anyone more trustworthy than you."

"I'm leaving for Silverhawk," Kit declared, desperately trying to change the subject. "I don't expect to ever return to Aarall." She stood up from the high priest's chair and moved to the front of his desk to give him a hug. The old priest gladly accepted the gesture.

"You'll return," he said when Kit finally pulled away. "This is your home, and we are your family. Your feet will always find their way back."

"Father, about Silverhawk." She paused for a moment to gather herself. "Its City Watch is corrupted. I suspect it goes all the way to the ruling body. It needs to be corrected." The old man's eyes slowly closed shut, and he nodded. Perhaps it was something he was aware of but wasn't in a position to do anything about. He had no say in the goings on of other cities, except perhaps in his role as the head of the Titan's temples.

"Goodbye, Father," she exclaimed, as her shoulders slumped. "I love you, and I'll miss you." Without another word, Kit exited, leaving Father Hoarfrost on his own.

"Farewell, Kit," he said to an empty doorway. "Titan's blessings upon you."

CHAPTER THIRTY-THREE

DRAGON HAMMER

"I sincerely hope that was the last time you're going to just abandon me," Fury scolded as Kit entered her cell.

She completely ignored his comment. "How do I forge you to my hammer?"

"Finally," Fury exclaimed as he levitated from his place against the wall. "Put your hammer in the corner of your cell and remove anything that's *flammable*. I don't want to set the building on fire."

Kit considered the corner of her room and huffed. It was already completely barren. She took her hammer and leaned it in the corner.

"Excuse me," Fury said, bumping her in the middle of her back. "Time to work some dragon magic!"

Fury hovered for a moment or two before spewing a tight burst of blue flame at the hammer's handle. At first it appeared like nothing was happening, other than an azure fire engulfing the oak shaft.

"Performance problems?" Kit asked with a smirk. The color of the flame immediately brightened. The sudden burst of heat felt good on her skin. She held her palms outward as though warming her hands.

Moments later the handle turned to ash, crumbling into nothing, snuffing out the fire as it disintegrated. Fury moved his bone-cane body over the hammer head until his base was directly over the place where the oak handle used to be attached to the weapon. The cane suddenly burst into flames, leaving Fury's body wreathed in a sky-blue aura as the fire licked up and down the bone. With each passing second his fire got hotter and hotter, forcing Kit to retreat slightly from the heat; the once blue flames turning white as the intensity increased. She shielded her eyes from the now blinding light as Fury lowered himself onto the hammer, his base filling the spot once taken by the oaken handle. There was a brilliant flash which practically knocked Kit off her feet.

When her vision cleared, the weapon stood in the corner; Fury and the hammer were now one. Kit picked up the weapon, its handle was already cool to the touch. She slowly rolled it over in her hands, inspecting it closely. The connection between Fury and the hammer was a large claw, its bone fingers grasping the hammerhead. The bond between the two was so perfect that it was difficult to determine where the bone ended and the mithril began.

"Some of my best work," Fury said, his jeweled eyes spinning wildly.

"It's even lighter than it was before," Kit responded, spinning the hammer in her hand.

"Please don't ever refer to me as *it*." Fury threatened. "I am the hammer. The hammer is me. We are one."

"My apologies, oh mighty *Dragon Hammer*. I meant no disrespect," Kit giggled in response. "I've never seen a sentient weapon before, let alone owned one."

"You do not *own* me," Fury intoned, his voice full of... fury.

"Well," Kit replied with a playful tone. "I owned the hammer, and you are the hammer, so I own you."

"What has been made can be unmade just as easily." The hammer burst into blue flame with the statement. Kit watched in wonder as the flames licked her hands, traveling up her wrist to her elbow. There was no heat in the flames. They were cool against her skin, like a soothing balm. Her body suddenly wracked, like a lightning bolt had just shot up her arm.

"Sweet Titan," Kit exclaimed, as a sudden rush of power coursed through her body. "What did you just do?"

Fury laughed as the flamed died out. "A small taste of the power you can have when you wield me, if you treat me properly. By the way, I like the nickname you gave me. You may call me that if you wish."

"Nickname?" Kit asked. "Do you mean Dragon Hammer?"

"Precisely!" Fury exclaimed. "Just think of the epic tales the bards will sing, espousing the magnificence of the dragon hammer, and how a small girl carried him into battle, ensuring absolute victory."

"You're delusional," Kit said as she tossed him onto her straw mattress.

"Oh, Kit," Fury raised himself from the bed, hovering a few inches above the blankets. "You should have seen me in my glory... before I was ripped apart by Fate magic. I was truly splendiferous. I was absolutely breathtaking. I was..."

"Full of yourself, apparently," Kit jibed as she gathered up her belongings, stuffing them into her knapsack. She pulled out her bracers, remembering the merchant at Silverhawk who had gifted them to her. A small pang cut through her as she remembered the man. He had taken a great risk painting the Scarlet Tide tattoo on her neck. If the vampires discovered his role... She pushed the thought aside and tossed the bracers onto her bed. She pulled out her chainmail gloves and turned them over in her hands. These were a gift from Captain Harding. She still couldn't understand why the captain of the guard would give her a present for her birthday at all, but she was happy that he had. She tossed them onto the bed beside her bracers.

"My beauty rivaled even that of Ouroboros, the Black Dragon King himself. My scales were iridescent, my wings glorious, my maw terrifying. Even the gods feared me, feared what we dragon lords would do if we were freed of our shackles." The dragon hammer dropped dramatically onto the bed, next to the armor she had laid there.

Kit pulled her holy symbol from a drawer in her bedside desk and slipped it over her head. When she pulled out the necklace, a scroll fell to the floor. It was the letter Danny had written to her before he'd disappeared. She still hadn't read it. She wasn't sure if she wanted to read it. Her heart ached for her friend, her friend who had left without saying goodbye. She quickly scooped it up and stuffed it into her knapsack. She rolled Fury's words around in her head.

"Shackles? You're a captive, like Titan?" She paused her packing, Fury's words piquing her interest, at least those words that were not for the benefit of his self-adulations.

"I am not, but Ouroboros, the Dragon King is. He's been bound to his mountain range, unable to leave until the key is found. The key that will unlock the collar that binds him. As long as he remains confined to the mountains, so will all dragons be tied to his fate." Fury sighed, like he was resigned to his own destiny. "If my parts were gathered, it's possible that I could be reborn to my natural state. Oh, it felt good to be in draken form while I was in the secret library. Perhaps I could even free Ouroboros from his lofty prison."

"You were actually quite beautiful," Kit said with all seriousness.

"Thank you," Fury said, his voice sullen. "I'm even more wondrous in my dragon form."

"Where's the rest of you?" Kit asked as she returned to her packing. She pulled out the enchanted comb that Lin had made for her, passing it effortlessly through her thick black hair. She stepped in front of the mirror to see its effects. The red stripe in her hair was thicker than she'd remembered. It almost seemed to glisten with each stroke of the comb.

"I don't know where the rest of me is, but if I was to make a guess, an educated guess, I expect that each of the Fates is holding a piece of my soul." Fury flew over to Kit, where she stood looking at herself in the mirror. "You're also quite beautiful," he laughed. "You'll be even more beautiful when you reach your full potential. Not as beautiful as me, mind you, but glorious all the same." She ignored his final comment and continued to ready herself for departure.

She moved back to her bed where she had been piling her weapons and bits of armor. She slipped the comb into a pocket and picked up her bracers. As she fastened them to her forearms, she stared at the perfectly shaped symbols of Titan that had been carved into the metal. She tucked her chainmail gloves into her belt and headed for her wardrobe.

She pulled out her heavy hiking boots and tried stuffing them into her knapsack. There was no way in Helja they were going to fit. They were pretty beat up and not nearly as nice as the soft leather boots she had been gifted by the people of the fishing village. That had been her very first real mission. She had saved a boy, and, in doing so, caused another to be executed. She pushed the idea from her mind.

My robes are so nice. She loved those robes, but they wouldn't be practical, not if she was to be impersonating a slaver. The bracers were hard enough to explain, priestly robes would be impossible. She closed the doors and sighed. Being awarded those robes was a highlight in her life, and now she was walking away from them, likely never to return.

Fury hovered by her shoulder as Kit picked up her knapsack. She tossed it over her shoulder and snatched her hammer out of the air. She slid Fury into his holster and made for the door. She tucked her holy symbol into her tunic and buckled up her armor. She gave her cell, her home, one last look before pulling the door closed.

Her soft leather boots barely made any noise as she headed down the hallway towards the exit that would lead her to the stables. When she pushed open the doors to the courtyard she was met with a stiff, cold wind.

"May I walk with you?" asked a voice from behind Kit.

Kit spun around to see a Berrat warrior with painted whorls on her face and arms. Her blonde-white hair was tied in tight braids which cascaded over her shoulder. "Fenrir, how may I serve you?" Kit asked as she immediately took a knee. The small god took her chin in her hand and gently encouraged her back to her feet.

"I am here to offer you some assistance, though, not directly," she said in her melodic voice. As her eyes moved to Kit's dragon hammer, her demeanor darkened. "You've chosen an unexpected ally," she said, sneering at Fury. Her lips curled as a low growl passed between them.

"I think she'll make a wonderful ally," Fury replied with a mischievous note.

"I wasn't talking to you," Fenrir snarled, her mouth now filled with an impressive set of fangs.

"Fury's been helpful," Kit interrupted, "I expect he will continue to be, as long as it suits his purpose." The dragon hammer whined at the assertions.

"Being on the *winning* side suits my purpose," he declared, pretending to be hurt by the women's words. "I do not hide the fact that I want to be whole again, and Kit is my best chance for that to happen. If I am right, I probably won't even have to look for my parts, they'll come to us willingly."

Fenrir rolled her eyes. "Be wary of him, Kit. Dragons only serve themselves." She waved her hand, dismissing Fury and the distraction he'd caused. "Allies will approach you in Silverhawk. You will *know* their hearts are true when you meet them. They are in league with your mother, your birthmother. They will be able to provide you with both information and support."

Kit's eyes went wide when Fenrir spoke of her birthmother. Might she finally get to meet her? So much was happening. Her mind raced at the implications of what she'd been told in the last hour. Even though Fenrir had been speaking to Kit, telling her of the connections she should make in both Silverhawk and Cormorant, the young priest's mind was a thousand leagues away. She occasionally grunted in response to what Fenrir was saying, but none of it was actually getting through to her. By the time Kit finished her daydream, Fenrir was gone.

"Fenrir?" Kit asked, her head swiveling around as she searched for the deity.

"Welcome back," Fury laughed. "Did you know that her last words, before disappearing, were: *This girl is hopeless.*"

Kit and Fury engaged in banter for several minutes. She was trying to get Fury to explain what Fenrir had said, and Fury mocked her inability to focus on the here and now, especially when a god was present. The conversation continued until they reached the stables.

"Ready to go?" Indie asked, with both Runt and Lump at his side. Kit squealed with delight as she threw herself into Indie's arms, covering him with kisses. The boys were both jumping at Kit, trying desperately to get her attention.

"I missed you, too," Indie laughed when she finally pulled away from him. Lump managed to wheedle his way between the pair, making room for both him and Runt to give her a proper, excessively slobbery greeting. In moments she was on her back with the two canines smothering her body in thick gold and black fur.

When they finally let her up, her previously combed hair was back to its unruly, traditional mess.

"You know, I was just on my way to get you." She quickly wiped her face with her sleeve before spitting out copious amounts of dog slobber onto the ground. The boys rubbed up against her, wanting to freshen her scent on their fur.

"I know," Indie said with his easy smile. "That's why we're packed up and ready to ride." As if on queue, Amara and Silverleaf came out from the stables, leading Char and Angel.

"I'm so happy to see you," Angel said through their bond. *"But I had Char to keep me company. The acolytes even let us share a stall."* Kit didn't know how to reply to that last comment. The horses were always housed in separate stalls, except for... *"Exactly,"* Angel said. Even through the bond Kit could feel her coy smile.

Kit couldn't find it in her heart to say goodbye to her friends. Something deep inside tugged at her, telling her that they would meet again. There were hugs, and laughs, and a few tears as Kit explained that she would not be coming back to the Temple. Even though nobody believed her, they pretended they did, and gave Kit a fond, heart-filled send-off.

"I want to stop by to see Captain Harding before we leave," Kit said as they mounted up and headed away from the Temple grounds.

"He's expecting you," Indie nodded. "Lin's there, too. She's not herself today."

"It's a long story," Kit said, her voice filled with resignation. "I don't know if we can trust her."

"I think you can," Indie replied. "She told Harding everything. Just before I left for the stables, I heard Harding call for Lieutenant Karr to be delivered to his office. I don't know what came of it though."

Kit pressed her lips together into a hard line. "I hope so," she finally said. "She was instrumental in the success of our rescue mission. But..." Something about Lin was gnawing at Kit but she couldn't figure it out. She was like an iceberg. What you saw was only a small percentage of the whole. "I just don't think she's who she seems to be. She executed a man, sliding her sword into his neck, twisting the blade to make sure it wouldn't ever heal. He was down and beaten."

Indie's eyes went wide as she recounted the tale of how Lin had killed Jailer. "That might be exactly the person we need with us, Kit. All I know is, you are everything to her."

CHAPTER THIRTY-FOUR

REUNION

Kit and Indie rode in silence the rest of the way to the barracks. Kit allowed her mind to wander aimlessly for most of the ride, not even noticing when children were running up to play with the boys along the way.

"You didn't comment on my new look," Indie said with a mock-hurt voice, bringing Kit back to reality.

"You look nice," she replied absentmindedly, without actually looking up at him. Indie's eyebrows shot up and he cleared his throat, repeatedly. When she finally glared over at him, her eyebrows mirrored his and her mouth flopped open for good measure. "Sweet Titan, are you wearing obsidian armor?"

"From head to toe," he beamed back at her. "Harding gave a set to all of us who completed the training. He also gave me these cold-iron longswords." He pulled a blade a few inches out of its scabbard, enough to show the fine workmanship and the bold damascened pattern in the steel. To get such a rich pattern, at least two different types of metal needed to be combined. Indie said it was cold-iron, but there was a second metal folded into it during the forging process, a bright silver metal of some sort. Neither of the pair knew much about forging, but they could both appreciate the beauty of the craftsmanship.

Kit's brows furrowed. Obsidian armor was in the shipment that Karr had taken from the Moreden twins. She couldn't help but wonder if this armor was a part of that same shipment. She found the look of the armor mesmerizing, the way the ink-black glass caught the light, sometimes reflecting it, sometimes absorbing it. Even from a distance, the quality of the workmanship was obvious, the stitching of the leather, the way the obsidian was interleaved throughout. Indie's gloves, boots, and pauldrons were all made in a similar fashion.

How could I have missed this earlier? He's so... beautiful.

"It's very nice," she declared, her face heating furiously. She wanted to look away, without being obvious, but it was hopeless. She nudged Angel into a trot and blew out a breath. She hadn't realized she'd been holding it. A deep flush creeped up her neck.

"They're both beautiful," Angel declared through their connection. It was obvious that she was talking about Char, which made Kit laugh out loud. *"Laugh all you like, but you know I'm right."*

"How was your training?" Kit asked, trying to change the subject.

"It was intense. I have much more respect for vampires. I believed it was their compulsion that made them dangerous, but that's only one of their many weapons." Indie visibly shivered as he finished the sentence. "Some possess a talent known as *celerity*. It allows them to move at inhuman speeds. They move so fast, they're barely a blur. If they have that talent, you can't strike directly at them – you have to aim for where they're going to be."

"That seems impossible," Kit gasped. "How can you guess where they'll be?"

"*Knowing* where they'll be is the trick, not guessing. All vampires, regardless of their talents, are driven by blood. Some can manage their urges, allowing them to walk about without the living ever noticing them, but in combat – their blood rage takes over. Their instincts will force them into close combat. They want to get at your neck. It's where the blood is closest to the skin, and they'll always take the shortest path to it." Indie's hand involuntarily moved to his throat, his skin paled.

"Hullo, Sister," a brightly faced guard greeted Kit. He couldn't have been more than seventeen cycles, barely able to grow facial hair. Even in the City Watch armor he appeared willowy. "Captain Harding is expecting you. He's in his office."

"Thanks, Mullen," Indie replied. "How's his mood?" Mullen grimaced at the question. "Okay then, not good."

"Maybe you two should wait outside," Kit suggested to Runt and Lump. "We won't be long." The two canines immediately bounded off, heading towards the mess hall. Apparently, they knew where to grab a quick and easy snack. As the boys disappeared, Kit tried to dismount, only to find her leg getting tangled with her new, longer-handled, battle hammer. Without giving it any real consideration, she pulled the hammer from its holster and slid down from Angel's back.

"I don't know what you're expecting but I don't think you're going to be needing your battle hammer in there," Indie suggested. His head snapped back when he spied her hammer's new bone handle, his face pinched slightly.

"Fury gets prickly if I leave him behind," she said as she spun the hammer in her hand.

"Fury?" Indie asked, his tone incredulous.

"It's a long story," Kit said with a laugh. "Apparently, we're going to have a lot to talk about on our way to Silverhawk." She gave Indie a small, flirtatious wink before she walked into the barracks. The familiar scent of blood and sweat greeted her as she entered the barracks' massive indoor training grounds. The indoor arena made up a large part of the barracks' space, and it was full to capacity. There was a mix of City Watch guards, Temple priests, and acolytes. They all seemed to be running obstacle courses, while avoiding being hit by arrows launched at them from multiple directions. There was an infirmary set up, where medics immediately treated the wounds of the injured, before they headed straight back onto the grounds.

"The bugs have gotten worse," Indie commented, as though it was a complete explanation. "Every able body is being prepared for combat."

"I didn't know," Kit said as she turned back at Indie. "Should we be helping?"

"No," Indie replied shaking his head. "Our mission is just as important, maybe even more so. We need the Berrat on our side, and right now, stemming the slaver activity will do the most good."

"What about calling in the Royal Guard? Surely the King can help with Arnnor's defenses." Kit's eyes were still fixed on the melee happening on the training grounds. Soldiers were being hit by arrows repeatedly. Even blunted, they could cause serious damage.

"The King has not responded to a single request." Indie pulled Kit by the sleeve towards the captain's office. He practically had to push her through the open door when they arrived.

"Welcome back, Sister," Harding said in his booming voice, standing from his chair as she entered. "I believe you know Lieutenant Karr."

The lieutenant was sitting on a chair with two guards standing on either side of him. They were not restraining him but leaving didn't seem to be an option for him. He appeared fit and well, but his spirit was broken. Despite his precarious position, Kit's eyes narrowed, and a sneer pulled at her lip. She had never particularly liked Karr, but up until now, she believed him to be a devoted guard even if he was a colossal jerk.

Harding slowly lowered himself back into his chair. "Lieutenant, I want you to recount what you told me about the weapons shipment you liberated from the merchants."

Whatever broken look Karr had disappeared immediately from his face. He set his jaw, like he was about to strike out at the guards standing next to him.

"Captain, as I said, we acted on information we received from some of the new recruits. We were told that a shipment of weapons coming in was going to be robbed." The lieutenant paused for a moment, giving everyone a chance to object to his statement of fact.

"You murdered them!" Kit snarled, her neck corded, spittle flying from her lips. "I watched as you killed them all."

"My men murdered nobody." Karr practically spat back at her as he denounced her attack. "We executed criminals; men sworn to the Watch. When they joined our ranks, they swore an oath to abide by the laws of this land. The people we executed, each and every one of them, deserved exactly what they got."

Kit was suddenly unsure of herself, of what she had seen with her own eyes. Karr was speaking truthfully to her. She knew he was. At her core, she could absolutely feel it. "And what of the Moreden twins? They were not members of the Watch, and yet you killed them, in cold blood."

The lieutenant took a deep breath, trying to calm himself before he continued. The look of loathing he had for the girl never diminished. "I executed two murderers. We are charged with the same duties as the Temple priests. We have authority to dispense justice, immediately and without reservation. We must make an accounting of our actions, and if we contravene the vows we took, our lives are forfeit. The Moreden twins were directly responsible for the deaths of eight caravan guards, and for treason against the Watch when they bribed my men into breaking the law."

"Has any part of his recounting rung false with you, Sister Standing Bear?" Harding's face resembled a block of granite, showing no emotion whatsoever. "You are the only true witness to the events, to the death of the merchants."

Kit bowed her head for a moment as she replayed the events in her mind, wondering to herself how she could have seen the incident so differently. "What lieutenant Karr describes is in line with what I witnessed. I *know* he is speaking the truth."

"You mean, you *believe* he's speaking the truth," Harding interjected, questioning Kit's choice of words.

"No, Captain, I *know* he's speaking true." She had a grim look on her face. The notion of standing up for Karr made her skin crawl. It made her feel dirty, like she was now somehow complicit with his actions.

The big man settled deeper into his chair, leaning back like he was about to have some fun with the girl. "Please, little sister, enlighten me as to how you can *know* this."

"Call it a gift," Kit said, smiling back at the now smug-faced captain.

The captain sat back up in his chair and leaned in towards the girl. "Okay, let's test this gift of yours. Ask me a question, one that you don't know if I'll know the answer to, and then tell me if I am speaking true."

Kit pondered for a moment, a question, a meaningful question that would prove her point. Her eyes lit up when she fell upon the query that she wanted an answer to.

"Do you know who my father is?"

The captain scoffed and a small smirk appeared on his face, his left eye twitched ever so slightly. "No! How could I possibly know him?"

Kit's eyes practically bulged out of her head. They almost immediately turned glassy. "You're lying to me," she said. Her heart raced so hard that she feared it would pound out of her chest and right through her armor. "You do know who my father is!"

The captain sat bolt upright in his chair; his neck flushed. His eyes flashed to Indie just a moment before his commander's face kicked in. His breathing returned to normal, but his jaw was still set tight.

"Lieutenant, you're cleared of any wrongdoing. Everybody out!" Not a single person moved, they were too dumbstruck by Kit's last statement. The captain stood from his chair, bringing his two meaty fists down on his desk in a thunderous boom. The top of the desk practically exploded on contact. "I SAID, OUT!" Like smoke in a breeze, everybody disappeared from the room without a word. All, except Kit and Indie, who both stood defiantly in front of the captain.

"Indie, I need time with Sister Kit," the captain's voice was now quiet, almost pleading.

"I'll be outside. Find me when you're ready," Indie whispered to Kit, giving her a quick kiss on the cheek. As he walked out, he gently closed the door behind him.

The captain stared down at his ruined desk, blood dripping heavily from both of his hands. Without a word, Kit moved in front of him and took his hands in hers; the size difference was astounding. The captain tried to pull his hands away, but she maintained a firm grip. A moment later, her hands were glowing a pale gold, the familiar warmth spreading through her body as the radiance fully engulfed the captain's hands and forearms. She winced as the aura spread out, but she maintained her hold. A moment later she pulled away, leaving the big man's hands fully healed.

"The desk is beyond my ability," Kit said with her patented smile, batting her eyelashes at him for extra effect. When she stopped playing around, she finally noticed that Harding's lower lip was quivering, and his hands were shaking badly. He quickly grasped them together to stop their trembling. He could not assuage the tears gathering in his eyes.

"You remind me so much of your mother, I can't stand it," he finally said, his tears now flowing freely over his cheeks. "I've wanted to tell you since the day you arrived at the city gates, when you were nothing more than a dirty pile of rags."

"You?" Kit asked, her own face now suddenly wet with tears. Harding lowered his head and nodded slowly.

"Why?" Kit stammered, "Why didn't you tell me? I've lived my whole life without a father, never knowing his love." As Harding's shoulders slumped, Kit's heart shattered. She pushed through his defenses and wrapped her arms around him. "What I just said was wrong. You have cared for me and loved me since the day I arrived. You have taught me more than you'll ever know. You let me be me."

Harding wrapped his arms around the girl, his daughter, practically crushing her with his embrace. "Your mother and I are so proud of you. What we have done, keeping you away from us, was for your protection. It killed me to not hold you, to not tell you that I loved you, but..."

"How could my knowing my parents be dangerous?" Kit asked, even though she knew her father was telling her the truth. Knowing what he had sacrificed all these years, for her, made Kit's heart swell.

"I cannot explain it," he said, as he pulled away to look at his daughter. "Your mother will tell you when the time is right."

"Where is she?" Kit asked, the first of a million questions that were now racing through her mind.

The man's giant shoulder's shrugged, a pained look crossed his face. "I don't know, not exactly anyway. I haven't seen her since you were born. I have been giving messages to Riva, and she's been taking care of getting them to your mother." Harding gave Kit a bit of a smile. "We've both been keeping her apprised of your life."

Kit's eyes suddenly went wide. "But you're married! You have a son. I have a brother!"

Harding rubbed his hand across the back of his neck, scrubbing it harder by the second. "It's complicated," he finally said, hoping it would be enough of an explanation. The look of expectation on Kit's face said that it clearly wasn't.

"I love your mother, with all my heart. I wanted to spend my life with her, but it wasn't possible. She told me, just before leaving for Berrathia with you, that we would never see each other again. She said that, where she was going, I couldn't follow." Kit's face crumpled and unbidden tears flowed once again.

"That's the very same thing that Riva told me. My mother said that she couldn't take me where she was going." This whole conversation was hard to take in. She was starting to swoon, so she quickly found a chair before she fell down. Harding leapt to her side, helping to ease her into the chair. He took a knee beside her and gently took her hands in his.

"Who is she? Why did she leave us?"

"You will meet her, very soon, I expect." He gazed deeply into her eyes and sighed. "I know very little about her, except that I love her completely." He stared down at his hands, inspecting them for any residual damage from demolishing his desk. "I met her on the battlefield during the Gizmo uprising. My hands had been mauled by a hill gizmo, one of the wolf types. I could no longer hold my weapon. She healed me. She came out of nowhere. Her healing power, it, it was the same as yours. We fought side by side for hours. When the battle was over, we…"

"On the battlefield?" Kit couldn't help but laugh, although the mental image of the captain and her mother on the blood-soaked countryside sobered her right up.

"Titan's snowballs, girl," he exclaimed, his face immediately turning bright red. He waved his hands about like he was trying to shoo away the topic. "We were inseparable for the next ten moons, but less than a moon after you were born, she insisted that we separate and never see each other again." The big man settled back onto his heels, his chin at his chest. "I waited a full cycle for her to return, but she never did. The day before you arrived in Aarall, Riva showed up and sought me out. She said you were coming, and that I should prepare a place for you in the city."

Kit wiped her nose with the back of her hand. "I came here to say goodbye." She teared up yet again. "I just found out I have a father, and that he's been here with me all along, and now I'm leaving."

"Life's funny like that," Harding said. "Wherever you are, piece of my heart, I will be with you."

"What will happen to Lin?" Kit asked, changing the subject before she started bawling. She swiped at her nose again with her sleeve.

Harding shrugged. "She should be held on conspiracy, but I'm not sure she actually broke any laws. She's free to join you if you want to have her along. She cares deeply for you." A wide grin broke out on his face, and he nodded slowly. "A father knows these things." The grin continued to widen until it fully split his face making Kit's eyes well up yet again.

"I guess we should get going then, if we're to make it to Silverhawk before the moon is gone." She stood from her chair and offered her hand to her father. She liked the sound of that, her father.

"I guess so." He got to his feet and immediately pulled Kit in for another hug; a deep, fatherly, hug. "Your man is probably wondering what's happening right now."

"Daddy!" Kit swatted at her father's beefy arm. She liked the sound of that, too. It wasn't a term typically used by Nomads, but she had heard it from westerners from time to time. It slid nicely from her tongue. It made her heart happy.

"He's a good man, and he loves you very much. I might even consider him *worthy*." The captain's words came to an end just as he opened the door, to discover Indie, Runt and Lump all standing there, staring at Kit and the captain. "And if he does anything to hurt my little girl, I'll snap him like kindling for a fire."

"Sir?" Indie squeaked. The color drained from his face.

"C'mon, let's get going," Kit said, grabbing Indie by the arm, dragging him away from her father's office. "Bye, Daddy," she called out over her shoulder.

Kit didn't know if anybody was watching or listening, but she simply didn't care. She had a father, a man she had respected for as long as she had known him.

She suddenly felt more whole, like a piece of herself that she never realized was missing, was suddenly there.

"That was very touching, young Kit," Fury said as he swung from Kit's waist. "It also confirms everything that I had expected."

THE STORY CONTINUES...

The story continues with *Eyes of Titan*, the next novel in the Priest of Titan series on Amazon.

Read on to discover more about how Silverleaf and Amara repaid Father Hoarfrost for the little mare they gave to Kit for her 16th birthday.

Silverleaf & Amara's Graveyard Shift

Silverleaf grumbled as he pulled his furs tighter around himself. Sitting on a granite headstone was doing nothing to warm him. Even though it was spring, and he was wearing his winter furs, the frigid wind still managed to find its way through every seam.

"Don't disrespect the dead," Amara said, looking down on the half elf. Unlike her fur-bundled friend, the young Gigas was dressed in light leathers, reveling in the crisp night air.

"Because I'm sitting on a headstone? Whoever this is, they've passed on to the Great Cycle. It's just a wooden box with bones buried here, and a piece of stone to mark their location." The young man needed to crane his neck to look up at the Gigas woman. Even though she was a cycle younger than the half elf, she stood more than two heads taller than him.

"That's the kind of talk that'll get you kicked out of the Temple," Amara said, taking a few steps back from her friend. As she stroked her long, blonde braid, her eyes went wide. The look on her face suggested that Titan himself might smite Silverleaf for his words.

"It's not like I'm ever going to become a full priest anyway," Silverleaf said with a huff. "We're both overage acolytes now and we'll never get a chance to try again."

Amara shivered.

"I don't ever want to climb that accursed mountain ever again."

"I still don't understand how you failed the test. You're practically immune to the cold. How did you not beat the Rite of Abandonment?" Silverleaf asked, his green eyes twinkling with mischief. "You've never told me the story."

"And I never will. The experience atop Mount Uha was personal, not meant to be shared. If it means that I will forever be an acolyte, then so be it."

"The only one of us who had any hope of becoming a priest was Kit. Father Hoarfrost has been grooming her to become High Priest some day. She's gotten special treatment since the day she arrived here."

"You sound like a jealous child," Amara scolded. "You have no idea what she went through to earn her place in the priesthood."

"No, no I don't. Because she got sent off on important missions, while we stayed tucked away doing chores in the Temple. What was your last task, cataloging scrolls in the Temple library?"

"I volunteered for that assignment," Amara said with a huff. "I like being around all those books and scrolls. They contain the wisdom of the ages. How could I not want to be there? Besides, your last assignment was helping Brother Powder in the apothecary. Are you going to tell me that was a task you didn't enjoy?"

"It wasn't a mission, not like what they send Sister Kit Standing Bear on." The half elf jumped down from the headstone, landing lithely on the mostly dead grass growing between the rows of graves. As his soft leather boots touched down, a gentle clinking noise escaped his cloak.

"What have you got in your coat?" Amara asked, curious as to why the young man would tinkle.

"Just some muffins, some cheese, and some bread that I picked up from the kitchens," Silverleaf responded, quickly wrapping his furs around himself. "In case I get hungry."

"That was not the sound of muffins or bread."

"I might also have a potion or three tucked into my pockets," he said with a shy grin. Amara shook her head.

"Expecting trouble, are we?" She knew that the young acolyte had a penchant for brewing potions, but he rarely shared the details of what he was creating, even with his best friend.

Silverleaf was immediately grateful for the darkness covering up his reddening face. He snatched up a clump of dried mud and tossed it at a nearby tree. He gave it a satisfied grin when it exploded against the tree's heavy-barked trunk. In his head, he was still considering Amara's comment, that he was jealous of their friend.

"I'm not jealous," he replied eventually, "but Father Hoarfrost sends her on missions, actual missions. He sends us out on babysitting jobs, hoping to see who might be knocking over headstones and robbing graves. I mean, really, who cares? These people are dead. What do they care if there is some jewelry buried with them in the box? He doesn't even trust us enough to send us here alone."

"He sent us on this mission because it's payment for the horse the Temple gave us, the one we gave to Kit for her birthday. Surely a few nights of lost sleep are worth the look of joy on Kit's face when she saw Angel and the ridiculous bow on her head." Amara's comment made Silverleaf smile. Doing the graveyard shift for a few nights really was worth the look on their friend's face.

"And, if you would rather do this duty on your own, I can go to the other side of the cemetery." Amara kicked at the low-hanging fog, causing it to swirl about her. Silverleaf considered her suggestion and frowned.

"No, I'm glad you're here. I hate this place."

"Because you're afraid something's going to come crawling up out of the ground?" the young Gigas laughed, her baritone voice carrying in the silence.

"*No,*" Silverleaf replied, straightening out his furs. "It's boring here. There is nothing to do, and besides, it's a sad place. These were all someone's loved ones, and now they're gone and they're never coming back. It makes me think of me, us really, getting dumped off at the Temple as babies because nobody wanted us."

"We are nothing like these dead people. We were given a chance at a better life. My parents were killed in a slaver raid and yours died of the wasting disease. Do you really think we have it so bad?"

"No, our life isn't bad. I'm just ..."

"Bored." The giantess said, finishing the young half elf's sentence.

Silverleaf smiled as he pulled one of his small battle hammers from its sheath at his hip. He twirled it a few times before he waggled his eyebrows at the Gigas. "If we catch whoever it is that's vandalizing the cemetery and we have to fight, are you going to use that glaive you're holding?"

Amara looked at the nearly twelve-foot polearm she was carrying, giving it her absolute best frown. "You know I'm a pacifist, and I will not intentionally bring harm onto another person. You know it's the way of my people. It's *always* been the way of my people."

"But you'll fight in our sparring classes," Silverleaf said, his eyebrows raised to ridiculous heights. "You nearly broke my back the last time we fought."

"That's for fun and competition," she added, as though it made perfect sense.

"So, you'll beat me up for fun, but you won't fight someone to protect yourself?"

"I am permitted to defend myself," she said, curling her lip slightly, "but I will not ever try to take somebody's life. Look around. The dead surround us. This is a sad place, you said so yourself. I will not be a part of ending someone's existence."

"It's just a waste," the half elf said as he tossed his hammer at the same tree he had accosted with the mud clump, embedding the pointy side of the hammer deeply into the tree's thick bark.

"You're probably the best fighter in the whole Temple. You've even bested Kit during training." Silverleaf crossed over to the tree and tried to extricate his hammer. After several heavy grunts, tugging to the point of turning red, the young Gigas went over and blithely pulled it out.

"I fight for fun, and I fight for exercise, and I fight because it's expected of me," Amara said, spinning her massive glaive like it was nothing more than a baton. "But I will not fight to kill. Ever."

Silverleaf shook his head. "If you won't kill, why, in the name of Titan, would you carry a glaive. It's basically designed to separate someone's head from their shoulders."

Amara got an evil look in her eye and, after performing a perfect spinning attack, swung the glaive's ax barely an inch over Silverleaf's head, causing his eyes to bug out from his face. Dropping down to the ground, well after the blade had already passed him by, he screamed out at the Gigas, asking why she would risk killing him.

"You know I won't kill you, and yet you're still frightened by my weapon," she laughed, spinning the weapon around with another flourish. "Consider somebody who doesn't know I won't kill them. It will make them soil themselves for sure."

Silverleaf said something under his breath that, if she had heard him, would have likely resulted in Amara kicking the half elf across the graveyard and back again.

∞∞∞∞◊∞∞∞

Several quiet, utterly boring hours passed by without incident. Amara needed to rouse Silverleaf several times when he'd dozed off, his back propped up against the tree he had been hitting with his hammer.

"Let's patrol the area," Amara said brightly. "If nothing else, the walk will help keep you awake."

After a good deal of protestation, Silverleaf finally agreed, and the pair began patrolling the graveyard. After spending nearly an hour walking the cemetery's perimeter, Silverleaf started becoming bored again. He fumbled around in his pockets and pulled out a large chunk of cheese. As he unwrapped the paper holding it, Amara made a sound of utter disgust.

"How can you eat that?" she asked, wrinkling her nose and turning away. "It smells like old feet that walked through a dung pile." Silverleaf smiled and took a big, noisy bite. He followed it up with exaggerated chewing sounds before swallowing the odoriferous chunk of food.

"It's delicious. Sam's Cheeserie has the best cheese in all of Arnnor," he said just before biting off another chunk. Amara gagged.

"Please put it away, it's going to make me hurl." Silverleaf did as his friend asked, wrapping it in its paper and stowing it away in his furs.

"Are you up to playing a game?" the half elf asked, licking his fingers. "There's hardly any moon out tonight, so why don't we play some hide and seek? Since it will force us both to be silent while we seek each other, we'll still be able to catch anyone who decides to vandalize the graveyard."

Amara, one who would typically never shirk her responsibilities, was immediately sucked in by the idea of having a competition.

"What do I get when I best you?" Amara asked, twiddling with her long, blonde braid. "I think maybe I'd like you to clean and polish all my gear."

The half elf considered her wager.

"Deal," he said brightly. "I accept."

"And what do you want, in the unlikely event that you win?" she asked, leaning on the haft of her glaive.

"I'll tell you when I win," he said with a wink.

After a brief discussion, they decided to keep the rules simple. They would split up, moving to opposite sides of the graveyard. When they reached the boundary, they would begin seeking the other player. The object was to strike the opponent with a mud clump, without the other player seeing them. When Amara picked up a mud clump larger than Silverleaf's head, he grimaced, knowing that if he lost, it was going to hurt ... bad. But he also knew, when it came to sneaking in the dark, he was definitely better than Amara. His having excellent night vision didn't hurt either.

Silverleaf watched as the enormous Gigas girl raced across the graveyard. His head snapped back when he noticed that she was barely making any noise as she moved. Apparently, she had been practicing her stealth skills. The half elf shivered slightly when he thought he may in fact lose this competition unless he was completely committed to remaining silent and unseen.

It only took Silverleaf a few minutes to get to the west side of the graveyard. As soon as he reached the boundary, he spun around and slowly headed north, towards the cemetery's main gate. He figured that even though Amara was the most competitive person he knew, she was also the most duty-bound person he had ever met. So, if those assertions were true, then she would stay close to the cemetery's most heavily trafficked point of entry.

A gust of wind kicked up, shaking the limbs of the tallest of trees. The clacking of the branches sounded like the footfalls of some fell creature hunting in the hallowed fields of the dead, its insatiable hunger for flesh and blood driving it forward, searching for those who may wander the cemetery after the sun had set. The wind died off and the footfalls died away with it, but the thought that he was not alone had already crept into the half elf's mind.

Get a grip.

Silverleaf pulled his furs around himself, causing the vials within his pockets to tinkle together. He quickly pressed his hand over them to silence the bell-like noises. If there was a creature in the graveyard, which he was certain there wasn't, there was no sense in ringing a dinner bell for it.

Staying in the deepest shadows, the young acolyte picked his way through the burial sites, using trees and the largest gravestones for concealment. Anytime he managed to slip into deep cover, he paused long enough to scan the area, hoping to catch a glimpse of the giant. At times, he found himself holding his breath, hoping to hear her moving about.

Groaning silently to himself, the half elf continued on, ducking and weaving in the darkness.

⌘

After what felt like an hour of searching, Silverleaf was about ready to give up. It was entirely possible they were both wandering about on opposite ends of the cemetery, and they would never run into each other. The sliver of a yellow-silver moon was lowering in the night sky, and the first rays of dawn would be upon them in a little more than an hour. The rising sun would mark the start of a new day and the end of their babysitting duty, so he decided to continue playing, if for no other reason than because it was more entertaining than sitting around, doing nothing.

It was when Silverleaf passed by the stately Moreden mausoleum, he heard a noise. This wasn't his imagination playing tricks on him. This was definitely the sound of somebody walking through dead grass. Finally, his patience had paid off and he had a chance of winning the competition. As best as he could tell, the noise came from somewhere in front of the ostentatious white-stone structure. Ducking around the east side of the crypt, the side that would afford him the best shadows to move through, he moved silently along until he approached the front corner of the building.

From behind a heavily thorned barberry hedge he peered out towards the mausoleum's portico. In addition to its thick, ornately carved pillars, there were also two statues of Titan at each corner. The sculptures were exact replicas of the enormous ice-statue of Titan that had been built into the face of Mount Toka, to the east of Aarall's city walls. Silverleaf grinned slightly when he considered that he would be using Titan to keep himself hidden.

After skulking between the pillars and the great stone figures, Silverleaf took a knee behind one of the statues. He waited intently to hear the slightest of sounds or to catch the briefest of movements. As he waited, he slowed his breathing, and when he reached a state of complete relaxation, he finally picked up Amara's footfalls.

Even as acolytes, Titan granted powers to his followers. Where most acolytes would choose strength or fighting prowess, Silverleaf chose the skills of stealth and observation. Where full priests could call on Titan's aid several times a day, acolytes could only cast a single spell, or *miracle*, as they were often referred to. The new day would start at sunrise and seeing as how he had not yet used his daily miracle; the half elf bowed his head in silent prayer.

"Titan, hear me," he said, his voice barely louder than a gentle, summer breeze. "I call upon thee to grant me your favor that I may serve you. I call upon thee to grant me the power of stealth, that I may move among the wicked and be unseen until I deliver unto them your divine justice."

Almost instantly, a surge of energy flowed through him, as wisps of inky-black smoke swirled around his body. Silverleaf loved the feeling of calling upon his deity. It reminded him of when he had to be heavily sedated after taking an ax to his stomach during sparring practice. There was a moment, barely lasting a second or two, as the effects of the spell coursed through his system, that he felt invulnerable. The feeling was completely addictive, and he surmised it was a big part of how the Temple attracted and kept the acolytes in the service of Titan.

With Titan's blessing enhancing his stealth skills, the half elf slipped out of his hiding place and slunk in the direction he had last heard the noise.

⚜

Another gust of wind kicked up, blowing old leaf litter across the entrance to the mausoleum. The sounds of dried leaves rolling haplessly over the ground would help cover any noise Silverleaf might make as he scampered towards one of the many small crypts that surrounded the larger, white marble structure. He pressed his back tightly against the smaller building, clutching the pocket-full of potions to make sure they made no noise. Dipping closer to the ground, he loosened a clump of dirt and clutched it lightly. He rolled it over several times in his fingers until he had a good grip.

A cloud rolled across the sliver of a moon, obscuring what little light had been illuminating the grounds. Even though the half elf had excellent night vision, it was so dark that he could barely see ten paces.

If I can't see well, then Amara can't see at all.

He slipped out from his position, and with the aid of his stealth spell, nary made a noise. A grim smile spread across his face when he caught the silhouette of Amara standing between two large headstones. With one smooth motion, he launched his mud clump at the woman, striking her squarely in the back of the head.

"Victory!" Silverleaf shouted. "I claim victory!"

Amara turned, a low rumbling growl coming from her throat. She would not be happy about losing, but she sounded furious.

"C'mon, Amara, I won fair."

The cloud that had covered the sliver of moon passed by, allowing its pale-yellow light to fall upon the woman. Silverleaf's blood ran cold. This wasn't Amara. The two headstones that were on either side of this person unfurled, revealing two, thick-bodied people. They were much shorter than the first, but they appeared much more powerful. They each took a menacing step towards the young half elf. They were making an odd, snuffling noise. He took a step backwards as his hands slipped towards his battle hammers. Their leather wrapped handles gave him a sense of security. He had trained under Sister Gale for many years. He had won and lost many of his sparring matches in her classes, but he had never fought anyone who had true, deadly intent. Losing here meant dying.

The two shorter, heavier people moved off to the sides in a flanking maneuver while the taller person moved straight at him. A slight shift in the breeze carried the rank scent of decay with it. A deep, raspy rattle came from one of the people flanking him. The other responded in kind.

"By the power of Titan, I command you to stop!" Silverleaf said, his voice not carrying nearly the level of authority he had hoped. The two people flanking him laughed, if you could call it that. It sounded like a metal grate being pulled slowly over rough stone.

The taller person, the one coming straight for him, threw back his hood. Silverleaf recoiled at the sight. His head resembled a skull with skin stretched tightly over it. Tall, pointed ears protruded well beyond the top of the creature's head. A gravelly noise came from one of the two flanking him, drawing the half elf's attention away from the horrid looking man before him. He was almost within arm's reach. The man's hood was still up, but like his taller cohort, his face looked like that of a skeleton. The stench that poured off him nearly made Silverleaf retch.

Once again, a cloud drifted across the moon, casting the cemetery into total darkness. His three attackers fell into shadow and Silverleaf took the opportunity to duck low under what he perceived to be the outstretched hand of one of his attackers. He swung wildly with his battle hammer at his unseen enemy. He continued to swing until his lungs burned from the exertion, but he never made contact with anything. The clouds traveled past the moon, its pale glow once again chasing away the darkness. He was standing alone. His enemies had vanished.

What the Helja?

Silverleaf spun on the spot, searching for the three men, or creatures, or whatever they were. How could they have disappeared? They were right beside him. His mouth dropped open as he tried to deduce what had just happened. A sudden sharp pain exploded in the back of his head, knocking him several steps forward. He stumbled awkwardly before falling to his hands and knees.

"I claim victory!" The sonorous voice of Amara brought him back from the edge of unconsciousness. "You'd better do a good job cleaning my gear."

"Shush," he said, gripping the back of his head where the mud-clump had struck him. He took a quick check to see if he was bleeding, but all he had on his hand was dirt.

"Don't shush me. I won."

"Shush," he repeated, his voice a harsh whisper. "The grave-robbers were just here."

"Liar," she whispered back. "I've been following you for nearly twenty minutes. I saw nobody."

"What do you mean, you were following me?" The idea that she had been toying with him bothered Silverleaf much more than it should have. "How could you not have seen the three men who were here, not two minutes ago?" Amara shrugged at the question.

"I couldn't see you very well, but I could smell that cheese from a mile off. When the clouds blocked the moon, I lost sight of you." She paused for several moments, studying Silverleaf's expression. "You're serious, aren't you."

"Yes, I'm serious," he hissed back. "They were just here, three of them." The young man's face went pale.

"What?" Amara whispered, looking around.

"The graves," he whispered, "they're all dug up." All around where they were standing, coffins had been unearthed. Bone-white burial shrouds lay across their broken wooden tops.

"How had we not heard them?" Amara asked, picking up one of the death shrouds. It stunk of mold and decay, and it left a bitter taste in her mouth. She threw it back to the ground and spun around.

The pair were turning in circles, their backs to one another, hoping to catch a glimpse of the three men. The wind was picking up, rattling the branches high above, making hearing anything nearly impossible. The screech of metal grinding over stone echoed across the graveyard.

"The mausoleum," Silverleaf said, as he hunched down and started skulking towards the grand building. Amara swung out wide, separating herself from her friend, but still keeping him in view. Silverleaf paused briefly at the back of a tall, thin monument before sneaking a peek around its corner. He yanked his head back immediately and motioned to Amara to stay low. The half elf was trying to give her hand signals, but the Gigas couldn't see well enough in the dark to make them out. He peered again around the base of the monument to get another look, and when he turned back, Amara was gone.

He called out with a hushed voice for his friend, but the Gigas was nowhere to be seen. Keeping himself low enough to the ground that he could smell the earth beneath his feet, Silverleaf scampered to where he had last seen his friend. He skidded to a halt when he saw the woman's glaive laying across a patch of dead flowers.

"Amara?" he called out in a heavy whisper. "Amara, we need to leave – now!" A bank of clouds blew across the moon, casting the area in complete darkness yet again. He searched the ground in vain for footprints, but without any moonlight, it was impossible to discover anything meaningful. With a shake of his head, he ran back to the monument he'd been hiding behind just minutes earlier. Taking a deep breath, he moved around to the front of it, giving him a full-on view of the mausoleum and the procession of black-robed people filing into it. Under the cover of clouds, it was difficult to tell for sure, but it looked like several of the people were carrying something over their shoulders. The half elf's blood froze when two of the people seemed to be dragging something behind them, something that appeared to be the general size and shape of Amara.

A darkness much deeper than a moonless night crept into the young man's soul. His breathing quickened to match his out-of-control racing heart. He needed to help his friend, his best friend, but how? He was one and they were many, and the young half elf was not the best of fighters. The best fighter he knew was unconscious and being dragged into Titan knows what.

Titan, help me.

He had no idea what help he needed, but right now Silverleaf was drowning in a sea of doubt and indecision.

I'm coming, Amara. I won't let you down.

He waited until the last of the robed bodies entered the crypt before bolting across the clearing towards the door. He had to slip past them before the door was closed. The chance of succeeding was incredibly small, but he didn't care. He took the three steps leading up to the portico in a single bound, trying to keep a statue of Titan between himself and the door. Another gust of wind kicked up, raising a cloud of dust, making the tree limbs clack against each other. Keeping himself as low to the ground as his body would let him, he skulked to the wall and quickly peered inside the still open door. He had expected guards, but there was only a damp silence. The young man pressed his hand to his chest, fearing his heart's thunderous thumping might give away his presence.

Again, he quickly poked his head into the doorway and pulled it back once more. He could see nothing, except for a pale, flickering light beyond what appeared to be statues of Titan, Ymir, and Fenrir. Beads of sweat that had been gathering along his hairline dripped over his heavy eyebrows and into his eyes. He quickly rubbed them away, his eyes now burning badly.

I'm coming, Amara.

He slipped through the still open iron-clad door and into the building. It was dank, and musty, and reeked of death and decay. The flickering lights beyond the statues of the gods seemed to give life to their forms, the face of Titan appearing particularly grim.

To his left and right were rows of sarcophaguses. These were the resting places of the city's rich and powerful. These were people who'd likely been buried with their riches and yet none of the great stone caskets appeared to be disturbed. A sudden chill ran up the young man's spine. The room made for a natural choke point, a perfect trap. The enemy could be lurking behind any of these tombs. He quickly slipped his hammers from their slings and took a combat stance. The time between each of his heartbeats felt like an eternity. He waited and listened, expecting one or more assailants to leap out at him at any moment.

That moment never came.

His catlike footfalls barely disturbed the dust covered floor as he moved quickly between the statues towards the light. The room continued on for a good distance beyond the stone likenesses of the gods, with rows of sarcophaguses lining each side as they did at the room's entrance. The dancing light seemed to be coming up from a hole in the floor, likely a stairway leading to the catacombs.

If there were braziers or torches lit in the burial warrens, there was no way he was going to be able to hide his descent down the stairway. His stealth spell boosted his ability to move silently and hide in the shadows, but it wasn't an invisibility spell.

Sweet Titan, how could I be so dense?

After placing his hammers on the tiled floor beside him, the half elf dug into the recesses of his furs and felt around for the vials tucked within. The tiny glass jars tinkled lightly as he disturbed them, his fingers feeling each one until he came across the round, fluted jar. He pulled it out and shook his head. It was an invisibility potion, of sorts. He lacked the skill to make a true potion of invisibility, but he had managed to create a concoction that came fairly close. It had a bad side-effect, however. It would completely destroy his night vision. He could only surmise that the cloud of obscurity that it would create around him would also interfere with his ability to look through it.

He didn't care. He needed to walk down a well-lit hallway, possibly filled with enemies, and he had no choice if he was going to try and save his friend. He pulled the tiny stopper and raised the bottle to his lips. The familiar scents of licorice and nightshade tickled his nose. This potion, if mixed improperly, was deadly, but again, he didn't care. In a single gulp he downed the contents of the vial and slipped the empty bottle into another pocket. The liquid burned his tongue and throat, but it would pass. He just needed to wait a few minutes. When the burning subsided, the potion would be fully active.

The young man reached down, picked up his hammers, and slunk down the stairs.

∽∾∾⧉∾∾∽

The wooden stairs groaned lightly under the half elf's weight. Where the mausoleum's upper floor was tile and stone, the lower level seemed to be wood and dried mud. The guttering light of a torch thirty paces further down the hall cast dancing shadows over the shelves hosting the bodies of those long since passed. Most of the corpses were wrapped in shrouds, but many had been disturbed by rats and other vermin. The cloth had been eaten away, revealing the darkly stained bones beneath.

The air in the catacomb was dank and reeked of mold and mildew. It left a sour taste on Silverleaf's tongue. With a grimace, he licked his lips and tried to see further down the hall. As much as he wanted the benefits of his invisibility potion, his reduced vision was a hinderance. The sound of constantly dripping water from somewhere up ahead would help mask any noise he might make, but there was no real place to hide should trouble appear. Nevertheless, the young acolyte did his best to hug the endless shelves of the dead and stay in the shadows.

The half elf continued skulking along the corridor until he was directly under the sconce holding the torch. It was only at this point that he could clearly see the shelves of dead bodies. Each shelf was deep enough to hold six bodies, side by side. There were five shelves on each wall, made of rough-cut timbers. The wood showed signs of insect damage, but they still looked like they would last a thousand cycles. The floor was constructed of short, thick planks. The wood was worn and twisted, making the footing uneven. He peered further down the hallway, only to discover that he could barely see twenty paces into the darkness.

What little night vision he had was ruined by the light of the torch and the time he spent examining his surroundings. It would take a while for his eyes to adjust to the darkness once again. He took a deep breath and renewed his grip on his hammers. He blew out his cheeks and started trotting further down the hall, timing his footfalls to match the pattern of the ceaselessly dripping water.

After heading deeper into the darkness, Silverleaf's night vision was returning slightly. He was now standing over the source of the dripping noise. There was a thin ribbon of river running across the hallway, several feet beneath the floorboards. Beyond the wall of dead bodies, the tiny stream fell away, the water splashing some distance below. The air there was marginally fresher, giving the young man's nose a welcome respite from the ever-growing stench of mold.

Squeaking, and the sound of tiny feet pattering beneath the floorboards, said there was a healthy population of rats living along the water source. A shiver ran up his spine at the thought of them infesting the dead. The possibility of one or more of them leaping on him from the death-lined walls forced Silverleaf to move more towards the middle of the warren. He wrapped his furs tightly around himself and started heading further down the corridor.

In the darkness, the half elf didn't see that the corridor came to an end. He ran headlong into the wall, his head crashing into a shelf holding yet another stack of dead bodies. Several rats squealed and scampered away. He held his breath, fearing the noise would have given away his presence, but all was silent, except for the tiny gnawing noises coming from the shelf above his head.

To his left was total darkness. To his right, a faint light could be seen at the end of another very long corridor. He took a few timid steps to his left, holding his arms out before him, his outstretched fingers probing in the blackness. He took several hesitant steps into the inky tunnel, only to find the space completely empty. It was curious that he could see nothing, not even so much as a shadow ahead of him. His night vision was badly impaired by his invisibility potion, but he would not have expected it to be so bad that the darkness of the tunnel would appear as a void.

He turned back towards the lighted hallway, only to find that the light had gone out. He quickly moved to the wall, pressing his back against the shelves.

The thought of a rat climbing onto him made his insides twitch, but standing out in the open, even in darkness, was a bad idea. He took a few tentative steps in the direction the light had been when it suddenly winked on. He instinctively ducked back, and the light winked out.

The young man's heart was now hammering in his chest. He had to forcibly calm his breathing which was becoming erratic. He waited, and listened, but there were no sounds other than that of his heartbeat and patter of tiny paws inches away from his ear.

He slipped his hammers back into their scabbards and dropped down to his hands and knees. The floorboards here were smooth and dry, with significant gaps running between them. Lowering his belly until it was flush with the ground, he crept forward, a few inches at a time. As he pulled himself along the floor, the light up ahead winked on again. He quickly retracted himself and the light was immediately extinguished.

What in Helja?

He slowly leaned forward, and the light was once again visible. He blinked at it for a moment, retracted his head again and the light winked out.

Sweet Titan, someone had cast a darkness spell in the hallway. The light at the other end was a ruse, designed to lure anyone who might have followed them down the wrong path.

He spun around and stared into the never-ending darkness. He was about to start heading off when the sound of footfalls and a steady thumping noise drew his attention back from where he had come. He slowly pressed his face in that direction, stopping as soon as the light at the far end of the tunnel came into view. A moment later, a tall figure appeared, thumping something on the ground. Even though the light was very dim, it looked to be Amara's glaive. His heart jumped up into his throat thinking that perhaps, beyond reason, the dark figure was his friend and perhaps she was coming to look for him.

The shape turned and walked towards him at an ominous pace. Friend or foe, whoever it was, would be on him in mere seconds. Silverleaf pulled himself back into the darkness and tucked himself into a tight ball. As the footsteps neared, he held his breath, fearing that it might be enough to give away his position.

A tiny weight landed on his shoulder and a set of fine, hair-like whiskers tickled his ear. Every nerve in his body screamed at him to brush the rat away, but the footsteps were now within arms reach. He shook his shoulder slightly, hoping to dissuade the animal. Instead of leaving, the furry creature slipped beneath his furs and ran down his chest. Its tiny claws were digging into his skin as it scurried about. A moment later, it traveled into one of his many pockets.

The thump of the glaive landed a breath away from him and whoever was holding it stopped. The thick stench of death rolled off whoever it was standing next to him. He could hear a snuffling noise. Perhaps it was trying to sniff him. Silverleaf quickly squeezed his furs, causing the rat within to squeal out. Whoever, or whatever it was standing next to him hissed and slowly continued walking into the inky blackness.

The half elf waited for several long seconds as the sound of footsteps and the thumping of the weapon's haft slowly receded. He slowly let out his breath and sucked hard, filling his lungs with air. He had no idea how long he had been holding his breath, but it was only at the last second that he realized he was nearly ready to pass out. He quickly reached into his pocket and grabbed the rat by the tail. He dropped the animal to the ground beside him. He couldn't see it, but he gave it a small nod of thanks for the roll it had played in getting him past whatever that was that had walked by.

He reached into the pocket where the creature had been and grimaced. It had found his supply of snacks that he had stowed away just in case he got hungry during his graveyard shift. With a shrug, he headed into the darkness, following whoever or whatever had just walked past.

Thankfully, the darkness spell was localized, and it only took a dozen paces to pass through it. Even though it had no effect on air quality, he took a deep breath when he finally emerged. Being within the spell's aura of darkness felt like he had been buried alive. A weak light was leaking up through the floorboards, illuminating the tunnel enough that Silverleaf could get a clear view of the shelves and the entombed bodies that had been haphazardly crammed together. Their death shrouds were tattered and worn, likely the result of more rat activity.

Why drag bodies down here? What was wrong with these people?

He placed his hand on the exposed shoulder of a corpse. The bones were cold and dry. He pressed his lips into a thin line and continued down the hallway. The light seeping up through the floorboards got brighter the further along he went. He didn't know if it was actually brighter, or whether the spacing between the floorboards had increased. Either way, it gave him an uneasy feeling.

What if my invisibility spell is wearing off, and that's why I can see better?

He really had no way of telling what the state of his invisibility was. Even invisible, he'd be able to see himself. Such was the nature of the spell. He shook off the idea. The spell was active. It had to be. They simply didn't wear off that quickly.

The half elf dropped to his knees where the light shining up through the floorboards was particularly bright. The gap in the wood here was wide enough that he could put his fingers between them. He looked from as many angles as he could manage, but all he could see was the wooden floor beneath him. He picked himself up off the ground and continued down the corridor.

It was difficult to tell how far he'd traveled or how long he'd been below the mausoleum. There was no point of reference and the changing light conditions played tricks on his mind. So much so, that he thought the skeletal hand of one of the corpses reached out for him as he passed.

A rat likely, moving within the death shroud.

He took a peek over his shoulder after he was several paces past and waited. He stared at it for more than a few seconds, watching intently for any movement, but it remained still. The sudden realization that he was in a tunnel beneath a mausoleum surrounded by dead bodies sent a shiver up his spine.

Get a grip.

He turned and started heading down the hallway again. He had taken no more than four paces when a hollow, rattling noise made his head snap around. He stood transfixed, staring at the skeleton that was dragging itself off its shelf. It fell to the floor with a clatter. For several seconds, it lay in a heap.

What the Helja? How?

His thought was cut off when the bones began moving, rattling about like they were engaged in a bizarre, uncoordinated dance. At an inexorable pace the skeleton continued until it stood erect, its body a full head shorter than Silverleaf. The half elf's hand slipped down to his hammer while his heart thundered in his chest. He clenched his butt-cheeks together when he felt his bowels starting to loosen.

He slid his hammer from its sheath and gripped it tightly, waiting for the skeleton to move towards him, but it never did. It remained motionless, staring at him through empty, lifeless eye sockets. Silverleaf raised his hammer to shoulder height and took a step towards the animated bones. They remained still.

"What are you?" he hissed at the skeleton. It continued to stand, frozen in place. He raised his hammer higher and took another step forward. The muscles in his neck, shoulders, and back were tense, ready to unleash a strike hard enough to crush its skull. The skeleton took a half-step back and thrust its arms out to its side, as though blocking the half elf from exiting. Silverleaf practically jumped at the clatter of bones coming from behind him. He spun around to see two sets of bones tangled with each other trying to right themselves.

Do not face enemies on two fronts. Divide and conquer. These were the warnings of his combat instructor, Sister Gale. Unless you had advanced combat skills, which he certainly didn't, fighting with an enemy at your back was certain death. He didn't wait to think this through any further.

With a single fluid motion, he spun back to the lone skeleton and brought his hammer down on its skull. The bones shattered like eggshells, exploding in a cloud of shards and dust. The animated corpse dropped down to the floor in a heap, its numerous parts spraying across the wooden boards.

Boney fingers wrapped themselves around his neck and pulled the half elf off balance. He swung wildly with his hammer, hitting nothing but air. A second hand grabbed the haft of his hammer. With ungodly strength it tugged. The skeleton was unnaturally strong, and it ripped the weapon from his hand with ease. Another hand shoved him hard, sending him sprawling across the bone-littered ground. He tried to spring to his feet, but the myriad of bones on the floor made the footing treacherous.

Silverleaf reached for his second hammer. A sigh of relief spread through him as his fingers gripped its leather-wrapped handle.

When facing two opponents in close quarters, try to use one of them as a shield from the other. This was yet more advice given by his combat instructor.

The young acolyte stepped over the bones, careful to not have his foot land on one. He quickly slid to the right, isolating one of the two skeletons standing before him. With surprising speed, it reached out to grasp him, but Silverleaf was faster, bringing his hammer down onto the corpse's head. Like the first, its skull exploded on contact and its collection of bones fell in a heap, adding to the pile already there.

The remaining skeleton lurched forward, both hands outstretched, ready to grasp onto anything within reach of its boney fingers. The footing was as equally precarious for the dead as it was for the living. As the skeleton got a hold of Silverleaf's furs, it lost its balance and crashed heavily to the floor, dragging the half elf down with it. The pair tumbled around on the wooden path, knocking bones in every direction.

The creature had his back, making it difficult for the half elf to swing his hammer at him. He felt a sharp pain in his neck, like a great vice had just clamped down on him. He could see the skeleton's hands gripping his furs at his chest.

Holy Helja, it's trying to eat me.

Using the butt of his hammer, he rammed it over his shoulder, slamming it into the skeleton's face. The pressure on his neck increased significantly. He wanted to scream out in pain, but instead, he gritted his teeth, desperately trying to not draw any more attention to himself from anybody, or anything, further down the corridor. He quickly spun the hammer around in his hand and slammed its iron point into the skeleton's face. There was a satisfying crack on impact and the pain in his neck instantly abated.

The skeleton still had a bear-like grip around his chest, making it difficult for Silverleaf to breathe. He managed to get his weight under himself, and with little effort, got up onto his feet, dragging the skeleton with him. With more room to maneuver, he blindly threw his hammer over his shoulder, making solid contact with the creature's skull. The loosened grip on his furs told him that the strike had been fatal.

Did I kill them? Can you kill something that's already dead?

His random musings were cut short by the sound of a scream. It sounded like it came from a man, but Amara's voice was so deep that it might well have been hers. Silverleaf scooped up the hammer the skeleton had ripped from his hands, and with both weapons at the ready, he ran headlong down the hallway. The sound of his feet slamming into the wooden floor echoed down the tunnel.

The hallway came to an end, and like before, branched off in two directions. To the right, the hallway was dark. To the left, light continued to seep up through the floorboards. The darkness to the right was not absolute, it was not magical in nature. Without giving it a great deal of thought, he turned left and continued to run headlong between the shelves of the dead. If any more skeletons appeared, he would hopefully be long past them before they were ready to fight.

Up ahead, perhaps thirty paces or so, there was a large light in the floor, likely another set of stairs leading down. Standing in front of the stairway was the silhouette of a what looked like a man wielding a longsword. Silverleaf skidded to a halt some twenty paces from the silhouette.

"Who's there?" the shape called out. Its voice was masculine. Silverleaf stood perfectly still, his breathing was rapid and much too loud. He desperately tried to get it under control, but it was impossible to maintain. He quickly took a deep breath and tried to hold it. The man-shape took a few steps forward, his sword swinging lightly at his side.

"Show yourself," the man said, his voice having a hint of uneasiness to it. The air whooshed out of Silverleaf's lungs as he was forced to draw a breath. The man's progress stopped. He stood very still for several seconds before slowly taking a step back.

"Who's there?" he asked again, holding his sword tip in front of himself. It was wavering badly.

He can't see me. He's frightened.

The half elf did his best to lower his voice and make it as raspy as he could manage.

"Leave. Now," he rattled out.

The silhouette peered down the stairs and then back towards the disembod-
ied voice.

"I wasn't paid enough for this. Not nearly enough." The man's sword clattered on the wooden floor just before he started running directly at the half elf.
If Silverleaf hadn't pressed himself against the shelves, the man would have run
directly into him.

Once the footfalls had receded in the distance, Silverleaf turned and walked
towards the next set of stairs and the warm yellow light that was pouring up
from below.

⚜

The stairs leading down to the next level were rotting badly. With each step, the
wood groaned heavily under Silverleaf's weight. With each step, he feared he was
going to be found. With each step, he was closer to wherever it was that Amara
had been taken. He was sure of it. He could feel it in his bones.

When his feet finally met with the hard dirt floor, he quickly surveyed the
area, only to find it to be yet another hallway with shelves upon shelves of dead
bodies. There was a hint of death and decay here. The bodies on the shelves
appeared mummified, but somewhere here, there were bodies of the recently
deceased.

There was only one corridor, leading away from the stairs. Torches in sconces
guttered along the way, spaced evenly at twenty paces or so. The ceiling was the
floorboards of the hallway above. With only one direction to go, the half elf
crept down the hallway, trying to not let his boots scuffle too loudly along the
packed dirt floor.

Silverleaf was about to increase his speed when he came upon a tunnel that
crossed his own. He slowly poked his head around the corner, hoping to get a
look at who or what might be there. He blew out a breath when he realized they
were only alcoves, or perhaps the beginnings of new hallways for storing more
dead. The half elf shuddered. Sure, death was a part of life, but he had never

really considered what happened to the people's bodies after they had passed to the Great Cycle.

Amara's scream filled the hallway. He couldn't be sure if it was pain, terror, or anger, but if she was screaming, she needed help.

Unsure if his potion of invisibility or spell of stealth were still active, Silverleaf increased his speed and started running down the hallway. His battle hammers were at the ready as the warrens turned. Torches along the walls continued to light the way. He no longer cared that he was surrounded by the dead. He no longer cared if the enemy was going to jump out at him. He was going to help his friend, regardless of the risk.

The hallway suddenly opened to a huge circular chamber. Its walls looked to be about twenty feet high with a stone balcony perhaps ten feet from the ground. At the center of the room was a raised dais with a large black stone altar at its center. Behind the altar was a tall, thin man dressed in black robes with his hands raised above his head. Behind the man was the statue of Ymir, the ice god, the chosen of Titan. The statue was perhaps twelve feet tall, with his bone trident in one hand, and his other hand extended out over the altar. To the left of the statue, a chain hung from the ceiling. Amara was at the end of the chain, dangling from a pair of manacles. Below her were eight flesh-rotten people, reaching up at her. She was keeping her knees tucked up, trying to stay clear of their outstretched arms. Blood dripped from deep scratches on her legs. With each drip, the corpse-things clambered to lick it up.

Upon the altar was a corpse still wrapped in its burial shroud. The robed man reached down to the dead body and began tearing the fabric away from its remains. As the veil fell away, it revealed the corpse of a recently dead woman. Her skin was pale and covered in what looked like open sores. The man raised his hands and began chanting. The words he spoke were foreign, a language Silverleaf had never heard before.

Six other black robed people who were kneeling before the altar raised up their arms in unison and joined in the chanting. Their words were different, their cadence creating a counterpoint to the other's chant. Small wisps of black smoke appeared around Ymir's outstretched hand. The smoke flowed down to the widespread arms of the man. It swirled and twirled around him, looking like tiny tentacles that were probing his body, searching for a place to enter. When the man was nearly entirely obscured by the smoke, he pressed his hands upon the chest of the corpse before him. Those swirling tentacles immediately began pushing their way into every open crevasse of the dead woman. The voices of the cantors raised to a horrible screeching crescendo. A moment later, the corpse's chest heaved, and its eyes snapped open, milky white and vacant. The dead body screamed. It was a horrible, blood-curdling noise that made Silverleaf stumble backwards.

He's a necromancer, a death wizard.

The animated corpse made snuffling noises as though it was testing the air. With a jerky motion, it rolled to the side of the altar, falling in a heap onto the floor. It continued to snuffle, its head turning towards the six cantors. After several failed attempts to get itself to its feet, the corpse pulled itself to the edge of the dais and tumbled down the stairs. The cantors continued their strange chorus while the creature continued to slowly creep towards them, its lifeless legs dragging along behind in a bizarre macabre display. When the corpse was nearly upon them, a circle around the altar burst forth with a dark green light. Again, it shrieked out, this time in pain. It immediately withdrew from the lighted edge of the circle, staring at the cantors through vacant eyes. Its insatiable hunger for flesh pressed it forward and again the green light burst forth. It recoiled yet again and raised its snuffling nose into the air. The creature's face snapped towards Amara, and it started dragging itself across the cold stone floor towards her.

While the cantors continued their horrid chant, the necromancer moved towards a pile of dead bodies that were stacked next to the altar. He picked up one of the corpses, this one smaller than the others, and placed it on the stone slab. He pulled at the coverings, tearing them away from the cadaver, revealing a young boy within.

Silverleaf didn't know how long he had been standing at the back of the room, watching the proceedings, but at that very moment, something inside him snapped.

"Get away from that child," he screamed at the top of his lungs. "By the power of Titan, I command you." A great power surged through the half elf's body, filling him with righteous fury. With his twin battle hammers at the ready, he raced towards the altar. His chest felt like it was on fire, and he was going to unleash Titan's wrath upon those who would befoul this holy place.

The six cantors turned to face him. Like the creatures he had encountered in the graveyard, they looked to be skeletal, with skin stretched over their skulls. Their dead, lifeless eye sockets stared back at him. The tallest of the lot, who was nearly seven feet tall, held Amara's glaive. It cackled out with a clicking sort of noise and his cohorts immediately started to spread out, to circle him. They all had no nose to speak of, and yet the skin around what might have been a nose scrunched, like they were trying to smell him.

Silverleaf crouched low, ready to strike when the first of the cantors neared. He leapt up from the ground and brought the first of his hammers to bear. The creature threw up an arm, blocking his attack before reaching out with his other hand and grabbing him by the furs.

With his second hammer, Silverleaf struck out at the creature holding his cloak, catching it cleanly on the side of the head. The pick-head of his hammer embedded deeply into the creature's skull. It fell to the ground, dragging Silverleaf with it. Despite his hammer being embedded in its head, it still maintained a death-grip on his furs.

Amara screamed out a warning. The half elf looked up just in time to see a weapon arcing towards him. With a quick twisting action, he pulled away from the still grasping hand and slipped out of his furs. The vials within, as well as his food supply, came spilling out. The potions clattered in multiple directions while his food stash sprayed across the floor. The pungent odor of his cheese filled the area, drawing the attention of the five remaining cantors.

They're blind. They operate on smell.

He stepped away, catching his heel on Amara's glaive. The weapon clattered about as he fell on his backside. All of the cantors turned towards him before returning to feasting on the cheese and other foods he had dropped.

They're blind, but they hear well enough.

He wasn't sure how long his food stash would keep the cantors busy, so Silverleaf snatched up Amara's glaive and dashed towards her. Using the polearm like a lance, he ran headlong into the first of the animated corpses, the weapon's long, pointed tip puncturing the creature's chest. With his battle hammer, he used the flat side to crush the head of another.

The impaled corpse writhed and screamed, while the one whose head he had caved in fell into a heap on the floor. He tried to extricate the glaive from the chest of the other, but it was writing so heavily that he couldn't get a grip on the weapon's handle.

"Release me," Amara screamed. "The lever to lower me is on the far side of the room."

Silverleaf looked to where his friend was motioning with her chin. It was beyond the cantors who were now sniffing the air, likely in search of the half elf. There was another horrible scream, drawing Silverleaf's attention. He looked towards the altar. The corpse of the young boy was now standing on the stone table, wailing at the ceiling.

"Feast," the necromancer yelled. "Feast. Fulfill your purpose." The boy's head turned towards Silverleaf and Amara. With deadly intent, it leapt from the altar and ambled towards what may have been the only two beating hearts in the room.

"Run," Amara screamed. "They can't leave the circle."

Without thinking it through, Silverleaf made a dash towards the cantors. He had only one battle hammer and there were five of them. Even though they lacked sight, they were still effective fighters.

"Titan, hear me," Silverleaf screamed as he ran headlong into the cantors. Their heads immediately snapped towards him at his words. The half elf's hammer head was immediately covered in frost. He stretched his arm out before him, unleashing a spray of snow and ice pellets. The cantors seemed unaffected by his attack, but the frosty spray covered the ground with a thin sheet of ice. The half elf threw himself to the floor and slid along the now icy surface. As he came within range, he slammed his hammer into the knee of the cantor nearest him. The creature bellowed out and fell hard to the ground. The others, trying to react to the sound of the half elf skidding through their midst, lost their footing and the entire group fell into a tangled mass. They screeched out, making clicking noises, as they tried to right themselves. When Silverleaf's slide came to an end, he hopped up onto his feet and bolted for the lever.

The noise of the chain clattering over pulleys filled the room. The cantors covered their long, pointed ears and screeched in agony. Amara's own baritone scream filled the hall. She had dropped directly into the midst of the corpses who were now viciously biting and clawing at her. Her hands were still bound by her manacles and her arms were still trapped over her head. She kicked as best she could to keep the corpse things away from herself, but they were many and she was exhausted.

Silverleaf sheathed his hammer and sprinted towards his friend. He stomped on the head of the glaive-impaled corpse and yanked the weapon from her torso. Holding the twelve-foot polearm across his chest, he ran full out into the group of corpses that were clutching at his friend. The impact knocked most of them over, including Amara, who was now dangling oddly from the chain. With a quick spin, the half elf brought the heavy ax blade around, cutting Amara's chain, sending her crashing to the ground. The momentum of the swing threw him off balance and he too fell, spread eagle, onto the room's stone floor.

A strong hand wrapped around Silverleaf's upper arm and started dragging him to his feet. He couldn't reach his hammer quickly enough, so he resorted to swinging a back-fist as his attacker. A surprised Amara released her grip on the young man to avoid him striking her with his clenched hand. Silverleaf landed hard onto the ground, his forehead bouncing off the cold stone floor. Somewhere in the distance, he could hear his friend screaming. A searing pain exploded in his leg, bringing him back to the moment.

One of the corpses, the young boy, was laying across his legs, sinking his horrible teeth into his flesh. The surrounding skin of each bite immediately blackened. Whatever magic was bringing the dead back to life included giving them a necrotic venom. Silverleaf was trying to kick him off when another of the corpse things grabbed him by the hair and twisted his head away, exposing his neck. With its rotted mouth gaping wide, the creature moved in, ready to sink its horrendous teeth into his flesh.

Titan, protect me.

The head of the creature exploded as a chain ripped through it, covering Silverleaf with a brown, viscous sludge. He frantically swiped at the muck, spitting and sputtering. A moment later, there was another wave of sludge spraying across his face. He quickly swiped at his eyes, trying to clear his vision.

Amara was standing over him, her body covered in gore with bits of dead flesh hanging from the links of the chain still attached to her manacles. Her face was contorted with rage, her eyes wild, her teeth bared. Her head slowly swiveled until her gaze fell directly on the necromancer. He already had another corpse on his altar, summoning it back from the Great Cycle. The corpse, a man in his prime, jolted as though it had just been struck by lighting. The Gigas growled something unintelligible just before she bolted towards the necromancer, closing the distance between them with just a few long strides. As she reached out for him, he vanished in a puff of black smoke. Silverleaf immediately recognized the spell.

"He's still there," he cried out. "He's just invisible." He tried to stand, to help his friend catch the necromancer, but Silverleaf stumbled and fell. The wounds he had taken were severe and he was having trouble maintaining consciousness. He called out again just before the room went dark and the stone floor once again greeted his face with a sickening thud.

The creature on the altar cried out, its face raised, snuffling at the air. Its head turned towards the oncoming Gigas. With decayed and blackened hands, it reached out, its fingers grasping towards the woman, its mouth opening and closing with a hollow, clacking noise.

"Back to the Great Cycle with you," Amara screamed as she swung her chain, severing the corpse's head from its neck with a single blow. Without slowing down, she leapt over the headless corpse to the far side of the altar, the place she had last seen the necromancer. Before her feet even touched the floor, she was already swinging her chain in a wide, flat arc, hoping to cut the man in half. The chain whirred aimlessly, hitting nothing but air.

The woman's rage turned to terror when her eyes fell upon her friend, laying face first on the ground, a pool of blood spreading out from his body. Even from this distance, she could see the large hunk of flesh hanging loosely from his thigh.

As quickly as she had given chase to the necromancer, the woman returned to her friend. Ripping off one of her sleeves, she quickly wrapped it around Silverleaf's leg. Her blood-slick hands were shaking so badly she struggled to tie it off. She took a quick look over her shoulder, making sure that there was not another attack coming. It was then that she saw the potion bottles strewn across the floor. With a great tug, she tightened the tourniquet around his leg, rousing the half elf.

"I'll be back," she choked out, barely able to get the words out of her throat. She skidded across the floor, scooping up the three potions. In a heartbeat she was back at his side. "A healing potion will fix that right up she said," a nervous smile on her face.

"Won't work," Silverleaf ground out, his eyes closed tight, his teeth gritted. "The wounds are necrotic. My flesh is dying, and it can't be repaired by a healing potion." He tried to push her hand away. "Use it on yourself. It will heal most of your wounds." The last of his words fell away as he lost consciousness.

"Don't you do it," she screamed at her friend. "Don't you dare leave me." The giant's hands were trembling badly, making it difficult to handle the tiny bottles. In the dim light of the room, she couldn't be sure which of the three potions to choose. Healing potions are red. The strongest ones are so red they're nearly black. The potions in her hand were all varying shades of red. She couldn't see well enough to easily differentiate their colors.

"Which one?" she screamed out. She grabbed the half elf by his tunic and gave him a good shake. "Which one is the healing potion?" Silverleaf's head lolled to the side, his mouth flopping open.

"Titan, guide my hand," she called out. "You can't have him yet. I still need him. He can't go." She struggled trying to manipulate the potions, her wrists still bound tightly together by the manacles she was wearing. Her eyes were drawn to the darkest of the red vials. An inner confidence told her that she was making the right decision and she pulled the cork with her teeth. Her lips tingled where the cork touched her skin. She poured a few drops of it onto his leg wound, which was already bleeding through the tourniquet. When the liquid contacted his skin, it bubbled and boiled, but seemed to have no other effect. She stared down at the two remaining potions. They looked identical. She was about to pull the stopper from another bottle when the potion on the acolyte's leg began to sizzle, and Silverleaf's eyes bulged. His mouth opened silently for a moment, and then the screams of agony peeled through the room. The wound was still bad, but it had improved considerably. She quickly poured more of the liquid onto his leg, and Silverleaf renewed his screams of anguish. The acrid stench of burning flesh filled Amara's senses.

"Healing potions shouldn't burn like this," she said, staring at the last of the potion remaining in the vial.

"That wasn't a healing potion," Silverleaf gritted out, his body convulsing. "That was my hot sauce." He pointed weakly to one of the two unopened potions in her hand. "That's the healing potion."

Amara glanced at the potion and then back at the wound. It wasn't knitting closed, but the spreading blackness of his skin was abating, the color returning to normal. She corked the hot sauce and uncorked the healing potion. She poured a generous amount on the young man's leg. Silverleaf's wracked body suddenly relaxed. The edges of the wound were already knitting together. He blew out a sigh of relief. Amara was about to apply some more when a hand covered her mouth and dragged her away from her friend. Whoever was holding her was incredibly strong. She slammed her head backwards, making solid contact with whoever it was behind her. There was a loud crack and an unearthly scream.

Silverleaf rolled over to find Amara struggling against an unseen adversary. The chain that was dangling from her manacles was winding itself around her throat. She was clutching at the links, trying to create enough space to open her airways. Snatching up one of the potion bottles, Silverleaf ran to his friend.

Invisible didn't mean insubstantial. The necromancer was there, Silverleaf just couldn't see him. From the way Amara was fighting, he could tell the man was behind her. Silverleaf slipped in behind the pair, groping with his hands until he felt the head of the necromancer. He let his arm slip beneath the man's chin. Like a constrictor, his arm snaked around the man's neck and then locked tightly onto it. However, no matter how much pressure he applied, the man would not release his hold on Amara. The acolyte looked down at the potion in his hand and grinned. He changed his grip on the man, moving his arm up to cover the bottom of his chin. With all his might, Silverleaf yanked down, stretching his back to gain as much leverage as he could. As soon as he felt the man's mouth open, he rammed the glass vial past his teeth. He quickly lowered his grip to drop below the necromancers chin and yanked up again.

There was an unmistakable sound of glass shattering. Amara slumped forward and Silverleaf pushed the necromancer away from himself. A moment later, the man's skull erupted into a ball of fire. The cantors screeched out. The sound was so loud that the half elf was forced to cover his ears. He stole a glance in their direction, but he couldn't find them.

Amara lay on her side, her chain still wrapped around her neck.

"Sweet Titan, no!" Silverleaf tilted her head up enough that he could unwrap the chain from her throat. Any concern for the cantors immediately fell away. If they attacked, he'd deal with them when it happened. Loop after loop he went, exposing deep, dark bruising beneath. When the last of the chains were removed, he breathed a sigh of relief. The joy turned to ash when he saw that his friend was not breathing on her own.

The young acolyte would have called on Titan's powers of healing if he knew how. While many acolytes chose the path of the healer, the half elf busied himself with learning potions. He had only ever learned the basics of restorative treatments. Her face looked so pale.

Savior's breath. It was one of the techniques that he had learned. It was intended to help revive a drowning victim, but it might work here as well.

He slipped out to the woman's side and tilted her head back. He took a deep breath and placed his lips against hers. With all his might, Silverleaf blew into her mouth. The woman's chest rose slightly and fell away just as quickly. He pulled away and repeated the steps. He watched as Amara's chest rose and fell, hoping that it might induce her to breathe on her own. It did not.

"I won't let you leave me," he said as he took another deep breath and blew it into her mouth. This time, he let his lips linger for several seconds. The warmth of her skin against his lips made his heart skip a beat. He pulled away, tears flowing freely down his cheeks. He dropped his head to her chest, his emotions now getting the better of him. He pulled her close, hugging her for all he was worth.

Thump-thump.

He heard it. It wasn't his imagination; he was almost positive. Taking another deep breath, he wrapped his lips around hers and blew. Her chest rose once again and fell slowly when he pulled away. He took yet another deep breath and blew into her mouth. Her chest rose again, but his time it didn't fall.

"I can smell that damned cheese on your breath," she whispered to him. "It's disgusting." Amara wrapped her arms around the half elf and drew him against her. They held each other in a tight embrace for several minutes before the Gigas finally released her friend.

"Do you have any more of the hot sauce?" she asked, a crooked smile on her lips. "I took quite a few bites, and my legs are killing me." Silverleaf hopped up and scrambled to get the vile. As he looked around, he saw that the chamber was empty.

"They've left," he said, his head swiveling about. "The cantors, they've run away."

"Hot sauce, please," Amara called out, clutching her leg.

"This is going to hurt," Silverleaf said as he uncorked the bottle. "A lot."

He poured a little onto the worst of her wounds. It was black and smelled of rot. As soon as the liquid hit her skin, the giant grimaced. While the liquid started to burn away at the dead flesh, he moved to the next worse wound and repeated the process. The cords in Amara's neck were protruding from her skin as he continued to pour the rest of the liquid over her wounds.

Amara opened her hand, revealing the last of the healing potion. She had poured the majority of it on Silverleaf's leg, but there were still a few precious drops left.

"If you wouldn't mind," she said.

He quickly took the remainder of the vial and dripped it carefully over the worst of her wounds. The look of agony on the woman's face lessened significantly.

"Can you walk?" Silverleaf asked, holding out his hand to help pick her up. "We should get back to the Temple and let Sister Alyce look at that." He looked down at his own leg which was almost nearly healed. "We need to report this to the high priest."

"Father Hoarfrost can wait," she replied with a strange look on her face. "I know what you did."

"What do you mean?" The young man pulled back his hand and wiped his palms on his trousers.

"You kissed me." The woman's face was utterly flat, expressionless.

"I ... I did no such thing," he stammered. "I ... I gave you savior's breath, like we were taught at the Temple."

"Is that what that was," she said, her eyebrow cocked ever so slightly. The muscles at the corner of her mouth twitched. The woman hopped up onto her feet, looking refreshed and ready to fight.

"Too bad," she said with a shrug. She walked calmly over to where her glaive was and picked it up. She paused for a moment next to one of the dead corpses and yanked Silverleaf's hammer from its skull.

"You dropped this," she said, still smiling, and tossed it at the young man's feet. "Let's get you to the infirmary and then we can go report to Hoarfrost."

Silverleaf's brow knit together as he looked down at the blood-covered weapon at his feet. When he looked back up, Amara was already halfway across the burial chamber.

∽∾∾◈∾∾∽

After spending the rest of the morning in the infirmary, two priests brought Silverleaf and Amara to see Father Hoarfrost, the high priest. The news of their encounter had already reached his ears, but he wanted to hear about the events from them both, firsthand. While the pair's wounds were being treated, he had sent a group of priests into the catacombs to retrieve the dead bodies and return them to their eternal resting places.

"Tell me about the necromancer," the old priest said.

"There wasn't much left of him." Amara screwed up her face and she looked down at Silverleaf.

"I shoved a fire potion into his mouth," the half elf said. "It was the only thing I could think of to get him off Amara. When I closed his mouth on the bottle, it broke open and ..." Father Hoarfrost grunted. His facial expression said nothing. His reaction seemed, flat.

"Have you ever seen the man before?" the high priest asked. Both of the acolytes shook their heads.

"Tell me of the Grimmorcs," Father Hoarfrost continued. "What role did they play in this?"

"Grimmorcs, Father?" Amara asked.

"There was a dead Grimmorc in the burial chapel," Father Hoarfrost said, cocking an eyebrow. "His head had been caved in."

"Oh, the cantors," Silverleaf said. "They seemed to be helping the necromancer raise the dead. They were singing a strange song while he performed his foul ritual."

"Those creatures do not belong on the surface," Father Hoarfrost said, his features grim. "We know little of them, except that the dwarven miners first encountered them when they delved too deeply. Is there nothing more about them that you can tell me?" Amara and Silverleaf shook their heads in unison.

Father Hoarfrost leaned back in his chair and knitted his fingers together. He looked carefully at the two acolytes standing before him. His gaze lingered for several seconds before he turned his attention to Sister Gale, their combat instructor, and Brother Snowpack, the infirmary attendant who had administered care to them upon their arrival. Sister Gale nodded lightly, as did Brother Snowpack.

"Tell me more of this hot sauce," Father Hoarfrost said, his deep blue eyes alight with wonder. He pulled on his long, gray ponytail. "According to Brother

Snowpack, it has completely cured the necrotic wounds you both suffered." The question made Amara groan.

"I made it from firebug ichor," Silverleaf replied. His fingers were fidgeting uncontrollably at his sides.

"Firebugs?" Father's eyebrows shot upwards. "You made it from the creatures that the City Watch have been battling for the past three moons? What would possess you to do such a thing?" Silverleaf's fingers twitched faster, his chin dipping down to his chest.

"I was examining a carcass," he said, his eyes still downcast. "I thought they might have something useful to use as reagents for making potions."

"And?" Father Hoarfrost pressed him, leaning forward in his chair, splaying his fingers across his highly polished dragonwood desk.

"And their blood smelled like demon peppers." He looked up to see the now confused look on the high priest's face. "I tasted it."

"You tasted the firebug's blood?" Silverleaf nodded and dipped his chin back to his chest. "And?"

"And it tasted just like pepper juice, but it burned my tongue – badly. I just thought that if I could tame it a bit, it would be … delicious."

"And how exactly did you tame it?" Brother Snowpack asked. He had covered his mouth to hide the grin on his face.

"Mandrake root," Silverleaf said. "I used its pulp to reduce how badly the blood burned." The priest's eyes widened.

"Mandrake root is the primary ingredient for making healing potions," Brother Snowpack stated, still covering his mouth to hide his mirth. "You made a spicy healing potion? One that burns your mouth and heals it at the same time?"

Silverleaf nodded slightly.

"That was ingenious," Sister Gale said. She too had her hand over her mouth, but the way her shoulders were bobbing said she was laughing hard. She finally got control of herself and turned her attention to Amara.

"And our gentle giant here finally made her first kill." The combat priest gave her a mock bow.

"I did no such thing." Amara's face was red with fury. "I killed no living being."

"She didn't," Silverleaf added. "She only killed the animated corpses." Sister Gale frowned and shook her head.

"How will you ever dole out Titan's justice if you are unable or unwilling to take a life?" the combat instructor asked.

"It's lucky for us then that we won't have to do that," Silverleaf said, stepping between Sister Gale and Amara. His willingness to use himself as a living shield for the giant made all the priests grin. "We both failed the Rite of Abandonment on Mount Uha. We will never be priests."

Father Hoarfrost cleared his throat, drawing the attention of the entire room.

"The purpose of the Rite of Abandonment," the high priest said, leaning back into his chair, knitting his fingers over his stomach, "is to put your faith in Titan against what feels like insurmountable odds. When the night comes and the winds blow so hard that they will freeze you in your tracks, it is your faith that will save you. It brings you warmth and it brings you hope. You may think you love and believe in Titan, but it's when things are at their worst that you will discover if you truly believe – or not."

The two acolytes stared blankly at the high priest. They had never heard this about the rite before. All they were ever told was, if you survive three days on the mountaintop, you will be given the title *Priest of Titan*.

"You each faced death, hardship, and sorrow while performing this assignment. In each case, it was your faith that saw you through it. It was your faith that made you strong. It was your faith that allowed you to call upon Titan's miracles, miracles that are only available to full priests."

The high priest rummaged through the many pockets in his silver robes and pulled out two holy symbols of Titan. He turned to Sister Gale and Brother Snowpack, holding out the necklaces. "If you would be so kind."

"I don't understand," Silverleaf said as he watched the two priests retrieve the wooden symbols from Father Hoarfrost.

"You are both now, officially, priests of Titan," Sister Gale said. "Amara, if you would please lower your head for me, it would be my honor to place this gift upon you."

Brother Snowpack slipped the cold-iron chain over Silverleaf's head. "Welcome, Brother Silverleaf."

"Welcome, Sister Amara," Sister Gale said, looking up at the Gigas woman.

"We're priests?" Amara asked. She glanced over at Silverleaf who was absolutely beaming. "But I cannot ever deliver Titan's justice. How can I?"

"Delivering justice across Aarall is but one of your duties as a priest," Father Hoarfrost said, his eyes sparkling with joy. "I have every faith in you to do the right thing at the right time. Afterall, faith is what makes us priests. What we choose to do with that faith is what makes us who we are as people."

"If it's all the same to you," Amara said, "I'd be good to work in the library and not be out delivering justice to the kingdom."

"This was a once in a lifetime event," Silverleaf scoffed. "You can bet that Kit never had to endure anything so horrific on her assignments." It was Father Hoarfrost's turn to scoff.

"Then you have no idea what Sister Standing Bear has endured on her assignments," he said with a bemused look. "As for your request, Sister Amara, you are welcome to work in the library, if that's what you want, but you will perform whatever duties I set out for you, for you both." The temperature in the room dropped rapidly as the old priest glared at them. The frosty chill dissipated as quickly as it started. The old priest stood from his chair and straightened his silver robes.

"Now, I hear Sister Miyuki has prepared a special meal, in honor of your new station in the Temple. Why don't we all head down to the dining hall to see what she has prepared for you."

"I could eat," Silverleaf said, enthusiastically.

"As long as it's not that foul cheese you had with you, I could eat as well." Amara punched her friend in the arm and strode past him to the doorway. "And I don't want any of that hot sauce, either."

AFTERWORD

Thank you for reading my novel. Reviews are critical to the success of every indie author. I would ask that you leave a review on Amazon, GoodReads, and Book-Bub. If you have any thoughts or comments that you'd like to share directly with me, I would love to hear from you. You can email me at paul@paulmouchet.ca.

Do you want more stories? You find links to all my novels on my website. You can also sign up for my newsletter, Marvelous Mondays, which I send out every other week. They're full of fun pics, snippets of what's going on in my life, and book news.

Also, if you'd like to discuss my stories with me and other fans, in a safe, friendly environment, please connect with me on my Facebook group ~ Paul Mouchet's Reader's Group.

You'll find the link to all my social media accounts on my website. I look forward to chatting with you.

Happy Reading!